D1465514

THE FARM
EDGE OF THE

Cornwall 1939. Will and Alice ar
granite farm, perched on a windsw
they meet the farmer's daughter,
against fields of shimmering barley, er
hood largely protected from the ravag
But in the sweltering summer of 1943, so
happens that will have far-reaching consequ
Over 70 years on, Alice is determined to aton
her behaviour – but has she left it too late? Me
while Maggie's granddaughter, Lucy, returns
her crumbling childhood home after a failed
marriage and on leave from work after a terrible
mistake. Can she rebuild herself, the family farm
and help her grandmother find some peace?

The Farm At The Edge Of The World

by

Sarah Vaughan

Magna Large Print Books
Long Preston, North Yorkshire,
BD23 4ND, England.

British Library Cataloguing in Publication Data.

A catalogue record of this book is
available from the British Library

ISBN   978-0-7505-4423-8

First published in Great Britain in 2016 by Hodder & Stoughton
An Hachette UK company

Copyright © Sarah Vaughan 2016

Cover illustration © Sandra Cunningham/Arcangel by arrangement
with Arcangel Images

The right of Sarah Vaughan to be identified as the Author of the work
has been asserted by her in accordance with the Copyright, Designs
and Patents Act, 1988

Published in Large Print 2017 by arrangement with
Headline Publishing Group Ltd.

Magna Large Print is an imprint of Library Magna Books Ltd.

Printed and bound in Great Britain by
T.J. (International) Ltd., Cornwall, PL28 8RW

To Bobby,
with love.

She would concern herself with the business of the farm; rise early ... bend her back to labour and count the strain a joy and an antidote to pain... She belonged to the soil, and would return to it again, rooted to the earth as her forefathers had been.

Daphne du Maurier, *Jamaica Inn*

Because the road is rough and long,
Shall we despise the skylark's song?

Anne Brontë, *Poems by Currer, Ellis, and Acton Bell*

Prologue

The farm sits with its back to the sea, and the sharp winds that gust off the Atlantic: a long stretch of granite, hunkering down. For over three hundred years it has stood here, looking in at its fields of barley and its herd of Ayrshires, which amble, slowly cropping, russet bulks shifting against the lush, verdant green.

It watches, this farmhouse, as permanent as the rocks, more so than the shifting sand dunes; sees the hedgerow that spills out to ensnare a rare driver – for few make their way to this spot, high above the sea. The details change with the seasons – the hawthorn burnishing then falling bare; the sky bruising then lightening after rain; the crops placed in shocks then gathered in – but the view remains the same: a ribbon of lane leading up and away from this lonely patch of coast, through a tapestry of fields, towards the heart of Cornwall and the rest of Britain. And, above it, always, hulking in the distance, the moor – brooding ochre and peat and grey.

In the sunshine, all looks idyllic. This is a farm a child might draw: slate roof, whitewashed porch, near-symmetrical windows; one either side of the door with an extra one tacked on in the eighteenth century when the house was stretched. The proportions are good. A house assured of itself and built to withstand a wind that whips the trees

11

into right angles, that blasts the panes with fat plashes of rain, that endures winter after winter. Two chimneys stand, and, from October to May, the tang of woodsmoke mingles with the ripe stench of the farmyard and the gentler smells of the coastline: the fruity reek of silage, of honeyed gorse and sea salt, wet grass and cowpats, camomile and vetch.

On sunny days, the granite walls of the house, barns and workers' cottages glow, warm and gentle, the stone glinting against the blue of the sea. Walkers, rooting out cream teas, drink in the view from the back garden – the fat-eared crops, the full-bellied cows, the surfers riding white horses across the bay. And then they hear the birdsong. A glorious melody so irrepressible, so unrelenting that it gives the place its nickname. No longer Polblazey, but Skylark Farm.

Yet, when the skylarks stop singing, and the sky turns grey, the granite dulls to a dark charcoal. The farm becomes less inviting: bleak if not austere. Then, it is clear that the casements are in need of a paint, and that the garden – with its close-cropped grass fringed with clumps of woody lavender and thrift – is untended. A wizened crab apple bends over a rotting bench, and a tamarisk stripped of its leaves by a vicious wind, points inland. Skylark Farm – run by the same family for six generations, steeped in its history and secrets – shrugs on its traditional Cornish name. Becomes Polblazey once again.

On such days, when the earth has been ploughed into great clods of soil, when the cobbles are slick with manure, when a murder of crows follows the tractor, the farm is at its most remote and unforgiving. For nothing lies beyond its cliffs and headland but the petrol-blue Atlantic – and then America, unknown and unseen. Then, it is a farm at the edge of the world. The sort of place where the usual rules can be bent, just a little, and any secrets stay hidden. For who there would tell? And who would hear?

One

Now: 30 June 2014, London

She takes the opened letter and smooths it out on the kitchen table. It was never going to be good news. She knew that, as soon as she saw the official frank across the top of the envelope. This was it: the confirmation of Monday's appointment in black and white with the trust's name emblazoned in that institutional cobalt blue that conjures up the smell of disinfectant and tepid, overcooked food, and plump young nurses who call her 'dear' – as if her age and diagnosis gives them the right to bestow not just sympathy but affection. She does not want either. Just the thought of their eyes, brimming with understanding, makes her want to rage.

Still. Just for a moment she had allowed herself to hope. To imagine a reprieve. That there had been a mix-up – and some other poor woman was receiving the news she had dreaded to hear.

But no, here it is, in a letter to her GP, copied in to her. *'Further to yesterday's consultation with Mrs Coates...'* the oncologist, Dr Freedman, begins, and for a moment the use of the third person throws her: as if he is referring to somebody else. And then comes the crucial bit: *'Following the liver ultrasound, it appears the malignant melanoma on her upper back that we removed has metastasised. A few spots were found on her liver. Surgery, at her age, is not advised.'*

She blinks. Inoperable. Not that she wants further surgery. The wound, which had required a general anaesthetic, itches, and was deep.

'I have discussed biological therapies with Mrs Coates, but she declined them after raising concerns about the side effects. She understood that they would extend her life by a year at best. During our discussion, she was most insistent that I give a prognosis. I advised her that, without treatment, the average outlook would be less than a year.'

Actually, Dr Freedman, she thinks, you gave the impression that a lot less was far more probable. 'How long before it begins to affect me?' she had pressed, and her voice – so dry throughout the consultation – had quavered, just the once, at that point.

She did not want to envisage the pain, the extreme fatigue, the sickness, but she would rather know what she was up against. 'Six months – even less?'

'We can only give you the average outlook,' Dr Freedman had said, and then he had nodded slightly: just the gentlest of nods, almost inadmissible. 'No one can tell, but that's not an un-

14

likely scenario.'

'Thank you,' she had said.

Death – something she had been so aware of since Pam, the last of her siblings, had died – had jumped a little closer. Six months. After eighty-three years, it would feel like such a short time. She tries to force a laugh at the thought that she has always been someone who puts things off; who needs a deadline. But though she can do a stiff upper lip, she doesn't do black humour. It comes out as a mirthless cough.

The only good she can find in all this – and she is trying so hard to do so – is that at least she *knows*. And while dying in her sleep, like Ron, her husband, might be the ideal way for it to happen, perhaps it is better to prepare. Maybe this is what she needs: this prompt to tie up loose ends. And to think this should come today of all days. June thirtieth. She has been dreading this anniversary. Seventy years. Most of her lifetime. The coincidence chills her. As if a shard of ice has pierced her core and remains, still frozen there.

A drill whines. The builders next door are hard at work. Another loft conversion and kitchen extension to push a Victorian terrace upwards and outwards, though her neighbours – a young couple who work in the City – have only one child. Her parents brought up five of them in a terrace this size before the war. Then they were all evacuated – even Robert, ever the baby. And life irrevocably changed.

She pours a mug of tea from a glazed brown teapot and warms her fingers around it. How has it come to this: that it is only now, with death so

15

imminent, that she is considering trying to put right something she should have done years before? Everything – each recollection; every throwaway thought – leads back to that summer, that time she has tried so hard to forget.

Her eyes flit to the PC sitting on her small mahogany table in the corner. Who is she trying to protect? Someone she once loved, or herself: ever fearful of recrimination, as cowardly as she was at thirteen? A lump forms in the back of her throat and she swallows. No time like the present. And she has so very little time.

The computer takes a while to start up. Her hand grasps the mouse and she concentrates, the tip of her tongue out like a stalking cat's, as she navigates to where she has saved the link. She smiles, a little sardonic. They are still using its nickname, though its more forbidding Cornish name seems more in keeping with the nightmares that have started to wake her: heart palpitating, nightdress soaked through with sweat. *'Skylark Farm, Trecothan, north Cornwall. Run by the Petherick family for six generations. Offering self-catering and cream teas.'* For a moment, she is back in the sand dunes, listening to peals of birdsong – rapid, repeated, joyous. Fresh from London, she had been mesmerised by the speck that hovered, and anxious. 'That swallow's a bit high,' she had said.

She had been eight then: wide-eyed and entirely innocent. By the time she left, all that would have changed. And yet the farm remained the same. She looks at it now: solid, seventeenth-century. She glances at Maggie's bedroom window – the room of the daughter of the house; decorated with

16

rose wallpaper and that cast-iron bed – and then at her own, at the very end of the house, closest to the sea.

It's largely a dairy farm, now, according to the website. So no lambs bounding across the lush spring grass, no chill March nights spent lambing. A sudden memory and she is back in the lambing shed: the air ripe with crushed straw and mucus, the metallic stench of blood and brine. She has a flash of Aunt Evelyn: all thin-lipped dissatisfaction and disapproval as she watched her baby an orphaned lamb. She shuts away the image – and the others, the ones that surface in the early hours of the morning when the nightmares press upon her. She would never romanticise Skylark, or the family that lived there.

And yet, for all that, it had been a place of refuge for an evacuee escaping the horrors of the Blitz. Quite literally, as the WRVS woman had told her mother, 'a safer place to be'. It certainly felt cut off from the rest of Britain, towards the very end of a peninsula: the farm's fields running to the edge of England, right down into the crystalline, tempestuous, unpredictable sea.

She opens the timetable of weeks when the two cottages are available, and their surprisingly reasonable prices. Not completely booked up yet, which is curious given that it's late June. The last two weeks in August are free. She hesitates. Should she really do this? She has terminal cancer: enough to contend with. She pauses for a moment, willing away the tears that prick and burn her eyes so that the image wobbles and blurs.

If she does nothing she will die never knowing

if she might have made things better, if she could have exorcised the demons that harangue her, not just at night, now, but during the day. She craves peace at the end of her life. And reconciliation. If there is a possibility she could achieve that, well, then it is worth the risk.

With a sudden click, she highlights the box and is directed to the next page. Judith Petherick – Maggie's daughter? – will email her back to confirm her booking if she will leave her details. She does, before her nerve fails.

There. It is done. A couple of tears seep from her eyes before she wipes them brusquely away. She cannot quite believe it.

After seventy years, she is going back to the farm.

Two

It is terrifying, Lucy thinks later, when she tries to be rational, how life can change at a single moment: as if a coin is spun to decide if it should continue merrily – or teeter and fall.

As a nurse she knows this. Has seen the impact of a split-second's loss of concentration: the mangled limbs and paralysis when a driver ploughs into another on the motorway; the drunken arguments that start with a shove and end with a knife; the prank – free-running along a rooftop, diving into a shallow lake – that seems such a good idea at the time, then ends as anything but.

18

She knows it as a daughter, too. An accident – tragic, needless and preventable – took her father from her. Fred Petherick: killed when he slipped while running on the north Cornish cliffs.

But she has never felt it as clearly as she has today: that sense of the mercurial nature of life. How one simple mistake – a 'near miss' in clinical terms – could shatter her entire world and expose its painful, terrible fragility; could lead to her wailing on her bathroom floor so that she barely recognises the woman staring back at her from the mirror, crimson-eyed, swollen-faced.

One shift you can get over, she thinks, as she pulls her knees to her chest and hugs them tightly. But two: a mistake on top of a life-changing discovery? Two is too much, it seems. For it's this combination that has made her world shatter – and exposed her seemingly happy life, here in London, as groundless. As insubstantial as a dandelion clock puffed by the breeze.

She rocks her knees tighter as a fresh volley of sobs racks her body. She needs to get a grip. Her mind whirs; her heart skips, jumps, flutters. Wired on caffeine, sugar and misery or a cocktail of all three. She hasn't slept in forty-eight hours. And in that time, her life has been wrenched apart like a suitcase of inappropriate clothes: the contents turned upside down, sneered at, discarded.

It had started yesterday morning. She had come in off her Sunday night shift, in the neonatal unit of the hospital where she works, bones weary, eyes aching, and had gone to take a shower upstairs. The disposable contact lens case on the edge of the sink had niggled; it wasn't hers

19

and Matt's eyesight was perfect. A sliver of cold crept inside her; wormed its way in tight.

Perhaps one of their friends had been around and had changed a lens? She ran through who it could be as she dried and dressed herself, but could think of no one. Better not to fret but to grab a couple of hours' sleep. She stretched out, and tried to relax. Imagine you are back home, she told herself. Back at Skylark. Think of the headland – and imagine standing there: at the edge of the world, the very edge of the cliff. Drink in the view: Land's End to your left, Devon to your right, the Atlantic stretching in front of you: aquamarine, then teal, then a deep, dark blue as it hits the horizon. Feel the stiff onshore breeze temper the heat of the sun, then blast you backwards. See the seagulls drift upwards; and a pair of seals, sleek and slippery, bask on the rocks beneath.

It was no good. Though her body was weary, her mind whirred: feverish, over-analytic. Even the state of her bed bugged her: the sheets needed changing; Matt's pillow was tinged with sweat. Perhaps she should just do it now. She swept back the duvet and, as she did so, saw a long hair curled midway down: just one hair, innocuous and easily dismissed, except that she was fair and this was dark. A luxuriant hair: the sort that belonged to a Spanish woman like Matt's colleague, Suzi. And in that second, she saw them at the advertising agency's Christmas drinks. Her head flung back as she laughed at something Matt had said. Her hand lightly touching his forearm to emphasise a point. Her whole manner just oozing sexual confidence. 'She eats men alive,' Matt had laughed, later, when Lucy had mentioned it. 'Completely terrifying.' Only now, he didn't seem to mind being terrified.

She sprang from the bed. It was so clichéd and predictable: the cruelty so casual it was almost as if Matt wanted her to know. She thought of her husband – for whom the passion had gone, yes, but isn't that what happened seven years into a relationship, when both of you were working hard? – and wondered if she even knew him. Who was he, this advertising creative? A supposedly sensitive, *Guardian* reader who liked Hilary Mantel novels, Vietnamese not Thai food, cinnamon not chocolate on his cappuccino; who pushed his heavy-rimmed glasses up when he was nervous, but was irritated when she once told him he was almost too pretty. 'So – not handsome?' he had probed. 'Well ... yes, of course ... but daintier.' He had pulled his slim-fitting cardigan tight.

He wasn't some aggressive alpha male, but her friend: the person who'd held her after her father died, and had proposed six months afterwards; who had helped put her back together again.

That hair – the fact he hadn't checked for any telltale traces; the fact he had fucked his lover here, in her bed, apparently oblivious to whether she would notice – made a mockery of them.

He hadn't even bothered to deny it. When he came home on Monday at lunchtime – after she'd called and said they needed to talk – she was, for some unfathomable reason, slicing peppers, thoughts tumbling with each knock of the knife. As he entered, she put it down. Her hand was

21

quivering and the blade trembled against the slivered fans of red and orange. Please deny it, she willed him, as he took in her eyes pooling with tears. Tell me it's a mistake, that I've imagined it. That there's some other explanation for this?

But: 'I need some time to think,' he said, calmly, infuriatingly, as she stood there, convulsed with sobs, just wanting him to make it better somehow. Couldn't you just hold me? She felt like screaming, even though she knew that if he did so, she would push him away. For a moment she craved a bear hug from her tall, broad-chested farmer father: the sort of hug that made her feel as if no harm could ever come to her, as if she was buttressed against the world. Matt could never give her that: their bodies are mismatched – hers soft against his, his, too slight and slim. Insubstantial.

At the door, he had paused.

'I'll be in touch,' he said.

She had gone straight to her night shift. They were too short-staffed for her to cancel, and it was her last night in a row of three. The last of five long shifts. But she was exhausted and distracted. They nearly lost a patient. Yet another extremely fragile baby: born at twenty-five weeks, clinging on for a further three. She watched this child they'd had to resuscitate: more skinned chick than baby boy, his nappy and cap dwarfing his scrap of a body: veins pumping gold beneath his translucent skin, not one ounce of fat or muscle. And, despite knowing it was unprofessional to let herself be affected, she found it hard not to cry.

There wasn't time to be distressed, though. She

was too busy looking after two other babies. Both needed to be monitored: drugs dispensed, tubes suctioned, ventilation levels altered and assessed. Little Jacob Wright was late in having his morphine topped up – and it was then that she made her mistake.

'Um, Lucy?' Emma Parker, the most junior of her colleagues, was flushing as she double-checked the dose Lucy had measured just before the infusion was administered.

'I think you've added 1ml of morphine not 0.1ml to the saline. Isn't that ten times the amount it should be...?'

The world spun: the always-stuffy atmosphere of the neonatal intensive care unit pushed down on her, bright stars crowding her vision.

'I ... I can't have, can I?'

And then she looked at the empty vial and in that split second her bowels turned cold and she could see her world come tumbling down in such a way that she didn't know how it could be rebuilt again.

For Emma was right. Of course she was. Out of practice at regularly making up infusions, she had filled a 1ml syringe, instead of drawing out just the 0.1ml and mixing it with 0.9ml of sodium chloride. Such a tiny, fatal difference. Such an easy, terrible mistake.

'Glad we double-checked.' Emma gave an uneasy laugh, embarrassed on her behalf. 'No harm done.' She glanced at her superior, chewed her bottom lip.

Oh, but there could have been! How there could have been. If she had given it to Jacob, he would have died. No question of it. Her chest tightened at the thought of him going into cardiac arrest. Then she imagined telling his parents: his father who insists his son is a 'fighter', his beautiful, fragile mother. How would they react if they discovered that, through human error – through *her* error – their tiny son had died?

'I'll fill out a DATIX form; tell the manager.' She cleared her throat, tried to breathe deeply, to think clearly. Her palms were sweating; her armpits pricked.

'There's no need; I won't say anything, I promise.' Emma was insistent, and she could see her trying to cover up her shock at what her superior had done; was perhaps running through the consequences if she hadn't noticed. A baby's death meant suspension and possible disciplinary action – for both of them.

'No.' She was firm about this. As the sister on the ward, she had to set an example, however humiliating. 'This is serious; it counts as a "near miss".'

'Well, if you're sure,' Emma said, and she could see the relief on the younger woman's face that she was doing the right thing.

Lucy, shamefaced, looked away.

It wasn't the first time she had made a mistake, as Ruth Rodgers, the manager, pointed out when she suggested Lucy take some sick leave. She had recently placed a junior nurse with an intensely sick baby who later required resuscitation, and had made other rota errors. Nothing this serious, but still: did she feel her judgement was a little shaky, these days?

'It's not like you,' Ruth went on. 'You're usually

24

so focused, which we'd expect from a sister with your experience.' She paused and tipped her head to one side as if the next question was delicate. 'Can I ask: is everything all right at home?'

And it was then that Lucy knew that their trust in her had gone; that they no longer viewed her as a conscientious, thorough, clinically safe employee. Her eyes filmed as tears began to brim.

'Let's set you up with your GP and occupational health; get you some sick leave.' Ruth was brisk, no-nonsense. 'Perhaps you need a few weeks off. A couple of months. Sick leave not suspension. Time to get yourself back together again.'

Within a couple of hours, she had traded the security of the hospital she had worked in for five years for the warm anonymity of a crowded London street: her badge gone, her uniform off, her status as a nurse in question, whatever occupational health might say. The late June heat, choked with exhaust fumes, pressed against her, and she felt overwhelmed. No longer a nurse. No longer a wife. Who was she – and why was she here?

She was drifting, rudderless, far out to sea.

Later, safe in the privacy of her home, she dry retches into the toilet, the shock of what has happened striking her with the force of a rogue wave pounding a beach. She clutches the cold enamel, trying to calm herself, waiting for the nausea to subside. Her body shivers. She heaves again.

It is early afternoon now. Sunshine streams in from the street and pools on the carpet. She slips onto the sagging sofa; hides herself away. Her knees curl up and she shifts so that she is lying in

25

a foetal position, holding her grief tightly inside her so that it cannot spill into the sunny front room of her maisonette; the home that is her sanctuary from London's hustle and bustle. The home she shared with Matt until yesterday. Was it only then? That time belongs to a different era. She wipes at the tears and the snot that keep sliding down her face.

As the light shifts, she paces the room; her insides hollowed out at the thought of everything she has lost: husband, reputation, possibly – for she does not know how she can go back to nursing at the moment – career.

When she comes to the mantelpiece, she turns down the smiling photos of herself and Matt, and picks up one of her father, standing, beaming in front of the family farm. Dearest Dad. The last time I felt such grief was for you. Four years ago and yet, at times, it could be yesterday. She traces a face that will never age beyond fifty; peers at his eyes. Deep brown, they seem to crinkle. 'How bloody fantastic,' she can hear him roar.

Behind him the sea glints against the gold of the barley, the green of the hedgerows, the soft grey of the farm. The tug of homesickness takes her by surprise. She couldn't wait to get away from the place – ravaged by foot-and-mouth the summer she left: so desolate and *boring,* she felt as a teenager. Yet now, she is sick with longing for it. The only place she wants to be is standing on the top of the headland, arms outstretched, with a stiff cross onshore wind blowing, all fears and sadness buffeted away.

Could she run back home? Help them out over

the busy summer months while she licks her wounds and puts herself back together again?

The idea ferments. Her mother would welcome her with open arms. For a moment, she sees Judith flying up the slate path towards her, her face an open question, as she pulls her tightly into an embrace. There would be unconditional support and love. And so what? It might be regressive. Not something someone nearing thirty-two should ever want to do. But her life isn't what it was two days ago – and the old rules and expectations no longer hold. Skylark Farm, the home of her childhood, is the only place she wants to be.

Trembling, she reaches for her phone.

'Trecothan 87641?' The voice at the end of the line has a Cornish lilt and is gentle.

'Mum?' Lucy says, and her voice breaks with relief.

'Lucy? Is everything all right?'

And the tears are falling now, warm and wet. She has to pause for a moment before she can get out the sentence.

'Lucy?' Her mother's concern deepens.

'Mum. Please can I come home?'

Three

Then: 30 June 1944, Cornwall

The sea was a deep navy when Maggie clambered down to the empty cove for a swim, late in the evening. She was supposed to be up in her bedroom, revising for her Higher Certificate exams next week.

She picked her way carefully, choosing the route she always used, with the fewest torturous leaps and only a smattering of mussels and barnacles to stab her feet. No gelatinous seaweed. She had scrambled over these rocks since she was little, but still feared the slip and slither of those rogue, damp strands of green.

The tide was high and coated the rocks where they dropped, not shelved. She eased herself in gently, the cold burning as it spread over her crotch, her navel, her breasts. She ducked her shoulders, unable to bear its iciness any longer, keen to curb the sensation. If only she could disappear, be swallowed up by it, deep where no one could see her, bar the odd crab and the glimmering shoals of fish.

She swam strongly: a brisk breaststroke, eyes wide open. The salt stung them, but she needed to immerse herself entirely. The sea silvered her ears and she blew fat bubbles that filled her head with a gurgle that would be comical were her stomach

28

not churning with grief. She rose and swam down again, aware that she had left the cove now and was swimming out to sea and that first cave, where they had hidden; then towards the second, and the spot where they had first kissed.

A wave lifted and dropped her. The sea was becoming choppy: the sky, a blue filleted with mackerel clouds just a few hours earlier, was turning a sheet-metal grey. The air was chill, and she trod water, bicycling her legs. Better to swim down once more, where she would be entirely hidden and where she could cry in private, her tears mingling with the salt of the sea.

For grief wasn't something that was discussed at home where her father might give her a sympathetic glance but didn't know how to address the matter, and her mother refused to acknowledge it or even look at her with a smidgeon of compassion, or so it seemed. Joanna had moved to work elsewhere – *She knows too much,* her mother had said – and Alice had been rehoused with a family down in St Agnes. Next week, two new evacuees – brothers aged seven and eight – were moving in.

Nothing had occurred, or so her mother would have everyone think; and yet Maggie's world had changed entirely. She let out a howl of disbelief. The noise was pitiful: a lamb's bleat when what she felt was a lion's roar of rage so immense that, at times, she could barely contain it. Distress, too: that had been her overriding feeling for the past ten weeks, and a terrible deadening numbness. Guilt – sharp, relentless – and desperation. A sense of panic: that she could do nothing.

At times, these emotions felt overwhelming. At lunchtime, she had hidden in the school music cupboard quaking, so intense was her distress. *Please God,* she had prayed to a Lord whose existence she increasingly doubted. *Keep him safe; keep him safe.* As if something terrible, at that moment, was happening to him.

She rolled onto her back, and for a moment let herself float: watching the clouds swell and burgeon. Her curls unravelled in a halo; her limbs formed a cross as she drifted further out to sea.

I could just let myself go, she thought, dispassionate. And then the cloud above her broke and the surface of the water began to be spattered, the drops bouncing and plashing off her face.

The rain hadn't yet reached the farm, and as she looked at it, high up on the hill, she saw that it was lit by a shaft of freak sunlight.

She turned towards the shore and began swimming in.

Four

Now: 3 July 2014, Cornwall

Maggie, perched on her bench under the crab apple, peers up the track from the farmhouse, waiting for her granddaughter to return. The lane is empty; the air still. Only the song of a skylark and the tread of her daughter's boots tramping down the lane break the calm of the summer's morning. The gate clicks and Judith comes up the worn slate path.

'I keep telling you. She texted at Exeter. She won't be here for at least another hour.' Her daughter smiles as she comes towards her, her face a mix of exasperation and concern.

A pretty girl, Judith, though she crops her hair now for practical reasons. No good having long hair if you're a farmer. Still, she makes an effort: small Celtic knots in her ears and a flick of mascara. When she stops doing that, they will know that something has gone very wrong.

'Do you want a cup of tea? I'm putting the kettle on.'

Maggie shakes her head.

Judith Petherick, up since a quarter to six, gives a tight, bright smile and exhales audibly. 'Right. Well I've two more batches of scones and a Victoria sponge to make before she gets here, so I'd better get on.'

'I'll come and help.'

'No, you stay here. I'm fine.'

'Well, just sit with me for a moment.' Maggie leans back and watches the leaves and tight green marbles of the crab apple dapple her skirt. After a pause, Judith sits down.

'So she seemed in a state?'

Judith nods, her face grim. 'I've never heard her like it – well, not since Fred died. Inconsolable. Kept going on about what could have happened. Seemed convinced she wasn't up to her job and terrified that, when or *if* she goes back to nursing, a baby will die.'

'Was she as upset about her husband?' Maggie

31

has never approved of Matt. Too much of a Londoner; too scathing about Cornwall and the farm, which he barely visited. Perturbed by the reek of silage and the lack of a signal for his mobile phone.

'Hard to know. But at least she can be rid of him – not like the guilt if something happens to a baby or her shame if she gives up her career.'

'Perhaps she might move back here?' Maggie voices the wish she is sure they have both had.

'Oh, Mum. There's not much to keep her here, is there?'

'You don't mean that, Judith.'

'Not for us, no. But for Lucy? She's hardly been racing to come back here before now.'

'Perhaps not, but it's like a magnet this place. Draws us back if we leave. It did with me.'

'Not sure about Lucy.'

'No?' Maggie pauses. 'Yes ... you may be right.'

She takes in the view: the same as when she was born here, bar the wind turbines on the horizon. It is beautiful, yes, but a hard existence. Getting up for the six o'clock milking, day in, day out, is not for everyone – and who would want the financial burden of a farm past its best? She thinks of the latest overdraft statement that Judith had tried to hide in her pile on the dresser. The sum had shocked her. She twists her wedding ring, loose now, against her knuckles, and wonders when to bring that up again. For discussing it will mean looking at Richard's proposal, once again.

'Perhaps she will want to stay this time,' she persists. 'She needs us now, but we need her too. Tom must be thrilled to have the help?'

'Well there is that,' says Judith, thinking of her

son, who gave up his cheffing when it was clear the farm would fail if one of her children didn't return.

'And maybe this is a chance for her to make up for not coming back four years ago,' says Maggie, thinking of the aftermath of Fred's death, when Judith was consumed with grief. 'When you really needed her.'

Oh, what is she doing? The fear that running home is a stupid idea – something regressive and infantile and pitiful – grows stronger once Lucy leaves the M5 at Exeter and ploughs down the A30. She can't pretend she is in the Home Counties or anywhere close to her old life. With every mile, the landscape becomes more verdant, agricultural and desolate. A cloud chases across the moor, and turns the peat dark, purple and ominous; transforms luminous green into dingy grey.

A mile from the farm, she pulls over. The anxiety is now overwhelming, clutching at her stomach so that she feels physically sick. Breathe slowly, she tells herself, but it's no good. The panic always hits her here: when she spies the stretch of coastline where her father died.

She tries to focus on the barley shimmering in the breeze, the skylarks spiralling overhead, and the sea sleek behind them. A green John Deere tractor crawls down a lane. For a moment, she sees her father driving the combine, his face ruddied as the corn is gathered in. Then she remembers the cool of the local church. The pale wood of his coffin.

She blinks through eyes that prick and burn.

Don't do this now. Not when you're minutes from home. Mum won't want to see you with reddened eyes, to know that you've been crying. She peers through the dust-flecked screen. The tractor is coming back, continuing its gentle crawl, like a child's toy pushed around a farm set. Focus on that. Breathe slowly and deeply; and for God's sake get a grip.

A flash of red appears around the corner. The sight makes her wipe her eyes, stem the tears that are threatening to spill over. She knows him. Sam, the postman who delivered letters throughout her childhood and long before then, freewheeling down then cycling back up the hill most days.

Surely he's not still going? He must be close to retirement. She watches him pedal his bike: panniers bulging, tanned calves pumping below his incongruous, dark grey shorts.

Don't let him notice me, she prays, but as he draws alongside her he glances at the car and his face breaks into a grin of recognition. She smiles back, face tight. A London smile.

He stops the bike and wheels it back to the car. 'Lucy? Lucy Petherick?'

'Hello, Sam.'

'Your mother said you were back for the summer.'

'Well, yes. No point being in London when the weather's this good.'

'Good that you're here when the emmets come down.'

'Run off their feet, are they?'

'Well not at the moment. Still the effects of this bloody recession.'

'Oh, quite.' She finds herself curiously calmed by him and their gentle chatter. 'Tourists still the best crop, though?'

'Let's hope so, though last year were dire, weren't he? Better weather this summer. Looks like he'll be a scorcher.' He rubs a streak of sweat from his forehead and wipes his hand on his legs. 'Bet you're pleased to be out of London, anyway?'

She had forgotten that he didn't stop talking.

'Different world here, isn't it?'

'The edge of the world,' she says.

He looks at her quizzically.

'Only world I'll ever need. Just look at it.' He gestures at the view: the tide in, the sea calm and sparkling. The coast at its idyllic best. 'Well, better let you get on. Your grandmother would never forgive me if I kept you from her.'

'No, that's right.' She smiles.

He swings a leg over the saddle, and heaves himself off again. Eventually, she restarts the engine and drives down the single-track lane. The air smells salty, cool and fresh. The road ends and she joins a potholed track – far worse than when she last came down in November. The Renault jolts from non-potholed patch to non-potholed patch, and then is up and away, straining to reach the top of the hill in third gear.

And there it is. Skylark Farm. Its back to the sea to protect it from the elements, its eyes – for she thinks of the windows as these – looking inwards across its land and towards the moor. Behind it, the fields are filled with their summer corn; in front with their cattle: a patchwork quilt of russet, gold and green.

Some things have altered. The Jerseys have long gone, as have the six pigs that were turned into sausages. And yet, really, little has changed. Milking still takes place twice a day; the barley is harvested each summer; the silage is made, and the cauliflowers are grown. The cattle still run with the bulls throughout the year, and the bull calves are sent to be fattened and slaughtered. The rhythm of the farming year continues, just as it has always done.

She thought she was immune to all this; that Matt and her work at the hospital was her real life now, and her Cornish heritage – something she barely referred to, that she seemed to shrug off along with her accent – belonged to a different, childish age.

But it doesn't. And as she drinks in the view, she finds that her chest is constricting with regret, and, yes, a fragile happiness; and her eyes are brimming with tears.

Five

'Lucy!'

Judith's face is flushed as she runs down the slate path through the garden. She wipes red hands on her apron and catches her daughter in delight.

'Look at you – you've gone too thin!' She pulls away from Lucy, eyes narrowing with concern as she clasps her slight wrists, takes in the dip of her waist, her hollowed cheeks. 'Oh, my love. Is this because of all the stress?'

'Something like that.' Lucy tries to laugh at the predictability of her mother's concern, but moves back into her arms, unable to answer. For a few seconds they just stand there. No one has touched her since Sunday evening: a dutiful hug from Matt before she set off for work and he met Suzi for a drink.

For a moment, she sees his face: the frank self-absorption as he said he needed 'some time', the insubstantial – meaningless – apology. 'Look, I'm sorry you had to find that,' he had said, defensive and self-righteous, as if his lover's hair had nothing to do with him. 'But perhaps this has happened for the best.'

A sob bubbles up.

'There, there,' Judith soothes her like a child.

'I'm sorry, Mum.' Her tears dampen her mother's T-shirt, a patch that blooms over her angular shoulder.

'There, there. You're home now.' Her mother, half a head shorter than her, pulls her tight. 'You come inside and we'll fatten you up. Tom's created a new ice cream in your honour: lavender and honey, or cardamom and orange.'

'Oh – is he around?' She half-laughs and feels a stab of apprehension. She owes Tom, the good sibling, who came back to farming, three months after Dad died.

'He's hay-baling, but he's going to catch you before the afternoon milking.' Her mother smiles, and Lucy catches the hint of a strain around her mouth, the suggestion of extreme tiredness. 'He's so pleased you've come back.

Well, we all are,' she says.

She pushes open the heavy oak door and they walk through the flagstoned hall towards the heart of the farmhouse. It is all much tattier than she remembers: the wallpaper in the hallway peeling off the walls; cobwebs stroking the ceiling; the corners blotched with mould.

In the chaotic, cluttered kitchen, the air is scented with scones baking for the tourists, and something else: an earthy, animal smell beyond the usual undertow of cow and muck. Lucy glances to the side of the Aga and the grubby dog basket, now home to Champ, the three-year-old sheepdog. For more than a decade, Floss, the dog of her teenage years, had filled it.

'I can't get used to her not being here,' she says.

Judith starts to load up a tea tray with the Snowman mug used by Lucy throughout her childhood, and the matching plate. She chooses a vast scone, and loads plates with pots of jam and cream – then hesitates over the choice of tea.

'Are you OK with normal? I'm afraid we don't have anything fancier.'

'Normal is perfect. Here: let me help.' Lucy moves to the cupboard and hides her face as she selects the caddy, moved by her mother's desire to make her feel instantly at home, but embarrassed by the distance between them: the fact her mother might think she is too refined to drink the tea of her childhood, the tea she has always drunk with them.

'Mum – I'm sorry I've been distant.' The apology bursts out, unplanned and unexpected. 'I was so caught up with work, and Matt,' her voice trembles. 'Well, you know Cornwall isn't really his thing.

'I should just have come down without him at Easter, but he was so keen to go somewhere hot for a break.' Lucy can hear herself over-explaining. 'Perhaps I knew, deep down, that I shouldn't leave him alone too much. But I should have popped down at Christmas after my shifts.'

She risks looking properly at her mother then and sees that Judith's eyes have lost the film of hurt and anxiety that was clouding them.

'Oh, Lucy,' she says, and moves closer to her daughter. 'I've missed you, of course I have, but that's the last thing you should be worrying about now, isn't it?'

Lucy blinks away tears. This unconditional support is more than she would have hoped for given her reluctance to visit since Fred's death.

Her mother puts her arm around her again. 'What matters is that you're here now and that this was the place you felt you could come to when you needed it.'

Ava Petherick, sturdy-legged and soft-cheeked, is chasing ducks across the lawn and chortling as the mallards race away. 'Duck, duck, duck!' she sings, pointing at them and then turning to her father for confirmation.

'Duck, Ava. Duck.'

'Duck, duck, duck,' she repeats. She runs in the opposite direction, now, spying a goose that has found a quiet spot in which to peck, under a hedge.

'Not duck, goose,' Tom corrects her as he turns

back to his sister.

'–Oose?' Ava tries it out. '–Oosey, oose?'

She runs up to her aunt and looks, enquiringly, at her. 'Oosey?'

'Lucy,' her father says.

'Oosey,' she says, emphatic. 'Oosey,' and climbs into her father's arms, confident that she is right; and that she is loved.

'She really is gorgeous, Tom,' Lucy says as her niece squirrels into him and beams the smile of a small child familiar with adoration. 'Even lovelier than when she was a baby. I can't believe how much she's changed.'

She drinks in her honey blonde whorls of hair and those big, questioning eyes.

'Seems mad my little brother's the responsible parent, now!' She smiles at the tall, broad-chested man opposite her who seems to have aged dramatically in the last year.

He rubs a hand over his face, embarrassed. 'Yeah, well. She can be a little terror.'

They are sitting at a rickety picnic table, used in the afternoon for customers. Behind him, a flock of seagulls wheel down the estuary, and dinghies draw lines of spume across the bay. Lucy rubs her fingers over the lichen on the table, and the mossy green dampening the bench. They used to build dens in this spot, draping rugs over it before gravitating to the blackened broom bushes. Years later, they would perch here and plan where to go, with their mates and cider, on a Saturday night.

Every feature here is packed tightly with memories: the hedges where she and Tom lay in the dappled shade as their parents harvested; the

40

tree-house their father built one quiet autumn; the barns where they bottle-fed lambs and scooped up chicks.

There are the spots where significant things happened, too: the dip in the track where she tumbled and broke her arm; the tamarisk tree, behind which she opened her letter from UCAS; the barn in which she almost lost her virginity, before Tom and his best friend, Ben, came blundering in. She grimaces at the memory and looks beyond, to the headland: the spot where she always imagines standing. The land turns wild there and nothing grows except the grass cropped by a neighbour's sheep, and a mass of hardy vegetation: seagrass, camomile, thrift and vetch.

'Sorry to hear about your work – and that bastard.' Tom breaks into her thoughts.

'Do you mind if we don't talk about it?' Her stomach tightens. For a moment, she had kept reality at bay. She cannot bear to think of Matt and his casual 'perhaps it's for the best'. And as for Jacob? She cannot think of that tiny body, ringed with wires, clinging to life.

'Tell me what you've been up to.' Her voice is unnaturally bright. 'I don't suppose you're managing to windsurf?'

'Not a chance.' He jerks his head at the cows in the field. 'Too busy with all this.'

'And this – it's excellent.' She takes a mouthful of the ice cream.

'You like it?' His face lightens.

She nods. 'It's got such a delicate flavour. You should be selling it.'

'Not got the money – or the time.'

41

There is a pause. For a moment, he looks so like Fred it is uncanny. A blond version – with the same way of wrinkling his nose, and the same breadth and height. She blinks and sees her father repeat Tom's mannerism before his face breaks into a smile. *'Proper job,'* Fred tells her, playing up to the caricature of the Cornishman he was far from, really. *'All right me 'ansom,'* he adds, winking. Then he stands up, tips a pre-teen Lucy over his shoulder and races down the field with her, a young Tom running in his wake.

'How's Mum?' she says abruptly, blocking out the memories. 'She seems a bit low. What's up? I mean ... beside worrying about me, and missing Dad.'

Tom flushes.

'What?' She has a crushing sense that something big is going on and that she has been woefully naïve.

'You really don't know? She hasn't told you yet?'

'Told me what? She hasn't got cancer, has she?' Her mouth fills with a metallic taste.

'No ... nothing like that.' He pauses, and she has a stronger-than-ever sense that she has been negligent: that a whole different reality has been going on while she has been absorbed with her problems. When he looks up, she sees he is close to tears.

'We've got money worries. Big ones,' Tom explains, looking down at his calloused fingers. 'We've reached the £150,000 overdraft on the farm; and we're having real difficulties paying it back.'

It takes a second for the sum to make sense.

'A hundred and fifty grand?' She feels winded. 'But how did it get so big?'

'A bad harvest last year; sixteen thousand on replacing the pipes for the milking parlour. Then we lost six milkers this winter, and it cost us another eighteen to replace them,' he says.

'You knew about the restriction order?'

She nods: one cow was found to have TB, and so the bull calves that would have been shifted at two weeks had to remain on the farm for an extra two months while they waited to discover the results of their tests.

'We only managed to shift the bull calves in April, and we'd had the cost of feeding them for those extra months.

'So ... it's just mounted up. Mum had a £100,000 overdraft anyway: the buffer we use over the winter and that the bank's been happy to lend us, as long as we manage to cut into it each year. But we've had such a run of bad luck. And then, since March, the dairy's dropped its prices to compete with the supermarkets.'

'Why didn't you tell me?' she says.

'You couldn't be much help in London – and you've got your own problems.'

'But I didn't then, and I'd have done all I could to help if I'd known.'

He smiles a small smile. 'Not really much you could do, is there? It's hard physical work that's needed, and even that's not going to be enough to shift this debt.'

He pauses. 'On top of that, we've another problem: this suggestion from Uncle Richard.'

'What suggestion?' She thinks of her mother's

43

younger brother, an accountant living in Guildford. Suave, suburban, materialistic; he left
Cornwall at eighteen and has never shown any
inclination to return.

'He wants to sell the farm so it can be developed into luxury holiday accommodation with a
play barn and swimming pool; put Granny in
some sheltered accommodation in Wadebridge;
give Mum one of the cottages, and keep one for
himself.'

'And what about you?'

'I could go back to cheffing. An easier way to
earn a living – and at least I'd get Flo off my back.'

'But you don't want to do that, do you?'

'Nah ... I might not have chosen to do this, but
now I'm here I don't want to be the one who
can't make a good job of it.'

'Even if Flo's unhappy?' She thinks of his girlfriend, who seems frequently sulky.

'She'll come around to it.' He sounds as if he is
trying to convince...

'Well, what about Mum? She won't agree, will
she?' Her chest feels tight.

'It'll break her heart, but she can see the benefits.
She's tired. Uncle Richard's talking about getting
over two million. More if we sell off all the land, far
higher if he can organise the development. No
more having to get up early to do the milking; or
worrying about this overdraft; or about not being
able to pay the council tax. She could take it easy
if she could just forgive herself and not feel guilty
about being the fifth-generation farmer who gave
it all up; the one who lost the farm.

'But the big sticking point is Granny. She just

won't go, and so, while she's alive, I don't see he can chuck her out. He might be a heartless bastard with absolutely no interest in offering any practical help down here, but I don't think even he's that much of a shit.'

Lucy thinks of her grandmother and her determination to stay at the farm that seems as strong as ever. 'She seems absolutely insistent on staying here,' Lucy says. 'Quite panicky about it.'

'Yes. So the farm should be safe while she's alive or lucid – unless he manages to bully her into giving him power of attorney. But when he and Mum inherit? Well, he'll force Mum into it if the farm's not successful – and he'll probably persuade her anyway.'

He pauses and presses his lips together. The studiedly offhand look he used to adopt as a little boy when trying to fight off tears.

'Dada sad?' Ava peers intently at her father, then reaches up to hug his neck.

'Yes, it is sad, Ava.' He loosens her grip a little. 'Daddy grew up here, and Auntie Lucy. I don't want you to miss out on this.'

'Well – we'll just have to make it a success then.' Lucy feels suddenly, ridiculously, galvanised. 'Show Uncle Richard it's a farm worth hanging on to: a farm in which he might want to invest.'

'I am trying!' Tom is suddenly frustrated. 'I've planted ten acres of thatching reed, this year. If the weather holds, it could bring in fifteen grand.'

'And if it doesn't?'

'We're in even deeper shit.'

'I don't know what to say,' she says, aware that her optimism – her belief she can somehow make things better – is presumptuous. And yet she cannot think of this world slipping away. The farm is somewhere she has always imagined she could return: as permanent and unquestioningly present as her mother; or perhaps more so, for Fred's death has taught her no parent should be taken for granted. Their family has been here for more than a hundred years – and the fact that her great-great-grandfather worked these fields moves and reassures her. This farm is part of her identity.

'Oosey?' Ava is looking at her now, stretching plump hands towards her.

'Can I?' she asks her brother.

'Of course.'

He releases his grip, and his daughter springs into her arms and burrows into her: as wriggly and forceful as a puppy but with a sweeter scent.

'We'll try to find a way to stay here, Ava,' she whispers into hair that smells of baby shampoo with just a slick of sweat. Then: 'We will stay here.' But she hasn't the slightest idea how they will manage it.

Six

Then: 20 July 1940, Cornwall

It came out of a clear blue sky. One moment, Will was watching the Heinkel sneak up the estuary and roar over the small fishing town of Padstow, the next it was aiming straight at him; a fourteen-year-old boy, just minding his own business, cycling back to the farm.

He had stopped to watch: not fearful, for this was exciting, wasn't it, a real German bomber? And, all of a sudden, he was crouching down; heart in mouth, as it veered over the houses towards Prideaux Place and the deer park. The sound scorched the air and he could see the swastika on its tail, and the pilot, through the fishbowl nose of his aircraft. He's looking me in the eye, he thought. And his first instinct – after flinging himself against a wall, for he wasn't brave enough just to stand there, despite whatever he might claim afterwards – was to think of what he would tell Maggie. Then came the bombs that blasted a doe, cratered the grass, disturbed the view – a sweep of a lawn running to the sea that had remained the same for centuries. The Heinkel veered off along the coast; the drone rumbling, then growing gradually fainter. The Elizabethan manor stood, undamaged, save for the tinkle of falling glass.

Will crouched there, heart thudding, blood whooshing through his head, before straightening, giddy. A plume of black smoke rose from the craters, smudging the sky. This was more like it! The Battle of Britain had started: Spitfires were charging off from RAF St Eval, just along the coast, and German raiders had been targeting the base, dropping three bombs and machine-gunning it last week, but this was the closest Will had been to a German bomber. Eye to eye, they'd been: man to man. That's what he would tell Maggie. War – the thing he'd been evacuated from, that Cornwall was supposed to be keeping him safe from – had arrived with all the swagger and disregard of a Luftwaffe pilot.

He found his bike and started back up the lane. A mile and a half to home, it was: he'd be there in no time, powered by this news he had to tell. Eye to eye, he'd been: man to man. He could see the evil in the Hun's face: his determination to kill him. 'So why didn't he then?' he imagined Maggie asking, her mouth curving into a smile: not dismissive or mean, just teasing him, as she often did. Well, I scared him off, he would say. Even as he practised saying it, he knew that answer wouldn't wash. Maggie was no fool. Six months older than him, and at the county school – the one you had to be clever to get into, not the elementary one he went to and was due to leave, to work on the farm, this summer. Aunt Evelyn wanted her to be a teacher. In an argument, Maggie usually won.

His legs powered round. Strong and tanned beneath his grey flannel shorts; a bit of a contrast to the mimsy white legs he'd had nine months ago when he and his three sisters had arrived down here – the twins billeted to a house in Wadebridge; Alice and he sent to the farm.

Nine months was long enough to know that he never wanted to leave. The smog of London, the cramped terrace where he and his baby brother Robert bunked up in one room, their sisters in the other, their parents downstairs; all this was a world away from the sea and the countryside, the animals, and the *freedom* he was experiencing here.

He wheeled down the hill, legs flexed straight, standing high off the seat, bombing towards the farmhouse. He thought his lungs might burst, though he was fit; used to cycling back and forth to school. He could swim too; had been practising since May so that Maggie didn't rib him – though the chill of the water still took his breath away.

The barley fields parted to reveal the farm, and he grinned, as he always did, every single time he saw it. Mad to think that this was his life now: Padstow, Trecothan, Skylark Farm. He missed his mum, still in London with Robert, and his dad, of course, but he still had one sister with him, and he had Maggie: his best friend, though he wouldn't admit it. He couldn't tell the lads that a girl, and a clever one at that, was worth hanging around with, but without her how would he have learned to swim or hunt for mussels or find the most secretive parts of the cliff? The ledges you had to scramble up to, testing your weight against the slate; trusting that it would hold, until you had reached the hollows and crevices where you could hide and watch the wheeling seabirds, marvel at the crashing of the waves?

He screeched to a halt. Less than six minutes from the deer park to the farm. Not bad. Wait till he found the girls and told them. They'd have seen the bombs dropping, perhaps been worried? He started running: he hadn't thought of that. At fourteen, he thought he was invincible. One of the lucky ones, not sent back home at Christmas when the war didn't appear to start, for his mum had shown no signs of wanting that. Too young to be fighting – and, if he carried on working on the farm, exempt from ever having to do so, it seemed.

'Guess what?' His voice rang ahead of him as

he ran through the cobbled farmyard into the garden, to the side of the house, behind the farm cottages. Maggie and Alice were perched at the wrought-iron table, laughing and shelling broad beans. Behind them, leaning against the tamarisk tree that marked the end of the garden and the beginning of the fields, was Edward, Maggie's second cousin: slim, sixteen, a bit ginger. Will barely glanced at him.

'What?' said Maggie, and she wrinkled her nose and squinted at him.

'I saw the bomber! I was right there. He dived low and almost got me. He stared me in the eyes and everything.'

'Down in Padstow? Oh Will!' Alice, just nine, was gratifyingly impressed. 'He could have got you, Will! You could have been bombed – or gunned at.'

'Nah.' He felt embarrassed now; didn't want his little sister to be scared.

'How low was it?' Maggie was interested.

'Well, I could see the swastika – and his face!'

'You couldn't have seen his face.' Edward peeled himself away from the tree, and came towards him. 'Not really. Bombers can't come that close – not unless they're going to crash, and we saw it roar off again.'

Will felt himself deflate.

'I did see him. I did. Honest. It was a Heinkel – with the windows wrapped around the nose? – so I could see him clearly. He had piercing blue eyes that went straight through me. It was if he was gloating; he just *knew* I was there.'

'Then why didn't he bomb you or machine-gun

50

you down?'

'I dunno.' Will felt as if he was being cross-examined. Edward wanted to be a lawyer, though his dad was a farmer like Uncle Joe. He liked making points, quoting poetry, having debates. Anything that made clear he was planning to go to university. Maggie admired him. Will thought him a bit of a prig.

'Perhaps it wasn't as close as it felt, Will.' Maggie smiled at him, trying to make it better. Her hazel eyes crinkled and she pushed her thick curls behind her ears, as she did when she was embarrassed or wanted to get on with things.

'Why don't you believe me?' He was bemused. 'It was that close' – he held his hands a yard apart, a possible exaggeration. 'Well three or four yards at least.' He gestured to the tamarisk. 'As close as I am to that tree.'

'Not sure you'd have been able to see his eyes if he was that far,' Edward said, and he smiled; a patronising sort of smile as if to say, sorry old chap, you've got that wrong.

'Are you calling me a liar?'

Will had had enough. The most exciting thing that had ever happened to him was being challenged by someone who loafed around in a cricket jumper reading poetry. 'Say that again and I'll deck you,' he said.

Behind him, the girls seemed stunned. Then he heard Alice whimper. Will wasn't sure where the words had come from; this wasn't the usual sort of thing he said. He'd never challenged anyone to a fight before, but adrenalin was coursing through him and he couldn't bear to be disbelieved. Above them a skylark chirruped: a joyful, relentless call that spiralled on and on, telling him not to be stupid, to forget about it; utterly oblivious to the tension beneath.

'I don't want to fight, Will,' said Edward, and the look he gave him was one of faint amusement. 'If you think he looked you in the eye, then I don't doubt you. I just wondered why he didn't machine-gun you down if he saw you, as you said?'

'Perhaps he had a conscience.'

'Well, yes, that's possible.' Edward walked back to the tamarisk as if mulling over this point. 'Perhaps the Hun doesn't kill when he comes face to face with the enemy?'

He gave Will a mock-apologetic smile, and, at that moment, Will absolutely hated him.

'You still don't believe me!' His voice rose like a child's and he felt, all too clearly, fourteen to Edward's sixteen.

'Well, I think you might have exaggerated.' Edward gave a small shrug and held up his palms; a simple gesture that said he was sorry but Will's story just didn't make sense.

'Right. You're having it.'

He marched towards the older boy, who stood a head taller than him. Edward raised an eyebrow. Even at that point, he would have backed down had Edward said let's talk about something else. But no: the other boy just smiled at him.

Will charged, barrelling towards his stomach, and knocked them both sideways.

'Steady on.' Edward's voice came as a gasp. Will flailed at him, his right fist connecting with Edward's left arm, then the left with his stomach.

Edward shot Maggie a look of alarm, then, arms up, backed away.

'Will!' Maggie rushed at them and tried to pull him back.

'Get off.' He shrugged off her hands, for he didn't want to hurt her. He didn't want to hurt anyone, really. He glanced back, trying to convey this, to make clear that he wasn't angry with *her*, but she stared back, eyes wide with disappointment. Alice, tearful, had run away.

Ooof! So Edward had decided to fight back. The shove, to his chest, took Will by surprise. The older boy grabbed his arms, wrestling him away rather than punching, for Edward wouldn't want to inflict real harm. It wasn't cricket. And Edward would want to play fair.

He was stronger than he looked, though. Surprised, Will found himself pushed back, then knocked to the ground, his nose thrust into crushed camomile and rabbit droppings. Then Edward was upon him. He kicked out, in a fury, getting Edward in the shin.

'Aargh!' The older boy's pain came out in a breath. 'That hurt.'

'It was meant to.' He tried to wrestle him over and away from him. For a minute they grappled, and then Will had him. He clambered on top as Edward thrust against him in a mindless flurry of arms and legs and fists.

Will's shoulder hurt from where he'd been flung, and his shins were buggered. He suddenly felt immensely weary, for this wasn't about not being believed. This was about being the incomer. The boy who was welcomed on the farm but who wasn't entitled to be here.

'Get off me,' his opponent snarled, for his nose was bloodied now. 'For God's sake, stop.'

Will clambered off, staring at the blood that was dripping onto the cream of Edward's jumper, shaken by the effect of his strength.

'I'm sorry,' he said. 'I didn't mean...'

'You were like a savage.' Edward's light blue eyes had narrowed into slits.

Will's head fizzed, and he wanted to lunge at him again, but a sharp voice, incensed and increasing in volume, pulled him up short.

'What on *earth* do you think you are doing?'

Aunt Evelyn, Maggie's mother, was running into the yard with the maid, Joanna. Her eyes bored into him: two black beetles. Her mouth twisted in a hiss.

'Well?'

They were silent.

'I'm s-sorry,' Will eventually managed. His intermittent stutter – gone these past six months – re-emerging.

'It was just a scrap, Aunt Evelyn. Emotions running high. Will has apologised,' Edward said.

'That's very good of you, but you're bleeding.' Aunt Evelyn's eyes hardened. 'William, I will not tolerate such behaviour. You are a guest in our house and I will not hesitate to ring the billeting officer and get you rehoused if this happens again.'

'S-sorry,' he said.

'Your uncle will deal with this. In the meantime, shouldn't you be helping with the milking?'

'Yes.'

'Well, get to it.'

'Th-thank you.' He glanced at Evelyn. Her lips, pulled thin, were unsmiling, her forehead furrowed into a crease.

She nodded, curtly, preoccupied with the blood blotching Edward. And, before she could change her mind, he slipped away.

Later, much later, he ran from the farm, down the track, and out along the coast path. Past the concrete pillbox; up towards the headland; out towards the sea. He flew past the cove, where the water lay petrol-blue and deep, and beyond the old fisherman's hut. It was early evening, but the paths were empty. The perfect time to disappear.

The tendrils of goosegrass grew thicker, and the brambles scratched as he pushed past them. His legs were coated with spittle and juices, branded with nettles, itchy and red. He needed to be alone, to brood on Uncle Joe's words – he was 'disappointed', the farmer said, and that disappointment was worse than the thrashing he had feared – and to overcome his embarrassment and work out how he could face them again.

The ledge was a hiding place Maggie had shown him last September, soon after they'd arrived. They'd been blackberrying: picking the last choice berries, cramming them into their mouths and sucking the juices, heady and sweet. It had been a balmy day – and he had been stunned by the view and by the sea blurring into the horizon. 'Look!' She had grabbed him and turned him round. Far below, a couple of seals were sunning themselves, on rocks thrust high above the waves.

'I'll show you a better spot,' she went on, and had led him to this ledge, halfway along the side of the cliff; found by leaning in, and moving low; by trusting that the footholds would hold; that the wind wouldn't pick up and unsteady them. They had scrambled up then hunkered down, shuffling on their stomachs to spy on the world from under a canopy of seagrass and thrift.

'No one knows about this,' she had said.

'Well I do,' he had smiled.

'Yes,' she had said. 'You do, now. It could be our secret place. Just you and me.'

He hadn't been here since the start of June, but it was the place he came to when he needed to think things through. He hadn't expected her to follow, but it came as little surprise when he spotted her an hour later. She wriggled in beside him, tanned legs flexing beneath her shorts, more like a younger boy than a girl; still flat-chested, as far as he could see.

'You can't go hitting people, you know.'

'I know.'

'I didn't like it – and it wasn't fair on Edward.'

'He made me feel stupid.'

'He didn't mean to. He was just puzzling it out. That's just his way.'

Will was quiet. Beyond them, the sky was changing: lilac spreading into the blue with just a hint of copper. The tide now coated the sand, inching its way in. He fiddled with a stalk of seagrass, bending it into a loop then knotting it into a bracelet. Anything to avoid her seeing that he was close to crying. She was peering at him intently and reached out a hand to touch his lightly.

'We'd better go back,' she said. 'Mother will worry.'

'I can't go back.'

'Oh don't be ridiculous.' For a moment she sounded just like Aunt Evelyn. Then she smiled and a dimple stabbed her cheek.

How to explain that he was terrified of being sent from the farm; that, though he knew Uncle Joe liked him, he sensed that Evelyn was the stronger of the two; the one who would get her own way if she was determined. She was the one he needed to be wary of, to make it up to. The person he needed to impress.

'What if she hates me?'

'She doesn't hate you. She just doesn't want you fighting. All you need to do is apologise to *her* – be really *really* sorry – and make sure you *never* do it again.'

He looked at her, wanting to believe it. Her face had flushed, and she traced a pattern in the grit with her fingers. He watched and realised that it was his initials: the comical W. C.

'I don't want you to go. It was lonely before you and Alice came. You don't want to, do you?' She looked up at him, suddenly.

'No.' His voice was hoarse, for he could think of nothing worse. 'Of course I want to stay.'

'Well come on, then,' she said. 'Time to go back.' She slid out from the ledge and held a hand out to him as he clambered up. Her fingers were slim and warm, and her touch – quickly given, for he dropped her hand as soon as he was up – was comforting. Alice still hugged him, but affection wasn't something he often received.

57

'Race you back?' she said, with a backward glance, and a smile that seemed to say that everything would be all right. And she was off: dark curls bouncing, slim shoulders weaving through the banks of gold and green.

He waited until she had disappeared from sight, in the dip of the cove, then started after her, aiming for the farm, perched on the opposite hill's crest.

Seven

Now: 3 July 2014, Cornwall

Early morning, and while Tom does the milking, Lucy slips from the farm, guilt at not helping adding to her sorrow, anger, fear and shame. She runs briskly and with purpose, driving through the gently rotting vegetation, up along the coast path, out towards the cliffs.

The tide is high: a mass of deep blue, ebbing and flowing, not yet choppy, for the breeze that will pick up this morning is light at the moment, just pimpling her skin. She drives on, lungs straining as she pounds up the hill. She is working too hard to cry outright, but her face is tense as she concentrates on pushing her body and on forcing away the images of Matt and Suzi – who becomes increasingly seductive. The hedgerows whip her, a stinging nettle smarts, a fly whips into her mouth and is spat out, and yet she doesn't stop, for if she does she will crumble, and her self-respect – so fragile, now, so vulnerable – will fall away.

And then she is up at the top of the path with only a gentle incline leading up to the headland. She slows, legs burning, breath ragged, and bends over, her hands on the tops of her knees. The view is stunning – stretching one way to Devon, the other to the end of Britain, for the early morning sea mist has lifted and the pale blue sky becomes more defined with every moment. Dad must have run this way, the very last day he was alive; though it was April, then, the paths not compacted dust, but wet and slippery. A sob catches in her throat, and, finally, she gives in to tears.

Consumed now, she stumbles to the spot she always thinks of when she cannot sleep: the headland, where the wind blusters and pummels on all but the calmest of days. A trickle of sweat runs to the base of her back, and she tugs her top away, but it turns chill and soon she is shivering. She cradles herself, feeling her ribs rise and fall with each gulp of a cry.

And now that she is here, she finds that she does not want to stand, arms outstretched, trusting to the wind, pretending to be invincible. For it might drop and trick her into staggering backwards, or change direction and try to drive her from the cliff. She peers at the waves swirling around the rocks, the white spray crashing up and drenching the seagulls, and at the jagged granite that would rip you to shreds if you swam too near and got caught in the current.

And if you fell? For just the slimmest of moments, she imagines that death. Would it be quick, her skull impaled? Or slow, the blood seeping from her before the sea took pity and dragged her deep into its blackened depths?

She steps back. The tears have stopped. She has frightened herself. Really frightened herself. She did not contemplate it. Not really, even though she saw not just the rocks but her manager's face steeped in disappointment – *It's not like you. You're usually so focused*' – and Matt's, cloaked with self-pity: '*I need some time to think*'.

In that split second, she knows that she wants to live. That however shameful Matt's affair and her mistake, neither is so immense it should cause oblivion. The grief and self-loathing will ease, eventually.

She wipes her eyes and starts to walk back. The sun beats down now and, as she nears the farm, the dairy herd ambles from the parlour. She sees Tom close the gate and make for the farmhouse. Breakfast. She had better get going.

She starts to jog and as she reaches the cove, her pace picks up. And she finds, as she pounds along the coast path, that she is almost smiling.

Her moment on the headland, as she later thinks of it, is what she needs to kick her into action. No more obsessing over her problems, but plenty of hard, physical work to distract her from her guilt and grief.

She starts with the kitchen: scrubbing the Edwardian floor tiles, worn over a century and engrained with a sheen of dirt that hasn't been eradicated for years. From this angle, she can get some idea of the kitchen's grime: the whitewashed walls encrusted with stickiness where they meet the floor; the Aga slick with grease; the ropes of the drying racks yellowed by the cooking odours of the past hundred years.

She worries away at the particles of black lodged between the tessellated black and terracotta, trying to distract herself from thinking of her relationship: seven years seemingly thrown away. The disinfectant-infused steam stings her eyes, and she tries to focus on the pain. *'Perhaps it's for the best,'* he had said, as he left. Where did he go then? To Suzi's? She imagines him in another woman's home, another woman's bed. A slip of a woman with long, thick hair and an affected name. A woman who might put him first – for he had said she only thought of work. *'Well of course I do. When a baby dies.'* She scrubs even harder. His feminist principles – 'I'm more feminist than many of your friends,' he had said when one confided she just wanted to get married – didn't stand for much, in the end.

She sits back on her heels again and looks at the tiles. She *mustn't* obsess. She makes herself focus. Now: were they always this bad? From somewhere in her distant memory, she remembers a photo of her great-grandmother standing by the scrubbed pine table, and she knows – from Maggie's tales of her ferocious mother – that they wouldn't have been this grimy then.

Where are those pictures now? There was a whole set that captured the farm in its heyday – flourishing before, during and just after the war. Photos of cows being hand milked, and of her great-grandfather driving a plough. Of a wagon piled high with straw, an unknown teenage boy tossing it with a pitchfork, and of Maggie, as a young woman, squinting into the sun. Snapshots of a not-too-distant past when the farm could employ three men as well as a maid, and her great-grandfather could boast not just a team of shire horses, but a Fordson tractor.

Well, those days of relative affluence are long gone. A hundred and fifty thousand pounds in debt. The sum reverberates as she refills buckets of water and scours her way across the floor. She straightens, her eyes level with the top of the oil-clothed table, and then her stomach caves in. Surely not? And yet: of course.

The end of the kitchen table has always been piled high with papers – seed catalogues, machinery manuals, letters from the feed supplier, business correspondence. It teeters in two-foot-high piles. Lucy had assumed that Tom had been through this when he catalogued the debt. But who's to say that Judith hasn't shoved some unopened envelopes in their midst, or in the dresser drawers; that there's not more debt lurking, brooding, accumulating interest, while they have gone about their day-to-day business?

The floor finished now, she approaches the piles and begins sifting through the documents. And amid all the ephemera, there are sealed brown and white envelopes from the feed suppliers, the bank and the utility companies, indicating that the farm is a further £14,758 in debt.

There are payments too. Cheques dating back three or four years: the milk cheque for the month after her dad died, one for a load of cauliflowers, another for silage. Cheques that, if honoured, would bring in over eleven thousand pounds. But can she claim back such sums – or do they have to be discounted? She slumps on to the settle. She is no financial expert, and has no idea how to pull her family out of this mess.

On autopilot, she throws out the bin bag; moves the catalogues and brochures into the dining room to be filed, and lays the unpaid bills and unclaimed payments on the table where they will have to be seen. And then she turns to the very final pile. Happily, there are no more unpleasant surprises, but stuffed at the very bottom is the photo album she had been thinking of: the evidence that the farm was once a thriving concern.

She turns one stiffened cardboard page. Her teenage grandmother plays catch in the yard in front of the farm workers' cottages, with a far younger, clearly excited small girl. Another shot, and there are cows in the milking parlour; her great-grandfather Joe grinning broadly, and a young boy smiling more hesitantly as he crouches on a milking stool, as if the whole experience is new.

There are further pictures: a shire horse hoeing marigolds; the same horse standing by a corn-heaped wagon; and then some of the dairy. Her grandmother posing as she churned butter; and the smaller girl ladling milk, her tongue poked out in concentration like a cat contemplating cream.

One particular photo captures her attention. A meal, perhaps a Harvest Supper, the table heaped with food: pork pies, pasties, a roast chicken, tureens of potatoes, carrots and beans. The family and farm workers are gathered around: faces upturned to the camera, smiles betraying their exhaustion and relief. In the foreground is Evelyn, her face relaxed for once, calm with the certainty that she has provided a generous meal. Opposite her, at the head of the table, Joe beams in appreciation: this is his farm, and it is thanks to his graft and good management that they are enjoying this plenty.

But it is Lucy's grandmother, Maggie, who really draws her into the photo. Seated next to her father, she radiates excitement, her dark eyes sparkling, her surprisingly sensuous mouth stretched tight. She must be seventeen or eighteen here: a young woman brimming with happiness, and, more than that, with expectation. She looks as if she is plotting something: humming with anticipation, teetering on the cusp of her adult life.

More than anything, the photo conveys happiness – ranging from her great-grandmother's contentment to her grandmother's elation. This is a profitable, successful farm. And as the memories of an industrious past offer themselves up, the fragile skeleton of an idea begins to emerge.

Eight

Lucy takes the photo of the Harvest Supper and lays it in front of her family on the scrubbed pine kitchen table.

Her grandmother peers at it – then picks it up

and holds it close to her face.

'Do you remember it, Granny?'

Maggie, eyes skimming the picture, nods.

'You look so happy.'

'I was.' Her voice is dry. She puts the photo down with a shrug, but continues looking at her younger self captured in sepia. 'That was taken at one of the happiest points of my life.'

'It looks like it was a great occasion,' Tom says. 'It's such a lovely photo and it proves the farm was profitable.'

'Well, it was, once.'

'And not that long ago?'

'1943. A very different time. Farming was valued, then, seen as crucial to feeding a nation during the war. Every spare inch of this place was dug up: new potatoes dug into the tracks. Even the lawn wrecked, eventually, for the caulies. It was a different world.'

'You're quite right.' Tom defers to his grandmother's judgement. 'Farming's not valued, now, and we're not the least bit profitable. But we want to try and return to those more successful years.

'We know Uncle Richard has an idea for getting us out of this – has even talked to property developers, apparently, and to the estate agents about possible prices...' Judith gives a small click of indignation, 'but I think we're clear, aren't we, that we don't want to give up yet?'

'We've got a few ideas that we think will help,' Lucy says, her voice quavering as she looks at her family. They have called a meeting to discuss a possible overhaul but she is not convinced they are ready for change. Her grandmother looks defensive, and Flo, Tom's partner, distinctly bored. Head down, she examines her chipped fingernails and swings her crossed leg as if she is still the teenager of eight years ago. Every inch of her suggests she would rather be in the fish restaurant, where she waitresses four days a week, or with Ava. Anywhere other than discussing the future of a farm she only lives on because she is in a relationship with the farmer, and in which she has little interest at all.

Only Judith seems the least bit enthusiastic: perched on the edge of her seat, taking notes, trying to atone for the unopened bills and her subsequent shame. Lucy focuses on her. It is for her that they need to resurrect the farm – for its loss would mean not just the loss of her livelihood but of her identity.

She runs through the need to improve the farm's website and to spruce up the tired cottages – and offers to contribute her savings to buy new ovens, fresh white linen and Cornish blue crockery.

'Then we can put up the prices,' she says.

'What's wrong with the prices?' Judith looks appalled.

'Mum – you haven't changed them for ten years. You're charging the same in August as you are in May, when you could be charging double or, in peak season, even triple.'

'I don't know... It just seems a bit greedy.'

'At the moment the cottages are so cheap people will wonder what's wrong with them!'

After this, it doesn't take much to persuade Judith that they should increase the prices of the cream teas, and provide more picnic tables for customers.

'We had to turn two sets away yesterday,' adds Flo, showing some interest. 'They were proper pissed off at not getting a cup of tea.'

'We should also make more of our heritage,' Lucy says. 'So, longer-term we could spruce up the dairy – with photos of Great-Grandpa Joe milking, and perhaps old butter churns and milk churns as decoration – so that we can serve people if it rains, and during Easter and the October half-term: for a longer period of the year.

'Perhaps we could make the most of photos like this,' she adds, gesturing at the Harvest Supper. 'People are fascinated by a sense of history and identity. It suggests that we have credibility: that we know what we're doing, that we are successful – and we should make the most of it.'

'We also wondered about selling ice cream,' Tom says. 'We know that customers like knowing the provenance of food: that they'll pay more for that. If we could sell them something where the ingredients – milk, cream, even strawberries – originated just a few feet from where they sit, I think we'd really be on to something. We'd only need three or four flavours to start with, but, if they take off, perhaps we could try selling them further afield: Tredinnick farm shop – and other delis.'

'It's a lot of change,' Lucy tells her mother. But there is no need to tread gently.

'No, no. I can see it's necessary.' Judith smiles, and a hint of the old Judith – the one who existed before Fred's death – shines through. 'They're fantastic ideas,' she says, and her smile broadens.

'We can do this. Absolutely.'

The sea is as sleek as satin, and the beach almost empty, when Lucy manages to slip from the farm. The air is cooler, now: within an hour and a half the sun will have set and the sky will have faded to a muted indigo before imperceptibly turning a dark blue.

She pauses on the stile at the end of the field, and runs her hand over the granite gatepost, etched with the initials of past generations of lovers. She traces the JP and FP of her parents, lingering over a delicate, almost hidden heart. Tom and Flo's initials are entwined in Flo's creative flourish. But no one has ever inscribed Lucy's name.

She jumps from the stile, and walks through the coarse grass of the sand dunes, then reaches the beach and takes a deep breath of pure salt air. A wave of relief flows over her, and something deeper: the faint promise of happiness, that's what it is. The sensation takes some getting used to. When did she last feel happy? Not for quite some time.

It has been a busy day – and an emotional one – in which the magnitude of what she and Tom are trying to do has borne down on her. And yet, on this beach, in front of these fields, she feels, at least briefly, if not happy then content. The anxieties of her London life ease away like marks in the sand swallowed by the tide. They matter, of course they matter, but, just for this moment, they can be held at bay.

She slips off her Birkenstocks and feels the

silvery sand seep between her toes, then stands at the edge of a pool of water. Her feet squelch, the sand sucking her ankles and pressing heavy, cool and wet. She moves on, watching shrimps, surprised by her bright red toenails, scurry away. *Splosh, splosh, splosh:* the rhythmic splashing prompts a smile, just as it did when she scampered along the beach as a child after Fred. For a second she remembers her father's size twelve footprints, broad and long compared to hers when she placed them inside them. Feet like pasties, he'd called them. She couldn't ever imagine being so big.

She looks up. It's a good light for taking pictures or – hopefully – for capturing a sunset. Her digital camera hangs heavy round her neck and she fiddles with the zoom. *Snap, snap, snap.* She closes in on textures: cockleshells washed up on ridges of sand, bladderwrack unfurling in a rock pool. The everyday captured in black and white.

It is the sea – empty but for a swimmer streaking towards the horizon – that is the most breathtaking part of this landscape but, somehow, it doesn't look the least impressive when caught by a lens. Perhaps it just needs to be more dramatic. Like the weather, she has always loved the sea at its most stormy: white horses under charcoal skies; waves that pick you up and carry you along, exhilarating and terrifying – and which always threaten to crash over your head.

For a moment she is back bodyboarding with her dad: reliving the fear of having a wave tumble over her head and pound her into the sand, and then the whoosh of relief as his broad arms caught her and pushed her high above the next one so that she could ride it; mouth filled with salt, body surging with the thrill of being eight, nine, ten.

A sudden image of Matt and Suzi intrudes – an imagined clinch in her bed – and she scrubs at her forehead; then tiny, vulnerable Jacob appears. She feels befuddled, as if her ears are blocked with salt water, tilting her off balance. She needs to escape such thoughts by immersing herself in something so exhausting she doesn't have the energy to think. There is a selfishness to what she proposed to her mother – for herself, as much as for any other reason, she needs to revitalise this farm.

She turns and walks towards the shore. In the time she has been taking the photos, the swimmer has emerged and is now wading through the shallows. Who swims at this time of year without a wetsuit? A hardy local who swims every day, without fail? Without thinking, she raises her camera, zooms in and captures him in her aperture. He is young – and he looks as if he is fit. No pigeon-chested tourist shivering in baggy swimming trunks, but a younger, sleeker figure emerging from the sea.

She pretends to take a few shots in a different direction, then flits back, though she knows it is voyeuristic. Thick hair, dripping salt water, good cheekbones – a strong, though not classically beautiful, face. There is something familiar about him, as well. As if she has seen his features before, perhaps rearranged on someone else, or spotted, smudged, out of focus, on a younger, more unformed face.

The main thing is to get off the beach before he sees her, standing there with her camera. She reaches the dunes and almost trips in her eagerness to get out of his sight. Of course, she didn't take any pictures. But the water trickling down the V of his chest, the curve of his buttocks as he waded through the water, the white of his tan line: all this is imprinted on her mind.

Nine

Maggie readjusts her smartest cardigan and eases herself into the garden chair. The afternoon sun caresses her wrinkles. For a moment, she imagines it seeping into her bones. She closes her eyes. She dreads going blind – and yet with eyes tight shut, her other senses are sharper: the seagulls are raucous and there is a particularly pungent smell of thyme.

A voice grates – a Midlands accent: another tourist – and her eyelids flicker, roused by the chatter of a couple making their way across the lawn. She glances at the middle-aged man who is easing his wide thighs beneath the picnic table and sighing with relief as his bottom thumps on the slats of the bench. Could that be him? She asks that of every man who tramps the footpath, who visits the farm, who drops by for a cream tea or to deliver the feed; and who could conceivably be seventy. But he is far too young: too fat and florid and – well – too vulgar. She doesn't know who will materialise, but she is pretty sure it won't be someone from Wolverhampton with a sizeable belly straining against his sweat-drenched polo shirt.

His wife is fussing over him now. A small bird-like woman chirruping away, asking if he wants tea, or coffee, or a glass of water. Usually, customers just relax when they reach the tables, relieved to sit down after the climb up the cliff. 'This is the life,' they smile at one another as they gaze down at the calm slick of the sea and indulge in their annual fantasy. 'We could do this, couldn't we? Escape to Cornwall? Set up a B&B with a smallholding, or run a gift shop? Wouldn't it be marvellous if we lived here!'

They haven't a clue. Well, some of them manage it if they've made enough before coming down here. They accept there will be a lengthy quiet season, and that their project may not work financially; they may not even break even. But others sell up within a couple of years. Unable to cope with the rain and isolation; unprepared for the sheer hard graft of working on the land or with animals. If you haven't been brought up with it, it can be a real shock.

She doubts this couple would ever want to make a fist of it. The woman is still bustling around, peering intently at her husband. One thing she never did with her husband was fuss. For a second, she thinks of someone else: a peal of laughter; an arm slipped round her waist. A long-forgotten memory swims up from the depths of her past and emerges with such sudden clarity that it is as if he is in front of her. A pair of blue eyes smiling into hers, in the depths of the sand dunes, as he pulled her down on to him and kissed her with such passion that she hoped, even now, it meant he loved her. This boy – this young man really – who would never age beyond eighteen, who was eternally beautiful, and golden. Snatched in the prime of his life. Seventy years ago.

'We'll order a cream tea now,' the woman, voice bossy as well as concerned, breaks into her reveries. The sound wrenches her back to the present: the memory dispersing like ripples in a pool. She needs to get up, and sharpish. She shifts her weight over her knees, as the GP suggested, and grips the chair's plastic arms.

'Two cream teas, is it?' she asks.

'If it's no bother.' The woman looks perturbed at realising she has forced an elderly lady from her seat. 'And a glass of water? But perhaps I should get someone else?'

Margaret shakes her head. 'I'll tell my granddaughter.' Head held high, she shuffles into the kitchen, one hand clutching at the gatepost then the doorframe to steady herself.

'Lu-cy?' her voice quavers now, in the sanctuary of the kitchen.

'Granny? What are you doing up?'

'Don't fuss, dear. There are customers. Two cream teas and a glass of water. You do the tea, I'll do the scones.'

She moves to the table, holding on to it for support, and begins putting scones in a basket, spooning jam, shimmering with sugar, into a bowl.

Lucy takes the tray, piled with a pot of steaming English Breakfast tea, out into the sunshine, and she follows. No reason to stay inside on a glorious summer's day, and Lucy has gently made it clear – with her efficiency; the speed with which she

73

warmed the teapot – that there is no real need to help. Silly really. She can do all this with her eyes closed. She first made cream teas before the war when her mother provided B&B for hikers and members of the Cyclists' Union. From the age of eight, she'd be spooning jam and making scones. She had a light touch, said Evelyn – one of the few things she ever complimented her on. She pulled her weight, even as a girl.

She shuffles back into the garden. Something is wrong. The man – the florid, fat-faced customer – is hunched forwards, breathing heavily, clutching his arm.

A heart attack. Just like Edward. She is moving back into the kitchen, towards the phone, faster than she would have thought possible. Her fingers stab at the buttons of the handset. Nine nine nine.

By the time she gets outside, the man is lying on the ground; keeled over and apparently unconscious. Lucy is leaning over him, the heels of her hands interlocked and placed over the centre of his chest.

She watches her slight granddaughter perform CPR: arms stiff and pushing rhythmically. 'One and two and three and four and five and six and seven and eight,' Lucy counts, as his poor wife whimpers by his side. There is a ferocity to her movements as she pumps, then bends to breathe into his mouth, then resumes pumping. For this is about Lucy's capability as a nurse. About whether she can make things right or, rather, perform miracles. She wonders why she feels dizzy, then realises she is holding her breath.

The air is heavy with expectation seguing into

74

dread. 'One and two and three and four,' Lucy counts all the way to thirty, then two more rescue breaths, and back to pumping again.

'Where's the ambulance? Where's the ambulance?' The man's wife wails, her face blank with incomprehension.

'It's coming,' Maggie tries to reassure her. 'But we're quite a way away.'

'One and two and three and four,' Lucy continues: a mantra that she keeps up, unflagging, though now there is a catch to her voice.

'Keep going, they're almost here,' Maggie urges as the woman whimpers in accompaniment. 'Seven and eight and nine and ten,' Lucy chants. 'Eleven and twelve and thirteen and fourteen.'

And just as Maggie is beginning to lose all hope, the man coughs and splutters into life.

Later, after the ambulance has roared out of the yard taking the couple off to hospital, after the paramedics have praised Lucy, Maggie makes them a cup of sweet tea. Her granddaughter looks shaken.

'At least I didn't do anything wrong with *him.*' She unfurls from the tense position she has adopted. 'For a while I thought we had a death on our hands, there. I was starting to wonder if I was jinxed. As if everything I've ever learned as a nurse had left me. Not sure how I would have coped if he hadn't made it.'

Her grandmother tries to imagine the level of anxiety buzzing through her brain.

'No use thinking about what might have happened. You saved his life; that's all that matters.

He'd be dead if you hadn't been here.'

'I suppose he might...You were fantastic, by the way.'

'Bah!' Maggie puffs out her cheeks. 'It was nothing; a quick phone call, that's all.'

'You moved so swiftly.'

'Well.' She pauses. 'I don't like deaths on my farm.'

'Granny!' Lucy is appalled.

'Well, do you?' Maggie raises an eyebrow, then flushes slightly, the answer all too evident. 'No, I didn't think so,' she says.

They sit in silence for a minute, watching the low tide lick the sand. A guillemot wheels upwards. A list of deaths – the collateral damage of a farm – hangs in the air. There was her Great-Uncle Frank, flung to the apex of the barn when a threshing machine caught the back of his coat and tossed him like a rag doll; her Uncle Ned, who blew his hand off when straddling a gate while shooting rabbits and later died of septicaemia.

And there was Fred Petherick: her son-in-law, and Lucy's father.

Ten

Then: 20 March 1943, Cornwall

Will placed a cauldron of water above the fire in the corner of the yard, then helped Arthur to construct the table with four thick, heavy planks bleached white from being scrubbed clean.

Doris, the pig, watched from her sty, and yet she was willing to be lured underneath the beam: following Aunt Evelyn with her bucket of warm gruel, trotting along, chomping away as if she couldn't get enough of it. Will's insides clenched. Any minute now her gentle contentment would tip into rage and fear.

Uncle Joe came forward, scratched the sow behind her ears, rubbed her back, then slipped a noose in her mouth to clamp her nose and upper jaw tight.

Doris squealed. Not just her usual growling but a high-pitched, frantic screeching as she tugged and tried to run in circles, foaming at the mouth. Will rushed to help: corralling the pig, holding her fast, feeling the panic coursing through her body as she strained. Then the farmer flung one end of the rope over the beam and pulled it tight so that the pig was on tiptoes, trotters just touching the floor.

She scrabbled properly then, shitting and pissing as her trotters failed to grip, but he and Arthur

77

held her: faces pressed into her rough, hairy flanks so that they could smell the stench of dung and fear. Uncle Joe took out his sharp, pointed knife and aimed for the jugular: one small cut and then the full knife. Four killings in, it still surprised him how much blood there was. The bright red liquid pumped and spurted into the bucket in a mass of velvet blackness, before Aunt Evelyn swapped the container for a second pail.

Once the pig was dead, they heaved her onto the boards to scald the carcass and scrape off the bristles, until poor Doris's skin was spotlessly smooth and clean. He and Arthur hung her hind legs far apart, and Uncle Joe took his knife and slit her down the belly, pulling out her innards. Aunt Evelyn, face like a twisted lemon, for she wasn't born to this, you could just tell, scraped off the fat to be clarified into soft, white lard, and started to clean the intestines, which would later be used for hog's pudding.

The other men went, for this was largely a woman's job, but Will worked with her, handling the slippery, greasy intestines; squeezing out the waste – so rank the smell caught the back of your throat; piling them up to be cleaned and rinsed. There was a nip in the air, but Aunt Evelyn wanted to stay in the yard. No point dirtying the kitchen with such waste, and as long as they kept moving they wouldn't feel the cold. He watched her mouth purse as she grappled with the pig's guts, her hands smeared with blood and the khaki mulch Doris had been trying to digest.

She wiped a hair from her forehead with the back of her hand, her cheeks flushed, mouth thinned in concentration, and he realised that she must have been beautiful once, with those fine cheekbones and Maggie's large, almond-shaped eyes. She seemed too slight to be a farmer's wife: so thin, he feared she might snap when she helped haul Doris up or carried a covered pail after milking. And yet her determination made her strong.

She smiled at him now, and her praise was worth all the more for its rareness. 'You're doing well.'

He reddened. Nearly three years he'd been working as a farm apprentice. He'd settled down after that fight with Edward; worked hard, learned all he could about a trade he wasn't born to but which he loved.

Around him, the world was changing. The war seemed to be going better since the fall of Stalingrad, though each month brought news of neighbours who were missing presumed dead, captured or killed. Here he was protected: tending the land, harvesting the crops, milking the cows. He wondered if he would enlist, despite being exempt if Uncle Joe argued his case as a farm boy. Part of him was intrigued. The Allies were in North Africa, now, pushing through Libya and Tunisia, forcing the Hun back, and it would be a thrill to travel, wouldn't it? To feel that sun on your back, to see those sights?

But his stronger feeling was that he wanted to stay here, where few bombs had fallen in the past two years – apart from at the airfield at St Eval, where Spitfires roared off daily with their full-throated throttle, and along the coast, at Davidstow, from where the B24s of coastal command droned out to sea. This was his home: the place where his little sister lived, and where he had friends of sorts. Arthur, a couple of years older than him, pig ugly but with a wicked sense of humour; James, the cowman, experienced and kindly; even Joanna, who would slip him the most generous helpings of pie – 'I swear you're still growing' – but then boss him, as if he were one of her many brothers.

And there was Maggie. More distant, now that she boarded in Bodmin, but still warm: her presence enough to remind him of their shared stock of memories. He could see her now: eyes bright as she taught him to milk properly, two fingers and a thumb caressing the milk from a teat when he had wanted to tug, and her delight when he'd got it right. 'That's it,' she'd whispered, crouched by the side of the Guernsey, for he hadn't wanted to admit to James he was getting it wrong. The dribble and spurt of milk became a steady stream, and she had grinned. 'You'll be a farm boy yet.'

She was back for the Easter holidays in two days' time: Doris was being killed in preparation. His stomach fizzed with excitement but also apprehension, for Maggie was becoming a young woman. Her boyishness swapped for curves: hips, a waist and breasts. He felt himself stir and bent over the bucket, squeezing out Doris's intestines, reddening at the thought that Evelyn might see. He would have to hope that she still spared him the time of day, that she would still want to be his friend. But what if she didn't? If she had grown right away from him? The stench of Doris's guts struck him, and he felt suddenly sick.

As soon as she was back, she mucked in. In that respect, she was still the old Maggie. Always willing to get her hands dirty.

They were still dealing with the pig. Cutting it up and salting it for bacon before it could be bagged in muslin and hung from the rafters. Joanna handled the meat briskly: rubbing salt into the flesh of the sides and forcing it next to the bone so that no flies could lay eggs. Maggie copied: slim fingers probing the cavities, caressing the flesh. She bit her lip as she did so, but there was something dreamlike about her actions. As if she were thinking of something else entirely.

'You're stroking it ever so gentle.' Joanna, sturdy and no-nonsense, noticed. 'You don't normally do it so loving.'

'That better?'

'A bit. It needs more of a slap than a tickle.' Joanna, only four years older than Maggie, burst into laughter. 'Imagine some young man who needs knocking into shape.'

Maggie looked quizzical, her eyes wide open. 'Don't think I know one of those,' she said and paused so that Will wondered if she was going through her classmates.

Joanna caught his eye, gave him a wink. Four younger brothers she had: plenty of practice at picking up on a boy's weak points. He shot her a look: Don't say anything else, he willed her. Just don't. Not, of course, that there was anything to say.

'Imagine it's Will.' Joanna looked at him slyly, getting into her stride.

'Why would I want to slap Will?'

'You're quite right. Far better to tickle. In fact, I might just do that...' Joanna held up her red palms, glistening with the wet of the pig. She started around the table, skirting the end more quickly than he might have imagined, and he deftly swapped sides.

'I wouldn't if I were you,' he warned. 'I can tickle hard. Just ask Alice.'

'Well, there's an invitation!' Joanna whooped, her eyes glowing with laughter. 'Fancy taking it up, Maggie?'

'No, thanks.' Maggie, the sensible, county schoolgirl, went back to her salting. 'No offence, Will.' She gave a quick, friendly smile.

'None taken.' His breath eased out in relief.

'Well, I reckon we're missing out,' said Joanna, snorting with laughter, her small, red face aglow now. 'He could do with the tickle if not the slap! Any time you fancy it, Will...'

What had got into her? She'd never flirted with him before. He kept his tone light though he was burning with humiliation. 'I'll bear it in mind,' he said.

They carried on in near silence, bar Joanna's occasional chuckle. She seemed intent on creating or stoking some kind of *atmosphere*. For once, he was grateful when Aunt Evelyn joined them and worked away at the fleshy pinkness, fingers jamming the salt, her face particularly grim.

She smiled, though, when a tall, graceful figure knocked at the open back door.

'May I come in?' Patrick Trescothick, the local vet, gave her an apologetic smile, as if to say he was sorry to catch her like this, and entered the kitchen, ducking his head.

Will glanced at Maggie, but she was still working. Joanna, flushed and good-tempered, had stopped and was simpering at the vet.

He didn't like Mr Trescothick. He had last seen him at a livestock market a week ago when he'd been his usual self: courteous to the farmers, but a touch arrogant to those like Will he had no need to impress. 'Still enjoying the country life?' he'd asked, and Will had felt a niggle of irritation. Or perhaps he was being prickly: he'd just heard that their mother had left Fulham to visit Robert, now five years old and with a family in Hampshire, and he'd felt a surprise pang of jealousy. She had only come to Cornwall the once.

'Joe in?' The vet asked.

'In the stables,' said Evelyn and flushed: a Methodist minister's daughter, she wouldn't want to be seen with her hands inside a joint of meat.

It always surprised Will that the vet referred to the farmer by his first name, though he couldn't have been thirty. But then everything about him suggested he felt entitled: from the way in which he carried himself, to the cut of his tweed jacket, to his voice – like a posh Londoner, though he was Cornish born and bred.

He was good-looking, Will had to admit, with thick dark hair that flopped just so, and a face that could still be described as boyish. Joanna adored him, and even Alice, twelve now, looked at him admiringly. He'd attracted more attention since two of his three brothers were killed. Both RAF pilots. 'Tragic,' Aunt Evelyn had murmured to Uncle Joe. 'His poor parents. Thank goodness they have one son who can stay here.'

Will knew he should feel huge sympathy, and yet he still didn't trust him. Something about the way his eyes slid over Maggie; the curve of his lip as he laughed at something that didn't strike Will as funny, put him on edge.

He was doing it now. Eyes flitting over her as he mentioned his reason for calling, for Uncle Joe only used him if it was really necessary. But Noble, the youngest Shire horse, was suffering from the shivers and barely able to lift his rear hooves at the minute. The costliest animal on the farm, he needed to be checked.

'Lovely to see you, Maggie,' the vet called, as he started for the stables.

She smiled, and nodded politely. Will felt an immense rush of gratitude that she didn't seem the least bit affected by him, and wasn't simpering like the maid.

'And where's your sister, Will? She's fond of the horses. Thought she might like to see what the problem is?'

'She's at school,' said Will, stating the obvious, and feeling absurdly protective. For some reason, a shiver ran up the nape of his neck.

'What a shame,' said the vet, his bottom lip sticking out in an exaggerated pout that made his mouth look almost pretty. 'Looks like it's just me on my own then.'

He gave Evelyn and Joanna a mock bow, causing the maid to giggle and to bat her lashes, so stubby compared to his long ones. And, still with that infuriating smile, he turned away.

Eleven

Maggie Retallick smiled at the young woman staring out at her from the mirror.

The creature smiled back at her.

So it *is* me. She felt a jolt of surprise. She smiled again, less self-consciously this time, and reached to pat her curls, newly bobbed and set. I look so different, she thought, as she admired the curve of her neck, the delicacy of her profile. The hair and her lips – coated in a red lipstick her mother didn't know about – made her look distinctly older.

She turned to admire herself side-on, taking in her nipped-in waist and, well, a proper bosom. Amazing that she could have metamorphosed so. The silk fabric of her mother's green dress rippled over her breasts and caressed her hips. She was no longer Maggie, the county schoolgirl who blushed when American GIs called out to her in Bodmin, or Evelyn Retallick's daughter who was all set to take her Higher School Certificate and train to be a teacher, but Maggie: seventeen years old, elegant, sophisticated, and about to set off to an RAF dance with Edward Pascoe, her childhood playmate and second cousin.

She pulled the dress down a little and smiled again, though the smile was more equivocal this time, the excitement replaced by a hint of unease. A steady, reliable sort of chap, said her father, when she had announced that Edward was taking her to the dance. 'A good prospect,' her mother had added as if he was a type of livestock. Evelyn approved of Edward not just because he came from her side of the family but because, after the war, he meant to study law at university, making the sort of break she had never managed. Even if he returned eventually, he wouldn't waste his talents in a small north Cornwall town.

Despite – or perhaps because – of her mother's approval Maggie still found Edward a little earnest: her feelings for the boy she had tried to chide into swimming further or climbing higher were those of a sister for a slightly studious older brother. Still, there was no doubt he'd become more intriguing since enlisting and spending eight months training up in Scotland. And there was supposed to be something attractive about men in uniform, wasn't there? Or so Miss Jelbert, her French teacher and the most sophisticated woman she knew, had always commented. Certainly, many of the girls at school thought so.

This dance – the last time she'd see Edward before he set off for Glasgow and a ship to somewhere unspecified and secret – need not signify anything, Maggie reassured herself, as she pulled the dress back up again and wondered if the lipstick was, perhaps, too bright. A chance to send him on his way with a smile on his face and for her to escape the tedium of a long evening at the farm where her mother was becoming increasingly irascible, Alice was being irritating and Will... Well Will was making her distinctly uncomfortable.

Besides, there would be music and perhaps jitterbugging. She and Alice had tried to practise in the barn this afternoon as she hummed 'Tuxedo Junction' and 'Chattanooga Choo Choo', though it was hard to get a proper sense of the moves when she was always the man.

Alice had whooped and squealed as she'd swung her round, and Maggie had joined in, their cries startling the hens perched on the bales and the doves in the rafters who had stopped pecking to watch.

'Faster, faster,' Alice had squawked as Maggie swung her from one side to another, counting the beat in her head as she hummed loudly. And then, in a gasp of delight: 'Wiiiiiiiii-ll.'

She had stopped abruptly, mortified at the thought of someone watching.

He had grinned, leaning against the bales with a lazy smile.

'Have you been there long?'

'Long enough,' he had said. 'Enough to know you don't do it like that, you do it like this,' and he did a little shimmy, surprisingly agile in his overalls and heavy boots.

'Yes, well, we're just learning.' She had been defensive. 'It's very difficult.' She had paused: 'Come on then: you show me if you think you can do it better.'

'Well I dunno,' he had admitted. 'But I've seen Joanna doing it like this, down in Padstow,' and he had stepped forward, with some hesitation, put one hand on her waist and, with the other warm, slightly calloused hand, held hers.

He was a head taller than her now, which still came as a bit of a shock. He seemed to have shot up in the past few months, as well as broadened, with a smattering of light stubble on his jaw and a not unpleasant but distinctly male smell.

She could feel his breath on her hair and then on her forehead: a light breeze that brushed against her and synchronised with her breathing. For one long moment, she forgot Alice and the rustlings in the barn; was only aware of the warmth of his hand on her waist, his long fingers, just inches from her breast, touching her curves.

She broke away. 'Yes, well. I'm not sure this is going to be that helpful. Come on, Alice.' And she had turned to his sister. 'Let's try it again: a one and a two and a three and a four.'

She flushed again, just thinking about it now. A distance had grown between them. It wasn't just that she no longer knew what to say to him; it was that he seemed so different. Distinct from the boys in her class, their pale bodies packed into blazers, and a world away from the child who had turned up three and a half years ago: shy, gangling, ready, if teased, to flush. Time – and farming – had made a man of Will, and she found this disconcerting. How to respond to this new Will when what she missed was the old, familiar one?

The door inched open and she rubbed at her lips in case it was her mother. The crimson lipstick gashed her mouth like a stain.

'Maggie...'

'Oh, it's only you.' She opened the door to reveal Alice hesitating to enter her *boudoir*, as they jokingly called it.

'You look beautiful.' The younger girl seemed awestruck. 'Like a ... sea nymph, or something.'

'Oh, really?' Maggie never quite knew how to

take Alice's flights of fancy. 'Not quite the look I was hoping for.'

'It's meant as a compliment! You're just so ... slinky.' Alice reached out to touch the fabric, stroking it lightly, before Maggie, anticipating Evelyn's response should the fingers be sticky, moved sharply away.

'How are my lips? Too bright?'

'Dab a bit more... There, that's better. No one will be able to accuse you of being "garish" this way.'

She had got the inflection of Evelyn's voice just right. Maggie glanced at her as she perched on the side of her bed, stroking the eiderdown, taking in the bedroom with its rosebud wallpaper and heavy velvet curtains, decorated before the war began. Sometimes Alice surprised her. Just when you thought she was a mere child, she said something far more observant – far worldlier – than you would ever think.

'Edward's here. Waiting for you in the drawing room,' Alice revealed with a new air of solemnity. Then, more boldly: 'Do you like him?'

'Like him?'

'Is he your ... *beau?*' She half-laughed the word.

'My *beau?* How Victorian. He's my second cousin, Alice, and a friend.'

'Well, that's good,' Alice's voice floated down the staircase in front of her as Maggie followed her out of the room and down to meet Edward.

'How so?' Maggie shot back, practising her new, arch tone, and irritated by Alice's disarming *knowingness.*

Alice remained silent.

'Alice?'

But the girl was suddenly reticent. And, turning, she ran down the stairs.

The evening was a huge success. Maggie practised saying this as Edward took her hand on the dance floor and led her into a quickstep that almost took her breath away. The hall at RAF Davidstow was heaving with young couples: the girls bussed in from as far afield as Launceston as well as Camelford, and the men – American, English and even Polish pilots – taking their pick. Edward and, a couple of other Duke of Cornwall boys stood out, as much for their callowness – they hadn't seen any action yet, unlike the Americans smoking their Player Lights – as for their khaki uniforms. Perhaps they shouldn't have been there, but who was to begrudge three local lads, green and anxious, on the eve of their first tour?

Maggie wasn't quite sure what was expected of her tonight. She knew she shouldn't be standoffish, suspected that Edward might want her to be more than just friendly. So why did the thought of kissing him leave her cold or – worse – make her want to laugh?

She looked at him now, concentrating next to her as he moved her lightly between the other couples through the crowded aeroplane hangar. He was a competent dancer. The result of ballroom dancing classes, insisted upon by his mother when he was a boy. His grip was light and his tread delicate. But she couldn't help thinking he approached dancing much as he might a legal conundrum: something to be mastered after applying considerable thought.

'Is everything all right?' he asked, glancing at her quickly, a hint of anxiety in his blue eyes. His tongue peeped between his teeth – a mannerism that suggested he was concentrating hard.

'Glorious – wish I could go faster.'

As it was, her heart was hammering in her chest, though whether from the vigorous exercise or slight nervousness she couldn't be sure.

The music came to a stop and 'Chattanooga Choo Choo' started up. Maggie, humming it under her breath, would have liked to continue, but Edward seemed to want to pause.

'May I get you a drink? A lemonade – or a punch?' He was looking at her in a way she couldn't quite get used to. If he weren't Edward – a regular fixture in her early years, before he was sent off to boarding school – she would describe it as *beseeching*. No, that was wrong. A soldier, with wind-chapped skin from training in the wilds of Scotland and newly acquired muscles, didn't need to beseech anyone. But it wasn't the way he usually looked at her.

'Oh, a punch would be delicious!' She imagined this was the sort of thing Miss Jelbert would say. She felt slightly reckless. Aware that she had the chance – away from the farm and Evelyn's sharp eyes – of doing something completely forbidden.

'Not a word to your mother.'

'Evelyn Retallick would *not* approve.'

'Do you remember when she caught us in the stream?' Evelyn had discovered them, aged six and eight, in the copse by the beach, stripped to their underpants.

91

Edward blushed. Oh, come on, she wanted to tease him. We were *children*. Evelyn had given her a brisk thrashing, but she could hardly respond like that now.

'What about one small punch – and a lemonade to disguise it, later?' She sought to reassure him.

'Do I seem terribly cautious?'

'You just know my mother.'

'I think very highly of Aunt Evelyn. I just have absolutely no desire to offend her in any way at all.'

'Well you won't. You can do no wrong, these days. Not since you've said you'll apply for Oxford, once this is over.'

'You sound a little ... cross?' He gave a slight cough.

'Of course not.' She touched his arm to reassure him, then dropped her hand. 'It's just ... you know Mother. You've set the bar high. Still, at least she doesn't want me to languish – even if I wanted to.'

'No. Well, quite.'

'Nothing short of headmistress will be good enough for me, the way she's talking at the moment.'

'Well, it *is* an admirable job.'

'I know ... though I'm not sure it's really what I want to do.'

She was quiet for a moment, wondering if she should admit that, really, she just wanted to remain on the farm, or at least stay in farming. In this, she was her father's daughter: someone who loved the excitement of harvest, and enjoyed the day-in, day-out routine of milking, the hiss of warm milk squirting into a pail, the comfort of resting your head against the side of a cow.

The strange thing was, Evelyn didn't want the farm to go elsewhere: to Joe's younger brother or his sons. Skylark – or Polblazey as her mother insisted on calling it: 'Can we *please* use its proper name' – would be farmed by Maggie when he retired. But she didn't want Maggie to be constrained by it. She was to experience a different world first – the world denied to Evelyn by the first war, and an early marriage – before she did her duty and came home.

'The thing is,' she went on in a rush, 'I'm not sure that being a farmer, or a farmer's wife, would be so terrible. I mean, I can see the point of getting away for a bit, but I can't imagine life away from the farm.'

She wrinkled her nose, half-embarrassed by this confession, and the arch air she had adopted all evening slid from her like a chrysalis shed by a butterfly. For a moment, she wanted to be sitting in the sand dunes, the silk of the sand soft against her thighs, the breeze buffeting her cheeks; or hiding in the milking parlour. The hangar, with its mass of excited young men and women, seemed claustrophobic all of a sudden.

'You think that now, but once you're at teacher training college you'll realise there's a whole world out there,' Edward said, with the air of someone who had now experienced such things. 'Now: about those drinks?'

'Yes. Quite.' She rallied herself. 'Punch, please. There's quite a crush. Hope you can squeeze through.'

'I'll see to it right away.' And he leaned forward, and, reddening quickly, brushed her cheek with his lips.

Two hours later, and the punch was proving most delicious. That initial burn was quickly over, and her arms and legs relaxed so that her dancing was faster, more fluid than before. Or at least, the second glass made everything more fluid: the third was making her feel a little woozy. The floor tipped suddenly, lurching up at her, though she didn't think she'd stumbled. But then the trumpets started blaring and the noise and the crush became unbearable.

'You're fine, you're fine.' A voice came at her through the blur of sound. 'Let's just go outside for a minute.'

Someone – Edward – was leading her out of the hangar into the chill early March night. The lush sound from the gramophone – a dense mesh of strings – grew softer and softer, and she found herself concentrating on not falling down on the tilting airfield. Above her, a velvet sky bore down then skittered away in a whirl.

'Here. Put this round you. It's cold.' Edward was placing her mother's best wool coat round her shoulders and holding it tightly to her, as if to stop her falling as much as to keep her warm.

'Just breathe gently. You're going to be fine. Here.' He was walking her away from the entrance, from which another couple, huddled against the night, were leaving, their laughter soft and intimate. 'You'll be OK here.' He glanced at the other lovers, now kissing passionately, then back at her, and she managed to register that his eyes were shot with concern.

The ground seemed to be righting itself, and she tried to focus on the stars, bright in a clear sky, and the full moon: a help for any passing Focke-Wulf. Her breath hit the air in steamy bursts then dissipated like mist, and, suddenly, she was overwhelmed: by the vast night sky, the emptiness of the moor, and her impotence. She tried to explain, but it came out as a sob.

'Maggie.' Edward's face was a pool of concern. 'My dear, is it Aunt Evelyn you're worried about? Or my going away from you?'

She looked at him, uncomprehending, but it seemed too much of an effort to make herself understood. How could she tell him that being a young woman in a country three and a half years into a conflict that everyone said had reached a turning point – with the fall of Stalingrad – but which was still continuing, was *wearing*. That she was tired of the nagging, low-level anxiety, the uncertainty, the sense that the end could not be foreseen – though the Allies had to win, didn't they, especially now they had started bombing factories – that came with being at war?

She knew that, compared to those who'd been through the Blitz – like those in Plymouth, where the flames lit the sky down to Cornwall – they were protected. But she still had this niggling nervousness she couldn't admit to someone about to experience it first-hand.

He gripped her shoulders more firmly, his head – not much taller than hers – now so close to hers that she could see the moonlight glint off

95

his pupils.

'I will take the blame with your mother,' he said, his voice sombre. 'And I will do my very best to return.'

The impossibility of his promising this struck her properly for the first time. He might not come back. Everyone knew of someone who had lost a loved one. Barely a month went by without the news that another acquaintance had been killed. Brenda Edvyean in the upper sixth had lost both her brothers; Patrick Trescothick, three of his.

Edward had always been in the background: as solidly predictable as lambing in February and March, and rain in March and April. His visits a part of the farming year: like harvest and ploughing and hoeing and sowing once more. But what if he never returned? If his name was added to the roll-call of the dead, read out in church, to silence and a few stifled tears, by the vicar. What if this was the last time she ever saw him?

The world seemed slightly less hazy now: the sky had stopped swaying; the grass no longer tipped beneath her feet. He leaned closer, and she thought, with the rum still spilling through her veins like liquid gold, that, really, he wasn't un-attractive. He was almost sweet if she could get over the fact he was barely taller than her, and that she had known him for ever.

She closed her eyes and tried imagining she was Merle Oberon to his Laurence Olivier as he pressed his mouth to hers. His lips were warm and moist, not unpleasant, and then with his tongue he tried to part her teeth.

She broke away.

'Sorry, dearest,' he muttered, then pulled her towards him, gently. Was this what kissing was all about? Perhaps it got better with practice? Tentative, she tried again.

The second kiss was better: less frenzied, more gentle, and he seemed to draw confidence from it.

'Perhaps I shouldn't rush you,' and here his eyes gleamed, 'but if you could somehow wait for me, until the war is over. Not an engagement, if you don't want that, but an understanding...'

'An understanding?'

'That you would be here for me to come back to? That would mean the world to me.' He looked embarrassed and scared: the boy who'd been caught stripped to his underpants by Evelyn. 'I suppose I'm scared, Maggie,' he said.

She didn't know quite what to say. How to tell him everything would be fine, when there were no certainties any more beyond the fact they were relatively safe in their small bubble in Cornwall? And so she said what she knew he wanted to hear.

'Of course I'll be here. Where else would I go?'

She could feel herself trying to make light of what he'd said, for if he was asking for some sort of *commitment* – less than an engagement but still, some sort of understanding – then she couldn't give that. Perhaps she should make that clear? But as she started to speak, he shook his head and his eyes filmed with tears.

'Edward...' she tried, desperate to correct any misunderstanding.

But: 'You have made me happier than I could ever have imagined,' he was saying. 'You do know

97

that, don't you?'

'But I...'

'You are wonderful,' he said.

He pulled her tight and she felt his heart pound through the coarse serge of his uniform. Beyond her the moor waited, silent, the stars winking at her.

And all she could do was nod.

Twelve

It was Joanna who alerted Will to Maggie's news.

'And what do you think of Maggie and Edward?'

He was off to do the afternoon milking. Had only stopped by the kitchen to grab a flask of tea, for the milking parlour was cold, despite the warmth of the cows.

Joanna gave him a wink, delighted at having some gossip to impart.

'You'd have thought she'd have given us a hint!'

'A hint of what?' He stopped filling the flask with the ribbon of thick, dark tea and put it down next to the milk jug. His throat was dry; his tongue thick in his mouth.

'Well, I suppose it's not an engagement so it's not official,' the maid continued, drawing out the release of information, making the most of her power. 'But then again, Mrs Retallick seems to think it's as good as.'

She paused, looked him up and down.

He returned her gaze, blankly, refusing to give

her the satisfaction of asking what she was talking about: incapable of articulating something, he had only just realised, that was his greatest fear.

With an effort, he resumed refilling the flask; screwed the lid on tight.

'Don't you want to know?' Her crab apple of a face scrunched up with frustration. 'Maggie and Edward. They've an *understanding.*'

Her voice lingered over the words, but if she continued talking, he didn't hear. He was out of the kitchen.

'Here. Don't you want your flask of tea?'

He found her leaning over the gate to the top field, watching the newborn lambs springing across the grass.

'Hello.' She gave a wide, open smile. 'Aren't they gorgeous? Look at that tiny, black-faced one.'

She pointed to one of the smallest, gambolling towards its mother; still wobbly on its soot-black legs. But he didn't want to talk about the lambs.

'Is it true?' He stood stock-still in front of her.

'Is what true?'

'That there's something going on between you and Edward. That there's some sort of *understanding?*' He searched her face, trying to detect if Joanna had been exaggerating. 'You're not ... you're not going to *wait* for him, are you?'

She shifted away from the gate, her lovely face pinched and closed.

'Has that girl being spreading rumours?'

'Is it true?' he persisted. To his shame, his voice wobbled, and he felt a flush of blood rush up his neck.

'And what if it is?' She tossed her head, and looked at him in a challenge. Her eyes were hard, and he could see Evelyn in her for a second, hear her in her high-handed tone with its potential for contempt.

'I haven't said I'll *marry* him or anything … just, you know, that I'll, well, *court* him, I suppose you'd call it, when he gets back.' She gave a little harrumph. 'The poor boy's going off to war. What was I supposed to say?'

He was silent. How could he explain what he had barely admitted to himself, and what could he do to make things better? He thought of how they had danced together, just the afternoon before, and briefly held hands. Of the warmth of her hip beneath his fingers, the curve of her waist. It had all been so fleeting: their chests primly apart, though he was all too aware of the rise and fall of her breasts just inches from him; the smell of her freshly washed hair, the top of her head within kissing distance. He must have touched her like that for just a couple of minutes, but they were the most intoxicating of his sixteen years.

'I just thought you might have told me,' he managed, at last.

'Oh, Will.' She gave a quick, affectionate laugh. 'Is that all it is? It only happened last night – and it's just a silly thing. Nothing official. Nothing formal that will bind me. Goodness!' Her tone was as bright as a hard-boiled sweet. 'I don't know why I'm having to explain it to you, at all!'

She reached out to touch his upper arm – the reassurance you might give a dog or a child. He shifted brusquely away before her fingers brushed him. He couldn't bear it: her treating him like this. Behaving as if everything was all right, all very jolly, and there wasn't a splintering in his heart.

'This won't change anything, you know. I'll still do my leaving certificate next year, then my teacher training, and get a job. And I'll still come back to Skylark. Crikey!' Her voice turned shinier than ever. 'The war might continue for ages – and goodness knows when Edward will get back.'

He might not come back at all, Will thought, and felt an automatic spasm of guilt at the idea, and the fact it filled him with sudden hope.

'S'all right,' he muttered, rubbing at some lichen at the top of the gate and wishing he could expunge Edward for ever. She wanted *Edward* of all people. 'Just came as a bit of a surprise... I wasn't expecting it, that's all.'

'It's not going to make a jot of difference,' she said, in that over-jolly voice she seemed to be using for him now. 'It won't happen for ages, and, even when it does, we'll still be just as firm friends.'

She looked at him, her smile wide and bright, though her eyes looked troubled and sought his reassurance.

He gave her a tight, polite smile, and wondered how someone so clever could be quite so stupid.

Thirteen

They were feeding the fortnight-old calves, when it happened. It was a two-person job: Will clamping a calf between his thighs while Alice scooped the milk into her mouth and helped her drink.

James was hosing down the muck in the milking parlour, and Uncle Joe was leading the cows back to the top field to graze. The grass was at its most lush at this time of year, sodden from the April showers and sprouting up thick and fast. The cows, kept in over the winter and fed on dredge corn and silage, couldn't get enough of it.

So Will didn't see the accident; didn't spot Clover slip on the wet slick of dung on the concrete standing, just before the yard's cobbles, and do the splits on the floor.

He heard her though. A frightened moo, her voice dipping then rising in a surprised cry as she crashed down, cracking her femur.

'Easy, girl. Easy, does it.' James, a herdsman with thirty years' experience, got to her first. 'We'll need to use a pulley.' He assessed the cow, which watched him, silent and trustful, only the grinding of her jaw indicating that she was in pain.

Will moved his hand to her belly and felt her rough hide quiver. Her sides kicked; she was due to calve in eight weeks' time, but her calf didn't seem distressed. If they could just get her upright, perhaps all would be well. But the process of righting a heavily pregnant cow weighing nearly ninety stone was always going to be hard.

Moo-oooo. She began to call again as they wheeled the pulley over to her, placed the harness under her front legs and tried to lever her upwards.

Moo-oooo, mmmmmoo-ooooo.

Her front legs slipped and skidded before the rope snapped under the strain of lifting such a heavily pregnant beast.

'I can't do it,' Will gasped as she came crashing down.

James wiped his face with his hand. 'See what Farmer Retallick says, but I think 'tis broken.'

'Her leg?'

'At the hip bone.'

'I couldn't hold her.' Will knew he sounded pitiful.

'Not your fault. She did the splits, didn't she? Just one of those things.'

They both looked at the cow, one hip poking higher than the other at a freakishly jaunty angle. Will crouched down to comfort her and turned his head so that James wouldn't see he was close to tears.

'What is it? What's the matter?' Maggie's voice rang across the yard as she half-ran from the kitchen.

His heart plummeted. She was the last person he wanted to see.

'Where's Father? Why can't you get her up?'

'We tried. The pulley broke. The two of us can't shift her.'

She looked at him, and smiled, as if the solution

were simple: 'Then we all will,' she said.

She grabbed at the broken rope, and crouched down to place it beneath the Guernsey's legs.

'It's all right, my darling. We're going to right you.' She patted the cow's flanks and stroked her head gently.

'Maggie.' Will bent down opposite her and stayed her hands. 'We think her leg's broken.'

'But it can't be.'

'We think it is.' He said it quietly, calmly.

She looked down at their hands, hers warm beneath his, and he dropped them abruptly.

'Sorry,' he said.

They had barely spoken since he had confronted her about Edward. That was two weeks ago, and, in three days, she would return to Bodmin. Frankly that was all he wanted. He didn't know how to behave around this new Maggie. This thing with Edward had made her unreachable. And then there was the way in which she spoke to him, when they did talk: like a jolly big sister. The girl who nestled next to him on their ledge, who taught him to swim, had disappeared for ever, and he didn't like the young woman who had appeared in her place.

The cow lowed again, ground her teeth and tried to struggle upwards.

'James?' Uncle Joe was running into the yard now. He crouched beside the milker, assessing her hip bone.

'We were about to dry her off, weren't we?'

'Last day of milking.'

'Ruddy hell.' The farmer chewed his bottom lip.

He looked at her hips again. 'Will I get the vet? See if we can save the calf.'

'Might be too early.'

'Sixty days; yes it will be.'

'And,' the herdsman gave a cough and glanced at Maggie and Alice. 'Not sure as I trust him. They weren't too pleased with him last week at Tredinnick.'

'Well. He's had a lot on his mind,' the farmer said.

They remained silent. The vet had killed a horse clumsily at the neighbouring farm the previous week, taking three shots to manage it. ''E e'dn much cop,' James had told Will afterwards. 'A shifty bugger,' the herdsman had added.

'I'll get him just in case we can save the calf.' The farmer paused. 'I'll get him now,' he repeated, and it was as if they all needed to be convinced.

Patrick Trescothick had a wild look in his eye as he peeled himself from his Talbot Sixteen and ambled into the farmyard. Will felt his usual irritation and something more perturbing: that distinct shiver of unease.

The third of his brothers had just died in action, and perhaps it was grief that had tipped his cockiness into something unnerving. His thick dark hair was dull with grease and his face grey, as if he hadn't washed recently. He was only twenty-eight, but suddenly seemed older. His beauty had become as tarnished as a shilling soaked and then offered up by the sea.

He seemed reckless, too. Yes, that was the word. From the way in which he pulled a shotgun from the back of the car, without seeming to check the safety catch, to his half-stumble over the cobbles, to the over-the-top nod of appreciation made to Maggie and Alice, who watched, intrigued.

Perhaps he had been drinking? James was watching him through narrowed eyes, and Will wondered if he thought the same. As he walked past, he caught a hint of whisky remembered from a London Christmas. It wasn't even nine in the morning.

'You wanted me, Joe?' Mr Trescothick stood the gun on the ground, and leaned against it as if it was a stick. He bent down next to the cow. 'Yes, I can see that you might do... Poor old girl. Well, there's nothing for it, is there?'

Uncle Joe nodded, his jaw jutting forwards like Maggie's when she was trying not to mind.

'You can't save the calf?'

'Wouldn't live this early. Would just burden you with another vet's bill.'

The farmer cleared his throat. He hated to lose any animal. 'Well, I have one of them already. Such a waste: of a good cow, and your time.'

'Do you want me to do it?' The vet looked up at the farmer and Will saw a challenge in his eyes. 'Not a problem. Killing seems to be all the rage, these days.' He stood up, his height filling the small space between them, and gestured, theatrically. 'Anything's fair game, isn't it? Cows, dogs. Even men.'

Will ducked his head. So this was what grief did to you. Allowed you to say what was usually kept quiet. He swallowed, wanting Mr Trescothick to shut up: to revert to being his usual flippant self again.

'Do you not think so, Will?' The vet came so close he could smell his breath, then raised a finger and let it hover near his chest. He didn't jab – there was no need – he just let it rest there, barely touching. Will glanced at the shotgun; the handle in the vet's left hand, his index finger stroking the trigger, lightly. For a moment, he felt a shot of intense fear.

Then Uncle Joe came forward, breaking the tension.

'The boy feels for your loss, Patrick. We all do. It's a terrible thing you've experienced.' He paused, his face impenetrable. 'But perhaps I'll deal with Clover, all the same.'

'No, I insist.' The vet smiled, his eyes steely. 'You've called me out anyway so there's no extra charge. And I'm a clean shot, whatever they're saying at Tredinnick.'

'I've no doubt you are.'

'Then that's settled.'

Will watched as Joe tried to assess which was the worst of two evils: offending a bereaved man by questioning his ability, or allowing him to shoot an animal, anyway.

To his surprise, the farmer nodded to the vet. 'Right you are then.'

'Fine.' The vet, so cocksure a moment earlier, suddenly seemed a little uncertain. He rubbed at his right eye with the back of his forefinger, ran his hand through his hair.

Will glanced at the girls. Alice looked pale; Maggie, pinched – her body shrunk in on itself, her usual bravado gone.

'Best be getting on with it,' the farmer said. 'Maggie, Alice: inside.'

'But I want to be with her.' Maggie looked from the cow to her father.

'I said go inside.' Joe Retallick, usually such a measured man, sounded angry. 'Go and help your mother. This isn't something you need to see.'

She turned and walked back to the farmhouse, her back rigid with fury, Alice racing away.

'Are we ready then?' Patrick Trescothick tossed his shotgun from his left hand to his right, as if bored.

The cow looked up at him and made one final effort to stagger up.

Uncle Joe bent to pat her side. Will crouched down on his haunches and stroked the velvet skin at her temple. She rolled her eyes, showing the whites.

'Come along, come along.' The vet was impatient. Will waited for the vet to bend down, too, to stroke her flanks and offer a brief word of reassurance, to calm her in the moments before death. But he was having none of it.

'Out of the way, boy.' He lifted the shotgun to take aim, and Will sprang up.

'Steady on there,' said Uncle Joe. The cow flared her nostrils. Will stood, heart ricocheting against his chest.

'Nooooooo!' Maggie ran from the house as the vet took aim.

The shots rang out across the farmyard. Two blasts to the head. A mass of blood and splintered bone and blasted flesh.

Uncle Joe looked sickened; the colour drained

from his cheeks so that Will could guess at the old man he might become. Maggie whimpered, a pitiful noise that sounded as if she was trying to keep it in, but which broke out regardless. Her shoulders trembled, and he wanted to put his arms round her and hold her tightly.

The vet stood, impassive, as smoke wreathed from the end of his gun.

'Not a bad job,' he said, surveying the carnage.

Uncle Joe cleared his throat, apparently at a loss as to what to say.

The cow, taken by surprise, was silent as the blood flowed from her. But her calf, kept tight inside her, twitched like a marionette jerking free of its master as her source of life ebbed away. One jerk, two, three, as if she was kicking to get out and gasp fresh air. The kicks, frenetic at first, became weaker. And then, nothing.

'Best be getting on, then,' said Patrick Trescothick with his air of false jollity. No one contradicted him. The atmosphere was as leaden as the mass of grey cloud that had obscured the sun and would soon lead to rain.

'I won't bother you with a bill for this,' he added, perhaps sensing the mass disapproval. And, the gun flung in the boot, he sauntered to the car door, wrenched it open and roared away.

Fourteen

Now: 20 July 2014, Cornwall

'I never see you, we never have any proper time together, you're always with your frigging cows or I'm with Ava or at the restaurant; I can't even wake up with you 'cos you're always up so early, bloody milking.' Flo's voice spirals upwards so that it is impossible for Lucy not to overhear the latest argument between her brother and his girlfriend, fought just outside the kitchen where Flo has caught up with Tom.

She moves away. She knows about Flo's resentment at staying on the farm: the fact she barely sees her partner, with her working in the restaurant at night, and Tom up so early each morning; her frustration that he has given up a job that paid more; her lack of understanding of the tug of the place – the sense that they cannot give up on Skylark; that to do so would betray past generations. But she has never witnessed this level of anger, heard the rawness and the pain behind it, the sense that Flo feels so neglected, before.

She should make it easier for them. Suggest she does alternate mornings milking; offer to babysit so they can get out for a full day together. Those early mornings on top of helping with the harvesting, when it starts, and dealing with the tourists will stretch her days to breaking point – but isn't that what she craves? Physical exhaustion that means she has no energy for self-analysis: hard work that proves she is doing her very best to help rebuild the farm? Besides, she doesn't want Tom to experience the gradual erosion and loss of a long-term relationship as she has done. Not if it could be prevented; if something could be done to stop it now.

She thinks of Matt and worries away at an itch: the fear that perhaps she had let their relationship slide, that she should have given him more attention. She had been so wrapped up in her work on the ward, so drained at the end of a twelve-hour shift, and, yes, perhaps a little unsympathetic when he'd told her his news. What had once seemed so glamorous – his work as a copywriter at an ad agency – had felt increasingly superficial compared to the day-to-day struggle being fought by the premature babies in her care. The gulf became insurmountable, six months ago, when a baby had died – and on the same day he had won a lucrative deal to advertise still bottled water.

'It's a massive account,' he had laughed as he'd cracked open the Prosecco and regaled her with his ideas to sell something that you could get free from a tap, but that could be bottled and marketed and sold for a vastly inflated price. And she had watched him, and thought of little Eloise, felled by a bowel infection, and of her parents, distraught and incredulous, though the odds had always been that their daughter wouldn't survive.

'I don't want a drink,' she had said, her insides twisting like a tangled rope.

'Oh, go on!' He had looked appalled, and so, as

111

ever, she had caved in, accepted a glass with an apologetic smile, toasted his creativity, his inevitable success. But the wine had tasted sweet and acidic, and she had hated herself for dissembling. A spurt of bile had filled her throat, and she had left the room.

She had withdrawn from him after that: felt herself watching him more critically, silently deriding his slogans to sell water: *'Aren't we all seeking clarity?'* Had become more distant – still affectionate but less responsive when he tried to initiate sex. In truth, she hadn't felt sexual. All too aware of the frailty of the human body, its inability to counter infections or to work without machinery or antibiotics or surgery, it felt somehow wrong to delight in her own – beyond being profoundly grateful for her health, her strength, when those around her were failing. It was just a phase, she had thought; she was just tired. He would understand, for he was a kind man, never excessively sexually demanding. She felt so ashamed now of her naïvety, for it hadn't occurred to her that he was taking the lead from her, or that he was hurt by her rejection. That being painfully right-on might be a guise, and he might be being sexual elsewhere.

Suzi – effortlessly sensual in a way that olive-skinned Mediterranean women often seemed to her to be – must have been a joy after months of her clamped-thigh frigidity. At the Christmas party, every man's eyes had been drawn to her: this woman who commanded attention in her sleek black jumpsuit while everyone else teetered in too many sequins and too-high heels. She

112

imagines them in bed: the sheets damp with the musk of sex; their limbs entwined as his lover cries out unapologetically. Not like Lucy with her quiet whimper. She flushes at the thought of it: starts, and sees that she has shoved a fork into the fleshy part of her palm. Four prong marks forced hard into the red.

And yet it wasn't always like that. If she thinks of their early days, there were moments of intense sexual excitement: a sultry weekend in Paris where they had teased one another for so long in the Jardins de Luxembourg that she thought she would combust just from his breath on her neck. Another in Brighton where they spent an entire day in bed, and rose, ravenous, to eat fish and chips. Long walks through Soho in the early hours, when they would drag each other into empty doorways, limbs wedged tight as they kissed.

She misses this, she realises with a jolt, and also the long-lost tenderness. His willingness to hold her for hours, when she woke in the night after her father's death, or just to lie next to her in the darkness, silent, unless she wanted to talk. It is the small acts of kindness she mourns the most: the cups of tea he would bring her on the mornings she didn't have to get up for work; the meals he would make when she returned exhausted; the scribbled love notes he would leave after a run of late shifts. That everyday gentleness has long since disappeared; but it was once there.

It is so much to give up, to throw away, this shared history of loving. To discard it for excellent sex – for a woman who looks as if she would make him feel like a god – is understandable. But it shouldn't be. Oh! How it shouldn't be. Her stomach tightens with its habitual low ache of shame and grief. Don't start crying again; please don't start crying. He isn't worth it. The bastard. But however much she tries to feed off her anger, the suspicion that if he has behaved like a bastard, then she might have inadvertently helped him become one, keeps creeping in.

She moves back into the kitchen. Flo and Tom seem to be talking more amicably: Flo looking up at him, smiling, just the hint of a tease on her lips. They make their way across the yard. Flo's arm is slung round Tom's waist, now, and tucked in his jeans pocket; Tom's is draped casually over her shoulders until he pulls her into an embrace. He looks exhausted, and yet there is still a spark of passion as he draws his girlfriend towards him and gives her a lingering kiss, then smacks her bottom. She dances away, pretending to be affronted, then pulls him back again.

Lucy turns back to her cooking, ashamed at having witnessed this moment. A baking tray bangs with an angry clatter. She slaps down a rolling pin, gives the table another dent.

She is embarrassed, yes, but also wistful and, well, jealous.

It has been quite a while since Matt made her behave like this.

The car, a six-month-old, dark-navy Audi estate, is blocking the way to the barn when Lucy comes back from negotiating the new milking rota. For a moment, she is thrown by it. She isn't expecting any guests today and anyone turning up on the off-chance of a B&B room is more likely to be on foot. The track leading to their farm is a no-through road, the farmhouse and cottages the only reason to brave its potholes and blind corners obscured by hedgerows. It isn't a place you stumble upon.

The car looks as if it has been newly cleaned, though a smear of muck caked with straw now clings to the rear left tyre. She leans to peer through the window and sees her face blur in the bonnet's gleam. It is the sort of car that is waxed: the pride and joy of a man with too much time on his hands and too big an inferiority complex to let its glossiness fade. A camel cashmere cardigan has been carefully laid on the back shelf of the car, and a road atlas is slotted in the side door of the passenger seat, but otherwise the inside, with its cream leather seats, is as immaculate as the exterior. She bets the owner wields a hand-held vacuum cleaner after each trip.

She moves to the back of the car, intrigued and irritated now in equal measure. Any tourist will need to shift it before the afternoon milking begins. And then she spies the sticker, neatly placed in the corner of the back windscreen, so that the downward strokes of its letters are parallel. Guildford Golf Club. Of course: Uncle Richard and Aunt Carrie. But what are they doing here now?

She leaves the heat of the yard for the cool of the kitchen. Uncle Rich's voice, all trace of a Cornish accent removed, spools from the room at the front of the house that her grandmother still refers to as the parlour: a deep ribbon of sound punctuated by his own sonorous laugh.

Richard Pascoe is sitting in Fred's old armchair in the window, his legs spread apart, hands resting expansively on the arms.

'Lucy!' He gets up as she enters and goes to hug her. But the fact he is sitting in Dad's chair riles her.

'Hello, Uncle Rich.' She offers him her cheek, then does the same with his wife. 'Hello, Carrie.' Her tone towards the slim woman who has had the misfortune to marry her uncle is far warmer.

They settle themselves down. Her grandmother is sitting on a straight-backed chair, since her son has taken the softest one, and is squinting at him, a shaft of sunlight striking her eyes.

'Are you all right there, Granny?'

'Quite all right, my dear,' Maggie starts to re-assure her, but her son butts in.

'You should have said, Mother!' Richard is all booming bonhomie. He gets up and takes his mother by the arm. 'You sit here. I insist.' He guides her into the armchair.

'Don't make a fuss.'

'Nonsense! That better? Quite comfy?' His voice is a couple of decibels too loud.

'I'm quite all right, thank you, and there's nothing wrong with my hearing.'

Lucy turns away, suppressing a smile.

'So ... what brings you here? Not that it's not lovely to see you,' she asks, determined to be friendly.

'Just passing through,' says Richard with a wink that acknowledges the lunacy of this statement. No one just passes through Trecothan. No one just passes through Cornwall.

'We'd popped down for a weekend in St Mawes. Old friend of Carrie's was getting married down there, for the second time. They sail there. Glorious hotel. Tressiney – do you know it?'

Lucy shakes her head. The boutique hotels and yachts of south Cornwall are somewhere she has never ventured, though they are a mere thirty miles away.

'Impressive refurbishment. Very high spec, though they've maintained the period details, the sense of history.' He pauses. 'Gave us some ideas for what we could do here.'

The room is suddenly airless, and she is acutely aware of how shabby it is: the furniture threadbare, the walls browned from years of woodsmoke seeping from the hearth. She knows that the farm would be a developer's dream – all those barns; the old dairy; the cottages – and feels a fierce urge to protect it. She reaches behind to stroke the sloping wall.

'Oh, really?' she manages at last, her voice coming out higher than she intended. 'Should we discuss any new ideas with Mum and Tom here? After all, they're the ones running the farm.'

'Oh, we'll discuss them all with them later.' He waves his hand airily. 'I assume we can stay?'

'Yes, of course.' She forces herself to sound generous. The bed in the spare room hasn't been made up since yesterday's customers and the linen's still on the line, but they can cope with unironed pillowcases.

'And I'd like to go through the accounts with the three of you this evening.' He sounds as if he is chairing a meeting. 'Mother, you're let off.'

117

'Oh, shouldn't Granny be involved?'

'Mother, you don't want to be bothered with any of this, do you?'

'Well, I rather think I would if there are things you think we should be concerned about.' Maggie watches him, her eyes steely.

'Well, that's the question, isn't it?' The hint of a threat thrusts through his bluster, and then he gives a bland, non-committal smile.

'Oh dear, oh dear, oh dear.' Richard, his broad shoulders hunched over Lucy's laptop, is shaking his head as he runs his eyes over her rudimentary spreadsheet.

Maggie, watching, wonders where she went so wrong with her son.

He was a difficult baby, an energetic toddler, and grew to become a boy who always pushed the boundaries. Then a bored and petulant teenager. But, however much she knew he would leave the farm, she never thought he would want to tear it apart.

'What's wrong, Richard?' She is not going to be manipulated by his melodrama; is determined to stay calm and realistic.

'What's wrong?' He gives a mock cough. 'These figures! It's all very well stating that you'll have reduced your overdraft substantially over the summer, but you haven't accounted for the winter costs. There's feed, maintenance, the purchase of new seed. Tom, what do those add up to?'

'Eh?' Tom rubs his hands together and looks sheepish.

'Forty thousand?' asks his uncle.

'Somewhere in the region of that.'

Richard sucks in his breath, and Maggie knows that, at that moment, she actively dislikes him. It shocks her that she could think that of her child. Where is his sense of affinity with the place, and, more than that, his kindness? For a minute, she remembers him as a small child, needling the bull: reaching through the gate to tickle his testicles with a broom; prompting the most almighty reaction. 'Why did you do that?' she had raged, after the bull had charged at him and had had to be put down. 'Why not?' he had said, refusing to admit to being ruffled. He had shrugged his shoulders, she remembers. Insouciant, even at eight. Deliberately dispassionate.

Perhaps it is her fault, for she has always been hard on him, she knows that. Well it was inevitable with Judith as a sister: such a good, loyal, caring child. But there were other comparisons she inevitably made too – and he sensed it. 'Just who do you want me to be?' he had asked, shortly before heading off to university and effectively leaving the farm for ever. And how could she possibly answer that?

She must focus on what he is saying now, for she will not let the farm be sold off even after her death, if she can help it. Though she cannot tell them why it is so imperative, she needs her family to stay here. Six generations have farmed at Skylark, stretching right back to the great-grandfather in the late nineteenth century who gave Polblazey its nickname. And yet, as far as Richard is concerned, that connection – the same family tending the same land over one hundred and fifty years – counts for nothing. A hard knot of fury forms in her chest.

Lucy is coming to Tom's aid now, bless her, arguing that they can reduce the overdraft with her plans for the cottages. Twenty-seven thousand pounds they could bring in, she seems to be suggesting before Richard knocks her predictions down.

'What if we have a dismal end of the summer, or a freezing winter, and the rents don't come in for next year? Or you fit new bathrooms and that swallows up another six or seven grand?'

'Well, we've been thinking of improving the dairy to offer cream throughout the year.'

'Who's going to be tramping here in November or January? Or even March? They've got to have a reason to come here, and a dairy won't be enough of a lure out of season – however lovely it seems.'

His objections are coming thick and fast; his speech, precise and emphatic. She clenches her skirt into balls with her fists, so angry that she doesn't trust herself to speak.

Tom clears his throat. 'What about developing the ice cream?' He looks diffident: not used to putting himself forward. 'That's what I'd like to do. We could use our milk, and some of my more unusual flavours and market it as a taste of Cornwall. We think the mark-up could be good.'

'Well that might work,' Richard looks sceptical, but for the first time isn't openly scornful. 'And if profitable I'd be willing to invest. But we'd need to get some proper figures for the cost of machinery and the set-up, and your projected turnover in a year's time. It's all very well having this idea that

120

you might like to make ice cream, but I'd only want to invest in it – or support any application to the bank manager to do the same – if it was not just viable but likely to make money in the medium to long term.' He fixes them with a hard stare.

'I must be frank,' he goes on, and here it is, she knows. The real reason he has come down here. 'I still think the best plan is to look at selling and redevelopment. I know you don't want to move Mother,' he holds up a hand as if stopping traffic, and she knows that she is glowering. 'But I think we should look at coming up with some architectural plans. Now, Mother, please don't object. I'll organise everything; pay all the costs: we can settle up later if we go ahead with it. But this is a much sought-after area, and I'm just suggesting we look at all the options. See how much all this could be worth. We'll be talking in the millions, especially if we did the development ourselves. Think how that would set you all up: take away all this worry and stress.'

'I am *Not* Moving From Here.' She enunciates distinctly, her voice clipped in the way her mother always wanted her to speak. She thinks of Evelyn's steeliness and inflexibility; tries to channel it into her manner, now. How to explain the real reason she cannot leave? She glances at her children and the impossibility of ever revealing her deepest secret strikes her afresh. Better, perhaps, to explain that she is Skylark? That at eighty-eight she relies on these animals, these fields, these views that anchor her here; that bind her to the place. For she is nothing without the memories they conjure up, good and bad, and she knows that, once removed from them she will simply cease to exist.

'Well let's just have a look.' Richard's tone is emollient, but there is an edge to it too, just as there often was with her mother. She wishes to God she had never accepted that £50,000 loan he gave them after Fred died – for it bolsters him, she can see that; makes him feel he has some leverage.

She holds firm. 'I am not interested in looking at any plans.'

'Well perhaps Judith and Tom would like to see them?' he says, encompassing them with a smile. 'Otherwise, Mother, I'm afraid that we will all be sitting here, repeating this conversation this time next year, even further in debt.'

Fifteen

Lucy vibrates with rage as she works, alone in the kitchen, baking scones and cakes for the afternoon teas. Carrie and Richard have set off early, leaving behind an atmosphere so unsettled it feels curdled. Flo and Tom have been rowing, and she was sure she heard her mother quietly sobbing when she passed her bedroom, late last night.

Now, as soon as she has slammed another batch of scones in the oven, she turns to her notepad to scrutinise the numbers. The outgoings seem endless: seed, cake for the cattle, the combine servicing. The bank is getting tetchy, and Uncle Richard is no fool. He knows another TB scare, or a harsh

122

winter with another glut of cows' deaths, could see this more manageable – but still worrying – overdraft burgeon over the winter months. Her grandmother remains defiant – but what if he wears the rest of them down?

They need to think of something to dazzle him: something innovative that will show they aren't just intent on slowing the farm's slide into decline, but in halting and reversing it. What about Tom's ice cream idea – the only suggestion he didn't automatically reject? Come to think of it, why hasn't she been taking Tom's ice creams to different farm shops and delis around here? She has been down here a fortnight now, and she should have achieved much more. Her GP signed her off for six weeks, which means returning in mid-August. She swallows. Less than a month. She has so little time.

She scratches at a bite from a horsefly that blooms, hot and angry, agitated at the thought of having to return to the hospital and her London life. The memory of Emma pointing out her drug mistake hits her again: her own stab of fear and the look of shock and pity in the other nurse's eyes. What if she had administered the dose?

She clutches the side of the table. She mustn't obsess: must get on with working before she lets herself dwell on Matt, too. For her anxiety about returning to London is fuelled by the state of their relationship. They haven't spoken since he left; their only communication a text when she said she was returning to Cornwall. *Hope you have a good break. Talk when you're back,* as if she were taking a short holiday. She had drafted a reply, but it was one of those texts – cold, sarcastic, filled with expletives – that she knew, as she composed it, she would never send.

She starts shaking at the thought of him, and what he's doing now. Perhaps he's moved in with Suzi? She wrenches the oven door open, incandescent at the thought of another woman in his arms or, worse, in her bed. And yet, perhaps she's partly to blame? It has been quite some time since she initiated making love. They were friends for two years before they started going out: Matt the person she regaled with her dating disasters, who she turned to when one boyfriend turned out to be gay, another, serially unfaithful, when she tired of moving from one six-month relationship to another. Perhaps, ultimately, friends are what they should have remained.

She must get on. A solid wall of heat smacks her as she bends down and she straightens up, dizzy. Then her left eyelid starts to twitch. So she is tired as well as stressed. She slams the baking tray on the table and begins to decant scones, her fingers scalding. Steam rises, bathing her cheeks in yet more perspiration, escalating her bad temper to something close to panic or fear. There's that feeling again: of teetering on the headland, unsure of whether the wind will buoy her up or abandon her and send her tumbling. Let nothing else go wrong. She needs this farm as an anchor: for her well-being is precarious, in the balance. If one more thing goes wrong, she will be pushed out of kilter, forced to the very edge.

The sound of a Land Rover towing a heavy horsebox comes from the yard, the rattle and grind of a heavy load coming to a halt, and then a gentle lowing and the thud of cloven hooves clattering down a metal ramp.

The new Ayrshire heifer. Tom and Judith are in the top field, hay baling, so she had better settle her in. She rubs at her red cheeks and smarting eyes, aware that her distress must be playing across her face. She does not want to face anybody, now or at any time in the future. If only she could stay in this womb of a kitchen, cocooned from the well-meaning looks of neighbours curious as to why she has returned from London, hidden from the harsh realities of life.

Outside, in the brilliant white sunshine, the cow's owner is pulling her from the trailer. A tall, broad-shouldered man, from what she can see of him: dark brown hair, strong arms and a voice that is firm with the hint of a Cornish accent. 'Easy girl, easy does it. C'mon. Easy now.'

The cow is a beautiful amber brown with a white diamond over her nose, two white legs and a pale underbelly. At two years old, she is slighter than many of the cattle in the herd. A cow that has not yet had a calf, nor been pregnant, but is ready to run with the bull and will do so in the next few months. By Christmas, her belly should be swelling: by next summer she should be ready to milk. Her calf will get just two days in which to suckle, and then she will join the rest of the milkers in the shed.

She really is a fabulous beast: following the man quietly now, just the occasional toss of the head to suggest she is not to be taken for granted. A cat streaks in front of her, dodging her hooves.

'Easy, easy.' The man is gentle and authoritative as he leads her towards the field, one hand resting on her flank as he does so. Lucy rushes forward to open the gate.

'Need some help?' Despite herself, he has piqued her interest.

'Yes – great. If you can just open it, I'll hold her back.' He glances across at her then, shooting a quick smile. Her chest tightens. It's him. The man from the beach: and he *is* familiar.

'Hello, Lucy.' He smiles at her as if waiting for the penny to drop.

'Ben? Ben Jose?'

He grins at her.

She re-adjusts her face, trying to shake off her extreme surprise.

'Just let me get her sorted.' He leads the heifer into the field and unties her rope. The cow crops the sweet, sleek grass, jaw chomping rhythmically, feet shuffling. At the other side of the field, a member of the herd raises her head and stares.

She glances sideways at Ben. Tom's old friend from secondary school: not seen since he was, what, sixteen and she, eighteen? An annoying sidekick of her little brother's, who tried to gatecrash her parties and who once stole her cider when he was fifteen. Fred had laughed it off: well, boys will be boys, he had said, with the infuriating double standards that allowed his son to get away with far more than his daughter. Judith had been upset: what would his mother say about him coming here and drinking so much he was sick? But Lucy had been livid – particularly since Judith had blamed her for stockpiling the drink, as if it was her fault the boys had got paralytic. He'd kept away from the farm for a while after that. Then, a few months later, in the September of 2001, she'd gone up to London – and escaped.

Well, he'd certainly changed a bit now. The dark blue eyes are the same. But the soft boyish face has gone, replaced by sharp cheekbones and a jaw that must have been hiding underneath. Of course he has bean-poled and broadened: little hint of the skinny slip of a lad she recalls, though he shot up that summer she left. She feels as if the sky has tipped. If Ben Jose can metamorphose like this, then she has certainly been away from the farm, or disconnected, for far too long.

'I'm sorry about the cider,' he says. The corner of his mouth twitches with laughter.

'Oh. That. Surprised you remember.'

'I had the biggest crush on you. Think I nicked it to make you notice me. Well, that and wanting to get legless.'

The confession confounds her. She would have no more looked at him than at the postman, Sam.

'I'm sorry. I had no idea you might have thought that,' she says.

'Don't worry about it. I was an obnoxious little twerp. I'm sure I deserved a bollocking.' He gives a laugh that is just the right side of self-confident, then walks back up the field towards the horse-box, leaving the heifer to graze.

Is that the end of their conversation? She finds she is disappointed, and catches up with him to wrest open the gate.

'So ... what are you doing now?'

'Working at Tredinnick – my uncle's farm. Went

127

to agricultural college, then, after a spell on a farm in Warwickshire, came back home.' He nods at the sea, petrol blue today and a little choppy. 'Couldn't really see a reason to stay away.'

He smiles. 'I work with livestock, mainly: beef, pigs, sheep – and one day a week in the farm shop.' He grimaces.

'Not your forte?' She can't imagine him behind a counter. He looks as if he belongs with an arm up a cow, or in a newly ploughed field.

'Just rather be on the land or with the animals. But I can see diversification is the answer. Food particularly: we butcher our own beef and lamb and make our own sausages.' He looks pensive. 'It's what modern farming's about, isn't it?'

'Well, talking of which...' She hates herself for this, but perhaps this is what she will have to learn to do. 'We're looking at diversifying. I wondered if the shop would try some of Tom's ice creams? Cardamom and orange? Or clotted cream and blackcurrant? And one of my carrot cakes.'

'Tom's been making ice cream, has he?' Ben looks surprised. 'He's kept that pretty quiet.'

'It's gorgeous,' she says, and at least now she sounds less of a saleswoman and is being honest. 'You're in for a treat.'

She races back to the kitchen and pulls three fresh tubs from the freezer; then decants a freshly-made carrot cake, topped with an orange-flecked buttercream.

'You want me to take this now?' He looks bemused.

'If you don't mind?' She smiles, self-consciously upbeat.

128

Oh, please, she thinks, as she places the box in his strong, tanned hands. Do like them and say Tredinnick will order some. Please let this be a good business opportunity.

'Well, great. Thanks. We'll try them out and get back to you … perhaps some time next week?'

She finds herself willing him to say something more positive that she can grasp on to. But with that flimsiest of promises, he backs away from her, and is off and away.

Sixteen

Then: 20 July, 1943, Cornwall

It was the noise that broke into her thoughts.

The deep growl of a British bomber, or more than one of them from the sounds of it: a throaty drone that grew steadily louder and louder until she could hold off no longer and had to open her eyes.

She had been leaning against the gnarled tamarisk at the bottom of the garden, basking in the mid-July heat, and it took a while to acclimatise to the brilliant sunlight. Black dots pulsed towards her before her vision adjusted, and then she saw them: a trail of B17s, flying nose to tail, in perfect formation. A ribbon of heat and power and metal rippling across the sky.

The sun glinted on their wings, then, as they tore up the coastline towards one of the airfields further up the coast: Davidstow, Cleave, or perhaps Chivenor, over in Devon. Coastal Command was not just bombing German U-boats deep in the Channel but was blasting French ports to stop German troops mobilising from there, her father had explained. There was something so carefree about their return: as if the pilots and crew were jubilant as they seared through the sky. The safety of Cornish land and waters lay beneath them. The golden strips of sand and rugged cliffs, the small green fields and granite grey hamlets and churches of England at its most beautiful. The England they were fighting to maintain.

She stood and began to wave, slightly self-conscious at first and then wholeheartedly, just in case any of those men could see her, this tiny speck to their right, in a cornfield, and would guess that she was grateful to them. As always, she felt her heart swell with relief for those who had returned, would not let herself think of those who had not done so, who were lucky if they'd managed to ditch before their planes plunged deep into the murky sea. Nor did she dwell on the destruction they might have caused deep in the Channel or to the ports over in France where ordinary French people lived. Trawlermen like those who unloaded their catch, down on the quay in Padstow. Perhaps even children and young women, like herself and Alice.

The drone was dying away now. The planes disappearing from sight over the headland, leaving a trail of exhaust that discoloured the blue and prompted her usual sensation of flatness, and then unease.

She shuffled back against the trunk of the tree and looked up at the feathery fronds of the leaves that dappled her. Her ankles, left out in the sun, would tan if she stayed here too long, and her skin turn a deep chestnut like her father's. Her mother would hate that. She pushed her shins out further and hitched her skirt up above her knees.

Keep thinking of things like that, things that are inane, and frivolous, she told herself. But instead she thought, as she always did when she saw a plane, of Edward: still in North Africa, working to clear a destroyed port and swimming in the Mediterranean, or so his heavily censored, relentlessly jolly letters seemed to suggest.

Dear Edward. The Duke of Cornwall's boys had been part of the first army: pushing east against the Germans from Algiers, contending with the heat and the dust to capture Tunis and precipitate the surrender of North Africa. It was a turning point in the Allied campaign, her father said, and Edward was a hero. The idea was ludicrous, though she kept that to herself, and tried to marry the image of him in his cricket jumper, reading *Brave New World*, with Edward sand-blasted and weary, streaked with sweat and dirt in his army fatigues.

She tried so hard to empathise with what he was going through: not just the fear – for how could she begin to imagine that? – but the extreme discomfort: the sand in his strawberry-blond eyelashes, the sunburn on his pale skin, the sweat-inducing, stultifying heat. It made her want to cosset him: to ease the heavy backpack from his back and carry his steel helmet and rifle, which must be near-crippling in the conditions of the desert. But it didn't make her love him, like a sweetheart. She still couldn't think of him in that way.

She tried. Oh, how she had tried! She would stare at the photograph of him in his fatigues; replay his kisses on Davidstow moor, which hadn't been *unpleasant,* they just hadn't provoked the reaction she had expected, and try to conjure up what she believed she should feel. Perhaps she was being unrealistic but, when she kissed, she wanted to feel consumed, as if she could crawl under the skin of the other person, so intense was her longing, as if she were overwhelmed by something bigger than the both of them. She was reading a lot of Hardy, and she wanted that overwhelming feeling Tess had for Angel Clare, or Gabriel Oak for Bathsheba, or Bathsheba for Sergeant Troy.

She smiled. Edward, of course, would be ever-so-slightly patronising if she ever referred to such lovers, for he didn't rate Hardy. 'Sentimental twaddle,' he would say. 'Mawkish; overindulgent. Look where such infatuation got Tess.'

And yet she clung to her conviction, wedged hard in her core, that this grand passion was what she wanted. Perhaps the war would change him, and when he returned she would see him as her hero.

She sighed. She ought to be getting back to the farm. Her mother was packing to leave for Falmouth, where her sister had just had a fourth baby and was run ragged. It was terrible timing – mid-July, nearing the corn harvest. For any mixed farm, one of the busiest times of the year. Still, needs must, her mother had said, when she announced she would be away for three weeks. Gwynnie – never the most practical of women – needed her. And Maggie was more than capable of pulling her weight, now she was back for the summer. Evelyn's habitual dissatisfaction had slipped, then, like a mask, to reveal a different woman: one who wouldn't spend the summer working under the blistering heat but would tend to her newborn nephew, and his small siblings. A woman who might have been a doting mother if it hadn't been for the relentless demands of the farm.

Maggie shifted her legs out of the sun and contemplated going back, but the thought of Evelyn flying around in a flurry stopped her. She wasn't going to spend the summer like her, in a whirl of bad-tempered energy, each chore accomplished in a manner that suggested she really should be – she *deserved* to be – elsewhere.

Depending on how long the weather held, there might be a fortnight or so before harvest, and, in this time, she was going to get her jobs done quickly: milking, preparing the lunchtime meal, doing the bake. And then she was going to slope off for an hour each afternoon: down to the beach to read in the dunes, up on the cliffs for a ramble with Alice. Or – if she had the energy after she'd washed the supper things, after no one needed her – for a late evening swim. The beach would be empty then and she could immerse herself without fear that anyone would see her in her knitted costume. If no one were there, she would run in in a slip and then pull it off once hidden by the water, so that she could swim, free and unencumbered, as weightless as air.

133

Of course, when harvest started she would be busy, but she didn't mind that. Harvest felt like a celebration, especially if the crop, barley and dredge corn, was going to be as good as it looked like this year.

It was exhausting work: binding the sheaves, forming the shocks, working in an ever-decreasing oval until all the barley was baled and the rabbits forced to scamper out. And yet she could cope with working under the hot sun, pushing herself until her arms and legs ached so that she slept deeply at night, her body so exhausted her mind stopped running in circles. She craved that oblivion. Anything to stop her fretting about the future: not about the war, but about what she was to do about Edward. She looked back at the farm, searching for a distraction from such troubling thoughts.

A figure was making its way towards her with a slightly diffident walk.

'Did you see the bombers?' Will's face was alight with the drama. Then: 'Your mother's looking for you.'

She groaned. His smile grew broad.

'Did she say what it was about?'

He shrugged. 'Just the usual.'

She smiled back, surprised that he might be critical of Evelyn, for Will tended to keep his head down.

'Sit down here with me for a minute?'

'Won't your mother get angry?'

'Probably, but no more than she is already.' She suddenly wanted to talk. It had been a long time since they had chatted properly. She had avoided him since Easter, when he was silly over Edward, but he seemed to have grown up since then, or forgotten about it. Besides, she couldn't maintain her offhand manner much longer.

'Budge over, then.' He lowered himself next to her and nestled his back against the trunk so that their shoulders and thighs were wedged against each other. She felt the warmth flow from him, enjoying the firmness of his thigh against hers.

She shifted slightly away.

'Are we both hiding now?' He almost whispered it.

'Is it that obvious?'

'Just a little.'

She gave a smile of complicity. 'I just wanted to avoid going back to all the bustle. She gets so tense it's better to stay away from her.' She sighed. 'I promise I'll go back in a bit.'

They gazed at the sea: so tranquil now there were no planes, no hint that a war was continuing. It wasn't always the case. Besides the aircraft flying past, the water turned green when a pilot jettisoned an aircraft, and the estuary boomed when mines were bombed, out in the Atlantic. Now there was just a sleek expanse of blue.

'I got distracted by the bombers,' she explained. 'And thinking about Edward. But before that I was thinking about swimming: about how, once Mother's away, I'll be able to do it as much as I like.'

'Do you remember teaching me to swim?'

His question took her by surprise.

'You were awful.'

'No need to swim in London.'

'You're much better at it now.'

'Well, no thanks to you. But, I'm all right at it. Yes.'

She glanced at him, remembering his frantic doggy-paddle that first full summer on the farm, and his embarrassment at being shown up.

''S'all right for you,' the fourteen-year-old Will had shouted, spitting out yet another mouthful of salt water. 'You've had all this,' and he'd gestured at the turquoise bay and golden sands, the evidence of her good fortune, 'on your doorstep. Course you can do everything much better than me.'

He had tried to storm through the water, then, but had been buffeted by a wave and pushed under. When he had emerged, his face was furious and crumpled, and Maggie couldn't tell if he was wiping away water or tears. He had pounded up the beach, legs pale and skinny from never having experienced a full Cornish summer. But the next day she spied him trying to teach himself: clinging to an old wooden board as he worked on his legs.

His arms, resting loosely on his knees, were long and muscular now; his shoulders broad and firm as shelled almonds. She imagined a fast, powerful crawl, those arms wheeling in and out of the sea.

She looked up at his face: the freckles merging with his farm boy's tan, his cheeks hollowed with none of the softness of last summer. Over the winter, he had spun himself a cocoon and emerged, more man than boy.

'Come on. Your mother will be furious.'

He jumped up in one movement and pulled her to her feet.

For a moment, she stood there, feeling the warmth pulsing between them, sensing the shape of his fingers, long and firm but with small callouses, imprinting themselves onto her skin.

He dropped her hand and turned to walk back to the farmhouse. Evelyn was standing at the top of the garden, peering down the fields. Even the way she stood – one hand to her forehead to shield her eyes from the sun, the other fiddling with the tie of her apron – suggested she was tense.

'Do you think she's seen us?' Maggie asked, drawing back into the shade of the tree.

'Nah. We're hidden here.'

For a split second, the air was taut with possibility. The breeze seemed to have dropped and Maggie felt as if she could hardly breathe.

Then Will turned and began to trudge up the track: a firm, steady pace that suggested he had work to be getting on with.

Maggie hung back a minute, and then followed, head down, as if she had had absolutely nothing to do with him.

Seventeen

The heat, which had been building steadily since ten, had reached a climax: one o'clock, Will reckoned, as a ball of fire sizzled overhead.

A trickle of sweat ran between his shoulder blades and stuck his shirt to his skin. He wiped his forehead with the back of his hand and felt his hair, damp with moisture. His stomach jabbed with hunger and his arms and lower back were beginning to ache from a morning's hard work, but what he most needed was a drink.

The girls, back at the farm, should be here by now, bringing fat pasties and jugs of lukewarm tea. The corn shimmered as if in a mirage. His throat rasped and he imagined gulping down the liquid, drinking so fast it dribbled down his chin.

Then he felt guilty. Edward must have experienced far more extreme heat at Tunis, and exhaustion and fear, while he was safe in a Cornish cornfield: safe, and living alongside the girl of Edward's dreams.

He scuffed his boot through the stubble, hating himself for his jealousy, and then for the hard glow of satisfaction that it was he who was here with Maggie, and not Edward – the lad she was courting. It all made him feel a bit of a worm, not to mention a wimp. The question of whether he would sign up next year kept nagging at him, as he paced up and down the field, gathering the sheaves and standing them in shocks. This was part of the war effort, too – but was it enough? Then again, he couldn't imagine not gathering in the harvest next year.

The mirage melted to reveal no Maggie and no tea, and so he carried on working. They had cleared a good half of this field now: Uncle Joe, driving the Shire horse and binder, himself, James, Arthur, and three men from the village gathering up the sheaves.

Uncle Joe would be thrilled. There was a dairy farm down at Lanlivet that was completely self-sufficient. Hay, they'd grown; clover, beans, peas, vetches and oats for silage; then spring wheat; marrow-stemmed kale and, for the best milkers, linseed. It had been praised in the *West Briton* for not putting demands on transport or convoys, and Uncle Joe wanted them to be equally economical and patriotic. Trouble was, every spare patch of grass was already planted: the verges running to the hedgerows; the valley dipping down to the sea; the flowerbeds, stuffed with potatoes, runners and green beans, kale and rhubarb. They'd be digging up the front lawn next.

'Dinner time!' A voice, high and bright, cut through his grumbling.

Alice was running through the corn, holding a small basket. Maggie, carrying a larger one, with a jug and enamel mugs, followed in her wake.

The crop seemed to part for her as she surged forward, her dark curls breaking free of the ties at the back of her neck, her face reddening. The stalks pressed against her, outlining her breasts and her long, strong legs. He flushed just thinking about it. Did she know why he and Arthur smiled broadly whenever she walked towards them, though never if her father was likely to spot them looking? Perhaps, but if she did she didn't know what to do about it. And, more to the point, neither did he.

It was fair to say that Maggie tormented him, now, even more than she had at Easter: this young woman who had once been a flat-chested tomboy, keen to show off her farm to them, and so eager to be his friend. He thought back to their first full day at the farm, when she had

139

inadvertently shown them a squashed piglet. 'Where's the runt, James? There were twelve,' she had said and then her voice had shrunk to a quiet 'Oh!' when Alice had pointed to the still, pink cylinder nestling in the straw. To cheer themselves up they had raced to the beach.

It was better than he could ever have imagined, stretching firm and almost white to the sea, which sparkled in the distance. The sand was soft where the thick stalks of seagrass met it, and finer than sugar when he bent and pushed his fingers in.

He had tried so hard not to appear overimpressed. But as the wind caught the waves and the sea glinted as if filled with diamonds, the strain of the last thirty-six hours lifted from him and he became just a young boy again.

'Race you!' he had cried, and, whooping and laughing, had charged across the beach.

'Wait for me!' Maggie had called after him.

He had turned and flashed a smile, but hadn't stopped running.

'Catch me if you can!' he had said.

He could remember that exhilaration now. His taunt had floated through the air as he wheeled and whirred towards the water. The nearby seagulls – great, cocky birds – had flown up, startled, as he charged towards them, then hung, suspended, buffeted by the wind.

Like skylarks circling one another, the two of them had flitted to and fro, whooping and whirling and eventually tumbling as they had streaked across the sand and then raced through the shallow waves. His lungs had banged against his ribs, and his heart had swelled – not just with the exertion but with the sheer thrill of finding a potential new friend to race with in such a glorious place.

She had shared that exhilaration then. He had seen it in her flushed cheeks and her eyes that laughed at him, daring him to run faster, challenging him to outstrip her – which at thirteen he could, though she was the better climber, the more confident swimmer. Well, the one who could swim.

She had shared it, too, that night, about a month after they'd arrived, when he'd experienced his first storm here and had lain in bed as the farm was buffeted. Rain seeped through the cracks of the window, soaking rags and licking sills slick with water, and the whole house had creaked, beams and floorboards groaning like a ship tossed on the high seas. But it was the wind that was the most exciting: an asthmatic whine that whistled through the casement fastenings, high-pitched and insistent like an old crone clamouring to be let in.

It rained in London, of course it did. Will had known the Thames, grey and swollen. But the wind didn't seem to blow there like it did here. The thought came to him that, if he could just open the window, he could test its force: see if he could resist. Of course he'd get wet. But he was always getting wet and filthy and sandy. And he had a towel to dry himself with. Better take off his pyjama top, though. No point irritating Aunt Evelyn, who had been livid about the muddy boot prints in the kitchen and the tear in his shorts where he'd caught them on the rocks when scrambling down from the cliffs. Now, if he could just open the casement latch – a bit stiff here – and push it...

'What *are* you doing?'

He had jumped. He couldn't help himself. She had stood there, waiting in the doorway. It gave him a fright, her creeping in like that and just standing there.

'It doesn't open like that.' She had come up to him and fumbled with the handle, wiggling it so that the lock came free.

One hand on the catch, she had turned to check.

'Are you sure you want to do this?'

He had nodded.

'It'll be strong?'

'I can handle it.' The valour of all vaccies rested with him.

'Ready then: one, two, three...' And she had forced open the fragile pane.

The wind was even fiercer than he had imagined it, the rain far wetter. It had lashed at his face, flaunting its power, sharp and sleek.

'Brilliant, isn't it?' Maggie had beamed at him, half hanging out of the casement, her eyes bright in the moonlight, her cheeks shiny and slick with wet.

He had nodded, unable to speak against the force of the storm as he flung his arms and torso out of the window, caught up in the intense, adrenalin-fuelled moment. Nothing in his life had prepared him for this: the exhilaration of courting danger so blatantly, of goading the elements to come and get him. This exquisite sense of being alive.

Later, once he'd handed her his dry pyjama top and they'd wrapped themselves in his rough blankets, they had squeezed onto the seat by the window. Her legs were warm against his, and she had tucked them both in.

'I love it when it's like this,' she had confided, watching a fresh flurry of rain strike the pane. 'When there's danger but it can't quite get to us.'

'Like the war?' he had said, thinking of how they'd yet to experience it in deepest Cornwall. Then he had thought of his parents and Robert, back in London, waiting for the war to really begin.

'No,' she had said, chewing her lip in concentration. 'Maybe a safer sort of danger than that. You know: when you know it's there – you can sense it, feel it – but you know you've got the better of it. Like managing to swim in a choppy sea.'

'I've never done that.' The thought filled him with fear.

'No?' She had looked at him, askance. 'Well, you should try it, sometime. I'll teach you. It's a delicious sort of danger, you'll see.'

A delicious sort of danger. That was what he felt now. Something completely exposing that made him feel vulnerable yet emboldened. Not so terrifying that he couldn't cope with it, yet enough to make him feel intensely alive. Did she feel the tiniest bit like this? Even when they'd sat together beneath the tamarisk? Well, of course not. She had Edward. But there was no doubting that he did.

He watched her filling the enamel mugs with tea and held out his own. Would she look at him,

143

now? Go on. Please. But she filled it up without a glance and carried on pouring the others; eyes downcast, measuring the liquid carefully.

'Thanks. Just what we needed.' Arthur, as sturdy as the Ayrshire bull and with the same thick neck, beamed down at her. She smiled back and he felt a wasp's sting of jealousy that he hadn't prompted such a response. He buried his head and gulped down the tepid liquid, emptying his mug in one go, he was so thirsty.

'Would you like some more, Will?' The jug was empty, but she was holding her mug out to him, looking straight at him now.

'What about you?'

'I can get more in the kitchen. Go on. You look like you need it more than me.'

She passed it over, and he found himself mesmerised by a drop of tea beading on her lip. He wanted to lick it. With a cat-like tongue, she swiped it away.

He turned the mug so that his lips touched the spot that had been touched by hers, and imagined tasting them. He daren't look at her. By the time he'd finished, she was busying herself with her tray.

'Well, I must go and fetch some more. I'll be back in five minutes.' She rose, not making eye contact, once again. Her cheeks were flushed a deep pink and her forehead gleamed with a light sheen of sweat. He felt a pang of guilt, now, at taking her tea, for she, too, must be feeling the heat.

He watched as she marched through the corn, the empty jug swinging from one hand, her back

144

stiff as if she sensed her progress was being followed. He glanced at Arthur, who gave him a fat, leering wink.

It was only later, in bed that night, as his limbs sank into the mattress, his body aching from a fourteen-hour day, his neck hot to the touch where the sun had scorched him that it struck him that perhaps she hadn't flushed just because of the sun. That perhaps she might feel as he did.

And that was intoxicating.

Eighteen

He was lying spreadeagled in the sand dunes when they came across him, looking for all the world as if he was asleep. The fields had been shocked: the sheaves of straw were standing upright, burnished by the sun, drying in the wind.

The afternoon milking was a couple of hours off and so he had sneaked down here just for a moment, he explained, when Alice jumped on him to shake him awake and Maggie stood there, wondering how tired he must be to be able to fall asleep so readily. He rubbed his eyes, and for a moment, she saw the young boy of nearly four years ago, embarrassed and tongue-tied that first morning, when they were introduced at break-fast. Then he stood up, stretching those long limbs and towering over her, and the thirteen-year-old vanished.

'Come on,' he said to his sister. 'What shall we

do now that you've caught me napping? Go for a ramble?'

'We could always rock-pool,' said Alice. She gestured at her fishing net and bucket. 'That's what Maggie and I were going to do anyway.'

'Rock-pooling it is then,' he said. Alice beamed and jumped from the dunes onto the beach before leading the way.

Despite Maggie's initial half-heartedness, the rock-pooling proved addictive. Will smashed a mussel for bait and pierced the slippery mollusc with a fish hook. A blenny was netted, then a couple of shrimps.

The crab line was dangled to the sandy floor of a shallow pool and a spider crab scuttled towards the bait. Alice held the net poised and secured it, then eased her trophy into a pail of water and soapy, lettucy seaweed. More and more fish followed, until the bucket became a heaving mass of crabs and shrimps and fish, swimming or clambering over each other – the largest con-suming the smallest in a survival of the fittest.

'Why are they doing that?' Alice looked per-turbed and yet she didn't fish out the offending crab as Maggie suggested.

'He's my best catch. He can't go.'

'Even though he's eating the little ones?' Maggie said.

The younger girl shrugged. Years of seeing her favourite lambs and chicks sold off, of realising that the baby rabbits would be shot and even the excess kittens drowned, had made her less sentimental, it seemed.

'I might just go for a walk,' Maggie suggested,

after they had peered into the pools for a good twenty minutes. The heat licked the back of her neck and the air was so still she felt clammy around her waistband. She wanted to walk to the sea to paddle or, even better, wade in.

'I'll come with you,' Will said, and gave her a quick smile. He glanced at his sister. 'Are you coming, Alice?'

Her heart sank, but Alice barely looked at them.

'You go. I just want to net this really tricky crab that's hiding from me,' and she jabbed at the wine-red fronds of a sea anemone. The crab scuttled and buried.

She looked so absorbed that they left her to it.

The sand was wrinkled with the previous tide's markings, and the ridges massaged Maggie's bare feet as she walked over them. Nearer the water, a slight breeze whipped her face. She closed her eyes, enjoying the sensation of it brushing her skin. The beads of perspiration that had formed at the top of her back as the sun refracted off the rocks had dried and disappeared as quickly as they had come. She felt, as she always did by the water, calmed and soothed by it.

'I will if you will?'

He was smiling at her with a look of broad mischief. The sort of smile she remembered from when he was a young boy. 'If I will what?'

He made it sound so simple. 'Swim.'

'I can't, can I?'

'You're wearing shorts.'

And so she was – for the first time ever since she had become a young woman: for Evelyn would not approve if she knew of them.

'You could jump in with them on, or,' and here he flushed a deep red so that his freckles were subsumed by the colour, 'I promise I won't look if you want to take them off and just dive in.'

She dithered and glanced up the beach towards Alice, straining to see if there was anyone on the footpath or in the fields – Arthur, James, her father – who could spy on her. The paths were empty: just Alice still bent over her net.

The water lapped and lulled around her ankles.

'Promise you won't look?'

'Of course not.'

She prevaricated.

'Not chicken, are you?'

That was it: the challenge she needed. And yet she still wanted reassurance. 'Promise you won't look and you won't tell?'

'Who? Your father? Aunt Evelyn?'

She flushed. There it was: the admission they were no longer children. That this was behaviour her mother would be appalled by.

He shrugged and turned his back. 'Tell me when I can come in.'

It looked so enticing. The waves glinted with shards of gold, and slid from aquamarine through to a deep turquoise. Days like this, when the sea failed to take your breath away but felt like a cool bath, were rare. Her mind made up, she scrambled out of her shorts and left them with her shoes on a rock, then raced through the water. The waves splashed up against her, drenching her blouse, spraying her hair, and with one ungainly whoosh, she was in.

'It's glorious! Come on in!' She rolled onto her back, sculling and kicking as she glanced back at the beach, then did some fierce, quick breast-strokes as she swam deeper. A wave picked her up and carried her, and she ducked her head under, eyes smarting, ears singing, as she swam underneath.

And suddenly he was there, swimming towards her. 'So you made it at last.'

He grinned, ducked his head under and ploughed towards her, biceps whirling, body streamlined. He surfaced and flicked the hair out of his eyes, droplets flying from him like an effusive dog or perhaps a seal.

'Race you?' It was her challenging him now. She turned away and plunged under the water, heart pounding as she fought against a small current, feet kicking ferociously as the old child-ish competitiveness reared up, once again. She could hear him coming up on the inside of her and it seemed ridiculously important that she beat him at this; that she assert that, though he had become another person physically, she was the better swimmer, all the same.

It was no good. He had caught her up, and swept in front of her, his face ablaze with laughter.

'Kiss me.'

Maggie wondered if she was imagining it.

'Go on, I dare you,' he said.

They were treading water now, having swum far further than they had intended. Will was so close she could see spots of salt water joining his freckles. She let her body drift towards him so that their chests were almost touching and their limbs knocked against each other, phosphorescent in the water, disembodied in the depths.

It struck her that this would be a clumsy kiss. Here, out of their depth. And so: 'No,' she told him. 'You'll have to catch me first.'

She ducked under a swelling wave, and surged towards the beach, helped by an onshore wind and the incoming tide. Her blouse clung to her breasts, but without her shorts she swam freely. She plunged deeper, and with three quick strokes was away.

A flurry of bubbles and she emerged to see that he was behind her, his face triumphant and then hesitant.

'You haven't caught me yet!' she said.

She carried on swimming, legs kicking fiercely as she led him in towards the shore. And then he had her: an arm circled her waist and she let herself be pulled towards him.

'You've won!' She laughed, allowing her body to twist and turn; disarmed by a sudden flurry of shivers that ran down her thighs as she glanced against him. With one swift gesture, she was buoyed, contained.

He could touch the sand, here, and her limbs wrapped round him so that they were entwined far more closely than if this had happened on dry land. His left hand rested on her buttocks, but with his right he wiped a frond of hair from her face.

'Now I can see you more clearly,' he said, and looked suddenly serious. No longer Will, the evacuee she had known since he was thirteen, but someone else entirely.

She could feel his chest pressed against her breasts, his thumb stroking the small of her back and then dipping down towards her bottom. A hard thing pushed against her. She put her arms round his neck, and pulled herself up to wriggle away. He held her high, hands below her hips, and, suspended by the water, she wrapped her legs round him so that they couldn't get much closer. We are held as fast, she thought, as an anemone anchored to a shelf of slate.

'You are beautiful,' he told her, his eyes dark now, his expression open and unwavering. She wondered if he had ever kissed anyone before, and thought that, perhaps, she should lead the way.

Their lips met and it was sweet and yielding, soft and delicious. She tasted the salt on his lips, the warmth of his tongue. She teased him, planting butterfly kisses on his open mouth, until he pulled away and coated her neck, ears and eyelids with kisses so light it felt as if he, too, was taunting.

'Kiss me properly,' she heard herself plead.

He stopped and gave her such a fierce kiss – hard and forceful and hot – that she wondered if he was angry. Her shivers intensified as she leaned in closer and tasted the salt on his skin.

'You're dangerous,' he whispered, as if he was confiding something.

'Dangerous?'

'Like a sea you can just about swim in – remember?' She shook her head.

'Never mind,' he said, and planted another kiss.

'Kiss me like you did a minute ago,' she said, frustrated with such tender pecking.

'Like this?' The kiss was so passionate she

151

wanted to melt into him.

'Yes – and again and again.'

His fingers grazed her left breast.

'Sorry,' he said.

'No – you can.' She kept her eyes shut tight, in case he judged such wantonness. His fingers stroked her nipple, tentatively at first; then, when she gave a sharp gasp of surprise, again.

'Kiss me,' she muttered, her lips searching for his. She held him tightly, clinging on to his shoulders, buoyed by the tide and his strength. This is dangerous, she thought. But no one can see us; we are hidden. And if all is secret, we can claim it isn't happening.

Under a setting sun, she forgot about Alice and her rock-pooling; forgot about her mother; forgot about Edward. Nothing was important but the here and now. The chill of the water. The soft taste of Will's lips.

Soon the cold became too much and they broke off. They left the water and the beach separately – Maggie searching for Alice, Will diving through the molten waves for a swim. But as he left her, with a final, lingering kiss that tasted of excitement and hope, she knew that something had started and that nothing would ever be the same again.

High up on the cliff, Alice watched Maggie gather her shorts and sandals together, saw her hunch to hide the way her wet blouse clung to her figure, tried to imagine, from the way she scurried, the expression on her face.

It had been a while before she noticed them swimming – and longer still before she realised what they were doing. She had been quite a way away – far too far to see their expressions – and, at first, she had tried to persuade herself that they were just talking.

She wiped her nose with the back of her hand, pushed a strand of hair from her eyes. Let them scour the beach, looking for her, late into the night, until they were really panicked. The longer they were out, the less likely they were to see that she had been crying; to understand that she might have seen. She turned her back, furious with herself as much as with them, though she couldn't explain the resentment that jostled with acute embarrassment at her naïvety and a stronger than ever sense of being left out of something.

The grasses whipped against her as she carried on up the path, stinging nettles pimpling her ankles, cuckoo spit wetting her legs with thick globules of phlegm. She wiped the stickiness, scrunching a dock leaf against the raging red hives clustering on her calves, and, head down, resumed her trudging, back up the stone track, towards the farm.

Nineteen

Now: 28 July 2014, Cornwall

Lucy watches the rogue rain cloud with trepidation. The gunmetal grey deepens to a charcoal,
smudging the darkening sky.

It is the worst thing that could happen: a sudden squall of rain or, worse, a downpour. For
Tom has just finished cutting his precious wheat
reed for thatching, and the fields are filled with
shocks that need drying. For two to three weeks
they must stand there while the wind whistles
through them and the sun bleaches them from a
pale greeny gold – the grain soft, the straw un-
ripened – to an almost white.

She can see them now, these sheaves, grouped
in eights, all touching: a straw cultivated by Joe,
her great-grandfather, and by his father too.
Before the war, the fields shimmered with this
high-value crop but it's labour-intensive and has
always proved to be a risk. If they get wet, the
grains in the ears will germinate and the tops of
the sheaves bind together, making thrashing or
combing impossible. It will rot and discolour and
be good for nothing but spreading as dung.

A fat raindrop plashes on her outstretched
hand and spreads like a wet toad. She swears.
This wasn't forecast. She looks up at the rain
cloud, willing it to shift and hang over the sea. Go

154

on move, she begs. The cloud refuses to budge and darkens even as she watches, as if reminding her not to take it for granted. Do remember: the weather will beat the best of farmers, it says.

Another drop falls, and then another. Her heart clutches as it begins to rain in earnest, hammering on the corrugated iron roof of the outbuilding with a hard, percussive beat. Silver stretches from sky to earth: mercury ricochets off the yard, streaming into puddles that swell, whisky brown and ominous. The downpour is furious and relentless: a freak of a cruel nature that, within moments, transforms an overcast sky into a mass of watery grey.

Trapped in the barn, Lucy is impotent. The wet sheaves can't be moved or covered – for then they would be fatally damaged – and all she can do is wait. After a drenching, they could be lain down to dry, butts to the wind, if it is windy and sunny – but the damp will remain deep inside, where each sheaf is bound tightly in the centre, like a festering, dangerous secret.

The rain is falling thick and fast, still: rivulets running over the cobbles, wetting the pats of dried manure, turning the ground into a coppery slick. In the fields, the cows will be hunched miserably, trying to shelter beside the hedgerows, waiting for it all to be over. In the farmhouse, Flo and Judith will be watching. She can see her mother's face at the kitchen window: a mirror of hers, or perhaps even bleaker as she contemplates what the loss of this crop will mean.

She cranes her neck out of the barn, and a torrent of rain soaks her, running straight down the back of her T-shirt. Where is Tom, who has invested so much energy in producing this crop – and so much hope? Through the sheets of rain, she sees a tall figure in the nearest field, fists clenched, body wound tight with exasperation – and more than that, with fury – standing stock-still, railing at the sky. He can do nothing to stop this happening: must feel utterly helpless. And yet, faced with the loss of the entire fifteen thousand pounds they had been relying on, what else can he do?

She runs through the downpour, the rain striking her shoulders and soaking her clothes within seconds. The stubble scratches her ankles, hair plasters her face.

'Come inside,' she shouts through the rain.

He turns to her, mouth twisted and wordless, and she sees utter desperation and disbelief in his eyes, though they both knew that this was possible: that the wheat reed was a gamble precisely because it must be dried outdoors for two to three weeks. The unpredictability of the Cornish weather, the reeds' vulnerability to the elements, the need to manage it precisely to make it as durable as possible are the very reasons it could have commanded such a high price – if only they had managed to conquer all these things.

'Come on, Tom,' she repeats, and holds her arms out.

'I can't.' For a moment, he is a small boy reluctant to be held by his big sister.

'Come on.' She tries to put her arms around him. 'You're getting soaked. You can't do anything here.'

He shrugs her off. 'How could this happen?'

Rage contorts his face. 'Why the fuck did this have to happen to us? On top of everything?'

She shakes her head for she can say nothing to make it better. 'I don't know,' is the best she can manage. Rain fills her mouth, making her words indistinct and pitiful. 'But you can't do anything. Please. Just come inside.'

He shakes his head and begins to walk from her, face flushed and ugly, head bowed against the taunting rain. In the centre of the field, he stops stock-still and shouts at the sky: expletives hurled into the impervious grey, which drowns him out with a roll of thunder. The rain continues, merciless, relentless: seeps through her jeans so that they cling, sodden, chilling her right to the bone.

This has always been a field packed with happy memories. The field where they made their dens as children. Not a field facing in the direction of where Fred died. But from now on, this will hold the memory of her brother raging at the sky: fists clenched, shoulders raised, all self-control surrendered – and something else: his self-belief.

Another roll of thunder. It's getting closer. A flash of sheet lightning illuminates Tom and he looks so like Fred, at that moment, that it chills her. She won't leave him alone here, she thinks, as she runs towards him to beg him to return indoors. But he turns, the fight gone from him – or the need for self-preservation stronger – and, shoulders hunched, trudges back towards her and their home.

Much later, drying out in the kitchen, she realises she hasn't seen Tom look so distressed since their father's funeral. Flo goes to him, and he lets her hold him tight.

'Shit, isn't it?' Flo says, handing him a towel and a mug of tea.

He nods slowly and loosens his grip on her; then turns away from them as if not trusting himself to speak.

'We'll try spraying the tops of the sheaves with Roundup, to stop the ears germinating,' he says, after a while, but Lucy can tell from his voice that he doesn't believe this'll be effective. 'Teach me to stick to what I'm good at. Not to gamble,' he adds.

'None of us can beat the weather,' Judith says. It is one of Fred's phrases. 'We couldn't foresee 'til afterwards.'

The truisms hang in the air. Fifteen thousand pounds has evaporated in less than an hour, and with it the slim possibility of convincing the bank manager – or Uncle Richard – that they have a realistic chance of tackling their debt. All that work, Lucy thinks: those hours spent cultivating the crop, binding the straw then building the shocks. The £300 cost of the seed and, far more, of Tom's labour: the physical energy expended and the emotion invested, the hope that it'd be the means by which the farm would start to succeed.

She leans against the Aga, feeling its warmth seep through her legs, and realises, far more clearly than she did as a child, that here, you are always at the mercy of the weather. In London, in the always-warm hospital and her centrally heated home, she had missed it: the changeable, mer-curial nature of it all. She had longed for the sudden squalls that chased white horses across the

158

bay; the fierce blasts that almost knocked you sideways; the sharp rays that shone through cerulean skies as tractors trawled through fields of gold and the crops were harvested. But here is the reality: a freak downpour that has ruined months of work within minutes and reduced a grown man to near tears.

She peers out of the window. The sky is brightening. A rainbow bleeds into the watery sky. It feels like a cruel joke: a jibe from a force that will always get the better of them, will always threaten to ruin their business, unless they can develop a means of outwitting it. She sees their mountain of debt stretching higher again and imagines them moving out of the foothills only to slither back down the scree.

'We have to convince Uncle Rich about the ice cream,' she says, slowly. 'We have to convince him that he should invest in the equipment – unless we think the bank will do so?'

'Not a chance. I spoke to them only this morning.' Her mother's words flood out in a rush of breath.

'Then he's the one we need to work on. Find out that there's sufficient demand among the farm shops and restaurants around here, and appeal to his better nature.'

'Not seen much sign of that,' Tom says.

The plans arrive in the post the next morning. With exquisitely painful timing, the A3 envelope with proposals from an architect friend of Richard's is delivered as Lucy comes back from milking.

'Got an important-looking one for you here.' The postman holds it deferentially like a tray of champagne.

She glances at it, sees the franking of an architect's firm, and feels her heart miss a beat.

'Thanks, Sam, but I don't think we want it.'

He tilts his head to one side. 'You mean you don't want to take it? It's addressed to your grandmother.'

She looks at it again. At least her uncle still recognises Maggie as the farm's owner: his moves to gain power of attorney or acquire the farm to circumvent inheritance tax, so far failing. 'I don't think she'll want it either,' she says.

Sam looks at her shrewdly, eyes crinkling through a web of crow's feet. She has the feeling he is suppressing a private joke. 'Your grandmother's very much her own lady, so I think I ought to ask her, if you don't mind.'

'No, it's all right. Of course I'll take it. Thank you. Though I suspect she'll put it straight in the bin.'

'Pity the fire's not lit: best way of getting rid of it.'

'I could always light one.' Despite herself, she smiles.

Her grandmother refuses to open it, and so Judith does that evening, once Maggie is safely out of the way.

'Just thought you might like a look at these,' Richard's note says. 'Just preliminary drafts. Very rough but they give us some idea of quite how extensive the farm estate is, and how many

160

dwellings we could get out of it. No need to get back to me yet. Mull it over. I'll be down in a couple of weeks to discuss them and see if there's any way we could move on from here.'

'Oh, he's clever. He's very, very clever.' Judith lets out her breath and smiles as if half-admiring her brother's chutzpah. 'Just leaving it for us to "mull over". Wearing us down gently, more like.' She shakes her head.

She puts the plans on the table, spreading them out so that her children can see them all. Despite herself, Lucy is drawn to them: intrigued by the neat, computer-generated images and the thought of the number of dwellings the architect has managed to conjure from the dairy, cottages, barns and old stables. Six, seven, eight.

It is a neatly sanitised world: most dwellings with two or three bedrooms. Individual, lawned gardens, each with a barbecue and picnic bench. The tamarisk tree has been pulled up, and the avenue of blackthorn bushes: all evidence of the ferocious wind erased. She could imagine children racing over the still-retained cobbles, and loving couples admiring the view of the bay while toasting each other with chilled white wine.

'He hasn't touched the house.' Tom points to the plans. *Farmhouse to be retained for the family's use,* they stipulate.

'The clever bugger.' Judith whistles. 'Or perhaps he does care about Mum's happiness, just a bit.'

'So, if the farmhouse remains, we could stay here?' Tom frowns as his finger traces the drawings.

'I suppose we could – but what would we do?'

says his mother. 'All the outbuildings have been used, and there's no milking parlour. Look, it would be pulled down, to make room for – what's that? A children's play barn?'

'So, we'd have a farmhouse but no farm.'

'Think of how much they'd be worth though.' Flo is staring at them, intrigued. 'Eight properties with a view like this. They've got to be worth, what, over two million? And we could hire out the land, or even work it for someone else. And you'd have no money worries, would you? All those early starts. All that stress. You could go back to cheffing if you liked.' She looks up at Tom, face alight with excitement, glimpsing the possibility of an easier life.

Tom wipes his face with his hand, masking a conflicting array of emotions – irritation, exhaustion, perhaps even temptation. Judith pores over the drawings, her face flushed and tense. She and any future generations of Pethericks will be wiped out, as farmers, if they agree to these plans, and Lucy feels a sudden burst of fury on her behalf.

'That's not the point,' she says, addressing Flo but encompassing them all. 'We farm this land. And if Tom and Mum, not to mention Granny, want to remain here, not as householders but as farmers, we'll try to continue to do so – until the bank refuses to let us. Isn't that right?'

'Quite right,' Judith says, though her voice breaks and her eyes flit back to the plans as though they are enticing. Tom, his spirit crushed in the last twenty-four hours, murmurs in agreement.

It is hardly the resounding endorsement that Lucy wants to hear.

Twenty

Then: 18 August 1943, Cornwall

Evelyn Retallick was busying herself in the kitchen, her back to her daughter. There was definitely something *up*. Her movements were swift, her posture stiff, her manner offhand. Perhaps she knew. She might just know. Three days she'd been home from Gwynnie's and she seemed more watchful and suspicious than ever before, Maggie thought, as she scrutinised her. It had been impossible to meet Will, but whether it was because the men were still harvesting the crops or because Evelyn was keen to keep her from him, she just couldn't tell.

She needed to see him, though. She just wanted to be alone with him, to be enveloped by his arms, feel his firm body held against her. She longed for him to cup her breasts, as if gauging their weight, then dip his head and kiss them, his mouth hot on her skin. She thought of the last time they had met in the barn. His mouth had snaked from her neck to her collarbone, and then, as she caught her breath, he took her nipple in his mouth and bit it, gently. She had never experienced anything so arousing or felt so rebellious; she was teetering on the very cusp of adulthood, it seemed.

A kiss on the lips would be enough, though, she

163

thought, as she gathered together the enamel mugs and filled a pitcher with tea. A snatched kiss as she locked the hens in for the night, ever alert to Alice creeping up on them as they hid behind the bales of hay. Such kisses were always urgent, their bodies pressed together as if they had to squeeze the maximum sensation out of the shortest amount of time. She would feel the blades scratch against her hair, hear the hens scrape, the mice scrabble, and she could tell with just one kiss, no, with him pressed up against her against the bales, she could *feel* just how much she excited him.

They hadn't kissed since Evelyn had come back. *Three whole days* during which he had barely looked at her. He was already worried that Arthur knew. The older boy looked at her with a leer, his upper lip curling as his pale blue eyes looked her up and down. But then he'd always behaved in that way. *We will just be careful,* she told Will. *Now: calm down and kiss me. No one need ever know.*

Now, though, she feared that perhaps he no longer wanted her? When they had kissed, she had sensed his desire, but, left unattended, had it withered away? How could it be that she was tormenting herself with the thought of the trace of his fingers, the touch of his tongue and lips, and he refused to make eye contact when she passed him the potatoes, or served him the leeks?

The only way she could think of meeting up with him, properly, with her mother back, was to engineer an after-dinner ramble: a walk along the beach at low tide, or better still, along the cliffs. The barley was still high further west, the sheaves

164

soaking up each ray of sun, and if it was a little trampled, the neighbouring farmer would think little of it. Or perhaps they should find a spot on the very cliff's edge, only spied by the circling seagulls. Or in the cleft of the rock – the cave beyond the cove, only accessible before the tide turned and swept in.

She glanced at her mother, now drawing pasties from the oven. This stage of the harvest was nearly finished: the barley in the last field being cut and bound into sheaves today and tomorrow, then left in shocks to dry for the next ten days. They would be working flat-out tonight, but tomorrow? To-morrow, she might just get the chance to see him.

'I'll take them for them, shall I?' she asked her mother, gesturing to the pasties, fresh out of the oven. Evelyn straightened up and put down the hot tray.

'Here are the cups. Don't stay out in this heat. There's so much to be done here.' She leaned briefly against the kitchen table, a wave of exhaustion clouding her face.

Out in the brilliant white sunshine, the men were working fast, gathering the sheaves left by the binder. The team of horses was uncomplaining. Heads down, they trawled the field, tails flicking the flies away.

'Food – and drink,' she called, stumbling a little under the weight of both. Her father raised his hand to indicate they should stop. James started towards her, but Will moved through the stubble faster, boots trampling it down, kicking up dust.

'All right?' He spoke in a whisper.

'I need to see you,' she said, her eyes on James, now ten yards from them. 'Walk on the cliffs tomorrow if you're finished here. Eight o'clock, after dinner? Meet you down the track?'

She had worked out what to tell him this morning, practising how forward her proposal might seem.

'Careful,' she muttered, handing over a pasty and gesturing with her eyes behind him. 'Here you go, James.' Her voice became brighter as the herdsman caught up with them. 'One big pasty and a flask of tea.'

'Thank you kindly.' James took them in his leathered hands.

'I'll leave these for Arthur and my father.'

'Won't you stay a bit?'

'There's too much to do,' she faltered. And, aware that she was flushing, she rushed away.

'I'm not sure why you need to go out now?' Her mother peered at her over the top of the spectacles she now wore for reading.

'It's a beautiful evening ... and I just wanted to stretch my legs.'

Outside the heat of the day had eased to a gentle temperature, but the sky was a muted blue: white streaks of cloud slipped and faded. It would be glorious tomorrow and, in a couple of hours, the sky would turn a vibrant pinky gold as the hot ball of sun slid into the sea.

Her mother took a sip of tea and glanced at *Frenchman's Creek* lying in her lap, half-read and open. It was the first time she had sat down for days.

'Well, take Alice with you, would you?' Evelyn gestured to the younger girl, curled up in an armchair, engrossed in her own novel.

'What was that?' Alice raised her head, blue eyes shifting into focus as she dragged them from the page.

'I said you'd enjoy a quick walk on the beach with Maggie, wouldn't you?' Evelyn encompassed both girls with a flinty smile.

There was no point complaining, she knew; that would only increase her mother's suspicions. And so: 'Of course you can come,' Maggie heard herself say.

He looked beautiful when they stumbled upon him at the bottom of the track that led from the fields to the sand dunes, his face open in expectation until he saw that there were two of them there.

'W–iiiiillll.' Alice flung herself into his arms, excessive in her delight.

'Hello, little sis.' Over the top of her head, he raised an eyebrow at Maggie as if to ask what she was playing at.

'Mother suggested Alice came when I said I needed a walk,' she explained, her voice bright and brittle. Then: 'What a surprise seeing you here.'

He looked taken aback.

'Perhaps the three of us could go for a walk,' she improvised. 'Out to the rock pools over there.' She gestured towards the cove. 'Or up onto the cliffs?'

'We could explore the caves?' Will caught on, and pointed to the very spot she had thought of.

167

'I didn't think we could reach them?' Alice looked intrigued.

'Only when the tide's this low – and one's a scramble.'

'I don't mind a scramble.'

'Come on then,' he said, taking the lead.

The three of them set off across the sand, Maggie walking briskly, for she could not wait to shake off Alice. Her eyes scoured the view, wondering if a large rock would afford them some privacy and how they might grab just a few minutes on their own. Will now trailed behind, and Maggie felt an irrational stab of jealousy that his sister was monopolising his attention. Then she looked back at them and saw Alice's beam as he flung an arm over her shoulders, and relented. The young girl gained little enough affection from her at the moment, so why should she resent her receiving some from Will?

'Here they are!' She had reached the first cave: smaller and deeper than she had remembered – a narrow crevice, really. Rivulets of condensation ran down the steep walls and pooled in the sinking sand at her feet. It was cool, verging on cold, with the sunlight so dramatically curbed, and it grew colder the deeper she went. A shaft of sunlight burst through the roof, towards the back of the cave, illuminating shards of broken mussel shells and slate on the ground, and catching on a stagnant pool of water. There was an insistent *drip, drip, drip* of moisture, pooling, and a pungent tang of discarded seaweed and rotting fish.

Instinctively, she called out: 'Hellooooo.' The sound ricocheted, reverberated back at her.

'*Oooooo*' went the echo, and she felt – though it must have been the cold – a distinct shiver run up her spine.

She could think of better spots for a romantic tryst, but at least it was private. A sliver cut into the cliff, only visited, at low tide, by a rare, adventurous child: at high tide, by seagulls and fish. Above her, walkers could be tramping, skylarks hovering, the grass seething with a mass of insects – and none of them would know of the lovers hidden underneath.

'Eurrgh. What's that smell?' Alice's voice reached her before she did. The girl, silhouetted against the beach, came towards her.

Maggie gestured at a large cod, lying beached by the tide. A fly buzzed around the broken gills, and sand collected over his dulled eyeball. Alice – so unsentimental, now, about the farm animals being killed – was still squeamish about dead fish.

'It's horrid. And this is creepy.' She glanced around the cave, her face guarded and fearful.

'I think it's rather peaceful,' Maggie said.

'Let's go out into the sunshine. I'm going back to the rock pools.' Alice ran out into the sunshine and into her brother. 'Don't go in, Will. It's horrid in there.'

'I just want to see if there are any stalactites,' he said, and Maggie wondered at the ease with which he, too, was able to lie to Alice. She felt a pang of guilt at their deception, quickly overridden by a desire to touch him as he brushed past her in the cave.

Nevertheless, she had a sudden premonition that perhaps she shouldn't let Alice wander off.

169

'You won't go to the other cave without us, will you?' she called out to her from the cave's entrance. 'It's tricky to clamber up to it: we'll have to show you how to get in.'

Alice looked at her, bemused. Her big, forget-me-not-blue eyes fixed on her face, unsmiling. She blinked. 'I was just going to rock-pool.'

'Well don't go far.' She looked up the beach to check. 'The tide's turned. It will reach here soon – and the caves even quicker.'

'But you won't be long?' Alice suddenly looked younger than her twelve years.

'No. A couple of minutes.' She flushed at the thought that she might appear transparent. 'That's all. Then, we'll go off and explore together, I promise.'

He was waiting for her as soon as she drew back into the cool of the cave.

'Oh, I've missed you!' The words spilled from her.

He silenced her with a kiss.

'Come here.' He pulled her towards him, her skirt scrunching up as he held her bottom with one hand and ran his fingers through her hair with the other. He paused and traced the curve of her cheek, his finger lingering on her lip until she couldn't help but kiss it. His eyes darkened with such a frank admission of desire that she had to look away.

He began to nuzzle her neck – his nose and lips buffeting her nape, her earlobe, her collarbone – and she felt the intoxicating shivers begin. One hand crept over her breast and she pressed

170

against him, as if to siphon off his heat and excitement. She heard her breath catch as his kisses became more urgent again.

'We mustn't be too long.' She could feel that time might become suspended here in this secret slit in the cliffs, where all was hidden away.

'We've plenty of time.' He looked at her enquiringly for a moment; then, eyes still on hers, began to unbutton the top of her dress.

'Here.' She guided his hand into her brassiere, looking straight at him, though she could feel herself blushing. In the gloom, he barely seemed to notice, or perhaps he wasn't as preoccupied as her with shame.

He stroked her nipple, then lowered his head and began to suck. She shifted against him and a wave of shivers ran across her breasts. His breath was hot and fast now, the kisses more furious. She was getting hot – unbearably hot – and, to her embarrassment, there was wetness between her legs. His hand, which had been circling her inner thigh, dipped between them. She gasped, and kissed his neck savagely, mortified at what he must think of her. He touched her again, and she shoved his hand away.

'Sorry.' He looked crestfallen.

'No. I just...' How to explain that she was scared of the intensity of her feelings? That she sensed she was teetering: behind her, the safety of a cornfield; beyond, the exhilaration – and danger – of the cliffs.

He resumed kissing her neck, lips closed and penitent.

'It's all right.' She pulled him close, feeling the

171

heft of him. One hand clutched his shoulders, the other stroked his thick, sea-scented hair. Her body pulsed, strange sensations running up through her stomach and down the length of her legs.

'Kiss me.' His voice was fierce as he looked at her and pulled her towards him, his tongue slipping over hers, his mouth hard and urgent.

But it was no good. Shame and confusion were pressing in.

'We can't. We need to stop. We've been too long. Alice.' She broke away.

'She'll be all right.'

'No. Really. We have to stop now.' She sounded shrill. It felt terribly wrong, them deceiving his sister. And she ran from the cave.

The beach was empty. The rock pools untended: no figure bent over them, peering through the fronds of seaweed to their sand-strewn depths. She knew something was wrong even as the tide began to lick her toes and she saw that it had risen to knee-height, at the foot of the cliffs leading to the second cave: the one that had to be reached by clambering up to it. The one she should never have mentioned to Alice.

'Alice.' She tried to keep calm as she ran towards the pools, in the hope that she was hidden behind a rock, that she hadn't seen her. But panic rapidly crept in. 'Alice? Alice!' Her voice escalated, veering from a question to a cry, as she ran towards the tide. Above her, the pale of the sky was seeping away. It was half eight, she reckoned; they had an hour and a half before dusk switched to darkness. They needed to find her before night fell properly.

She began wading through the water, still calling, her voice increasingly desperate.

'What is it? Where's she gone?' Will, flushed and bewildered, emerged from the cave.

'She's not at the pools. She's gone missing. Unless she's hiding?'

She had a sudden inkling that Alice might be looking down on her, observing – enjoying, even – her panic. She remembered those eyes, wide, open, appraising her; the sense that Alice was less naïve than she had assumed and might have guessed that something was going on between them. Was this her idea of a joke, or a means of punishing them? Perhaps she was lying behind a hillock of grass, watching now? Keep calm, don't act perturbed. And yet she couldn't help but scan the cliffs looking for a flash of a patterned skirt or an Arran jumper, a nut-brown face, a shock of mousey hair.

'Alice,' she called up. 'Please. Please, if you're hiding, come out. We won't be cross but it's not funny.'

Nothing.

A guillemot, whistling shrilly, drifted overhead.

The beach was eerie in its emptiness: the trawlers out, no pilots above them. A pale crescent of moon, thin as a fingernail paring, peeped through the blue; a warning that dusk was near.

There was nothing for it. She began to wade out properly, the water lapping her knees now, so that she had to tuck her skirt up into her knickers. She pushed forwards, focusing on the rocks below the second cave.

173

'Do you think she's really there?' Will had joined her, surging through the water to catch up. His face, so blissfully relaxed, so *loving* just a few moments ago, was tense.

'I don't know. I don't know.' Her agitation segued into a near-whimper. If Alice were lost, or worse, it was *her* fault. Her parents would never forgive her. She stumbled as she tried to run against the now choppy water, and the chill clarified her thinking. 'That's where I'd have gone,' she said.

The sea had reached her waist by the time they came to the cliff leading to the second cave. A wave picked her up and toppled her against the rocks so that her shin was grazed by the granite and bled crimson red. She clambered up, graze stinging, feet pricking on the barnacles as she tried to avoid the slippery, mossy seaweed that could send you crashing down. Keep low, keep dry, she told herself as she bent almost double, and yet she had to keep looking upwards. 'Alice ... Alice?' Her voice quavered, almost breaking, and she realised she no longer expected a reply.

And then, she heard it. A definite wail, filled with distress and a desperation to be heard.

'She's here!' Will bounded in front of her to reach the ledge at the lip of the cave.

'Is she hurt?' Her heart banged against her ribs as she clambered, unconcerned about the stabbing barnacles: just desperate to put everything right.

'Just frightened, I think.' He crouched down and the whimper increased to a heartfelt cry of relief, clotted with sobbing. 'I thought you'd never find me,' Alice seemed to be trying to say.

Maggie made it to the cave's entrance and peered down. Alice was resting on a shelf at the entrance to the cave, clinging to her brother.

'I couldn't get down,' she cried, her face a pale, grime-streaked oval. 'I couldn't work out which bits to stand on – and then I couldn't see how to get back down again. Then the tide came in.' She gulped back another sob. 'I thought I'd be safe if I just stayed here, but then the sea got choppier – and then I thought you'd forgotten me.'

'We weren't that long.' Now that Alice had been found, safe, Maggie felt she had to defend herself.

'Yes, you were. You were ages. Much longer than you said you'd be.' Her eyes bored into her, accusatory.

'We weren't long. Honest.' Will looked at his sister directly. 'Five minutes at most – then we came to look for you. You must have been pretty determined to get here.'

Her snivels began to subside and she started to calm down as he put his arms round her, stroking her hair and soothing her, as his mother must have once done to him. He was tender: his manner as gentle as when he rescued abandoned chicks and put them in the warming drawer of the Aga, or bottle-fed lambs disowned by their mothers. As loving as when he'd stroked her cheek.

I love him, thought Maggie. The realisation surged through her, filling her entirely, for there had never been any doubt of it. I love you, Will, she wanted to say. He caught her eye, but the smile he gave was devoid of complicity or sexual intent – and filled purely with relief at having found his sister. Then he looked at the water, now smashing against the rocks, beneath.

The waves were waist high now, or higher. They must head back or risk scrambling up the cliff towards the coast path, trusting that Alice wouldn't panic when told to stretch just a little further to a foothold, however precarious it seemed.

The younger girl was still quivering, her face flushed and beaded with sweat, her breath fluttering – and Maggie realised the climb wasn't worth risking.

Will seemed to have read her mind.

'If we head back now, you can swim on my back for the first bit and then I can carry you,' he promised his sister.

'But the waves!'

'It's that or the cliffs.'

Alice looked up and her face darkened as she took in the slivers of slate that had fallen like scree.

'The sea?'

She looked into its dark green-grey waters, then nodded, mutely.

Her brother took her hand and they inched their way down, her eyes flitting to the sea then darting back to the rocks, as if she feared they would shift and splinter beneath her feet.

Maggie followed, painfully aware that, though they had found Alice just in time to return home safely, their relief might be short-lived. The flash of resentment on Alice's face – eyes bugging, unblinking – and the explanation they would have to give her mother hinted at further troubles ahead.

Twenty-one

Then: 28 August 1943, Cornwall

Maggie looked around the heaving kitchen table, circled by everyone who was most important to her, and felt happiness flood her bones.

She was going back to Bodmin for her final school year tomorrow, and she wanted to catch hold of this memory: to remember it when life at Aunt Edith's was tedious, when her schoolwork was tricky, or when she felt a sharp pang of homesickness.

She watched her parents, now. Her mother, contented for once, quietly proud that she had put on such a good feast for her family and household; her father at his most jocular, relief that it had been such a good harvest evident in every gesture – from his back-slapping Arthur to his generous servings of food.

There had been little scolding when she and Will had brought back a subdued Alice from their cave expedition, ten days ago. Their mother had been preoccupied with news that a neighbour's son had died, out in Sicily. Mrs Tippett had been sobbing in their kitchen when they'd slipped back, and her anguish meant that their childish escapade went relatively unnoticed. 'How did you get quite so wet?' Evelyn had asked, distracted, the next morning. 'I slipped when we were paddling,' Alice had said, 'and Will grabbed me.' Maggie had felt her breath ease out in a rush.

Alice smiled at her now, as she passed her the potatoes. The younger girl had been distinctly cool for a few days after their adventure, but in the last week had thawed towards her. It must have helped that she and Will had barely spoken since that night. He hadn't come close, and she hadn't sought him out. She knew that, if they touched, her joy would play across her face and their secret would be out in the open. It was as if they had an unspoken pact: we got away with it, then, but we can't chance it, now.

Oh, but it was so hard not even to look at him, when she could feel his eyes on her; sense him diagonally opposite. She smiled at Arthur and, when he winked, focused on this celebratory harvest meal, instead. Though the cream, like the butter, was rationed, everything else spoke of plenty: the two roast chickens, freshly killed this morning; the tureens of runner beans and carrots; the piles of new potatoes, flecked with parsley and a scraping of butter to make them gleam. There was raised rabbit pie, the jelly glistening under the crust; soda bread; and, to wash it down, Cornish mead and home-made spruce – lemonade with added ginger. Beside her, Alice slurped at the sweet harvest drink.

For pudding there was blackberry and apple crumble, figgy duff, apple tart, or fat slabs of parkin. She and Alice had worked hard alongside Evelyn and Joanna, who now came in three times a week. They would have a feast, her mother said; and Maggie was touched that some of this was not

178

just because there had been a good harvest but because it was her last supper. We wanted to give you a good sending-off, Evelyn had said, with an uncharacteristic peck on the cheek. She had looked at her proudly, and Maggie had felt the burden of expectation being placed on her this year.

She looked up to say something to her father, but caught Will's eye and turned away abruptly. She couldn't bear it. The thought of leaving without touching him one last time. His gaze burned into her as she passed the salt, served the veg, chatted to Alice, and all she could think of was tasting his lips, his tongue, his mouth; the saltiness of his neck after a day working in the sun.

'Maggie?' She couldn't ignore him when he addressed her. 'Please could I have the water?'

Her cheeks flushed as she passed the jug, and she wondered if he could read her mind.

She risked a tentative smile back, and his face broke into a beam, eyes lightening so that she realised he might be taking the lead from her and have wanted to approach her, all along. She smiled more broadly, hoping he might guess at the complex jumble of emotions swirling inside her: guilt, sorrow, hope, desire.

This time tomorrow, she would be back at Aunt Edith's: safely out of touch or sight. Their glorious summer was fading: within a month, the air would be scented with woodsmoke, the mornings damp with mist. But like a bee sucking nectar from a flower, she wanted to eke out one last loving moment from this summer. And then she would bow to the inevitable and try not to think of him.

She didn't know how she got through the meal. And then, after she and her mother had doled out more cups of tea, and cake for James's wife, Ada, there was the washing-up and clearing away. Her father had got out his violin, and her mother – letting herself relax for once, for there was nothing to worry about now: the harvest was gathered in; her family had been well fed; her daughter was ready for school and was about to be off out of her hands – was persuaded to sit down at the piano and play with him. 'I can't remember anything. I haven't played for months,' she fussed, lifting the lid, and fumbling her way into a piece, fingers sliding over the keys and almost caressing them as she tried to remember. But, within a few minutes, she found her way in and, to Maggie's surprise, began accompanying her father, the violin soaring, the piano rippling, as they played 'A Nightingale Sang in Berkeley Square'.

Arthur and Will went off to check on the animals, and shortly afterwards, she wondered if she had left her cardigan in the barn. Her mother, distracted by a request from Ada and a compliment from her husband, only registered as she was leaving. 'Will you just check you've secured the hens properly?' she said.

Maggie nodded and slipped away from the music, the warmth, her parents at their best – everything she had known before now – and towards something more exciting and unsettling.

The barn was packed high with sheaves, and quiet except for scratchings in the corner. The moon was bright: within a week it would be as big and golden as a pumpkin. A real Harvest Moon.

She leaned against the straw and wondered if she was being presumptuous. Perhaps he wouldn't guess that she would find a way to follow him, and his fear of being thrown off the farm would override everything else?

And then, there he was: the moon casting the lower half of his face in shadow, hiding his smile as he moved towards her.

'All right?' he asked her.

She didn't answer, just drew him into an embrace. His lips were as firm and as soft as she'd remembered, his mouth just as sweet. She pulled him closer, desperate to feel the length of his body against hers; those arms tight around her, pulling her to him.

'Come here.' His voice was throaty and his eyes had darkened as he led her towards the back of the barn, the furthest corner. The straw rustled as they ran, almost stumbling in their haste.

She swallowed down a giggle.

'Better be quiet.'

'I know.'

'Oh ... I've missed you.' It was all she ever seemed to say to him.

He pulled away, his eyes filled with a sudden tenderness that softened the passion. 'Me too,' he said.

And then his mouth was snaking down her neck, sending tiny ripples through her body, and one hand was caressing her breast. She leaned against him, feeling the heat of his body and the tautness of his muscles, as the shivers pulsed

181

through her, light at first but gloriously there.

She ran a hand down his back and into the dip between his buttocks, and pulled him closer.

'I love you,' she whispered, as he kissed his way over her collarbone, peeling her blouse from her shoulders, struggling over a button before she helped him, smoothing away his embarrassment. Then he bent his head, took her nipple into his mouth, and sucked and teased.

They were grappling with each another now: him reaching up beneath her skirt and pulling her close, his fingers grabbing her bottom; her tugging his shirt up out of his trousers, feeling the leanness of his stomach, the definition of his muscles, the dip of his waist.

She stroked his chest: the tanned triangle and then the lily whiteness where he had been covered by a shirt for most of the summer. She could feel herself pushing against him, as his fingers slipped beneath her knickers and stroked the most intimate part of her, and she felt quite shameless, wanting them to fit together like pieces of a jigsaw, even though she knew that this was what wicked girls did.

It didn't matter, though, as he stroked the velvet skin at the top of her thighs then dipped his fingers between her legs. The war was jittering everything up, she told herself, as his fingers went deeper and she began to move against him. She gave a deep, grateful shiver as the ripples grew stronger, forcing all other thoughts away.

She buried her head in his neck, breathing him in, wanting to meld herself with him entirely. The ripples were rhythmic, regular, increasing in

182

intensity. He kissed her nipple again, pulling it upwards with a light bite, and she was catching a wave of excitement that carried her higher and higher, the sensation almost unbearable, thrill mingling with fear.

Dangerous. That's what he'd said it was. A delicious danger. Eyes closed, she reached down and let her fingers brush against the hardness at the front of his trousers. It strained against her and she heard his sharp intake of breath.

'Look at me.' His eyes were bright and questioning. 'Is this all right?' He was nudging against her now, emphatic and unapologetic, and she realised, with a shock, that he wanted to slip inside her.

She nodded and pulled him towards her, trying to convey that yes, of course it was. For how could it not be?

He paused, his face troubled. He looked so nervous. 'I don't want it to hurt you,' he said.

'Kiss me,' she said. And as he traced a line of kisses from her breasts to her lips, his mouth light and tender, then heavy and hot, and as the kisses became increasingly passionate, she opened up to him.

She didn't hear it until the very end; until after she had felt Will spasm inside her and she stood holding him. His body was soft and heavy, the force of the last minutes gone. He took her face in his hands and started to kiss her again, lazily, tenderly, softly, not hearing what she had and not seeming to care. But she moved away, alert as a cornered rabbit – and quivering like one.

'What?'

She gestured at him to be quiet.

It wasn't there now. That gentle rustle as if someone had been leaning against a hay bale and had then moved softly away.

'What was it? A dog?' As he said it, she knew he didn't believe it. 'Arthur went back into the house, so it couldn't be him.'

Her bowels dissolved inside her, and she knew who had been standing there, with icy clarity.

'Alice,' she said.

Twenty-two

Now: 3 August 2014, Cornwall

Six o'clock and Lucy is wishing she had got up a little earlier and made time for that instant coffee as she shepherds the first line of cows into their stalls.

Elsewhere, the farm sleeps, but she has been awake since dawn when the skylarks began their joyful chirruping. Still, she felt bleary, emerging into the cool of the early morning, and a world so fresh the grass was sopping with dew.

As a child, she had loved being up this early, watching her dad doing the milking in the summer months. Often so high-spirited, he was thoughtful with his cows; talking to them gently, patting rather than smacking their ample flanks.

They had some Guernseys then: longhaired, silky beasts that produced the richest milk from which to make the thickest clotted cream. Each had her own name, of course, and each her own personality. Fred would call them his 'Old Ladies'. 'I spend more time with them than with my younger ones,' he would say, glancing at Judith, somewhat ruefully, and bundling Lucy into his arms.

Perhaps that explained why he took their deaths quite so hard. When the Ministry of Agriculture declared there was foot-and-mouth on the farm, he had stormed off for six hours; running along the cliffs, as he often did when stressed, but staying out so long that his wife was frantic. 'I needed to get my head straight,' she had heard him tell Judith later. Then: 'I'm sorry.'

When the cows had been put on the pyres, he had cried. Yes, there was compensation, but the sense of generations of livestock going up in smoke, and the acrid smell of burning flesh, drove reason right away.

Lucy had been at her bolshiest then. Eighteen and desperate to leave Cornwall, the death and destruction wrought all around her just proved that she came from a nightmarish, apocalyptic land. And the sight of her father convulsed in sobs cut through her posturing and perturbed her in a way that she didn't like to admit. Fred never cried. Men like him didn't. It destroyed the natural order of things. And if he did, what was going on?

She wonders what he would think of his farm now. What would he be telling them to do: focus on the livestock or branch out into ice cream or tourism? He was never the shrewdest businessman – insufficiently ruthless to send a barren cow for slaughter, grim-faced when he sent the male calves. It was Judith who would phone the abattoir when one cow repeatedly failed to get pregnant or another proved hard to milk. 'There's a soft streak to him,' Uncle Richard would tell his sister – and he wasn't being complimentary. 'It's called compassion,' Judith had once, uncharacteristically, snapped back.

Lucy sees her father everywhere on the farm, now. The memories flood back as she checks that the teat cups are correctly attached and sprays the udders; when she whitewashes the cottages – for he put the last coat of paint on – when she takes a turn at hay baling or, yes, when she runs along the cliffs. And whereas his death haunted her before her return – the details of the accident she heard about from her mother, after she refused to attend the coroner's court – now it is the everyday details of his life that nudge at her, repeatedly. The positive memories – of him laughing as he collapsed in his threadbare armchair by the fireplace in the front room, or helping her to clamber to the top of the hay bales – drift up again and again, whispering to her: surely you remember? Don't make it all about his death. Fred was a father, a husband, a farmer. A hard-working, compassionate man, prone to fits of manic energy and the occasional low patch. Someone who felt things intensely but who always strove to do his best.

A figure stands silhouetted against the bright white light of the doorway and for a moment she thinks it is her father. Then Tom comes and stands beside her.

'Sorry I'm late. Barely slept, then couldn't get up.' He gives a smile that doesn't reach his eyes.

'Thinking about the crop?'

He nods. He has aged in the days since the storm: face cloaked in grey, his blue eyes dulled as if he were a truculent teenager. A heavy dusting of stubble grazes his chin.

There is no need to speak – and for a moment, it is too noisy. A heavy rattle and the feed rains down the hoppers in front of each cow. The vacuum pump begins its quiet drone, and then the cattle are silent, heads down as they chomp on their cake.

Lucy walks the length of them, checking the monitors behind each cow that weigh the milk which drips down the tube: three litres, four, five, six. The electronic figures rise for these most prolific of cows up to twenty – even twenty-two. Then: 'Home, home, home,' she calls. Tom releases the gates and they file out back into the farmyard while the next two lines are ushered in.

A rattle of feed, a lowering of their heads, and the next eighteen cows begin the process. It is comforting to do something so familiar and repetitive. The odd one stomps a hoof, but most are content to be milked, twice daily, for up to ten months a year, as long as they are well fed.

Tom joins her for a moment, waiting behind a bank of cows, jumping to avoid the streams of piss that gush towards them with regular frequency. She picks up a hose and aims it at the cowpats, washing them away.

'Luce–' He starts to say something that seems important, but there is the loud thud of a cow

187

trying to barge her way through a gate at the front of the line, and he sprints off to quieten it. Her neighbour shuffles, briefly disconcerted, but the rest continue to eat, uninterrupted.

For an hour and a half they milk, until all seventy cows have passed through the parlour. Tom leads them back to the fields while she fills a pail with milk to be fed to the calves held in their pens.

The three-week-old ones are her favourite. Still elegant, with slim legs and soft, liquid eyes, like a doe's, yet beginning to show their individual characters and strength. She slops the milk into the feeder and watches them drink frantically, eyes rolling back in pleasure, then lets the greediest suck on her milk-dipped fingers. Her tongue is rough and her mouth insistent as she cleanses them.

'No more. You've had your lot,' she laughs as she pulls her hand away, trailing a thread of milky spittle. The calf tries to barge her siblings from the bucket, buffeting them with her head.

'Oh, OK then.' She dips her fingers in the milk once more and the calf resumes sucking until, in her enthusiasm, she nips her with her sharp bottom teeth.

'You all right?' Her brother is back with a fresh pail of milk for the four-week-old calves, penned alongside them. He seems uncomfortable, and she remembers that there was something he had wanted to say.

'Fine. You?'

'Not really.' He gives a sigh, a long gush that makes it sound as if he has been holding something tightly inside for far too long. 'Just wonder what the fuck we're doing? Why we're bothering with all of this?'

'Oh, Tom.' She looks from him to the calves, their eyes soft and inquisitive. How can he doubt the validity of this?

'All right ... they're cute. But it's such a fucking struggle and it just keeps getting harder. The wheat reed makes me wonder if we should bow to the inevitable. Accept Uncle Richard's new idea – still living here but not farming – or consider it, at least.'

'Tom!' A hard knot wedges tightly in her chest. 'We can't give up on all this. What would Dad think?'

'Dad?' Tom is incredulous. 'What the hell's he got to do with this?'

She stares back at her brother. How can he be so stupid? 'Don't you remember foot-and-mouth? He never gave up when things were tough. He just picked himself up and carried on. So how could we do this to him?'

Tom shakes his head and lets out a low whistle, scuffs his boot against the straw poking from the calves' pen.

'I can't believe you can still think that.' His voice is low, as if he is trying very hard to control it. 'He was the last person to lecture anyone on not giving up on anything.'

The accusation jabs through the straw like a rusted blade.

'And what do you mean by that?' His anger takes her by surprise.

'Oh come on!' He laughs, openly derisive. 'He

left us properly in the lurch.'

'He had an accident.' Her words come out staccato and curt. 'A tragic accident. It could have happened to anyone. It was just his bad luck – and ours – that it happened to him.'

'Yeah, right.' Tom gives a bark of a laugh that is utterly unlike him. 'An accident that saw him just happen to slip from the cliff when he went out running.'

'The paths were sodden from a storm the night before. And he was running at dusk – when most accidents happen. The coroner said so.' She recites the facts, hurt and insistent, wondering why he has to dwell on this now, when going over the details won't change a thing.

'So, our dad – who'd run those cliffs, man and boy, for forty odd years – just happened to lose his footing and slip down the cliff after choosing to run at dusk, did he?'

Something is wrong. Tom's voice rings around the barn, dripping with sarcasm. This isn't the Tom she knows. His cheeks are flushed and he has that hard, trying-not-to-cry look that she remembers from Fred's funeral, and from many other occasions when he was a little boy.

'Why are you being like this?'

'It doesn't matter.'

'Yes, it does. What are you trying to tell me?' A cold streak of certainty works its way from her stomach and up through her chest. She knows what he is about to say, and she knows she could avoid it by fetching another pail, by closing down the conversation. But she has had enough of running away.

'Tom. Please. Say what you mean.'

He pauses, and when he speaks his voice is soft and sorrowful.

'He killed himself.'

'Noooooooo.' It is more of a bleat than a wail, this involuntary sound that comes from somewhere deep inside her body. She stares at him, frantic.

'But he couldn't have. The inquest found it was an accidental death. The coroner never once mentioned suicide, did he?'

'Well, there was no note, so he couldn't know for certain. No one ever will. But he gave that ruling so Mum would still get the compensation from the insurance company, and to save her feelings, though she knows: she just doesn't like to talk about it. Apparently that coroner's known for doing it with other farm deaths around here.'

He puts an arm round her and pulls her close. 'Someone like Dad, who's lived here all his life, who knows those cliffs back to front, who ran them at least twice a week, in most seasons, doesn't just slip on them. Doesn't choose to go running at dusk after a huge storm either, when he knows the paths will be thick with mud and impassable in places. You know how slippery they can get. There's another thing: they never found any sign of a slippage in the mud or a fall through the grass. And no sign of a fall of slate.'

'Perhaps they weren't looking for it.' She battles against his implication that Fred jumped.

Her brother sighs. 'Well, you believe that if you want, Lucy.'

'Well, I do, actually!' She pushes back against

him, standing defiant, as she did in childhood arguments. But the possibility that he is telling the truth bubbles up inside her and she finds herself grappling for certainties with which to force it down.

'He had nothing to feel suicidal about, did he? I mean I know he could get low – but the farm was OK, wasn't it? It wasn't like when we had foot-and-mouth. If he was going to kill himself, why didn't he do it then?'

For a moment, she is back to those terror-filled months in the spring of 2001 when the fields were eerily empty. The livestock killed or indoors, for fear they would catch the virus, blown on the wind. Each farm put bowls of pink disinfectant before each stile and gate, and infected farms had policemen standing outside them, their families effectively under house arrest; isolated, ostracised, unable to go out or receive visitors. When they discovered that one heifer had the disease, and the whole herd would have to be slaughtered, the Pethericks were in this position: bales steeped in disinfectant at the end of their drive, food left by a friendly neighbour in a dustbin and collected by the copper, Lucy and Tom unable to go to school, and the family faced with the certainty that their entire herd – and their flock of sheep as well – would have to be put to death.

Lucy had thought the killing would be the worst thing. These were cattle she had grown up with: some she had fed since they were two days old, others were expecting new calves – and delivered healthy ones, which had to be shot immediately. Even once it was clear a handful had succumbed

192

to the illness – their noses streaming and necks outstretched, a couple beginning to limp – it seemed barbaric to kill the lot. Judith and the children stayed inside, squirrelled away at the top of the house, as the Ministry of Agriculture slaughterman, with his single-bore shotgun, decimated their livestock – and their history.

But what happened next, if anything, was worse. The officials, wearing hoods drawn tightly, white boiler suits, and rubber boots and gloves, dug a trench in which to pile the cows and sheep, then left them for almost a week as they were ordered to kill infected beasts elsewhere. From time to time, an official would clamber over the rotting pile of flesh to spray it with disinfectant, and the bodies would pop with an audible *phut*. In the mornings, animal limbs would be strewn across the yard where badgers and foxes had worried them in the night. Once, a magpie flew past, an infected sheep's eyeball in its beak.

It was a relief when the pyres of rotting beasts, legs sticking out like matchsticks at all angles, were lit, and the stench of paraffin began to overwhelm the rottenness. For a moment, the air smelt of roast beef, then acrid, charring flesh. As the pyre continued to smoke, there was news that a neighbouring farmer had hanged himself in his cowshed. He had stood on a milking bucket, then kicked it away. Another farmer, nearer Truro, had rigged up his tractor to kill himself with his shotgun. But Fred had picked himself up, stopped keeping sheep and, with his compensation, rebuilt his dairy herd slowly but steadily.

'Why didn't he do it then?' She breaks off from

those pin-sharp memories.

'He was eight years younger. Fitter, more resilient. Perhaps more optimistic. Perhaps he didn't have depression – not depression like he had this time – then.

'The farm had had an inconclusive TB test a couple of days before he died. Another one was lined up, and, if that was inconclusive too, then, that was it: that animal would be killed. Perhaps he was worried that it would spread: that this would be it again? I think he couldn't face any more deaths on the farm – ironic, really, since his was the most tragic of all.'

He pulls away from her and looks into her blanched face. 'Did you really not know?'

'No. Well, perhaps.' Fragments of conversations and half-known facts tessellate to form a new truth, the edges becoming sharper with everything he says. She remembers Fred's fury when, aged seventeen and going through her goth stage, she had tried to paint her bedroom walls black. 'Isn't there enough darkness in life?' he had roared – and she had been shaken by the look on his face, and his uncharacteristic rage. Could he have done this to them? Bile rises in her mouth and she gulps it down.

'Yes,' she says. 'Perhaps I did.'

They feed the remaining calves together: the four-week-olds, the five-week-olds, then the six-month-old bullock they are rearing to sire cows that aren't closely related. He tries to head-butt Tom – his eyes filled with a promise of menace – and Tom slaps his huge head away.

The barn smells sweet: the straw fresh with

194

only a hint of manure, the early-morning air crisp and salt-tinged. Everything is as it should be and yet life has irrevocably changed. Her dad killed himself. He found life so bleak that he chose to leave all of this, and he chose to leave them.

A ball of cold hard fury replaces her heavy numbness. His family weren't enough to deter him, and her dad – the man she thought would protect her for ever – proved more fallible than most. Could not protect himself, let alone others, in the end.

How could he do it? However ashamed she has been of her mistake and of Matt's infidelity, she has never viewed life as unendurable, or death – especially a horrible, messy death – as an escape. She thinks of her one moment teetering on the headland, watching the spume swirling around the rocks beneath. She had shocked herself then, and in that split second when the wind offered to lift her, stumbled back, choosing life.

But this farm – a refuge for her, a place where she imagines she might eventually find happiness – was the very opposite for Fred. The relent-lessness of milking; the financial pressure; the fear it would all come tumbling down: he must have hated it.

'The fucker,' she says, more in sorrow than in anger.

'I know.' Tom takes the pail from her and puts an arm round her shoulders as they leave the barn and tramp towards the farmhouse. 'I know – but he wasn't really.'

'No. Of course he wasn't, really,' she says.

Twenty-three

Then: 5 September 1943, Cornwall

Maggie knew they had been found out, as soon as she arrived home from school on Friday evening. Evelyn and Alice were in the kitchen, preparing dinner. When Maggie entered, both stopped and looked up.

Alice's eyes were scorched red, as if she had been crying for days. Evelyn looked more implacable than usual. Even Joanna, who entered with a pile of laundry seconds after Maggie, froze in the doorway.

'What's wrong? Why are you all looking at me like that?' Maggie's voice changed from an attempt at wry amusement to near panic.

'Nothing's wrong.' Evelyn came forward to take the small suitcase. 'But just come through here a minute.' She guided Maggie by the elbow, leading her back into the hallway and through to the parlour at the front of the house.

'You're making me nervous. Has someone died?' The words spilled out. Her father's shotgun, used to kill badgers and foxes, burst unaccountably into her mind.

'No one's died.' Her mother remained as calm and controlled as usual.

'Then what?'

'Sit down for a moment, Margaret.' Her

196

mother gestured to a mahogany dining chair and, ramrod-straight, lowered herself into a second.

Margaret. She must know, of course she knew. So Alice *had* seen them. Her deepest fear erupted into life. All week, she had ricocheted between the hope that she had imagined that rustle, and the cold, hard certainty that they had been spotted and would be exposed. She had slept badly, fretting about what might be said, what might occur, when she got back to the farm-house, agonising as she had tried to hold herself tight in the stark bedroom at Aunt Edith's home.

And yet her mother seemed nervous rather than angry, her fingers twisting her wedding band round and round as if she dreaded speaking to her daughter. Maggie found that she was shaking, her heart battering against her chest so loudly she feared her mother would hear.

Time stretched. The grandfather clock in the corner of the room marked out the seconds between them, demarcating the silence, and she found that she was willing her mother to speak.

Eventually, Evelyn gave a small cough. 'Will has gone to work at another farm the other side of Bodmin. It will give him experience at a much larger dairy farm. Alice is understandably distressed, but it's an excellent apprenticeship: a wonderful opportunity for any young man.'

The words swirled around her: Will ... apprenticeship ... Bodmin.

'Which farm? And why's he gone already?' Her voice, small and incredulous, grew into a near wail as the immediate tragedy struck her. 'But I haven't even said goodbye!'

'Well.' Her mother looked discomfited. 'He went quickly because they needed someone as soon as possible. Your father took him on Wednesday. As to which farm it is, we think it's for the best that you don't know.'

Evelyn looked at her, grey eyes grave and unflinching. Maggie looked back, hating her mother at that moment.

'I don't know why you'd think that,' she said, her voice unnaturally prim, and strangled.

'Oh,' said her mother. 'I think you do.'

She waited for Evelyn to ask how long it had gone on – or how involved they had been. Anything that would let her gauge how much Alice had seen. But her mother was silent. Maggie looked down at her hands; the nails usually kept blunt and neat, but this week bitten down to the quick.

Her mother hadn't quite finished though.

'I was young once, you know,' she said, and her voice softened and was suddenly tinged with sadness. 'And I, too, fell in love.'

'With Father?'

'Not with your father, no.' She batted the idea away like a fly. 'With his younger brother, Isaac. We were very young, but we were going to be married. Then he was killed. August the third, 1918. The second battle of the Marne.

'Your father is a good man. The elder brother, saved from being called up because of the farm. He took care of me. Married me so that I wasn't left a spinster. And I will always be grateful to him for that.'

She paused, and Maggie waited, unsettled by

the news of this dead love and the fact that her mother might have loved someone apart from her father; wondering at her mother's hesitation. The implicit 'but'.

'Do you still think of him?' she ventured, after a while.

But Evelyn wouldn't be drawn and shook her head. 'Let's just say that your first love will always be special. Will always seem romantic. Perhaps even more so if it's cut short, as mine was.'

'Then why?' Maggie couldn't begin to express her sense of injustice. Why would her mother do this – stop her experiencing this intense, first, true love – if she understood how she might feel?

'Because first love doesn't last. It isn't real,' Evelyn said, emphatic. 'It changes, wanes – just like the passing of the summer. It's impermanent. Fragile. And so I won't let you throw away all the opportunities you have, that I never had, because of it.

'Besides which, there's Edward.' Her voice hardened and became more pragmatic. 'You're supposed to have an understanding with him. And he's a good man. Bright and with fine prospects. What would happen if he heard that you had affections for someone else, while he was away?'

'I don't think that's very likely. He's somewhere in North Africa.' It was hard not to sound sullen. She glanced at her mother. Would she write and tell him, or inform his father, her cousin? That would be vindictive and would hardly reflect well on Evelyn if it was known her daughter had behaved in this way.

The thought must have occurred to her mother.

'Well, I suppose it would hardly help his morale,' she sniffed. 'We'll say no more about it. But you are absolutely forbidden to try to contact Will in any way.'

She put her hands on either side of her daughter's upper arms and looked her straight in the eye: pinioning her, so that she was sure that she listened. Their moment of confidence was finished. She was back to being authoritarian, even severe.

'We've nipped this in the bud and we'll say no more about it. Or about this romantic ... *nonsense*.' She gave an emphatic sniff. 'You've been a very lucky girl,' she added, with a nod of dismissal. 'A very lucky girl indeed.'

Maggie felt her insides flip; a sharp twist of the gut. Lucky? Luck? What was the woman going on about? She stared at her, wondering how she could think – let alone say – such a thing. He was her world, her golden boy. As much a part of Skylark as James or Joanna. Or so she had thought. And though she had feared that they had been discovered, still she had clung to the certainty that she would see him this weekend. That she would taste him, touch him. Excitement at the prospect had jostled with fear and emerged triumphant: bright and optimistic and clear.

Her breath began to come out in short, light gasps, fluttering from her lips, tasting of panic; and the parlour seemed to press upon her: the smell of the woodsmoke, the dark of the furniture, the low-slung ceiling with its heavy oak beams. She ran into the gloom of the hall, the tears coming as she trod on each cool flagstone, and raced up the shallow, worn stairs to her bed.

The anger came properly the next morning. Long after the shuddering sobs that made her retch, then collapse, exhausted. After a fitful, fractious sleep.

At first, she felt hollowed out. Her eyes were tender from all the crying, her skin dehydrated. I cannot cry any more, she thought, looking at her blotched nose and the raw, puffy redness. I do not have the energy.

She curled up at the window and watched Arthur chain-harrowing in the closest field, his legs criss-crossing the stubble, up and down, back and forth, and imagined Will doing it, as he had last year. The September sun would light the copper in his hair, and the curve of his cheek-bones, and his whole body would move as he gave himself up to the rhythm of the harrowing. If man could be at one with nature – as the Romantic poets kept suggesting he should be – then Will had managed it.

She opened her eyes. The mirage dissolved. Of course he wasn't there – and never would be. And yet the farm would carry on just the same. Through wind, rain, sleet and high summer, the farming year would spin – the only variation which crop was sown in which field and when. The milking would continue twice a day, and the breeding. The animals would be born, and the crops grow in an endless cycle of creation and renewal. And yet nothing would ever be the same.

'He's gone,' she wanted to rail, at Arthur, her father and her mother. 'He's gone: and nothing else matters. How can you carry on as usual?

How can you just get on with things?'

But of course she didn't. She gnawed away at a cuticle, ripping it from the side of her nail and tasting blood, salty and sweet. Less than a week ago, she had felt such happiness and excitement. And now she knew she would never be happy again. Self-righteousness segued into a white-hot anger. Her mother was wrong. This wasn't a fragile, impermanent love. It was hard and durable: a pure, deep love her mother couldn't begin to understand.

The knock was tentative. Alice popped her head round the doorway.

'Go away.' Maggie turned back to the window, wanting to be left alone.

'I wondered if you wanted a cup of tea? You didn't come down to breakfast.'

Alice was carrying a tray with a cup and saucer, and a vase with three sprigs of lavender in it.

'I'm not thirsty.'

Still she hovered.

'I'll just leave it on your chest of drawers,' she said.

Maggie watched as she traipsed across the room. Her hand trembled as she transferred the cup and saucer and she slopped a bit of tea.

'I'll mop it up.' Head bowed, she dabbed at it with her hankie.

Her meekness niggled. Why couldn't she just leave her alone? She watched her, fussing and bowing, and all the thoughts she had tried to suppress as unfeeling and unreasonable, suddenly tumbled out of her in one great torrent of hate.

'Why did you do it, Alice?'

'Do what?' She half-jumped.

'Tell my mother about me and Will?'

'It wasn't like that,' Alice blurted. 'Really, it wasn't. I didn't mean to. Honest.'

'So you did tell her!' Maggie was triumphant at having winkled out a confession. 'How petty. How spiteful!'

It was Alice who had caused Will to be sent away – and she could take all the blame.

'Why didn't you come to talk to us? Ask us what was going on? We would have told you. We love each other, you see!' Her voice broke a little here, for Will had never said that, had he? 'It was love. Nothing to be ashamed of. And now you've gone and ruined everything!'

'I didn't say anything...' The younger girl was crying now: great sobs that racked her body. 'I didn't mean to ... and I didn't say what I'd seen in the barn ... what you were doing.'

'You saw us?'

'Just a little bit.' She reddened. 'I didn't mean to spy: I came looking for you. I wouldn't tell anyone about that. I wouldn't know what to say!'

'You must have said something.'

'Auntie Evelyn asked why I was upset and I said... I said...' Alice's sobs were so loud she was incoherent. 'She tricked me ... I didn't mean to say anything ... but she asked and I said I'd seen you kissing...'

'Just kissing?'

Alice sniffed and nodded, emphatic.

Maggie looked at her coldly, not entirely sure she could trust what she'd said.

'Well, you did enough damage.'

The words struck Alice as if they were drops of acid.

'I didn't mean...'

'I don't care what you meant! Get out!' she shouted. 'I don't want to see you and I don't want to listen to your apologies. Will has gone and you caused it! Do you hear?'

The girl stood there, wiping the tears away with the back of her sleeve, snivelling loudly. And yet there was still something she wanted to say.

'What is it?' Maggie's words were strung out like stones, cold and hard.

'It's not just you!' Alice was suddenly defiant. 'He's *my* brother and I miss him too!'

Twenty-four

Then: 28 October 1943, Cornwall

Late October and the farm basked in the glow of an Indian summer. The blackberries wizened in the hedgerows, but the land still clung to its warmth.

The ewes were being tupped for spring lambs. Those that had been covered were branded with the mustard-coloured dye dipped on the ram's stomach. As the week went on, more and more fleeces became discoloured until they matched the gorse fringing the cliff path: a sea of cream with mustard spots. After lambing, these blotches would change to signal the number of lambs. The ewes were marked whatever they did, so that her father knew exactly how fertile they were and exactly when they had been covered. There was nothing private in the life of a ewe.

Maggie, watching the sheep, wondered if her own secrets would soon be made this public. For something was happening inside her body, she was almost sure. A baby was growing there, beneath her ribs. There was no evidence yet – her stomach didn't dome, her breasts weren't full – but she had missed two periods, and she felt nauseous the whole time, as she had when she'd gone out fishing. A new life seemed to be growing: future – unwelcome – proof of the fecundity of the farm.

She didn't know for sure, of course she didn't. There was no one to ask and no way of checking. Perhaps if she limited the amount she ate, it wouldn't show for a while. At school, she could keep her blazer on at all times and, on the farm, wear overalls over a thick jumper to hide any change. But her mother was no fool. Come the spring, and the lambing, her belly would be tight as a ball, and it would be impossible to hide.

She felt sick at the very thought. If she were growing a baby, what would she do with it? What happened to babies with no fathers, or girls with no husbands? Wicked girls, *sinful* girls. They were sent away to 'relatives' for two or three months; or to the mother and baby home, Rosemundy House, down at St Agnes, where they could be squirrelled away until they gave up their baby for adoption. She only knew this from Joanna. Eileen Brooke was being sent there, she said, because of what she'd done with one of the Polish pilots up at Davidstow. Maggie had thought her absolutely wicked, but it seemed she was no different from her at all.

She wouldn't be like Eileen, though: she wouldn't be sent to the home – however well-meaning the ladies of the Cornwall Social and Moral Welfare Association. However determined her mother. She would have her child here, and present it to her parents as a grandchild. Faced with such a sweet offering – for the baby would be beautiful, she decided, a prettier version of herself, and she had looked angelic as an infant – then, surely, they wouldn't force her to give it away?

She thought of what happened to unwanted animals. The kittens from the last litter, drowned in a sack: no mercy shown, with a pack of cats already. The deformed lambs, or the cows, like Clover, who broke their bones. Then there were the pests: the rabbits, the badgers, the magpies. The gun, the water butt, or the snare – all dealt with the sick, the vulnerable, the pestilent and the surplus. There was no room for sentimentality on the farm.

Perhaps she could find Will, on this unknown farm the other side of Bodmin. But, even if she could somehow discover it, how could he help? He was, she saw it now, as much of a child as her. A farm boy. Seventeen, eighteen in June. Expected to do the work of a man, but not paid the wage of one. Her beautiful boy, with the body of a man, and all of the passion, but with none of the power.

She saw him now: his eyes darkening as he pulled her to him then softening as he traced her cheek with his finger. The way he had gripped her as he moved inside her; his mouth skimming her skin, planting deep hot kisses on her mouth, her neck, her breasts.

He had never told her that he loved her. The thought stung, though she knew – when he'd caught her in the cave, when he had held her in the barn – that he had felt something. But what did he feel now? Without their daily contact, the oxygen of sight and touch, had his feelings died away? Perhaps his was a fragile, impermanent love of the type her mother had talked of. He must have known that she wouldn't be told where he was, that she couldn't contact him if she wanted to, but why hadn't he written? For, if he'd wanted to send her a message, had wanted to reassure her, then he could find a way to do so, surely?

She had lost him, as simple as that. Perhaps this new farmer had a daughter, or some hearty, enthusiastic Land Girl, with far more experience and fabulous breasts.

He was only twenty odd miles away, but she had lost him as clearly as if he were in North Africa fighting alongside Edward.

But she could not bear to lose his baby.

Twenty-five

Now: 3 August 2014, Cornwall

Judith has started on the baking: hands coated in flour, cheeks turning pink as she rounds the dough, rolls it, then gently presses the cutters down.

Lucy watches a moment, trying to imagine her pain at her husband's death and then when her daughter stayed away, only flitting back rarely. Did it feel like a double rejection? Thank God Tom – more clear-sighted and perceptive – had been there for her.

Eventually, her mother looks up.

'Are you all right, my love?' She wipes her hands on her apron.

Lucy nods and takes one floury hand in hers.

'Things will work out in the end,' says her mother, her forehead creasing at her daughter's evident distress. 'Whatever happens with Matt or your work, in a couple of years you'll look back at this period and you won't feel the pain you're experiencing at the moment: or, at least, you'll remember just a shadow of it. I promise it will stop hurting quite so much.'

Lucy smiles. Her throat constricts and she can feel tears forming, not at the thought of the failure of her marriage and career, but at her failure as a daughter. Judith knows what she is talking about. Her eyes prick, hot and wet.

'I'm sorry, Mum. For not understanding – and for not being here for you.'

'What are you talking about?' Judith is bemused – and then a rush of blood floods up her neck.

'About Dad. Not knowing that he'd killed himself.' Her mother flinches. 'Tom told me earlier. I should have guessed the truth. I might have done – if I'd come and attended the inquest. If I hadn't tried to bury my head in the sand and been so self-absorbed.'

The words tumble out now as she tries to make sense of her behaviour. 'I believed the coroner's verdict because I wanted to – but I should have realised. Especially as it never quite added up to me. I feel such a child: carrying on believing what I wanted to believe while you and Tom knew the truth and felt you couldn't share it. I was so protected while you had so much to bear: not just his suicide but the practical responsibility for the farm and all this debt.'

'Oh, Lucy.' Judith folds her into her arms. 'That's what mothers do, isn't it? Protect their children. I'm so sorry, but I let you believe the coroner because it seemed the kindest thing to do. Better to think he'd had an accident than that he'd chosen to end his life, wasn't it? Perhaps I'd prefer to believe it was that as well.' There is a tremor in her voice but she masters it. 'No one wants to think that they couldn't help their husband. That life had become so unbearable for him and there was nothing I could do to help.'

She starts playing with an offcut of the dough,

rolling it into a worm beneath her fingers as if she cannot look at her daughter.

'It's painful to admit. I thought we had a good marriage and that that would somehow lift him. That I could help him see this darkness through.'

'You did have a good marriage.' Lucy puts her arm round her. 'You did have a good marriage,' she repeats, wanting to cling on to this certainty.

'Yes... I know we did. But a good marriage – or love – isn't always enough. His depression ... well, I underestimated how bad it was. Just how overwhelming, how all-encompassing, it could be.

'A couple of days before it happened – just after he'd got the positive TB test – he'd gone for one of his long walks and I thought he'd got things in perspective. I didn't realise he couldn't shake the depression off, not properly, particularly since he hadn't got any help – not gone to the GP and asked for medication, as I'd suggested time and time again. So, you see, it suited me for you to think it was an accident. It was what I wanted everyone to believe. What I wanted to believe, too, except, of course, I couldn't, knowing him as I did, knowing how low he could feel at times. But I didn't want you to know – or guess.'

'You weren't responsible in any way, Mum.' Her mother looks diminished: a slight figure crushed by so much emotional baggage.

'Oh, I know *that*.' Judith manages to muster up some indignation as she draws away to look at her. 'He was big enough and ugly enough to make his own decisions. But still, you're left wondering if you could have done things differently. There are the constant "what ifs": What if I'd made that appointment at the GPs and marched him to it? What if I'd begged him not to go for a run that evening – instead of just thinking he was in a black mood and it might make things better? What if we'd made love the night before, even? And that hurts. It really hurts. That's why I don't really want to talk about this. And part of me still wants to believe it was an accidental death.'

She starts rolling the dough properly now. 'Better get a wriggle on.' The moment for explanations seems to be over and she boxes up her emotion, sniffing as she lifts the dough, her movements light and quick.

But then she stops, perhaps aware that it feels too brutal to shut the conversation down so fast. 'It doesn't mean that he didn't love us – any of us,' she says, her eyes bright with tears as she glances at her daughter. 'It doesn't mean that at all – and you're not to think it.'

'Of course not,' Lucy says, though a childish part of her wants to scream: He couldn't have, or he wouldn't have left you. He wouldn't have left me.

'I thought that for a long time,' Judith says, as if reading her mind. 'How could he have done this if he loved us? And then I felt such anger. How the hell could he have taken that option? It felt cowardly, and for quite a while I hated him.

'But it helped to see it as an illness: something he couldn't help and that was distinct from his feelings for us, and so couldn't tarnish them. He loved us, and he loved this place,' Judith persists, her words hard and bright as glossy sloes, her fingers pushing against the table as if to impress on her this certainty. 'That's why I don't want to

211

leave here, don't want to give up on it – though Richard can't understand that. Can't see why I don't want to be shot of it, rid myself of the daily reminder of where it all happened,' she says.

'I don't know how you've managed to deal with it without feeling bitter,' says Lucy. 'You always sound so loving when you talk of him.'

'It still hurts. It hurts terribly sometimes. But his death, his,' Judith falters as if the word is still difficult to say, *'suicide* ... isn't the whole of him. It's not the thing I focus on. I think of the good times, the wonderful memories of him. And those outweigh the bad.' She gives a half-grimace. 'Well, most of the time, anyway.

'When I'm feeling bleak, I think of him racing down the field with you on his back when you were a little girl, or running along the cliff with Tom. His excitement at the end of harvest. And, yes, the way he could still make me feel girlish, right up until almost the very end.'

Lucy nods, barely trusting herself to speak.

'Do you remember his laugh?' she manages at last, as she thinks of his distinctive roar: a belly laugh that would fill a room so that people would stare at this larger-than-life giant. 'I'll try to think of that.'

Her mother's face brightens. 'Exactly. A man who could laugh like that could feel huge joy as well as despair. Of course, the two came together for him. He felt things strongly, intensely. Too intensely. But I suppose that at least he felt them. At least he experienced those highs while he lived.'

For a while they are silent, and then Judith slowly resumes her baking. Lucy watches, wondering at the repercussions of her father's suicide and who else knew of it. Whether it was only kept a secret from her – and tacitly understood elsewhere.

'Does Granny know?' she says.

'Yes,' her mother replies, as if there is no keeping anything from her mother. 'She knew at once. "A lot of deaths on a farm", was what she said, which seemed an odd thing to say about someone who'd fallen from the cliffs and drowned. And then: "It can be a soul-destroying way of life". For a moment, I thought she was just referring to the accidents she'd known over the years. And then I realised that, of course, she wasn't, at all.'

She looks up and manages a rueful smile. 'She's such a canny old bird. Might be worth talking to her. Not about Dad, necessarily, but about Matt or what you're going to do about your nursing – that's if you want to talk to someone other than Tom or me. She was so wise after Fred died that I can't help thinking she's experienced some intense heartache or loss.'

'Well, she lost your dad.'

'Yes, perhaps that's it, though I can't help thinking it was something different to that. Something she hasn't told us. An old secret.' Judith gives herself a little shake. 'Perhaps I'm imagining it, but she's always been so private, I've always thought she's experienced far more in life than she's ever let on, even to me.'

'I think her generation probably have,' Lucy says. 'The war must have meant that death was common.'

'Yes, maybe that's it,' Judith says, but she looks

213

pensive. 'Often I'll catch her, on her bench, deep in thought, and there's a sadness to her. Not a wistfulness, but something more intense. She'll shake it off when she sees me, insist on being cheery, but it's there all right and I'll see it again when she doesn't think I'm looking.'

She smiles, betraying the weight of anxiety on her shoulders, the burden of caring for her mother, daughter and granddaughter. Three generations of one family: an abundance of care.

'She may have seven or eight years left in her – but she may not. I would hate her to die with any kind of regret.'

Twenty-six

Then: 28 January 1944

It was freezing in her bedroom at Aunt Edith's. The tips of Maggie's fingers were so numb that she barely felt the needle prick her as she fumbled with the stiff folds of the material and it shot from her grasp.

Late evening, and she was supposed to be studying in her dark room in this Edwardian house, but the cold made it hard. No fire in the grate, for her aunt had limited means and lived frugally, despite the gentility implied by the solid granite villa. There was a range in the kitchen, but Maggie could hardly make such alterations there.

For she was letting out her pleated school skirt

214

and shifting the buttons on her blouse. Two inches she would gain on her waistband, if she did this. Perhaps an inch for her swelling breasts. Under a heavy school jumper and with her blazer pulled around her, she might just look as if she had become a little plump. As if Aunt Edith had, somehow, been overfeeding her, or she had over-indulged, back home at Christmas. Farming families never seemed to go hungry, despite the rigours of rationing.

She stroked her stomach, feeling her curves rather than seeing them by the glow of the Tilly lamp. It was just a tiny swell: probably not notice-able – though it soon would be as winter segued into spring. She had managed to convince her parents it was best if she stayed at her aunt's most weekends this term, given that it was the depths of winter and the lanes skirting the moor could be treacherous. Besides, her aunt was lonely, and she could work so hard towards her exams. Her par-ents had agreed, confounded by their daughter, who hid herself away in her room in the evenings and was uncommunicative, almost surly towards Alice. 'She's lost her spirit,' her father said. Her mother just watched her: eyes narrowed, lips pursed.

Evelyn didn't know: she was sure she didn't know. But how much longer could that continue, and what would she do come April or May when this baby was born? She would have to hope for a cruel spring after a harsh winter, one when she could bundle herself in knitted jumpers and handed-down overalls – her secret hidden over the Easter holidays until she could somehow give birth here, alone. And then what? A sob bubbled up, and she gulped it back down, ever alert to the possibility that her aunt – anxious, solicitous though mercifully shortsighted – might hear her. What *would* she do once she had a real-life baby in her arms?

She started to rock herself, clasping her hands round her slight shoulders, seeking warmth and comfort. What could she do with her baby? It was her constant refrain. Or rather, how could she keep him – for it was a he, she was sure it was. What could she say to persuade her parents that the baby shouldn't be given up for adoption? And what would she do if they refused to help? She thought of her aunt: seemingly mild and conventional, and yet with a quiet inner strength that came from having lived alone throughout adulthood. Unlikely though it seemed, could she be persuaded to provide a home for Maggie and help her bring up this illegitimate child?

A flurry of rain lashed against the window: percussive and insistent despite the heavy black-out curtains. Outside, the town would be shrouded in darkness. It would be even bleaker, out on the moor. Would Will be listening to the storm – or curled up with his Land Girl? Anger flared and, simultaneously, longing and regret. For a moment, she was back in the cornfield: watching him drink from her enamel mug, a bead of tea on his lip, the sweat licking his thick dark hair. Then she was in the hay barn watching his pupils darken with a look of intensity and earnestness, as she came towards him.

No use wishing for that now. Look where it had

216

got her. The sob forced its way up, insistent, and she swiped at the tears running hot down her cheeks. She had been such a fool. Such a stupid fool. A clever girl, but no sharper than Eileen in the village, who'd left school at fourteen and would go with anyone, provided they gave her enough cigarettes and chocolates, Arthur said. How could she have been caught? It had only happened the once and so she thought she could risk it. Hadn't really thought it could happen the first time – for it didn't always with cattle. (Though sometimes it did, a thought she had shoved to the back of her mind.) Held in his arms, she hadn't felt able to resist him. Or, if she was honest, she had wanted it so badly, it had barely occurred to her to resist.

She stabbed her finger again and the needle pierced her: a drop of blood beaded and threatened to smear across the worn cotton of her blouse. She sucked hard, the salt of the blood mingling with that of her tears, and her eyes pricked again. She was in the cave, his fingers brushing her lips so that she couldn't help but kiss them. From those intense feelings to the act of making love, it was just a few short steps.

Don't think about that any more. Those heightened moments that spooled through her mind, late at night, as she told herself she mustn't think of him: those images that tormented and reassured her, so that one moment she thought he loved her, the next, she knew he barely thought of her for there was still no news, no letter, at all. To her shame, her body still craved him, had become more unruly and lustful, even as she tried to focus on this new life. She stroked her stomach. Last week, she thought she had detected a flutter – further proof that there was something inside her that would have to come out.

She reached to open up the lamp. The light was too soft for such intricate work, but she peered intently at the needle, keen to be finished before Aunt Edith entered with a perfunctory knock and her nightly mug of Horlicks. She made a neat knot; bit the cotton with her teeth. There: that should see her through until Easter, though perhaps she had better further limit her eating. Easier to achieve here, away from her sharp-eyed mother, and with frugal, bird-like Edith in charge.

The sewing done, she lowered the lamp and shrank into the gloaming. Pulled her cardigan around her. Rearranged her knitted scarf. If only she could feel the sun beating down on the nape of her neck – the same sun that would bleach the barley and wheat reed, and join the dot-to-dot of Will's freckles so that he glowed with a farmer's tan. She tried to conjure it up: the high noon sun tempered by a light onshore breeze that cooled the sweat trickling down her back. It was no good. The heady heat of last summer belonged to a different age: one fuelled by hope and love and filled with joy and expectation. Now, she was tired and racked with a perpetual, low-lying fear. Perhaps this was what it felt like if someone you truly loved was away at war?

Which brought her, inevitably, to Edward. Oh, Edward. His name always slipped out in two syllables suffused with guilt and despair. His photograph was on her dresser, next to her silver-backed hairbrush and mirror. Propped up for propriety's sake – for what would Aunt Edith think if she didn't show some interest in the young man she was supposed to love?

'I never said I loved him,' she had whispered savagely, when her mother had made this point. Evelyn had gripped her wrist, as they'd packed, in her bedroom.

'Love isn't necessary. But you will show some loyalty to that poor boy.'

The photo, in its silver frame, was turned down at the moment. She couldn't bear to look at those blue eyes; that small, brave smile of trepidation, his thin lips pulled tight as if to convey confidence, the tension around his brow suggesting anything but.

'I suppose I'm scared, Maggie,' he had said, and she saw in this photo the sixteen-year-old who had come off worse when wrestling fourteen-year-old Will. The cricket-loving Edward who was destined for a partner's desk in a solicitor's office, not for sowing caulies on the north Cornwall coast. A young man who, despite the newly developed muscles, had never relished the thought of fighting. Would it be this cold in Italy, where the regiment was thought to have landed? She very much hoped not.

Perhaps he would fall for an Italian girl, and be secretly relieved when she let him down gently, as she would, as soon as he returned. But that still wouldn't justify her duplicity, her *wantonness*, the fact she had so callously betrayed him. She pulled her cardigan tighter and began her rhythmic, fevered rocking again.

Twenty-seven

Now: 6–7 August 2014

The farm looks at its best as Lucy leads the cows out of the parlour and back to the fields for grazing. Eight o'clock and the early morning sea mist has lifted away. The sky is clear after its blush pink start: a faded blue shot through with gold. She pauses for a moment, remembering how her father enjoyed this tranquillity.

Her mobile rings, brusque and intrusive, and for a moment she is disorientated, the ringtone a discordant blare. Matt's name flashes up and she considers ignoring it for she doesn't want anything to intrude into this moment of calm, nor to talk to him when her mind is full of her dad. Yet they have not spoken – spoken, as opposed to sending a few curt administrative texts – since he walked out on her five weeks ago, and so of course she answers it.

'Hey.' His voice is soft, caressing.

'Hello.' She is cold, uncomprehending.

'I was wondering how you were. How you were feeling.'

She doesn't trust herself to speak. Her throat thickens as she thinks back to the problems that have driven her here – not the revelation of Fred's suicide that preoccupies her now. But it seems he doesn't require an answer, for he is still talking.

'I was wondering when you were coming back

to London? We should meet and talk.'

'What about?' The words sound clotted.

'About us.' And for the first time he sounds sheepish.

'What about us?' She isn't going to make this easy for him.

'I miss you. I want to see you. Look ... I made a mistake. A stupid mistake and I regret it. I'm sorry ... really sorry.' He pauses. 'It seems so stupid giving up on seven years of us... Giving up on our marriage. We should talk about where we go from here...'

She is numb. His words wash over her – the apology she has longed to hear, the still equivocal suggestion that they resume their relationship. It is so incongruous, this painful conversation in a calm setting – the possibility of a new start while she is focused on the past – that she doesn't know what to think or say. A truth nudges towards her through the fog of her thoughts. She can't leave here, yet, and return to the clutter and noise of London – a setting she now associates with her professional and personal shame, where she knows her fragile self-belief is even more flimsy. Not while her mind is filled with Fred and with what Judith and Tom have had to experience without her. Not while she tries to help her brother and persuade him that the farm has a future. If she is to talk to Matt, it feels as if it should be on her terms, here.

'Luce – are you there? Say something.' His voice, gentle, persuasive, filters through to her.

'Yes. Sorry. Yes, I heard you. So. Did things not work out with Suzi?'

221

'It's over. A stupid fling. Ended as soon as it had started.'

'She finished with you, you mean?'

A long sigh. 'It was mutual. I realised I'd been stupid.'

She waits. He gives a low, you-can't-blame-me-for-trying laugh that betrays his embarrassment. 'All right. You win. She was the one who called it a day. But it was a relief. I just hadn't had the balls to do it myself. It was just sex, Luce. No – don't hang up on me. I mean: it meant nothing, absolutely nothing.' His breath comes out in one long whoosh and she hears a catch in his voice, before it softens. So: he is nervous. 'It meant nothing. Not like you and me.'

Her tongue feels dull in her mouth: her brain, befuddled. She wants to believe him, to imagine it would be easy to forgive and to step back into her old life again. For a moment, she remembers their first kiss: Waterloo Bridge at dusk, early December after ice-skating at Somerset House; the atmosphere charged as they slipped from being just friends to being a couple in a move that seemed to make perfect sense.

It doesn't now. *It was just sex.* Who is he? This man who thinks she wants to hear this, even though she is glad there was no emotional connection. But still, he is talking about a sexual relationship with someone else: wide-mouthed, sensual, lithe, taut-limbed. She looks at her jeans, splattered with mud, and her boots, powdered with dust. Down the phone, she hears the rattle of buses, the bustle of a street, the wail of a siren. He must be walking to the Tube. The cacophony of London confounds her, overloud, excessive, as it pushes in.

'Actually, I'm a bit busy at the moment. There's quite a lot going on,' she says, unable to think.

'Can I help?'

For a second, she is tempted to tell him about Fred's suicide, for he would be sympathetic, she knows that. He liked her dad, loved him even, and he has always been a good listener. He would understand, she thinks. But no, he can't help now. Her chest aches at the thought that she has lost her confidant: for she can't open up to someone who betrayed her so spectacularly, can't risk him seeing her so vulnerable.

'No, not really,' she says.

Her grandmother is sitting on her bench under the crab apple tree when she returns to the farmhouse.

'You look thoughtful.' Maggie looks at her shrewdly.

'Just enjoying this beautiful day.'

Maggie nods in agreement. 'I always think it's at its best early on, before it gets too hot or busy. When you have the world to yourself.'

Lucy smiles, and then tears start welling, for she has never been able to fool Maggie. She perches beside her and they sit in silence, Lucy focusing on the lichen-covered tree trunk, gnarled and distorted, and the bright green marbles of fruit above her. Her grandmother waits.

'Your mother told me that you knew about your father. That he killed himself,' Maggie says eventually.

'I feel so stupid. So selfish.'

'Oh, what rot! Nothing for *you* to feel foolish about, or Judith.' Maggie gives a sniff that suggests that were she to meet Fred Petherick in another life, she might not be so sympathetic to him.

'Do you want to talk about it?'

'Not really, if you don't mind. Just trying to think it all through.'

Her grandmother pats her knee. 'Very wise,' she says, approvingly. 'Sometimes you just need some quiet and space.'

They sit for a few minutes, and Lucy tries to empty her mind and concentrate on the surroundings: a skylark hovering above them, the smell of grass, moist with dew still, the scent of lavender, boiling with bees.

But Matt pushes his way in. The night they met, at a party held by an old colleague with whom he'd been at college, where she'd been stunned by his sharp one-liners. The excitement of being shown London by someone brought up there: who delighted in his 'manor', though his bit of Dulwich was closer to the college than Peckham and his estuarine twang affected. His enthusiasm and energy that, for a while, masked his stubborn streak. She misses those early days, when they would lie in bed, her tracing the dark whorls of hair on his chest, and plot what they would do that weekend. Her mid to late twenties, when time seemed endless. Before her dad died and she knew that it wasn't. Before life became shrouded in grief.

'I've just had a call from Matt,' she says, after a while.

'Ah.'

'I think he might want to get back with me.'

'And what do you want?'

'I don't know.' She lets out her breath and reaches forward, clutching the back of her knees. 'He's my husband, I should want to be back with him: I've been longing for him to apologise. But I'm so messed up, not just about Dad, but about what I'm doing with my life. I don't want to go back to London. I'm terrified of returning to work – scared of making the same mistake – and it feels as if everything's connected. I don't think I'm ready to leave here – and all of you. To embrace my old London life again.'

Her grandmother takes her time to answer, and when she does her words are weighed, considered. 'I think you seem to be in a bit of a muddle, if you don't mind me saying. They seem like different issues. If you don't feel ready to return to the hospital, that's one thing – perhaps you could go to a GP down here and explain that. See if you could be given some more sick leave?'

'Yes.' She chews at her bottom lip. 'I'm meant to be back in a fortnight, so I need to speak to occupational health anyway.'

'And if you're not sure about being with Matt, then give yourself some time to think. But do think about what you'd be giving up, won't you? You know he's never been my favourite person, but no one outside a marriage can judge it properly. If you really love him, then that's a lot to lose. Lost love can be so painful. That and wondering what might have been. Never having the chance to discover, well, I think that's the

225

most painful thing.' She pauses. 'Listen to me sticking my oar in. You know enough about loss. Don't need me lecturing you, at all.'

'No.' Lucy thinks of her father, but is distracted, conscious of Judith's suspicions: aware that her grandmother has been alluding to something in her own life, for her voice is anchored by a tug of pain.

She thinks of her grandfather, Edward, who died of cancer long before she was born. 'It must have been like that for you when Grandpa died.'

'Oh, *pff.*' Maggie is so dismissive Lucy is shocked. 'Well, I mean, of course I was distressed, then. But I was thinking about other losses.' She pauses. 'I've had quite a lot of those, in my life.'

Her face dissolves into blankness. Who is she thinking of? Lucy wonders if she can ask her, but she is so resolutely private any question would feel intrusive, and the moment slips away.

Maggie shakes herself from contemplation; forces a tight, bright smile.

'I don't want you to experience any more loss,' she says, and there is an urgency to her voice that says: Yes, I know what I'm talking about, here.

Her eyes bead, steely. 'If he's not right, walk away, but don't if you think that doing so is something you might regret. We get so few second chances in life that sometimes, if they come along, we should snap them up. You don't want to think, later in life: "Oh, if only". You don't want to be filled with regret.'

The day stretches, long and sorrowful as a damp winter Sunday. She manages to make an appoint-

226

ment to see the family GP, who extends her sick leave, so that she need not return to the hospital until September 13th. She mutters her thanks but does not know how she will manage even that. She feels so out of kilter that the thought of being responsible for a desperately sick child terrifies her. How will she deal with the pressure to be precise and conscientious at all times, even when preoccupied or exhausted? Her stomach churns at the memory of Jacob – poor skinned chick of a child – and the wrong infusion; of Emma's expression, the shock hastily covered up, and then the terrible pity. She cannot imagine ever feeling confident of being a good nurse again.

On edge, she slips from the farmhouse for a swim later in the evening. Her day's work is done, and she needs to clear her head. The tide is high. It will fill the cove along the cliff so that she can dive off the rocks and immerse herself completely. She wants the chill Atlantic to take her breath away, the swell of the tide to lift her, the strong pull to challenge her so that she doesn't have the headspace to obsess about Jacob or Matt or Fred: so that she has to concentrate to swim hard against the force of the sea.

The cove is deserted by the time she clambers down to it: the water deep and petrol blue, shadows darkening the surface, hidden rocks and fronds of bladderwrack lurking beneath. She picks out the path she always takes, with the fewest torturous leaps from rock to rock and only a smattering of mussels and barnacles to prick her feet; finds the spot where the rocks drop not shelve and she will not graze herself; readies herself; and plunges in.

The chill takes her breath away. She wants to scream, so intense is the sensation. She treads water, acclimatising to the cold that freezes then burns in pain. Her legs, beneath the water, gleam pale, and she kicks them away, plunging her head beneath a wave and swimming, eyes open. She surfaces, eyes stinging and, buffeted by a wave, takes in a mouthful: far saltier than she remembers. She spits it out and rolls onto her back, ears singing with the silvered sound of the sea.

The sky rocks, filled with vast, brooding clouds, and she drifts out, allowing herself to be buoyed up, suspended, cradled. This is what I need, she thinks. How I have missed this. And again: Why did I stay away?

Dad, she thinks, and the Fred-sized hole left by his death. Tears seep from her eyes, mingling with the salt of the water. Grief has infantilised her: made her persist in believing the tale she was told, though she knew that some secret remained unsaid. It has made her selfish, too: preventing her from coming home for fear of confronting the scene of his death. But loss has touched Judith and Tom just as keenly. Perhaps now there are no secrets, she can shoulder the responsibility for the farm as equally as her brother. No more hiding in London, closed to their troubles, ever again.

A wave lifts her up and lowers her down, gentle and rhapsodic. She is a child, once more, being rocked by a vast mass of sea. She thinks of her grandmother and what she said about loss, and more than that, the tone of her voice: that unmistakable anchoring of pain. She sculls lightly, as the waves buoy her up and knock her down, and Maggie's words fill her head once more. *Lost love can be so painful. That and wondering what might have been. Never having the chance to discover. You don't want to be filled with regret.*

Would she regret not getting back with Matt – or not returning to London? For the two don't have to be linked. One without the other could be possible, though the thought shocks her. Her body rocks as she puzzles over the possibilities. What does she want? A relationship that is warm and passionate; a career in which she feels confident; and this, a life immersed, supported and enriched by land and sea.

Even as she orders her thoughts, she realises she cannot have all three things with Matt. He would never live here, nor is their relationship passionate, though – and a fresh sob bubbles up – he has been capable of passion with Suzi, it seems. She thinks back to their good times: lazy brunches reading the papers over cappuccinos and fry-ups in ironic greasy spoons; autumn walks along the Thames; late-night drinking in Soho; city breaks – to Istanbul, Barcelona, Reykjavik. That heady weekend in Paris, kissing in the Jardins de Luxembourg, his breath on her neck. The way he held her after her dad died, just *being* there for her. *I miss you ... I made a mistake. I'm sorry.* Can she ever believe him again?

A wave surprises her, almost tips her up, and she swims further out then rolls back over, watching the sky arching over her, the greying clouds buffeting her way. There *were* languid Sunday afternoons when they would just potter, and any silence

lacked tension but hummed with quiet contentment, gentle mornings when they slept in late and
made love. But they were in the early days of their
relationship, quite some time ago. The stomach-
wrenching, palpitating agony of romantic love has
long gone, and what was left was affection and a
friendly tolerance sometimes marred by irritation
– or that was what she thought they had, before
Suzi. Is it a sufficient basis on which to try to
resurrect a relationship – especially if Matt has felt
something more powerful for another woman,
however fleetingly?

The cloud hangs over her now, chilling her to
the bone, and she thinks, briefly, dispassionately:
that means thunderstorms; that means rain. The
thought shocks her. She doesn't like swimming in
a storm. She rolls onto her front and tries to
power forwards but it's hard work: she has drifted
further than she thought and for each four
strokes she barely moves forward. Don't panic.
Don't panic. It's only the sea, you've swum here
since you were six. A vision of her dad, playing at
dolphins with her clinging to his back, rises up,
unbidden. He had spat salt water out in an arc as
she had laughed 'more, more' and 'faster'. Then
he'd ducked under, and she'd felt the terrifying
thrill of swimming under water for the first time.

He's not here now, though. She feels a sharp shot
of anger: You're not here, now, when I need you.
But all thoughts go as a wave slaps her in the face.

Spitting water, she fights against the drag, increasingly panicky. An ominous rumble. Thunder.
The water turns cooler, the sun hidden by a vast
mass of grey. She scans the cliffs, hoping that

someone might, miraculously, be walking their dog, but the path, fringed with darkening hedge-rows, remains empty. Not even a black Labrador bounding ahead of its holidaying owner. She ducks under a wave and pushes forwards, praying that there will be someone when she surfaces. Anyone. Anyone at all?

And, suddenly, there is. A dark head bobs along then disappears behind a thicket.

'Help!' She doesn't mean to shout, but the relief of seeing someone is so intense it is involuntary. 'Help!' Her voice echoes around the cove, but the person doesn't seem to hear. She treads water and cries out again. Nothing. Frustration and self-pity merge, and she ducks under the water, trying to fight against the pull, to swim inland. Don't panic, don't panic. A spasm of cramp grasps her left foot and she comes up for air.

'You all right?' Someone is shouting at her. The relief is so intense that, for a second, she cannot answer.

'No... Can you help?' Salt stings her eyes, her mouth tastes metallic with fear.

The man reaches into a small boat, dragged up on the slipway, then runs onto the rocks. Tall, dark, broad-shouldered, she can't make out his features without her contact lenses, but in his hand – mercifully, incredibly – is a length of rope.

'If I throw can you grab this?'

'Yes. Yes.' She almost laughs with relief. The rope whips the wave in front of her and she dives down to catch its hairy thickness before it sinks down into the deep.

Straddled on the rocks, he reels her in and, as

she is pulled closer, she recognises her rescuer. Ben Jose grabs her upper arms to pull her out of the water, his grip firm against her mottled skin.

'Here, have this.' He passes her the threadbare towel she brought down to the rocks, and watches as she pulls it around herself. She feels exposed, shivering alongside him, a snake of water spilling down her back, her legs two white sticks goose-pimpling.

'That was a bloody stupid thing to do, you know that, don't you?' His voice is tight. She pulls the towel tighter, feeling defensive.

'I didn't intend to be rescued.'

'What do you mean by that?' The colour drains from his face. She moves towards him, alarmed by his reaction. Does he know about her dad?

'I mean, I didn't think I'd need rescuing; I thought I'd just have a swim. Here – we'd better get going.' She begins to collect her things together, embarrassed, as thunder rumbles and she feels the first fat drop of rain.

She reaches for her cut-off jeans and T-shirt, pulls them on over her sodden swimming costume, and clambers over the rocks with Ben following. Did he really think she wanted to kill herself? Believe in some genetic predisposition? She thinks of her moment on the headland; shakes the memory away.

The cliff path is earthy beneath her bare, wet feet. Her toes, squelching, quickly darken. She walks faster, aware of the grey clouds rolling towards the farm half a mile away.

'What were you doing here, anyway?' she calls over her shoulder.

232

'I came looking for you.'

'Oh.' She carries on walking, heat rising in her cheeks as she takes this in.

'I'd gone to the farm to talk to you and Tom – but he couldn't find you. He was worried; mentioned that you seemed upset.'

The thought of being searched for like an errant teenager is humiliating and she half-runs forwards, a sob catching in her throat, her body shivering.

'Hey – wait a minute.' He catches her up. She turns, but his face has softened. 'He was worried about you. We both were. You know there's a strong current there or you should do. It's not a place to be swimming; not when the tide's on the turn and a storm's coming in.' He pauses and looks embarrassed. 'Perhaps I overreacted.'

'No,' she says. 'Really. it's fine.'

'There was a boy in my year. Mike Prouse. A good mate. Drowned the summer we did our A levels. We'd had a beach party. He'd drunk a bit. Not masses but enough. He said he was going swimming. It all seemed calm, but then the weather came in, suddenly – just like this. He didn't stand a chance. Makes me a bit jittery whenever someone's swimming and a storm's brewing.'

'That's OK.' Another death in the sea, around these cliffs. Another death in view of Skylark. She hugs her shoulders, not knowing what to say.

'Here – you're really shivering. Take this.' He pulls off his hoodie and puts it over her head. The heavy weight cocoons her as he pulls it over her shoulders, her arms and waist. The inside of the

233

fleece is warm with his body heat, and she moves it over her lips, feeling its softness. It smells of washing powder, of salt, and of him.

'We're going to get properly wet – come on.' He resumes walking as they hear a closer roll of thunder.

'Thank you,' she manages. 'That's much better.' And she catches up with him, half-running on the edge of the field as she matches his pace.

'You looked deep in thought when you were floating there,' he says.

'Oh – I just had some life stuff to think about.'

'Sounds heavy.'

'Something like that.' She cannot begin to talk about it.

'Do you want to hear something to cheer you up, then?'

'Please!' Her reply comes out in a rush, the tension held inside her for the past hour beginning to ease.

'It's about the ice cream. We'd love to stock it at Tredinnick. We'll take forty half-litre tubs a week, in season; not sure how much out of season.'

She stops, despite the rain starting to fall more heavily, trying to readjust her emotions and shake off thoughts of death. He wants to stock the ice cream. The suggestion seems bizarre: so left-field and unexpected that she does not know what to say. Ice cream? They want to stock their ice cream?

'That's fantastic. Thank you,' she manages, eventually.

He beams, then, to her frustration, resumes walking, briskly. 'I've also got a friend whose dad

234

owns a string of delis, Kernow's, throughout London. She's a buyer for him, is down at the moment and would love to meet to discuss a possible order, too.'

She stumbles on, the straw whipping her bare shins, nettles stinging her ankles, bemused by further possible good news; almost incapable of taking it in.

'What sort of quantity is she thinking of?' She tries to switch her brain into gear.

'Well, I'd have thought you'd need one of you making it full-time. It's early days, but Alex was talking about wanting up to 600 half-litre tubs a week if it proves successful.'

She catches him up, her mind reeling. This is a business-changing figure. The sort of news that might confound Uncle Richard and curb his development scheme. She tries to calculate the profit on 600 tubs at £3.95 each, but it's beyond her at the moment, so befuddled is she by the switch in emotions and the image of a farm that could be a success.

'Anyway,' he says, as he starts to jog up the last field, the rain gathering in momentum and falling thick and fast now. 'Will you come and talk to her? You and Tom? Meet us for a drink tomorrow evening? The Wreckers. Say, eight-thirty?'

They have reached the yard, and splatter through freshly wet muck to the kitchen. The rain is pounding, the air dense with the smell of soaked grass, crushed camomile and vetch.

They huddle inside the porch, and finally she grins up at him, as the rain falls from heaven to earth: grey sheets that section them off and contain them in the cool, intimate space between the yard and kitchen door. He is so close she can see the hairs on his forearm, and a small scar on the underneath of his chin from when he gashed it as a kid, rock-pooling with Tom. He smells of salt and earth and when he smiles at her she lets herself believe that, perhaps, the farm's fortunes might be changing.

'Eight-thirty it is,' she says.

They meet the next evening, as promised. Alex is petite, smartly dressed and classically beautiful – the sort of woman who would usually make Lucy wary, were it not for the fact she is warm and seems so interested in them.

At the next table outside the pub, a family are making the most of a balmy evening: the parents drinking cold white wine while their children – two boys and a girl – devour bags of crisps. Salty-haired, the boys start crabbing over the harbour wall: fixing pieces of bacon fat to lines and tossing them into the dark green gloom to entice crabs from the claggy algae.

'They'll be lucky to find anything in there,' Alex says.

But: 'Look, Dad, look. We've got a big one!' Within minutes there is a tug on a line and the older boy is scrabbling to pull it up.

'Well done, Oscar,' says his father.

'That's not fair. I want one too,' the little sister clamours as the second brother also draws up a crab and unhooks it into his bucket.

'Here, you can help.' Her big brother hands over the line as he inspects his catch. His sister –

236

who can't be more than four – sits patiently on the side of the harbour, waiting for the tell-tale tug to happen again.

Their excitement infects those around them. Lucy can see that Tom is just dying to peer into the bucket or join in, as he did as a boy. Ben is itching to do so, too.

'Can we have a look?' he asks, approaching the trio, and glancing at their parents first for approval. 'Cor. He's massive. You could almost eat him.'

'And Milo's got a good one.' Oscar proffers his brother's bucket, approval making him generous, both boys visibly swelling with pride.

'Do you have children?' Alex is watching her watching them.

'Oh no. I've left Tom to supply the grand-children.' Lucy trots out her usual line.

'But you're married?' Alex probes her.

'Yes. Err, yes, I am. Sort of.' She looks away as she says this and catches Ben's eye.

'I didn't realise you were married. You don't wear a ring,' he says.

She looks down at her long fingers, tanned brown by the sun.

'No, I don't,' she replies, not knowing what else to say. She feels dishonest for not mentioning this fact, surprised that Tom hadn't told him. She looks directly at him. 'It's a bit complicated.'

'Shall we talk about the proposal?' Alex rescues her. The quantities she suggests are impressive. The eight Kernow's delis would want to stock fifty litres a week each, at first, with a choice of flavours. The ice cream would need to be properly branded and marketed, and the flavours developed and finessed.

Tom becomes animated as he discusses possible options: rhubarb and custard; clotted cream and blackcurrant; raspberry with home-made meringue. Watching him, Lucy realises that she hasn't seen him so excited for years: not since he started his cheffing, when he was doing what he loved and was infatuated with Flo. Not since their dad died.

'We'll need more staff though, if we're to pull this off,' he is saying to Ben. 'I doubt Flo will come on board: she needs some distance from the farm. And obviously we won't have Lucy.'

'Why won't you have Lucy?' Ben looks startled.

'Well, she's only here until the end of the season. She'll be back working at her hospital in September.' Tom smiles at her, repeating the line she has given anyone who is interested. 'And then, obviously, she won't be here next year.'

The fact lands on the table between them, amid the finished peanut packets and their glasses. Lucy will have left the area in less than a month, once the heat of the summer has eased and the harvest has been gathered in. As the holiday season comes to a close and the Milos and Oscars return to school. As the ploughing and harrowing, the sowing and the maintenance resumes, as Cornwall becomes more desolate and less golden, Lucy will be living her old life, three hundred miles away.

'I don't have to go.' The words slip out without her thinking. She looks at her brother.

Surprise, and then pity, flit across his face.

'Probably a conversation for another time,' he

says with a nod, a warning – as if she needed it – to go no further. He downs his second pint, and she imagines his brain whirring as he works out how to protect his big sister from revealing more about her career absence, not to mention her marriage, than she intends.

'Lots to think about,' he says, with a business-like nod to Ben and Alex. 'I'm completely up for it. We just need to think about logistics. When we can get a shed prepared for the equipment; sourcing the machines – and persuading the bank, or possibly my uncle if you can give us this commitment in writing, to agree to a loan.'

'And do look into employing someone else,' says Ben, with an easy smile.

'Exactly – next year at least,' Tom says, and Lucy feels an intense sadness. This was an idea she had worked on and pushed him into pursuing, and she does not want to be sidelined at this point. Why would she be embroiled in the bustle of London, away from those she loves – struggling to make a relationship work, terrified of having to cannulate a tiny baby – while all this is happening here? Her throat thickens and she feels, childishly, as if she might cry.

'There's lots to be sorted – but it's all achievable,' Ben says. She can feel his eyes on her and knows that, if she looks at him, she might betray some of the emotions battling inside her: frustration, confusion, humiliation, perhaps even, perturbingly, just a flicker of desire.

'Yes,' she manages, getting up and managing a smile she hopes seems confident and collected to Alex. 'There's an awful lot to think about.'

Twenty-eight

Then: 18 March 1944, Cornwall

The lambing shed was cold. Seven in the morning, and outside the day was only just breaking. The grass was crisp with frost, the air tinged with dew. Inside, the barn was filled with the scent of straw and iodine. And something else: the iron-rich smell of blood as three ewes gave birth in quick succession: six lambs tumbling out in a confusion of cords and slippery sacs and, finally – once the lambs had started suckling – each ewe's plum-red placenta.

'Wait for one and they all come at once,' said Uncle Joe, as he and Alice watched the ewe which had birthed the triplets. The weakest, a female and a scrap compared to its sturdier brothers, shivered as it lay in the trampled straw.

'Come here.' The farmer picked up the lamb and pushed it right under the ewe's nose, then watched, brow furrowing for a second, as the mother nudged it to test if it was hers and bleated softly, as if murmuring a hello. The ewe began giving it small, quick licks, cleaning the mucus away, and, finally, the lamb tried to stand – foundering on bandied legs. The ewe nuzzled her young again, seemingly more affectionate. Stumbling, the lamb managed to find her teat and then, tentatively, began to suck.

Uncle Joe, meanwhile, had turned to the other two lambs and picked up the fatter male; then turned to the scene of the next birthing, where the ewe, a seasoned mother, had had just the one lamb. With a broad hand, he scooped up some of the bloodied musk spilling from the sheep and smeared it on the plump triplet, then thrust it towards the second ewe and waited for her to smell it.

'Go on.' His encouragement was low but intense.

'What? Why?' Alice, up since four to watch her first lambing, couldn't quite understand what he was doing.

'We do it with triplets. Take the sturdiest off and give it to one who's had a singleton if they've lambed close enough together. Best way of making sure the runt survives.'

He gestured to the pitiful lamb, still quivering with cold as it sucked. Its folds of skin were sticky and wet, its fleece thin and damp from its birthing. 'Poor little blighter doesn't stand much of a chance, if we don't help it like this.'

'It's the kindest thing,' he went on. 'You have to do it with the bigger lambs: more likely to get over the shock of fostering. It's like with humans. Sometimes it's necessary for the child to be taken from its mother.'

'Like Will and me.' She looked down as she said it.

The farmer looked uncomfortable and pulled at his earlobe. 'Well, these are unusual times. Special circumstances, you might say.'

They continued to watch the ousted lamb, now

241

being licked clean by the second ewe, apparently fooled by the farmer's deception. The lamb nuzzled in, gleaning warmth from its foster mother, whose own lamb began to suckle away.

For a moment, all was quiet, the drama of the lambings over as quickly as it started: three families of sheep, each ewe, now, with twins. Yet Alice couldn't shake away the thought of the rapid adoption. The lamb, befuddled by birth, might accept it, but what of the ewe whose sturdiest lamb had gone? Did she realise what had happened? And when she baaed her desperate, nasal bleat in the field, months later, would she be calling for her missing lamb?

'Your brother's doing well, you know.' Uncle Joe, usually a quiet man, seemed keen to talk, and she made sure she listened. Will couldn't be mentioned around Aunt Evelyn, and any snippets of news came from the farmer and were sparsely distributed: as rare as a double-yolked egg.

She knew the farm he was working on now, for instance – Farmer Eddy's at Polcarrow – but not if he missed them, or if he even thought about her. Her throat tightened at the thought that he might be lonely, and then at the thought that he might not be.

'I saw him and Farmer Eddy at market on Tuesday. He looked the proper farmer. Says he's taken to the bigger farm.'

'That's good.' Alice could barely speak. Her family had shrunk – William and Annie only visiting the once, when her father had leave; the twins in Wadebridge, though they might have been in Devon for the little she saw them. It was over

242

seven months since Will's departure but it still felt raw.

'He misses you.' He half-coughed the words.

'I miss him too.'

'Ahhh ... yes.' He cleared his throat. 'Well. I'm sorry.'

Alice looked at him in surprise. Was he apologising? Adults didn't do that sort of thing. For a moment, she wished he was her father and she could sidle up to him for a hug – but a light ruffling of the hair was the only affection he had ever shown her, and then only when she was younger. She swallowed, forcing down a hard lump at the back of her throat. She had felt so lonely since Will had gone. Maggie was neutral, at best; Aunt Evelyn, distant; Joanna, busy. And so it was the animals she turned to for comfort: Cocoa the kitten; Fly, the sheepdog; and a baby rabbit she had adopted, down by the broom bushes, who, quivering, would let her stroke its fur.

They couldn't make up for Will, though. She turned away from the farmer and the silence swelled as she tried to work out what she might say to him. The words weighed on her tongue; she could almost taste them. Did you send Will away because of what I told Auntie Evelyn? Is it really my fault, like Maggie says?

A sudden flurry on the other side of the shed. A commotion.

'She's in trouble.' Arthur, red in the face and apparently sweating, was bent over a ewe that was trying to stand.

'Bloody hell.' For a big man, the farmer moved swiftly, crossing the barn in three long strides, away from Alice and over to the ewe, cordoned off in the corner by a clump of bales.

A lamb's head was poking out of the rear of the sheep, bulging grotesquely as the sheep strained to push.

'Push it back in now; work against the contractions,' Uncle Joe barked at Arthur.

The boy tried to push the head back inside, and the ewe stamped, panicking.

'Here.' The farmer took over, placing his large hand over the head and pushing against the ewe, which stumbled and bleated.

'Got to get it in quick or it'll suffocate,' he panted, waiting for her contraction to be over. 'One more time girl,' he tried to reassure her as he pressed firmly again.

Alice held her breath. Uncle Joe strained, his arm slipped inside the sheep with the lamb's head and he grimaced. 'Now got to find the front legs and pull them through.'

He rummaged, face clenched in concentration; hand rearranging limbs inside the ewe's womb.

'Think there are three in here.' His eyes narrowed with the effort of working it out.

'Three?' Arthur sounded bewildered.

'I can't work out these hooves.'

Alice couldn't look at the rear end of the ewe, but watched her face, those eyes rolling with panic, head held fast by James.

'We knew she was big.' The farmer seemed to be trying to work out how this multiple birth could have gone unnoticed.

'Not this big,' Arthur murmured.

'Bugger, I've got one of each.' Uncle Joe, his

arm halfway inside the sheep now, seemed to have forgotten Alice. 'Damn,' he spat, and his brow furrowed deeper as he pulled.

Then: 'That's it.' He held one leg in his hand. 'Other's bent back. She should be able to get it out now.'

They paused. The ewe pushed, and the large lamb, head swollen, was forced out onto the straw.

'Now just got to get the other two,' said Uncle Joe, wiping beads of sweat from his forehead and bending down on all fours. But the ewe was looking exhausted, and had slumped back down as if unable to cope with the strain.

Uncle Joe reinserted his hand to find the forelegs of the next lamb.

''Tis a bugger: they keep slipping back.'

The sheep bleated, eyes rolling in panic.

'Will I get the vet?' said James.

Uncle Joe grunted and carried on rummaging.

'Think one has the cord around it.' He looked at his herdsman, his face bleak. 'Perhaps you ought... Alice, go back to the house,' the farmer barked. 'Help with the breakfast or something. No need for you to be out here.'

'But I want to stay...'

'Alice.' She saw a glint of steel: a hint of the man who could shoot a cow he had reared from a calf, or kill foxes or badgers without a moment's hesitation, who would snare magpies or drown kittens.

'Yes, of course.' She got up quickly and ran to the farmhouse, aware that she was being protected from something she might not want to see.

Twenty-nine

Then: 18 April 1944, Cornwall

The sensation was unlike anything she had ever experienced. A curious tightening, and then a deep, bowel-twisting throb of pain.

Maggie leaned against her wrought-iron bed-frame, her knuckles whitening as she gripped it and bit down on her bottom lip. I mustn't make a noise. Must keep this secret, but oh! The throb of pain came again: sharper this time. More acute. A stab of a knife, not a general, discontented grumbling. She could see her stomach tense, then quiver, and feel the baby push against her, no longer willing to be contained.

This must be it. The thing she had been dreading for the past six months was happening. Her baby was coming, at least a month early, and the secret she had managed to keep hidden – for her bump was small as if it knew it should remain invisible – was about to spill out in a tangled mess.

She paced the room. There was no pain now. Perhaps it was a false alarm and she could get out and have it in one of the more remote fields or hidden on the ledge on the headland? She grabbed a cardigan and a blanket, knowing that she wasn't being rational but desperate to avoid having it where she might be discovered. And then the pain came again.

It was harder this time, more insistent. An all-encompassing spasm that seemed to paralyse her body and then made her legs quiver. She clutched at the bedpost, concentrating on squeezing her fingers, and willing the baby to stay in. The mirror on her dressing table was tilted up and she caught sight of her face, tinged green, and her body hunched like an old woman's. What have I done, she wanted to whisper, though she seemed incapable of speaking, the pain was so total. Then, incredulous: What is happening to me?

A brief reprieve, and she found she could move again and think clearly. At least her mother was out, at Wadebridge market, for the day. Only James and her father were on the farm, and, in the house, Joanna and Alice. Perhaps it would be possible to flee? She could see why ewes hunkered down, found a private place in which to give birth. If she could just hide away from here, keep the trauma of birth away from the farmhouse and only return when she had safely delivered this baby, then perhaps her parents might be more willing to accept it.

She made for the door, blanket clutched in her hand, but as she did so there was a tentative knock and Alice sidled in.

'Shut the door.' Her words came out as a hiss.

Alice's mouth dropped and the colour drained from her face. 'Are you all right?' she said, hands flailing by her side, catching at air.

'I'm having a baby.' She spat the words before the pain surged once more: a wave that picked her up and carried her along. 'I'm having a baby,' she just managed, again, her voice softer and

247

more plaintive this time, before it cracked and she had to swallow to stop herself from sobbing.

Alice, in a fog of shock, just stood there.

'It hurts,' Maggie said, as the pain began to subside enough for her to speak. 'It hurts,' she repeated, suddenly furious that Alice couldn't see.

And then, finally, the pain pushed her so that she said something she would never have contemplated saying otherwise: 'You might have to help me.'

'But I know nothing about babies.'

'You know about lambs.'

'That's *lambs*.'

'And you've seen calvings.' She gasped. 'It's no different. Ah!' Another spasm and she was speechless, her silence stretched out with pain.

Alice lowered her voice and spoke gently, as if she were a small child, or simple. 'It's a baby, Maggie. It's different from an animal. I really think it is.'

'No... It's not.' The pain was gone, and she was able to speak normally, but she had to be quick. 'You've got to help me. There's no one else.' Her sharpness masked a biting fear.

Alice looked down at her stomach then up at her, eyes huge and brimming with anxiety. Maggie felt a rush of fury. 'I can't do this alone, can't you see? Besides,' she gasped as her stomach tightened and she clutched at the bedstead. 'You owe it to Will.'

'To Will?'

It came out in a rush. The truth: so clear and sweet and problematic. 'It will be your nephew or niece.'

She looked at Alice, willing her to understand, her eyes frank and frightened. Alice flushed – the unspoken truth acknowledged at last.

'Oh!' she said, and bent down, hiding her face. When she stood back up, her cheeks were still pink and she dragged her eyes towards Maggie as though it were an effort. 'Of course I'll help,' she said.

'You're going to have to help me cut the cord, when it comes out. Like Father does with the lambs.' In between gasps, Maggie began to be practical.

'I don't think I can cut you.'

'Not me – the cord. Yes, you can. You've watched Father, lots of times. Oh!' She bent forwards, doubled up in pain.

'Is it getting worse?'

She nodded, unable to speak.

'You'll need to clean my sewing scissors.' Her voice had returned to normal. 'With some water from the copper. Can you manage that?'

'Yes, of course. But I can't leave you.'

The words came far apart. 'Alice ... I'll be ... all right...'

Still Alice hovered.

'Go,' she said, once her voice had returned to normal. 'I'll be all right. Honest. Just go, please.'

She was keening by the time Alice had raced back from the kitchen, clinging onto the bedpost; her face, she could see from the mirror, beetroot and perspiring. The pain had grown more intense: as if she was being ripped apart or seared. The room tipped and righted itself; segued from a crisp chill to an oppressive heat.

'Oh, my Lord!' Joanna, all of a fluster, pushed past Alice and came to her side, put her arm round her to stroke her back as if she had done this many times.

'You told her!' she managed to get out, glaring at Alice.

'I didn't mean... She *saw* me.' The girl pointed at Joanna.

'And it's a bloody good job I did.'

Somehow, Joanna had found an old sheet and was placing it beneath her; mopping up the floor, which was slippery and wet.

The maid ducked down and glanced up beneath her legs.

'Oh, my love, I can see its head. It's starting to crown.'

She whimpered and then her embarrassment was forgotten in a fresh crest of pain.

'It's all right, my love. You've done so well. Now, I think that soon you're going to want to do some pushing.'

'Aaarrrgh.' She started weeping properly. Great big wet tears, for it suddenly seemed too much, this fear and pain.

'Now. When you think you need to push, you do so. Just like going to the privy.'

Alice flashed Joanna a look.

'It's no use being coy, Alice,' Joanna reprimanded her. 'Being coy didn't get her into this state.'

The tears came faster then: shame heaped on to pain.

'Oh, my lover, I'm not blaming you.' The maid

paused. 'Goodness knows but he was lovely.'

'Aarrgh ... I want to...'

'You push. That's right, you push. Alice, stroke her back.'

'Aaarrrgh...'

'That's right. It's coming! It's coming!'

She bent between her legs while Alice put her arm round her, and what might have felt irritating was curiously comforting.

'It's coming. It's coming. It's crowning!' Then: 'Here it comes; your baby!'

Something slithered out between her legs: hot and wet, more animal than human. A dark head, slick with a creamy grey waxiness, a bundle of tiny, wrinkled limbs.

'*Waaaaah.*' The bedroom filled with a different cry, tentative at first then swiftly furious. The baby was red, and its mouth, above a writhing body gripped by Joanna, was a black hole that seemed to take up its entire face.

'We need to keep it quiet.' She was trembling with shock.

'Here: the scissors – you do that bit, Alice.' Joanna smiled at the girl, who looked as if she was going to be sick. 'Go on: you need to do it.' And Alice cut the translucent cord, with its streak of red running through it, and separated her from this child.

'It's a beautiful boy.' Joanna was wrapping the baby in a towel, smoothing away some of the creaminess. 'Quite tiny, I'd say; a scrap of one. I think he's very early. Here – you take him.' The maid handed him over, and Maggie found herself holding her son.

251

It wasn't as she imagined, this first cuddle. He was red, squished, furious, and yet she couldn't get enough of him. She stroked his cheek with one finger and kissed his forehead, breathing in the heady stench of blood and brine.

She smelt his damp, dark hair, caressed his skull, as delicate and vulnerable as a bird's egg. Drank him in: her tiny, ugly-beautiful scrap of a baby; reading his face for any trace of his father, any clue that he wasn't just hers.

He was so small. That was what she kept thinking: his hands so wee, his fingernails minuscule, like the tiniest flecks of sand. His nose wrinkled in a snuffle, and his blue eyes – not Will's, not hers – stared at her, unsmiling.

'Hello, baby,' she whispered. His mouth opened as if he would mew, and she shushed him and held him tight.

'Does your mother really not know?' Joanna asked the question Maggie didn't want to contemplate.

'I don't think so.' She shuddered. 'He's so early. I thought he wouldn't be here for a month, at least. I think I thought I would have him at school or at Aunt Edith's.'

'Oh, dear Lord. That might have been worse.'

'Yes.' The strength seemed to have gone from her, and she felt her body hunch forwards, protecting the baby and her slackened stomach. She felt deflated and newly vulnerable.

'Here.' She realised that perhaps the others might like to hold him, and held him out to Alice. The baby's mouth opened and his tiny lips quivered. A burst of rage spilled out.

252

'It's all right. He wants you.' Alice looked fear-ful and shied away.

Maggie pulled him back towards her chest, where he started to forage.

'He wants to feed,' Joanna said, as the baby, mouth pursed, starting rooting. 'Here – you just put him on.'

Trembling, Maggie watched as Joanna helped him fumble his way across her breast to her nipple and he began to drink, as instinctively as a new-born piglet or lamb. Silence descended for Maggie was exhausted, and the other two seemed briefly overawed. Nothing could be heard save for the odd snuffle and then a gentle whimper of delight.

Thirty

In the end, she had six perfect hours with her baby. Joanna cooked the dinner, and told her father that Maggie had 'women's problems'. Well, it was hardly a lie. Alice had helped, but had been so quiet it was a wonder she hadn't given the game away. Then again, a new grandchild was the last thing Joe Retallick would expect to find hidden away upstairs.

While her father was preoccupied with a cow with milk fever, and her mother remained in Wadebridge, Maggie gazed at this perfect baby, so vulnerable and helpless he couldn't even hold his head up by himself.

If she put a finger in his hand, he would curl his

palm around it as if determined to cling on to her. And if she put him to her breast, he would suck obligingly. A trail of dark tar snaked across her puckered stomach and she marvelled at how efficiently his tiny body worked. He already knew how to feed and poo; how to sleep; how to secure affection. As long as he had her with him, he could survive.

After his second attempt at feeding, he slipped off her nipple, almost apologetic, and fell into a deep sleep. His breath came out in tiny sniffles as if he was taking in the scent of her skin. She traced the delicate curve of his cheek, afraid of touching him too heavily in case he woke up. The top of his scalp felt soft and almost unformed; the dark hairs fine and matted with some sort of lanolin. She kissed his head and breathed in the briny smell of herself and something sweeter: the milky, delectable smell of him.

When he woke, his eyes were bright and questioning. Babies weren't meant to focus when they were born, she had heard that somewhere, and yet he was alert and quizzical, searching her face as if to find some explanation for why he was here.

He didn't smile – perhaps that came later – but as his squashedness subsided a little, she began to make out a little of Will. His eyes weren't his, but his mouth was. She touched it lightly and imagined him kissing a girl one day. His ears were delicate curls, the veins glowing through the translucent skin, so that she could almost envisage the blood pumping through his body; carrying the milky goodness she had just given him.

'Little bunny,' she whispered, for there was

254

something so vulnerable about him, as though he were a baby rabbit, found cowering in its nest.

Her womb ached and the parts between her legs stung, where they had been stretched, Joanna had told her; it had burned when she'd used the bathroom, and Joanna, whose mother had only just stopped having babies, had got her to wash herself, after that final mess had come out of her, to rinse all the blood away.

The pink water had spiralled down the plug-hole, and Joanna had put the towels and her sheets straight into the copper still boiling down-stairs. Then she had scrubbed the floor clean with Jeyes Fluid, the smell of the disinfectant overpowering the stench of blood, and flung open the windows to waft away the medicinal tang. But no amount of boiling or disinfecting could disguise the fact that there was a baby in her bed, and it could only have arrived one way.

At first, the adrenalin of birth allowed her to ignore this. But once Joanna and Alice had gone downstairs, the exhaustion of the past six hours – and the strain of the past seven months – washed over her in vast, engulfing waves. How could she explain or hide him away? Her half-thought-through plan had been to have him in Bodmin, and then, somehow, to get herself and the baby to Will at Farmer Eddy's – where, Alice, in a rare moment of confidence, had recently revealed he was. Or, perhaps Aunt Edith – her father's sister, not her mother's – would be won over by this baby and persuaded to argue her case. Both scenarios had always seemed optimistic, but she couldn't believe she wouldn't manage to keep him. She needed to cling to that hope to exist.

But having this baby more than a month early, and at home, changed everything. To Evelyn, there was nothing more sinful than an unmarried mother. She would throw herself off the headland and be smashed on the rocks if Maggie ever brought such a shame on her family, she had said. The girls taking their babies to the Sisters of Mercy orphanage in Bodmin, or Rosemundy House down the coast at St Agnes, were a different type of girl from her daughter. Some were even put in the lunatic asylum. Girls weren't just wicked but *mad* if they behaved like that – and were caught doing it.

But looking at her baby, she couldn't believe that she had been so very wicked, for the closer she looked, the more of Will she could see – from the whorls of his hair to the perfection of his skin. She had loved him, and nothing had mattered but the intensity of her feelings. It was as simple as that. And so what they had done last summer couldn't be sinful, could it?

You're not an animal, though, are you? She could imagine her mother screeching the words, her self-control abandoned. You went through this, too, she wanted to say. You and Father did what Will and I did: you must have, to have me. And there were other babies: a son or two, who were supposed to take over the farm, who died before they were born, far too early. And what about Father's brother? Your first love, Isaac? You felt as I did, you said, though it was hard to envisage. She couldn't imagine saying any of this to Evelyn.

There was no way she could avoid her. She had

256

asked Joanna if she could get a horse saddled so that she could ride, with the baby, towards Bodmin and Farmer Eddy's, but was told she was foolish. There was still blood trailing from her, so how she could ride with a child was anyone's guess. Joanna couldn't drive there, even if she knew the way or there was enough red diesel, and as for Alice, she looked so petrified, she was worse than useless.

She looked at her bedside clock. It was three now. She had, perhaps, an hour before her mother returned: one single hour in which to nest with her baby, to drink in his features and memorise the snub of his nose, the dimple in his cheek.

She breathed in the sweet, milky smell of him, willing time to stretch or stop. A single hour before everything would change.

It was her mother's footsteps she heard first: light and insistent. The tread of a woman with something on her mind.

Ten past four. The door burst open. Dear Lord, she must have known. But her mother's face – slipping from irritation into incredulity – suggested that she hadn't.

Evelyn took in her daughter, lying propped against the pillows, and the bundle held tightly in her arms.

'What have you got there?' Her mouth fell, slack as the opening of a purse, and her eyes bulged as if staring would convince her that what she saw was just a figment of her imagination: the hump of a pillow, a fold in the sheet.

She staggered towards the bed.

'That's not a baby?' Even as she said it, reality struck.

'You've had a baby? You ... you.' Words seemed to fail her. Then: 'You wicked, wicked girl.' Her voice rose in disbelief.

Face contorted with rage, she reached for the bundle and, before Maggie could do anything, she had her hands on the baby – wrenching apart the towel in which she had wrapped him; exposing him to the chill air.

'Careful – be careful with him.' Maggie felt his heart flutter at the sudden disruption. His sleep broken, he opened his mouth and began to wail in indignation. The sound seemed to startle Evelyn, who shot away.

'You *slattern!*'

Maggie felt as if she had been slapped, her mother's venom striking her like the flat of her hand.

'You *little slattern.*'

The insult seemed to have startled even the baby, who suddenly stopped crying.

Evelyn seemed to be pulling herself together.

'How could you do this to me? To your father? How could you lower yourself like this? With all your chances?'

She paused, eyes blazing with contempt and what looked like betrayal.

'You stupid, stupid girl. You ... little *bitch!*'

There was a pause punctuated by a gasp of shock from Joanna, who had rushed in with Alice.

'You knew about this?' Her mother turned on the maid. 'Of course you did – and you!' Her contempt seemed to take in Alice, her face

258

blotched with shock, eyes filling with tears. 'Of course. You were her chaperone, her alibi.'

'No. It wasn't like that.' Maggie tried to object.

'Of course it was: *she* was the means of you conducting your *romance*.' Evelyn's voice was a vicious whisper. 'All those times when you were willing to play with her – and she was just making it easier for you to meet.'

The baby was quiet now, his mouth stilled with terror. She could feel his heart bumping, quick and light. His eyes, bright and watchful, never left her face, as if he was trying to read what she would do next. The air filled with the sound of Alice's barely suppressed sobs. The girl gave a hiccuped gulp and then began whimpering.

'Oh do be quiet.' Evelyn was merciless. 'Take some responsibility – on behalf of your brother. I should have known this would happen,' she went on, more to herself than anyone in the room. 'I warned your father it might have been more than a kiss, but he was only ever able to think the best of you – and him.'

She moved back towards the bed, and Maggie bent her arm fast round the baby.

'It can't stay here, you know.' Evelyn's mouth pinched as if she tasted something acidic. 'We could take it to the Sisters of Mercy. Joanna?'

'Yes, Mrs Retallick.' The maid rallied herself.

'Has the vet gone?'

'No ... he's just giving Daisy the calcium injection.'

'Good.' Her mother seemed to be thinking. 'Well, he can take it.'

'I'll need to get my stuff together.' Maggie tried

to swing her legs over the side of the bed, clutching the baby to her chest.

'Oh, you're not going anywhere, missy.' Her mother almost spat the words. 'You have to be booked in there three months before you have the baby. But the nuns should take it. Alice can go and get rid of it.'

'Me?' Alice spoke for the first time.

'We'll pass it off as yours. A thirteen-year-old evacuee with an illegitimate child? It's the sort of thing they're always getting up to, isn't it Joanna?' She didn't wait for an answer. 'I'm sure they're used to it.'

'You're not going to take him away from me.' Maggie was frantic, coldness creeping through her. Her mother had a strange, mad look on her face.

'Well, I'm afraid I am.' She reached for her grandchild and snatched him away as Maggie fumbled to pull her nightdress across her exposed breasts.

'Noooo. Give him back.' She tried to lunge at her mother, but her knees gave way and she slid to the floor.

'Maggie!' Joanna rushed to help her.

'The baby.' She tried to reach for him, but her mother was holding him up high and moving away.

'Alice.' Maggie turned to her, pleading. 'Get him, please.' Tears pooled in Alice's eyes and spilled from the corners. The impossibility of standing up to an enraged grown-up – especially one who had previously shown her kindness – appeared to be too much for her. Maggie felt a rush of rage.

'Get me up.' She tried to push herself off the ground, but Joanna was holding her tightly, and she felt weak and woozy.

'Get off me,' she lashed out. But something wasn't working: flashes of light, and then dark blotches kept pressing down, obscuring her sight.

'My baby. Get my baby.' She was slipping in and out of consciousness like a boat half-glimpsed on the horizon. Her voice must be getting weaker, for nobody was doing anything about it. No one seemed to be listening.

'Alice. Alice.' She tried one last time.

'She's fainting, dear love,' someone – Joanna? – said.

The baby's cry – frantic but growing weaker – filled the velvet thickness in her head. If only she could get to him.

Darkness descended.

Thirty-one

Now: 16 August 2014, Cornwall

Changeover day. Saturday, and there are two new guests moving into the cottages. Mid-August: traditionally the busiest time of the year.

Maggie casts her eye over the bookings printout her granddaughter has given her. A couple of months ago she lost interest in who was staying, but that customer's heart attack has bucked her up; made her realise she has a choice: whether to slip away now, when she has had, it has to be said, a good innings, or to cling on to life for a little while more.

She has chosen life. She will not give up yet, not this summer. Her limbs may be stiff, her body a shrivelled shadow of her once peachy self, but her heart is strong and her mind, her memory, is still good. Life – which has, at times, been tough – could yet surprise her. She does hope so. And while there is hope, she must go on.

There is a man staying this week, you see. Now, perhaps he could be life-changing. There's a woman, too. A Mrs Coates. But Maggie has no interest in the women who visit, at all.

It depends on his age. Impossible to tell from an Internet printout: better to speak on the phone, to assess their age and their background that way. Of course, few people use the telephone to communicate these days. It's all texts and emails – even from Richard, who seems to view her as a business proposition, and keeps sending Judith emails with bullet points in them, and even, for goodness sake, spreadsheets attached. As for letters – proper, handwritten letters, *missives* conveying news and love – well, they're as rare as hen's teeth. She can't remember when she last received a proper letter: not a birthday card or a postcard, something flimsy and trite, but a *letter*. Sealed up, secretive; conveying something of substance.

But this man. This male guest. Perhaps he could be the one. Her son. Her firstborn. She wonders if she will know him at first sight? She tends to dismiss most of the men of around retirement age who tip up, even before she has managed to slip in a question about where they were born or assess their Cornish heritage. Perhaps it is fanciful, but, seventy years after she last saw his father, she thinks she will recognise their son.

For she has never stopped thinking about her first, precious baby. Not really. Of course, there have been periods in her life when she just gave him a perfunctory prayer each evening, when she didn't *dwell* on him. But he has always been there.

She did try to block him out. In the early days with Edward, she told herself she shouldn't think of him any more: that it was a youthful mistake she could blame on the war and a freakishly hot summer. Her decision to give him up the result of her youth and her mother's narrow-minded fear of judgement.

It was easier before she returned to the farm. When she was teaching in St Austell and didn't have daily reminders of where it had all taken place. But then her mother died. And so, in 1956, she and Edward, whom she had finally married once she realised that their history counted for something, agreed to come back and help Joe run the farm.

It had been the right decision, and she was reconciled with her dear father, who, freed by Evelyn's death, had finally managed to apologise. 'Your mother was a stronger person than me, and I shouldn't have let that always be the case,' he had said. Neither had mentioned the baby, but there, in the milking parlour, cocooned by the smell of the warm beasts and the gentle hiss of the milk hitting the pail, she was grateful. He had given her a quick hug, suddenly sentimental. Until the last hours of his life, he never mentioned it again.

But, though it was the right thing to return, the memories – never that deeply buried – had, at first, almost overwhelmed her. Anything could spark them. Stacking bales in the barn where they had made love; resting against her tamarisk; walking on the beach at low tide and passing their cave, or the second one in which Alice hid. Even the daily renewal of a farm could prompt the deep throb of guilt, for how could she not think of her baby when she lived somewhere that depended on continual birth – of calves and lambs and even chicks – for its business; and especially once she became pregnant and had a baby again?

At times – when Judith was small and the similarities between her and this first child seemed most acute – she thought that grief might fell her. There had been a single moment when, dizzy with a lack of sleep, she had walked to the headland, past the ledge where she and Will had hidden together, and imagined falling onto the granite: toppled, then smashed, by the wind.

She had stood on the very edge, watching the spume buffeting against the rocks, listening to the hiss and slither of the tide dragging back, and she had wondered how much it would hurt. And then she had stepped back. Her breasts, ready to feed her six-week-old baby, were pricking and starting to leak. She had felt the milk soak into her brassiere, and she knew she had other duties. Another child to tend to. She had trudged back to the farm, arms cradling her smarting breasts, tears trickling

264

down her cheeks, with no one, bar the cows, to see them. By the time she had reached the farmhouse, her bloodshot eyes were the only sign of her grief.

She learned to manage it, this raw sadness. When Richard came, two years later, she contained it. The demands of a farm and of two small children meant she hadn't the energy to mourn another, anyway. Which didn't mean she forgot him. Over the years, she came to see her grief like a pool of water, fashioned in the sand by her children: for most of the time it was containable – just a deep puddle that, if abandoned, would eventually seep away. But then the tide would race in, or a child would throw in an extra bucket of water, and it would breach its sides, flooding out, anarchic, until she could shore it up again.

The intensity wore off over the years. It had been decades since she had felt that acute pang she had experienced before Judith and Richard were born, whenever she saw a small baby. That pain, as sharp as a paper cut, had – thank goodness – long gone away. But she still prayed for him each night. Keep him safe, she urged a God she wasn't sure she really believed in, in the slim hope of reassurance. Keep him safe, my sweet William. In her mind's eye, she always saw him as a tangle of red limbs, with slicked dark hair. A newborn baby. The grown-up version slipped and slithered in and out of her consciousness; part her, part his father; unknowable and never known.

For a long time, she believed that he would come looking for her. She just needed to be patient. And she persisted in thinking this even once she discovered that there was no record of him being handed in to the orphanage.

It was after Judith and Richard had left home. The late seventies. She remembers it now: that moment of despair in the county record office when she queried the missing paperwork and was told that there was none to connect her and him.

'The war,' an archivist had explained. 'Things were more chaotic then; there was a bigger turn-over of mothers and babies. And then all the records were cleared out ten years ago, when the orphanage moved.' But how could they lose something as fundamental as that piece of paper? The archivist, a scrawny young man who looked as if he spent too much time indoors, had shrugged. A bureaucratic mistake. One of those things. He was sorry, but it wasn't his problem. She had managed not to cry until she left the building. A scrap of paper could all too easily be discarded, it would appear.

Still, she hoped that he had been given the information before the move; that he knew her name, though she had no sense of his. But now that she is nearing the end of her life, that hope, that certainty she had clung to, knowing that it is *just* possible, is being eaten away.

And even if he knew her name, why on earth would he want to find her: the mother who aban-doned him seventy years ago and has made no apparent effort to find him? He might think her entirely heartless. Someone who handed him over like an unwanted puppy with barely another thought for him?

She looks down at her hands and sees that she is twisting her skirt between her fingers. She stops and makes herself smooth it out, deliberately. Her deepest fear – that her abandoned son hates her with a venom she can only imagine – bubbles up and she forces it back down again. Judith mustn't see her like this, or Lucy. She must pull herself together. A dinghy buffets across the bay, white horses streaking behind it, and she focuses on its speed compared to the fishing trawler ambling in beside it, chased by seagulls. There. That's better. Breathe this in and focus on this: on your world, your heritage, the life your parents and grand-parents built up for you and your children. Your *other* children. Not the child you let down. Your one, terrible mistake.

For he must know, this unknown son, that that's what young girls did if they were eighteen, and unmarried? If they faced the wrath of their mother, and the baby's father, a mere boy him-self, had been sent away?

What else could she do? He was wrenched from her and she couldn't get to him. She just *couldn't* reach him. The fatal combination of shock, pain and exhaustion meant her guard was down and she was vulnerable in a way she has never allowed herself to be since. But she still berates herself. How could she have let it happen? Her throat tightens: now almost a reflex whenever she thinks of it.

She has rerun that scene so many times, and also the memory of the next morning when she had inched her way to Alice's room.

Alice, eyes red-rimmed, face grey, had shrunk away up the bed, clutching her lemon eiderdown as if she thought she would be furious. And yet

Maggie was too exhausted – and dimly aware that she needed to keep Alice sweet.

'Did the nuns seem kind?' It was hard to get the words out. To speak without her voice breaking.

'They'll look after him really well. I know they will,' Alice had said.

She should have felt relief, for that was what any mother wanted to hear: that her child was being cared for. And yet she was unconvinced. It wasn't enough. Her baby deserved – her baby *needed* – to be loved.

She had sat, tracing the stitching on the counterpane with her finger, willing her surging helplessness and anger to subside. And yet it had boiled, hard and furious until she realised, as she looked at fearful, snivelling Alice that she just couldn't forgive. It was entirely unreasonable, she knows that now, and yet she had hoped that Alice would defy her mother – and would get the baby to her brother. Just for once, she wanted her to show some ingenuity, to act beyond her thirteen years.

Their relationship – so rocky since Will had been sent away – had never recovered after that. Perhaps Evelyn couldn't bear to see her, either: this girl she saw as collaborating in their love affair, this daily reminder of Will. It only took a little pressure on the billeting officer – and a generous side of bacon – to persuade him that the farm was far more suitable for younger evacuees, and within a month Alice had been rehoused with an older couple down the coast.

She remembers that departure now. Alice's face pinched white, and closed: no sign of the ruddiness or excitement it had worn the previous summer. Her big, blue eyes had looked unwaveringly at her.

'Well, goodbye then,' Maggie had said, and had held out a hand, suddenly abashed and ridiculously formal.

Alice had looked at it as if it were something alien, and then tears had filled those terrible eyes.

She had had to look away first, making an excuse to bend down and fiddle with Alice's old battered suitcase. Her father, noticing her discomfort, had lifted it as lightly as if it were a basket, and thrown it into the boot of the Austin Sixteen. Her mother had wanted Alice to be driven in the cob and cart to the station, but Joe had insisted she be treated better. 'She arrived here by car, and she'll leave that way. It's common courtesy.' He had looked intently at his wife, as if trying to impress something upon her, and had leaned forwards, his palms flat on the kitchen table. 'Evelyn: the child's done nothing wrong.'

Her mother had refused to watch as the car drew away, and so it was just herself, Joanna and James who had waved as it had set off up the track towards Padstow, stones and hay flying up, mud caking its tyres.

'It'll be quieter without her,' Joanna had said, which was strange, for Alice had known that the way to endear herself was to keep out of everyone's way. But perhaps it was just Maggie she had shied away from.

James had nodded, his craggy face impenetrable, and turned away, refusing to look at her. Each had trudged back to their jobs, heads down. Maggie had expected to feel relief or even an elation that the person she had blamed for revealing her love affair was out of sight and had effectively been punished. But she had just felt flat, and then a profound sadness had wormed its way inside her. The evacuees had slipped from the farm as quietly, and as unobtrusively, as they had arrived.

Thirty-two

Alice Coates parks the hire car she picked up from Bodmin Station and leans against the gate to the field in which the pigs once foraged. The sty is overgrown with nettles; the mud covered with ragged grass.

This is nothing like her first glimpse of the farm, for then it had been dark, the house unlit, the fields unseen but sensed, brooding in the distance. Only the sea, seen in the moonlight, had been heard lapping against the shore.

And yet this is the view she remembers, the scene she saw as she cycled home after school or caught a lift in the cob and cart: a seventeenth-century farmhouse with a slate roof and granite walls, neat whitewashed windows, a pillared porch. A house turned in from the sea, facing the fields and the ever-shifting shadows of the moor. Hedgerows running down to it, thick with black-thorn, honeysuckle and rosebay willowherb. A tangle of broom bushes; a clutch of outbuildings; and running down to the ever-changing aqua-marine then petrol-blue sea, the fields dotted with bales of straw.

Her heart hammers against her chest, so hard and frenetic she fears a palpitation. She jabs her palm with the dull prong of the car key, pressing metal against bone. Just calm yourself, she thinks, as she touches her handbag containing Will's letter, double-checking it is safe in there: her passport to a reconciliation should her bold plan not work out – for there is no guarantee it will do so. You do not need to be so anxious, she tells herself. There is no need to be scared, now.

For she has done the hard bit. Not just negotiating the clogged A-roads and twisting lanes from the car hire firm, her heart in her throat as she burned the clutch and tried not to stall on roads far steeper than those she is used to; or enduring the train journey from Paddington; but making the decision to come back, once more. Committing, with that first tentative email, the acknowledgement of acceptance and the cheque, to return to a place where the most formative years of her childhood were spent; where she felt the greatest happiness and the most intense pain: this spot at the edge of the world. Skylark Farm.

She takes a deep breath of Cornish air, so sharp compared to the warm fug of Paddington, with its smell of coffee and anticipation. She thinks of her sons, Ian and Rob, who she hasn't told about the cancer, let alone that she is coming to Cornwall – well, they have such busy lives. Her stomach hollows. A bird of prey hovers, scrutinising potential prey before swooping down, and she feels equally poised: on the cusp of achieving something daring, but so wary, so unconvinced, now that she is down here, that she is capable of achieving this, after all.

Well, she has to do it. This cancer is growing stealthily inside her: she imagines it spreading through her liver. These two weeks will be critical: perhaps the last when she will be able to travel and think clearly without experiencing the sickness, the extreme fatigue that she knows will come. She must stay out of Maggie's sight, while she does what she needs to do, while she works on her surprise. And only when she discovers if it is feasible or not – whether that letter, found in Pam's effects, is all that she can offer Maggie, or if she has managed something else, something incredible – will she risk approaching her.

She almost breaks her resolve when she reaches the cottage she is to hire and meets Lucy. The likeness is striking: she would have guessed she was Maggie's granddaughter even if they had met in a London street. There are those same almond-shaped, hazel eyes; and the dimple – the one that stabbed Maggie's left cheek. Her hair is lighter – a dark blonde, dyed she assumes – and she has less of an accent than she remembers Maggie having, for Evelyn had been unable to quash her lilt, despite her best efforts and her good education. It was as if she were determined to assert her Cornishness just a little; for to speak RP would be to distance herself from James and Joanna; from her father and even her mother; from herself and Will – whose voice had thickened, rising at the end of sentences, the longer he worked on the farm...

'Mrs Coates? Do you have everything you

need?' This pretty, smiling young woman makes her heart start: Maggie, as she would have looked, ten or more years after she had last seen her. A little sturdier perhaps – for Maggie was slight when Alice left, consumed with grief at losing her baby – but unmistakably her, or almost her.

'I've left you a welcome pack – milk, eggs, bread, jam and scones – but there are plenty of shops, and places to eat in Padstow. Do you know how to get there?'

'Of course,' she says, and it is on the tip of her tongue to say: 'It's just along the coast path; or I could walk over the hill and down the first lane.'

Lucy smiles and slightly raises an eyebrow. 'It sounds as if you know the area well. Have you stayed before?'

'Oh, no.' She fusses with the jacket she has taken off, unable to lie freely. 'I've been to this area years ago, but I don't know it well. Not at all.'

'Well, I'll leave you to explore then. There's a folder of visitors' attractions on the dresser, though perhaps you'd rather stay local and enjoy old haunts?'

'I'm quite all right.' She speaks more brusquely than she intended, for she has no intention of hanging around the farm, and she isn't here on holiday.

'I'll just leave you to settle in then, but do let me know if there's anything you need.'

'I won't.' She shuts down the conversation and the young woman's kindness. 'I mean: I'll be fine, thank you.' She smiles weakly, belatedly trying to apologise for her sharpness.

And Lucy smiles, and ducks out of the door.

It is when she is unpacking her clothes and placing them in an antique chest of drawers – Victorian pine and, she suspects, the one she had in her old bedroom – that she is overcome with doubt. For it suddenly seems melodramatic, her arriving like this, like a figure in one of her beloved Hardy novels. An Alec d'Urberville, perhaps; or a Sergeant Troy.

Perhaps she risks being cruel. She doesn't want to spring a surprise, and yet of course that is what she will do, turning up after seventy years with no communication at all. What was wrong with a phone call or an email? Or – more fitting for women of their age and the confessional nature of what she has to say – what was wrong, for goodness sake, with a *letter?*

Panic fells her as she dithers in front of the chest, wondering whether to put her underwear straight onto the lavender-scented drawer liners and risk unpacking properly. She should have just booked into a hotel in Bodmin – for if she is discovered before she is ready, before she has something positive to show her, she risks not just angering Maggie but destroying any happiness, or at least contentment, her one-time friend may have won. She needs to keep her head down and be absent as much as possible, at least until she establishes if the letter is all that she can offer. The consolation prize, if she cannot achieve the incredible and deliver up her son.

First thing tomorrow, then, she must be out of here; must set off to do her detective work, out on the moor. Apprehension fills her – for it would be a daunting task for someone twenty years younger, let alone someone who, with a cancer growing inside her, is definitely slowing down. And then she feels a tingle of excitement; a growing thrill at the thought that she is actually *doing* something after all this time. Tomorrow she will try to right a wrong – the only real regret of her life – or confront the possibility that it really is too late, after all.

She sleeps badly, of course, and when the dawn chorus bursts into her stark, light room she abandons any pretence that further sleep is possible. She settles herself with a cup of tea and watches the sky grow peachy pale through her tiny window, set low into the foot-deep wall.

Memories long suppressed come cascading back. Being Queen of the Harvest, perched astride Noble, swaying over the barley. The harvesting: Will beating rabbits from the crops as the men threshed inwards, the corn hissing as the stalks rubbed together and tumbled down. The food. Pasties, made with heaps of golden potato, onion and swede; copious rabbits; mackerel with newly dug potatoes, carrots and runner beans; sharp gooseberries and black- and redcurrants; and, for high teas and holidays, Cornish splits, saffron buns and an impossibly exotic blend of cream, sugar and gelatine, topped with raspberries or blackberries: Russian cream.

But all too soon the other memories creep in. If she thinks of a fox cub gambolling at dusk, she sees its mother wreaking havoc – the barn strewn with decapitated chickens and a pillowcase of feathers; the birds, broken-necked, puddled with blood. If she remembers Cocoa, she imagines her brothers and sisters, drowned: plunged in the butt, tight in their sack. And if she recalls jumping from hay bales, she sees herself spying, transfixed and frightened by Maggie and Will.

By seven, she has punished herself enough and so she gets up, has a tepid shower and makes her breakfast: the bread provided by Lucy, dabbed with butter and home-made jam. She makes herself eat, for she has a long day ahead, but finds her stomach is a pit of fear. Better just to get going. She packs a small rucksack with a flask, sandwiches, cagoule, map and her dog-eared copy of *Far from the Madding Crowd* – and yes, she knows she is being irrational in including this love story of a persistent shepherd and a more educated female farmer – and sets out, just like any tourist, for the moor.

It isn't as she remembers. The sun beats down on the coarse tussocks of grass and the soft granite outcrops, turns the pale green bracken luminous, greys the blackened branches of broom. The air fills with the song of skylarks, and the sky is so clear that when she parks high on the upper side of the moor – just to catch her breath – she can see the sea, glinting off the north coast, far in the distance. She is at the heart of this peninsula, high up on its ridge – the peak of Cornwall if not quite the edge of the world.

The moor's wildness rolls before her, and she finds a small stone circle, lying below Rough Tor, a ribbon of granite mounds, propped up like gravestones, emerging from the boggy marshes and scrubby grass. Pisky pits, Joanna used to call them. Those deceptive patches of lush green in between the rough grass and cotton grass that would suck your boot down and swallow you, or so she was told as a child. There were ghosts who stalked the tors, too: Charlotte Dymond, a Victorian serving maid, whose crippled suitor slit her throat when she dared to taunt him; and a wicked magistrate, tasked with emptying a moorland pool with a limpet shell with a hole in it. Phantom dogs would hound him if he stopped baling. Or was that the Beast of Bodmin? A giant cat that left the carcasses of cows and sheep strewn all over the moor.

Ridiculous tales. She has enough ghostly memories of her own to torment her. And enough to do in the present, she realises, as she picks her way from the stone circle back to the car. She had hoped she might find her way there instinctively, but the moor is different from how she remembers. Wild and open here – the narrow tracks fringed only with gorse bushes; the terrain entirely exposed to the elements. The tiny lanes, high hedgerows, avenue of trees and farmhouse found down a rough track and folded into the shadow of a tor have not materialised. She unfolds her map; realises she needs to be more systematic. To connect where she thinks they may have gone to where she is now.

But it is all so difficult. She finds herself driving down high-banked lanes thrusting with green shepherd's crooks of curling bracken; buttercups, greater stitchwort and red campions; potholed tracks that she can barely squeeze through, and that she drives down with her heart in her mouth at the thought of meeting another car.

Down she twists, disappearing to the bottom of valleys only to soar up the other side and find herself at another perplexing crossroads. Signposts point to hamlets, but she either misses the turning or interprets the Cornish miles too literally. She doubles back, disappears down another steep-banked lane, covered with a canopy of holm oak, beech and maple, and finds herself in a hamlet, folded into the crease of a hill, that time seems to have forgotten. A couple of granite cottages; a farmyard; a chapel where no one has worshipped for quite some while.

She manoeuvres the car, a complicated six-point turn, and sets off again. It becomes claustrophobic, this excessive lushness, and she starts to panic, for she has journeyed to the south-east of the moor and doesn't recognise the names: Bathpool, Slipperhill, Rilla Mill, Upton Cross.

And then the road bursts from a wooded dip and out onto a stretch of open moor, with Neolithic stones and the remains of an old copper mine. Disorientated, she parks and steps out onto the tufty grass, marvelling at how the ruined chimney enhances the bleak landscape, imagining the miners' harsh lives.

The moor is khaki: dotted with mustard gorse and the cream of sheep's wool. But as she watches, the colours fade, glazed sepia by a mizzle that creeps up on her, seeps into her bones and soaks through her shoes. The air fills with the lonely bleat of a lamb, the caw of a rook, the eerie moan of the wind picking up and wailing like a lost child. She makes for the car, suddenly unsettled and – more than that – frightened, and starts off once more.

It is late afternoon before she spies something that she thinks could have been it and makes her way towards it. A small ragged farmhouse, more compact than Skylark, but also made of slate and granite, snuggled below lonely Garrow Tor. For one painful moment, she believes this is it, and knows then that if it is, she has no way of finding him, for the place is deserted – the lichen-covered tiles slipping from the roof, the broken windows, empty eyes that stare blankly at the moor.

And then she sees that there is no evidence of stables or barns, no cobbles found when she scuffs at the grass. Nor has she come down a high-banked lane with oaks and ash bending over it, though perhaps the banks have been eroded? If clapper bridges have been destroyed and railway lines ripped up, then why should such details remain?

She walks stiffly to lean against the wall of the garden, feels the wind picking up as the sun disappears behind a cloud to cast her in shadow, making her pull her fleece around her and cradle her waist in a way she would not normally do.

And then the tears come. Not just because it seems insurmountable, this ridiculous search, but because the memories of that terrible night are flooding back now. A torrent of them. Like water from a weir, thrusting her under: relentless, furious, fast.

She cowers. Sinks down into the corner, so that

the dry-stone wall that has withstood the wind for more than two centuries can offer her partial shelter, and gives herself up to them, at last.

Thirty-three

Then: 18 April 1944, Cornwall

Alice was shaking. She hadn't really stopped since Aunt Evelyn had thrust the baby into her arms with a bottle of sheep's milk, the type she was used to feeding motherless lambs. At her feet was a bag with some cut-up towels to be fastened with a nappy pin: Joanna had already secured one to the baby and dressed him in a nightie that had once belonged to Maggie.

Alice stifled a sob and pulled the baby closer, breathing in the smell of his scalp, sweet and distinct; a clean smell compared to the earthiness of the manure-strewn farmyard or the unfamiliar scent of Mr Trescothick's car, where she was sitting now.

She sank down into the leather seat, hiding herself and the baby from view; trying hard not to look at the water butt that loomed just outside the window, or to fear the darkness pressing in around them. The dashboard was glossy walnut, and the dials gleamed. She focused on these, as she wrapped herself around the baby; trying to cocoon him, to keep him safe from harm.

From this spot, she could still spy on Aunt

Evelyn and Patrick Trescothick in the car's wing mirror. Aunt Evelyn looked formidable; the vet angry, and then sullen – like Will on the rare occasions when he had been told off.

Would he be coming soon? They had to get going as quickly as possible. Before Maggie woke and that dratted child started screaming again, she had heard Aunt Evelyn tell Joanna. Before, Joanna had muttered as she had struggled to put a fresh nappy on the baby, anyone had second thoughts about taking him away from the farm.

She dreaded a long, silent drive with the vet. Back in the house, he had given Maggie a sedative, plunged from a syringe similar to those he used for the horses. Well, she was hysterical, Aunt Evelyn had said, matter-of-factly; she needed something to calm her down.

'I'm not happy about this,' the vet had tried to object, as Maggie had sobbed uncontrollably: too weak to crawl after her baby, who had been whisked away from her by Joanna.

'I'm asking you to show some compassion for the girl.' Aunt Evelyn's voice was light though her eyes were hard and bright, as if it wouldn't do to cross her.

Then she had sensed Alice, still watching behind the door, and had turned on her. 'Alice? Go away, immediately. Go! With Joanna.'

And Alice had had to abandon Maggie as the vet stepped towards her.

She was scared of him, she realised now, as he jerked away from Aunt Evelyn and walked towards the car, his face set and unreadable. What was it Uncle Joe had said? *Not sure as I trust him.*

A shifty bugger. 'E e'dn much cop, James had added. And yet she and this tiny baby were relying on him to drive them to safety. Her knees knocked together as they did when she stayed too long in the sea because Maggie dared her. She hoped her teeth wouldn't start chattering.

He didn't look at her as he put the key in the ignition. The engine started up. A gentle *phut,* then a roar as he reversed swiftly and started up the track, the stench of burned rubber filling the air.

Alice's knuckles were white where she clutched the baby. He gave a whimper in his sleep, and she loosened her grip. You could smother babies, Joanna said, just as Doris had squashed her piglets by rolling onto them – or a sheep could butt a lamb it had rejected against a stone wall. She tried to breathe more steadily, concentrating on her breath going out in one long stretch, then worrying that the vet could hear her. At least she could try to keep the baby safe, for the time being: for the length of this journey. But after that? Well, then, she could be no help at all.

She began to well up with self-pity, and concentrated on peering through the windscreen. The road was empty and the sky a blue-black: just a few stars and a full moon lighting a cloud-smudged sky. The car's headlamps were dipped, and the hedgerows loomed as the car swung around the corners in the darkness. A rabbit bounded past, picked up by the car's beam at the very last moment. *Thud.* She squealed as the car jolted, the rabbit flung away from the wheels.

They peeled from their lane onto a main road towards the centre of Cornwall. The vet remained silent and Alice didn't dare speak. She risked looking at him, though. To think she had once thought him beautiful! Now, his face was all puffy, he had dirt beneath his nails, and dark smudges under his eyes. He was unshaven too, and jittery. He used to move as if entirely relaxed in his own body so that his clothes hung just so. But now his shoulders hunched and he kept peering forwards. Below his left eye, a nerve twitched.

'What a nightmare, eh?'

His voice, clipped and dry, took her by surprise. She felt herself redden.

He glanced at her, briefly. 'Poor kid. The last thing I imagine you ever thought you'd be involved in. Or perhaps you knew all along?'

She peered intently forwards. *Had* she known? Well, of course she had guessed. Maggie's reaction when she'd glimpsed her getting dressed earlier this month – the horror as her eyes had flitted to her turned-away stomach – had told her, really; and yet, until she'd come across her, earlier today in the bedroom, she hadn't accepted what she had known. She fiddled with the blanket, wrapping the baby close. Safer to deny all knowledge: she didn't want to get into further trouble or to cause problems for Maggie. And yet she didn't want him to think she was childish. After all, she was hardly being treated as a child now. Aunt Evelyn wanted her to pretend that *she* had had this baby. That she was old enough to have done that. The injustice, and the shame, began to smart.

'I sort of guessed,' she confessed. And the half-truth quickly became a truth.

'Really?' He looked at her again, as though

seeing her afresh. 'Well, that's more than I did, though of course I'd barely seen Maggie recently. I didn't know her like you.'

'She confides in me.'

She didn't know where that had come from: a definite half-truth, for Maggie never told her anything these days, and had behaved as if she could barely tolerate her since the summer.

'She tells me most things,' she said.

'So you'll know who the father is, then?' He looked at her, wolf-like. She wondered if he meant to be mocking. 'Don't worry: you don't have to betray any secrets, though I think I can guess.'

She shut up then, concentrating on the road emerging before them, the moor opening up on either side: an unseen expanse of gorse bushes, granite and rolling bleakness. Determined not to betray anyone or to make him mock her. For was she imagining a streak of laughter, when he asked: 'And how is your brother these days?'

'I'll drop you off here: you come down Higher Bore Street and meet me outside the Mason's Arms when you've finished.'

They were in Bodmin, on the road leading to the orphanage, the car's engine running as if he couldn't wait to be rid of her and was desperate for a drink.

'Aren't you coming with me?'

The reality of the situation, the fact that she would have to confront the nuns alone, hit her with the force of a gale blowing in off the headland.

'Why would I do that?' He looked genuinely surprised at the suggestion. 'I might as well wear a placard saying I impregnate thirteen-year-old girls.'

She felt a jolt of shock, then, at his brutal language, and the thought that a man could do that with someone her age.

'Just hand it in quickly. Then run away if need be. If you don't want to come in, just wait in the car outside.'

He roared off towards the pub, where she could already see a cluster of soldiers gathering. The streets were full of them, these days: some two thousand men, Uncle Joe said, parking their tanks up at the Beacon; swelling the five-thousand-strong town.

It started to drizzle, and she pulled Maggie's gabardine raincoat around her and the baby and tried to look inconspicuous: a young girl sheltering a bundle, scurrying up the hill towards the orphanage, on the road out towards the coast.

A couple of GIs walked past, more slick than the Duke of Cornwall's soldiers. Their velvet laughter filled the night air.

'Good evening, little lady,' said one.

'A little young, Bud. Even for you.'

She walked faster, away from the smell of them: their Brylcreem and soap, the whiff of their cigarettes. Their reek of definite manliness. Lifting her face to the rain, she tried to cleanse herself of the stench of them.

And then she was there, in front of the orphanage, perched at the top of a street of mean, flat-fronted terraces. There were hills behind, she was sure of it: a patchwork quilt backing into the darkness; but the street itself was built-up, crowded and dark.

The convent, or the orphanage, for the sign suggested they were the same, was a small castle. Not as old as the farm, but fancier, with turrets, a cross, and crenelated ramparts all made from chunks of granite, piled on top of each another. The mullioned windows glittered, and Alice tried to imagine what they hid. Was that a child crying? The cry grew louder – but it was the wind, keening with a rasping whistle that grew as it blew in from the moor.

The mizzle became thicker: fat droplets striking against the windows and running off her coat, licking her calves, soaking her ankles. She pulled the baby tighter. He carried on sleeping, lulled by her heartbeat, safe and warm.

She ought to hand him in now, she really ought. Before he got soaked and they both caught a chill. Before the wind grew fiercer. Before Mr Trescothick got angry. She stepped out of the shadows. The heavy oak door opened and a woman threw out a cat, which landed with a hiss and a yowl.

Alice stepped forwards and the door of this wicked fairy's castle slammed shut. The cat streaked past her, eyes wild in the dark and fur spiky, and she knew with absolute certainty that she could not leave this child here.

She drew him tighter, backing away, keeping the castle in view – poised to run if the woman should come out to grab him, having spotted her. She had lost everyone: Will, her parents, Baby Robert, her twin sisters, Pam and Susan. She had lost the love of Maggie, the occasional affection of Auntie

Evelyn and no doubt the goodwill of Uncle Joe. She had even lost the baby kittens, Flopsy the wild rabbit and Bert, her bottle-fed piglet. Everyone and everything she had ever loved had gone.

Her throat ached with the effort of keeping in all this loss, and she felt her grief well up inside her. She wouldn't give up this baby. She just couldn't. It was too much to ask of her. If they thought she was old enough to have a child, then she was old enough to decide that she couldn't give him up, too! She felt strangely elated as she turned from the orphanage and was blown down the street towards the town. She had never gone against a grown-up's wishes before, and yet she had no choice. They would have to drag this baby from her.

She would have to take it somewhere, though. The reality of what she had done grew on her as she ran down Higher Bore Street towards the pub where Mr Trescothick was drinking. Aunt Evelyn's face – the rage as she had screamed at Maggie – loomed in front of her and she knew she couldn't risk it. Couldn't risk bringing this baby back to the farm.

The germ of an idea she had had in the car began to grow and gain life. What if she was able to get the baby to Will, on the other side of Bodmin? If he saw it, she knew that he would take responsibility. He would love it and make a home for his son.

Happiness bubbled up and she hugged the baby tightly. Why hadn't she thought this through before? He would come and fetch Maggie and form a family. Uncle Joe might support them and help them marry. And Alice? Alice would be the fairy godmother. The supposed child who had made everything better and had brought about a happy ending, after all.

She could imagine it now. Will delighted to see her and proud that she had rescued his baby. Maggie, once they were reunited, so incredibly grateful – so sorry that she had tried to push her away. Her beam grew wider and she found that she was crying, but they were tears of relief that she had thought of a solution; that she would keep Baby Will in the family; that she wouldn't have to lose someone else she had loved. She kissed the top of his head, her tears wetting his cheeks as she shifted her grip on him. 'Baby Will,' she whispered, 'I'm going to take you to your daddy and you are going to be so loved.'

'What the hell do you think you're doing?' Patrick Trescothick, coming out of the Mason's Arms, lurched towards her. He was livid.

'I … I … I'm not giving the baby up. I can't. The woman was cruel.' Her voice trailed away.

'Get in the car.' He wrenched his door open and slammed it, then started the engine before she had a chance to settle down.

The car hurtled across the wide street and dipped away from the town in the opposite direction to the orphanage.

'Are you not taking me back there?' Her voice came out small and pinched.

'What's the point?' he snarled and the car filled with the smell of smoke and beer. 'I can't make you do it and I'm not handing it over. We'll just have to drive back to the farm.'

He took a sharp left, then did a U-turn before screeching back past the pub and out on the coast road. The nerve below his left eye was twitching again.

'Bloody woman! What the hell was I thinking?' he cried, slamming the steering wheel with the flats of his hands. Her heart thudded, but she stayed silent. Was the bloody woman Evelyn? Her breath came out, light and tense.

The car tore along a dark ribbon of road through woodland.

They were going the wrong way. The wrong way if she wanted to get this baby to Will and safety.

'Please,' she blurted out. 'Please. We could take the baby to my brother's. To Will's. He's at Farmer Eddy's at Polcarrow, the other side of Bodmin. Do you know it?' She didn't seem to be able to stop talking. 'Will would know what to do. He'd help us. He would take the baby. I know he would.'

Her words – out in the cold dark of the car – sounded ridiculous: the childish make-believe of a girl who wanted to play happy families and make everything better.

'Please,' she begged, again. She was frantic now. 'Please.'

There were tears running down her cheeks as he drove on regardless. 'Sorry,' she whimpered, then started hiccuping as she tried to stifle her sobs.

He put his foot on the accelerator and drove faster, the car weaving its way through dark patches of furze and gorse towards the mass of Brown Willy; the windscreen wipers scraping as the rain plashed down.

Panic overwhelmed her. She had ruined everything. Thrown away the chance of a home at the orphanage and the possibility of one with Will. And now she was taking him back to certain danger. She clung to the baby, her tears wetting his skin and seeping into the wool of his blanket. The baby stirred and gave a small bleat of indignation. Then a cough; then a full-on cry.

'*Waaaaaah... Waa ... aaaaah... Waaa ... aaaaaaaah.*'

'Can't you shut it up?' The vet looked appalled as the car lurched.

But it was as if someone had pulled a plug and she could not contain him.

'Shhh... shhh... baby...' she tried. 'Shhh... shhh... Please be quiet.'

The cries died down a little, then immediately grew.

She was shaking properly now. 'I don't know how to stop him.'

They were building to a furious crescendo.

'Can't you feed it or something?'

She strained to reach the bottle, but almost knocked the baby's head. 'I can't get to it. Please – could you stop a minute?'

'Oh, bloody hell.'

He swerved and the car lurched off the road onto the moorland before ploughing into a gorse bush. 'Bloody *hell*,' he repeated. 'Damn, damn, damn.'

She reached for the bottle and uncapped it, then tried to shove it in the newborn's mouth.

'Here, baby. Here ... please take it.' Her voice cracked with desperation.

'*Waaaah ... waagggh...*' And then a hesitant then

frantic gulping as the warm, creamy liquid began to go down.

She couldn't believe it. She had managed to make him quiet. Tears sprang again as she looked down at his small mouth, working away in the darkness. The terror that had gripped her since leaving the farm began to ease and she felt relief rush through her like sunshine, warming her insides, lifting her fear.

'He's so lovely, isn't he?' She felt bold enough to say that. She felt as if she needed to convey how precious he was: to mark this occasion. This might be the only time she could do this: watch him drink as she held him in her arms.

The vet grunted, tension vibrating from him. He lit a cigarette, grimy fingers fumbling in the packet, but grew calmer as his smoke rings filled the car.

The baby carried on drinking, eyes bright and fixed on her, mouth working away rhythmically, as he drained the bottle like a lamb. Eventually he fell asleep again, the teat slipping from his mouth, his lips occasionally twitching. He looked so peaceful, the trauma of the past hours eased by sleep and a belly full of milk.

'Couldn't we take him to Will?' The words slipped out without her intending them to. She glanced at him, but the cigarette and the sight of the sleeping baby seemed to have relaxed him.

'He wouldn't take him. What is he? Seventeen?'

'Eighteen in June.'

'The last thing he'd want at seventeen.'

She bit her lip, determined not to antagonise him, but how could he be so sure? And then she thought of how Will hadn't written to her since leaving, and of how he hadn't contacted Maggie. The fact niggled, ugly and insistent. Perhaps he had never loved Maggie – or even cared for her at all?

She waited for him to start the engine, but the vet sat still, almost mesmerised.

'I do know of another family who might take him. Other farmers with a farm on the moor.'

She didn't want anyone else to have this baby. But she'd refused to take him to the orphanage, and he wouldn't take her to Will. Another farm – familiar, and nearby – might be a safer option than their farm.

'Why would they want him?'

'They can't have a child. They tried for years, and they want one.'

She closed her eyes, trying to imagine this childless couple. What must it be like to want something so badly that you would accept it even if it wasn't yours? There had been a ewe whose lamb had died last spring and who spent her days trying to lure others' lambs to her. She had succeeded with one, and the lamb never went back to its mother. She sometimes wondered if the original mother missed her, or if the lamb ever realised. That was the difficulty with sheep bleating: they all sounded so plaintive it was impossible to tell.

She opened her eyes and caught Patrick Trescothick looking at her strangely. Something had shifted in the atmosphere between them, as if the sleeping baby and the silence of the moor around had created a new intimacy. Outside, the rain hammered on the window, but inside the car was quiet and calm.

'Of course it will cost you.'

'What do you mean?' She was puzzled. 'I don't have any money.'

He was leaning towards her now, with a determined look on his face and a silly, mocking smile. His mouth took her by surprise. That wide, taunting mouth tasted of smoke and beer and, just for a moment, she was too shocked to push him off.

'Just a kiss,' he said. 'And another.' His tongue was probing, thick and hard now, and his hand with its grimy fingers was forcing its way between her legs, pinching and grabbing between her thighs.

'No!' She came up for air – appalled and furious – and managed to push his fingers away.

'You help me, I help you,' he said, grabbing the back of her neck and pulling her back towards him. One hand clawed away at her knickers, rubbing beneath the material, and then he grabbed her right hand and pushed it down into his crotch.

'Touch me,' he said, furious, crushing her fingers and making her rub up and down the hardness at the front of his trousers, which stirred and strained.

'I don't know how to.'

'Just do it.' He sounded savage, and, loosening his trousers, thrust her fingers on to it again.

Blood galloped through her head. He is mad, she thought, quite mad. And yet, if I am to get out of here safely, with the baby, I need to do exactly as he says. She tried to remember what Will and Maggie had done, but the thought of that – and of what it could lead to – made tears brim and wet her cheeks. His face slid from hers, her tears coating it.

'Don't you dare cry!' He was shouting now. 'What have you to cry about? What the fuck have you got to cry about?'

And then his face crumpled like a small boy's: as if loss and anguish were battling rage.

'I'm sorry,' she said, and she tried to touch him as he'd said, moving her fingers up the disgusting thing. Let this be over soon, she prayed. Let him do the jolting soon; please, let it all be over. And don't let it get any worse. Please don't let him harm the baby or me.

But she didn't seem to be doing it right, for it was softening under her touch, and she feared that he would get angry. His face was red and squashed, and it was a while before she realised that, actually, he was crying.

Eventually, when it had shrunk to a mouse in her hand, he leaned over the steering wheel and became convulsed with sobs.

'I'm sorry,' she could just make out him saying. 'I'm so, so sorry.'

She sat very still, listening to the sleeping baby and the pounding rain, trying to work out if she could remove her hand without him noticing. Her insides were wound as tight as a spring.

'Look at the golden boy now!' he said, his face wet with tears. 'The only son left and I'm a dirty drunk. What a fuck-up. What a bloody fuck-up.' He grappled with the keys to the car and reversed abruptly, the car scratching along the side of the gorse bush before veering away.

Her heart thudded hard against the baby. She

looked down at him intently, hoping that he couldn't hear this and wouldn't wake and start screaming. With her right hand, she pulled down her skirt, rearranging it over her bare knees. There was an angry sore patch on her inner thigh where he'd grabbed at her, and her insides felt stretched and bruised where he'd tried to thrust in a finger. As the car accelerated, she felt very afraid.

And then suddenly, he braked so fiercely that she had to brace herself to stop slamming against the dashboard. The baby, tight in her arms, bleated awake.

Was he going to go for her once more? She felt for the handle. Better to fling herself out with the baby than for that to happen again.

He wasn't reaching for her, though, but manoeuvring the car so that they took a sharp right and plunged deep into the centre of the moor. She glanced out of the window at the moorland now rolling behind them. She had missed her chance to jump: if she did it now, she risked losing the baby. The thought of him falling from her arms into the scrubland – dark, unknowable and almost ghostly, with its boulders and bogland and silence, and the mist that enveloped you secretly – was absolutely terrifying.

'How will we explain it?' He seemed to be talking to her. 'The baby. If this other family take it.'

'We wouldn't need to.' She swallowed, her heart thudding. She needed to play this carefully. 'We could tell Aunt Evelyn I'd handed him in to the nuns. Just as she said.'

'And ... what happened.' He cleared his throat. 'You won't mention it?'

'Of course not.' She almost laughed. Who could she tell and who would believe her? There was no one she could trust even if she could find a way to explain.

'You suddenly looked much older ... with the baby. For a moment, I thought he was yours. It was ... a moment of madness.'

Liar, she thought, with a cold certainty that, at that moment, was clear as the ice that skimmed the puddles on crisp winter mornings. I am a little girl. You know I am. It shouldn't have happened. She kept her eyes on the baby. Her own eyes stared back, questioning her.

The car started to slow down now, and dipped through an avenue of branches, the trees gnarled, bare and twisted together – broom blackened and tortured by man and wind. The track was rough and potholed. The car bounced and jolted from one side of it to another before it rolled over cobbles and came to rest in a yard.

Through the windscreen she could see the softened granite of a farmhouse not unlike Skylark, though longer-slung and more dishevelled, the windows smaller casements, the frames in need of a paint. The garden was overgrown, the grass long, the bushes unkempt. A broken chair and some farm machinery had been dumped at the front of the house, and a water butt sat squat against the barn wall, water dripping into it.

'Are you sure this is the place?' She was suddenly filled with doubt. Who was to say they were good people? *You help me, I help you* – but perhaps it hadn't been a good bargain. *Not sure as I trust him,* said Uncle Joe; *'E e'dn much cop,* James had added.

'The very same,' he said, turning off the engine and reaching for the baby. 'You stay here. I'll take him to them.'

Thirty-four

Now: 22 August 2014, Cornwall

The next day, Alice sets out again, and the next. No longer driving in the same state of feverish frenzy, but taking a more systematic approach to retracing her steps. She paces herself, and organises proper supplies this time: a flask of sweet instant coffee; sandwiches, a banana, shortbread biscuits – though her appetite has gone. A warm fleece and her cagoule. *Far From the Madding Crowd*, and Will's letter, both carried as talismans, though to whom she intends to show them, she has no idea.

There are several false starts: more abandoned huts and weather-broken farmhouses whose early promise dissipates as soon as she gets close to them. The moor is riddled with evidence of lives spent and then abandoned here. The name Altarnum strikes a chord – and she descends to a remote granite village with a babbling brook and imposing church, only, to realise that she recognises it from a novel by du Maurier. A couple of mallards strut in a neat allotment, and rhododendrons bloom in a Georgian vicarage garden. The air is cool and fertile, scented with honey-

297

suckle and wild garlic, plump with moisture. But the spot is too pretty and too sheltered, safe in the crease of a valley, and she is searching for a more exposed and lonely place.

By the third day, she focuses on the highest parts of the moor to the east of the villages of St Breward and Blisland. Driving up another canopied track, she bursts on to open moorland – no trees here but gorse and blackthorn, and a lonely expanse of cropped grass populated by wild ponies, Highland cattle and a flock of tentative, black-faced sheep. She knows it is here somewhere, and so she drives on, seeing no one bar the odd horsewoman for, after her first attempt, she is too shy to venture into the rare village pubs promising real ale and roast dinners in which the locals stare when she dares to enter. She toys with her cheese and pickle sandwiches to the accompaniment of skylarks and the lambs' bleats.

By the end of the fourth day, she feels a dull ache in her heart, a hard certainty that this is a wild goose chase. And yet how can she give up now? A determination she barely knew she still possessed festers inside her, stronger than the tiredness that makes her draw up at the side of the road for a moment when she fears she will fall asleep at the wheel. She drifts off, then wakes, befuddled. An hour has slipped by and the landscape has changed. A charcoal cloud bruises the dull grey sky and fat raindrops plash down, not the fine spray of a sea mist but a proper rainstorm; and then, just as suddenly, they stop.

As a watery sun filters through the clouds, she drives on, knowing now that she will come out

298

each day, if necessary, to find him. She cannot go back to London without knowing she has exhausted every possibility, snuffed out all hope. And so she continues: retracing her steps; discovering new lanes; searing back and forth over the moor. For she knows she didn't imagine it, this hidden farmhouse: it has to be here, somewhere.

And then she sees it: an avenue of trees up a high-banked lane that seems even more secluded than all the others, the trees, more windswept, gnarled and wizened, their trunks crawling with ivy, wreathed in others' roots. She concentrates as the car bounces and jolts down the potholed track, ignoring the light that dapples through the leaves. For she has seen the farmhouse and there is something about its position that is familiar, that tells her that she has found the place that has haunted her for seventy years.

The car stalls to a halt. Through the windscreen she sees a house not unlike Skylark, though smaller and smarter. The casements are freshly painted and gleaming in the sunshine, the door a tasteful, sludgy green. There is a smart slate sign by the gatepost with the name chiselled deep. Trebartha Farm. She pauses, expecting the name to ring a bell. She never saw a sign as the car rolled into the yard, wouldn't have noticed in the dark. But perhaps it's a missing piece to her jigsaw; one more clue that will lead her closer to what she needs.

The door opens before she manages to knock: visitors must be rare and she had crunched the car's gears as she parked in the lane, not wanting to presume she could drive into the yard.

'May I help you?' The woman who opens the door is in her late forties. No trace of a Cornish accent. Slim, with her hair swept onto her head and a few tendrils tumbling; her eyes, beneath neat brows, appraising and grey.

'I was looking for a family who might have lived here years ago. Seventy years, in fact.' Her voice catches as she sees the woman's eyebrows rise almost imperceptibly. 'It must sound ridiculous. I think they lived here in 1944. A farmer and his wife, and their son – he'd have been a baby. But I'm afraid I can't remember their name.'

The woman – who could be one of her neighbours back home – smiles properly now warmth lighting her eyes.

'That sounds intriguing. Have you come a long way?' Her eyes run over her, taking in her age and the exhaustion and desperation that Alice knows must suffuse her face.

'Padstow. But I've been driving all over.'

'Oh, you poor dear. Here.' The woman moves back into the farmhouse, gesturing that she should follow. 'You'd better come in.'

She steps into the slate-tiled hall, feeling self-conscious in her old Peter Storm jacket. The hall is cool and a candle glows in a glass pot, emitting lavender and calm. It is all so tasteful. A house that is cherished by its proud owners – almost too polished to be a real home. She thinks of the dark, damp-infested farm she has imagined, with its neglected casements and scrubby garden, and of the changes wrought by fresh paint, money and time.

'What a lovely house.' She feels she must say

300

something as she stands there, her sensible slip-on shoes no doubt trampling dust into the hallway.

'Thank you.' The woman smiles more widely and she sees that she is not quite as imposing as she thought: there is a smudge of white paint on her forehead, smile lines around her mouth and eyes. 'We've only recently moved in. The family we bought it from had it as a holiday cottage for fifteen years and rarely used it. But we love it here.'

'And before them?' This is the place, she knows it, though she had never stepped into this hallway, had only watched as Patrick Trescothick went in. She imagines a phantom boy slipping past: a child of the fifties, short trousers above scabbed knees; a face, streaked with peat, as freckled as her brother's; and she knows she cannot leave without confirming that he lived here.

'It had quite a few owners in the eighties and nineties. People buying it as a second home then discovering they weren't quite so in love with life on the moor.' She pauses. 'But you're talking about way before then?'

'The nineteen forties. The end of the war.' Her voice cracks then tails away. She cannot tell this woman why she needs to track down this family. She is not the type to unburden herself – no one from her generation does – but she needs to impress on her that there is a point to her seemingly eccentric searching. 'If you know anything,' she begins, then pauses, steeling herself to say something confessional. 'You see: I don't have much time.'

'You'd better come right through.' The woman's voice softens and she leads her through a room

301

with a flagstone floor and battered leather sofas to the kitchen.

'The previous owners were history buffs and they left a file on Trebartha's history somewhere.'

She pulls at the drawer of a dresser and shakes a Manila folder free, then places it on a large wooden table. 'Here we are! I haven't gone through it properly – we've only just moved back in after the builders left – but I think it mentions the families who previously farmed here. The last owner, the wife, was fascinated with old agricultural practices, you see.' She pushes a lock of hair back from her eyes and gives a sniff. 'I think she was some sort of academic. She compiled a paper on the farm. It's terribly dry, I'm afraid – an awful lot on moorland sheep – but I think she might mention your family there.'

She pushes the file towards her as Alice fights back an impulse to snatch it. The notes are not a neat list of owners, but a lengthy document, in which Meredith Cooper, BA, MPhil, charts the demise of moorland farming in Cornwall in the mid to late twentieth century. And yet, hidden away, among a few statistics and some rather grandiose claims – for Alice is not completely naïve when it comes to social history – there are the gems she has been searching for: the names of the farmer and his wife who tended Trebartha from the early 1930s until the early 1960s, when they retired.

They were predominantly sheep farmers it seems, with a flock of a hundred ewes. And there is even a mention of a nameless son. Her heart jolts. Could this be him? The dates are vague: he

302

helped herd the sheep 'in the mid-1950s'. At ten or eleven, he could do that kind of work. She looks up at the yard and the moors outside. Why would a family, subsumed by this way of life, ever leave? And then she thinks of the loneliness, the harshness of farming on the moor; the way in which a rogue rain cloud can drench you to the bone and leave you quaking with cold, when the sun goes in; the bogs that suck you down to your knees, or even thighs; the carcasses of elderly or ill sheep, lying, scavenged. The isolation of a farmhouse, circled by rooks, whipped by the wind.

She has what she needs, though. A name. A family name, and this address. Tangible evidence. The crumbs that will lead her through the deepest thickets of genealogical research. The link that might allow her to find a current address, perhaps here in Cornwall. That might let her meet him, at last...

The possibilities are dizzying. A wave of tiredness tugs at her.

'Are you all right?' The woman touches her arm. 'Here, please. Sit down. You need a glass of water.' A wooden chair is pressed behind her legs.

The touch of this other woman is almost more than she can bear. How long is it since someone has touched her like that? A brisk hug from one of her sons. The guidance of a nurse, professional and calm. For a moment, the temptation to melt at the kindness of this touch almost overwhelms her. But there is no need – there is nothing to cry about, now.

For she has it. Here, in black and white. His family name. The crucial piece of the jigsaw without which she had no chance of finding him.

'Thank you,' she says, as a glass of water is put in front of her and a cup of tea materialises. She takes a sip, gaining strength from something hot and sweet.

The woman – Ali: a writer, she later says – is watching her intently, concern evidently tempered by an itch to know what she has discovered and why it is so important, this quest.

She cannot share it; but she smiles, emboldened by her new knowledge.

'Really,' she says. 'I'm absolutely fine.'

She is galvanised now and, the next day, is out by nine to discover more about Trebartha Farm's inhabitants – or, more specifically, to track down their only child. The local library is closed and so she finds she is drawn, despite herself, back to Bodmin to the street she ran down, wind and rain buffeting against her, with a baby in her arms.

She clutches her handbag, with the name, address and Will's letter, always the letter, and focuses on the solid, late Victorian library, refusing to look in the direction of the pub from which Patrick Trescothick had lurched. Moments before, she had been so certain she was doing the right thing: her heart bursting with that conviction; breath hot against the baby's face as she had whispered her promise. Baby Will, I'm going to take you to your daddy and you are going to be so loved.

The library is quiet and studious. The librarian, a helpful young girl, tells her that birth certificates have to be ordered, but that she can check all births within a three-month period in an index. She nods, disappointment seeping through her, for she had thought she would be able to see this proof of his identity today. Her fear that she may not accomplish her search in time increases as she watches the girl tap details into a computer. Come on, concentrate. This matters. But the despair she felt on the moor before finding the farm begins to press upon her. She is getting so close, and yet, in many ways, this baby feels as elusive as before.

'There we are.' The girl, for she is in her mid-twenties at most, looks at her brightly. 'There are seven births with that surname in that district in Cornwall in that period.'

Seven names to contemplate.

'But,' the girl continues, 'if you know if it's a boy or girl you could rule half of them out.'

'A boy.' She clears her throat. 'A man, now.'

'So just these four then.'

She looks at the entries, flashing on the screen. Her breath catches like a moth, fluttering in her chest.

'Are you sure you want me to order four birth certificates? That's forty pounds.' The girl looks incredulous that she might want to spend so much money.

'Yes, yes, of course. And as soon as possible, please. Could I pay more to have it speeded up?'

'Five to ten working days.'

'I can't wait that long.' She twists the strap of her handbag, feeling the fear rise up thickly.

The girl looks at her, her forehead furrowing. 'Well, I can't make any promises, but I could try marking it as urgent?'

'If you could? Thank you.' She nods with gratitude and fumbles with her purse, almost thrusting her card at her, so desperate is she to speed up the process. Four to one; and once she has that one, then the trawling of the phone books, the tracking down in earnest, the endless, exhausting search, will start up again. The effort is overwhelming and yet she is getting closer; she is still getting closer.

'I'll see what I can do,' the girl says.

The birth certificates arrive two days later. A knock at the door, and the postman stands there, blue eyes shining from a walnut of a face.

She blinks, confused. She had feared it would be Maggie, not this vision in grey shorts and bright Royal Mail red.

'Mrs Coates?' His voice is thick with a Cornish burr.

She nods, eyes fixed on the A4 Do Not Bend envelope in his hands.

'It's just people don't often get things sent to the cottages. I wanted to check it was definitely for you.'

'Yes, it's for me,' she says, reaching for the envelope, scarcely believing the answer is finally here.

He hands it over and she takes it greedily, forgetting to thank him in her eagerness to go somewhere private. She lays the four certificates out on the table that she knows she peeled potatoes on, out in the pantry, as a child.

Which one of these is you, she thinks, as she looks at the four male Joses. And the answer springs out at her: Trebartha Farm. Father, Jeremiah, mother, Emmeline. Date of birth:

18.4.1944. The name seems oddly formal for a baby. Biblical. Almost Victorian. No Will, as she half expected, but a Jeremiah Samuel Jose.

She prepares her rucksack with letter, novel, map and birth certificate, shortbread biscuits, a flask of weak coffee and a cagoule, just in case. The local library has the Cornish phone directory, the librarian said, and there will be J. S. Joses lurking there, as long as he hasn't strayed from Cornwall. She cannot bear to contemplate that possibility.

Thirty-five

She doesn't intend to be seen by Maggie until she has found her son; really she doesn't. She means to be able to present her with her child – or with the correct address, at the very least.

But there are five J Joses in the phone book in north Cornwall alone and having had no luck with the first two houses she found – bleak, greying bungalows with a John Jose and a Jason – she is utterly drained. The adrenalin that has brought her down from London and driven her up onto the moors, into libraries and onto unknown housing estates, is all entirely spent.

She gazes at the sea, a pool of French navy, through her window. Could she risk pottering around the garden? The sun beats invitingly on a bench. Gingerly, she perches on the wooden slats and tries to relax just a little while she steels herself for another long, potentially fruitless day.

She must have dozed off. When she wakes someone is in the farmhouse garden, hanging washing on a line. A grey-haired figure, bending over a basket then stretching up to peg out the items. Her hands arthritic, her arms wizened, her figure almost childishly thin. Gone are the curves she would once flaunt, without seeming the least bit conscious, in her mother's hand-knitted jumpers. Yet there is something about the way she tilts her head as she glances at the barley fields, the cows and down to the sea, that marks her out as the girl she was seventy years ago. That reveals her to be, undeniably, her.

Alice holds her breath as if she fears that, if she lets it out, the older woman will hear her. And yet she doesn't get up and slip back into the cool security of the house. Fear that any movement will attract attention pinions her there – but also, perhaps, a sense of fatalism, or even a secret wish to be found. She has dreaded this, but she is so tired of racing around and of skulking in fear that if exposure has to come, well, perhaps it had better come now, sooner than later, while she has some strength.

And then Maggie glances over the wall separating the two of them and into the garden, and in that second, their eyes meet. The look, which shifts from confusion to recognition, and then to something like fear, lasts perhaps three seconds. A chill runs through Alice's veins and then a bizarre sense of relief.

'Maggie!' She calls her name without intending to, but the syllables are certain: a call for attention caught on the breeze.

The other woman is startled.

'Maggie,' she repeats, emboldened by the fact that she hasn't moved yet. She stumbles up and starts to cross the garden towards her. Maggie, eyes on her face, starts to back away.

'Keep away from me,' the older woman says, her body stiff, her voice icy.

'Maggie.' She tries to pacify her. 'I've got some good news for you. I've something for you!' But her words are tossed by the wind.

And now Maggie is turning and stumbling, the peg bag abandoned, the washing strewn on the table, as she rushes from the garden at speed.

Alice stands at a loss, watching the washing fluttering on the line – the clothes of a family: hard-wearing trousers, faded shirts, a toddler's socks and leggings – and the jumble of wet boxers and T-shirts, lying discarded by a woman she harmed.

In the cool of the kitchen, Maggie finds that she cannot stop shaking. Her teeth chatter as she grips the kitchen table and tries to calm herself. It was *her*. It *was* her. No ghost of a young teenage girl, but a woman as solid as her standing there, as unapologetically as you like, calling out. 'Maggie' she said; and with that cry, unleashed a stream of memories she has tried so hard to suppress and that now cascade so swiftly that she trembles. Two syllables, no longer uttered in a child's voice, but still unmistakably Alice's. Her name, said by someone with the power to devastate her.

She manages to sit, her knees clattering against the underside of the table. Why has she come back now? And why not earlier, when she would have had the time and the energy to track her baby down?

She thinks of her own search: that moment with the archivist, and the countless hours she has spent since, wondering where he could be, how she could possibly find him. All those painful, fruitless hours. She slams a palm on the table: the initial shock seguing into something close to rage. How dare she arrive, uninvited and unannounced? If she has something to say, she could have sent a letter, or at least a note requesting that they meet. A letter would have given her time to think, could be read in private: lingered over, reread and maybe treasured. Such a letter could also be burned.

She must see if she can stand. Perhaps get a glass of water. She walks to the sink below the window, clinging to the worktop as she goes. The garden is empty. Perhaps she's hovering in the cottage? Damn Alice. Just what does she want from her? For a split second she sees her father raising his shotgun to a cluster of rabbits. *Bang, bang, bang:* a volley of shots blasting into the corn, smoke spiralling upwards. Run, rabbit; run, rabbit; run, run, run.

'Granny?' Lucy is standing in the doorway. 'Are you OK? I heard you talking to someone...' She comes closer and touches her arm, gently.

'See that woman–' She points and her finger shakes as she sees her, just visible behind the tamarisk. 'I don't want her here.'

'But that's Mrs Coates. She's staying in one of the cottages. We can't ask her to leave.' She looks perturbed. 'Why? Has she offended you in some way?'

Maggie shuffles back to her chair, the strain of carrying her secret weighing heavier than it has done for years. Should she just tell her? Her and Judith? It might be a relief to unburden herself: finally to confess to something that explains who she is today.

'She hasn't offended me, no,' she says, deliberately. 'But something she did – many years ago – caused me some pain.'

It is an exquisite understatement.

She reaches for her granddaughter's hand and gives it an uncharacteristic squeeze.

'Lucy. There's something I should have told you all,' she says.

Thirty-six

Judith is struggling to take in what she is telling them. Her daughter's forehead creases and she pulls at her bottom lip, as if she is trying to coax out the most appropriate words.

It was hard for Maggie to get them right. Or, rather, impossible. For nothing could take away from the brutality of the truth. 'I had another baby before you. I gave him away. And, each day, I wait, hoping that I'll see him. The child I've never known.'

Of course, she wouldn't dream of saying anything as overemotional as that. She managed the other baby bit – and the part about giving him up. But the sorrow, the endless, unrequited long-

311

ing to meet the child she had never known, her lost baby? That bit she kept to herself.

'You had another baby? And you never told any of us about it? Did Dad know?'

'No.'

She had never told Edward. When he returned from the war, it was clear that their 'understanding' was a childish promise, best forgotten, and it was a decade before they got together again and married. Just the once, he had mentioned their past 'embarrassments'. She took it to mean that he had visited an Italian brothel, and wondered if he had heard a rumour about the baby – but she couldn't bear to ask. 'The past is a foreign country,' he had said, quoting L. P. Hartley, for he was the most unlikely farmer, her bookish husband. He knew she wasn't a virgin, and she had taken his comment to refer to that; had just nodded and smiled.

She clears her throat, dry despite the sips of water she has forced down. She is immensely weary. 'It was a huge shame in those days; it ruined reputations. The family's, not just the girl's.' She pauses, remembering the intensity of her mother's anger. 'My mother, your grandmother, Evelyn, insisted the baby had to go.'

'What about your father? Grandpa Joe?'

'He didn't know when it happened. I think she said I had women's trouble. And when he realised and wanted to search for my baby, my mother was formidable and won the argument. Of course, I didn't know it at the time.'

She thinks back to the terrible aftermath of giving up her baby: when she'd gone back to the county school to take her Higher School Certificate. Not being able to confide in anyone, having to try to excise all thoughts of her baby from her mind. Her friends had thought her distant, detached, excessively studious, with no interest in the GIs circling the town, geed up in preparation for D-Day little more than a month away, though they didn't know it, then. She had kept her head down and worked obsessively in the bedroom at Aunt Edith's as an escape route. She needed to get away from everything she had once loved: to get away from the farm.

She sniffs. Lucy, a little more detached perhaps than Judith but still visibly shocked, is still grappling with the thought of this baby.

'And this woman, Alice ... the guest staying in the cottage she helped your mother get rid of him?'

Maggie looks down at her fingers, twisting her wedding ring up towards her lump of a knuckle and back. 'She was only a child. Thirteen. An evacuee. Terrified, I can see that now, of my mother's anger. She was supposed to take him to an orphanage in Bodmin – and yet I've never found a trace of him there.

'I know it's illogical, but I've never been able to stop blaming her for doing as my mother said. I suppose I thought that somehow she would defy her, side with me, refuse to take the baby – perhaps even tell my father, who might have been able to stop my mother at that point.'

She sees Alice's blanched face, streaked with tears, as she backed out of the bedroom. And earlier, her look of guilt when Maggie returned home from school to discover Will had been sent away.

'I blamed her for telling them about Will, too.'

'Will?' Judith looks bemused.

'Her brother. The baby's father.' The words are out: the father's identity. But the name – meaningless to her daughter and granddaughter – cannot convey what he meant.

'There was no one like him. There was never anyone else like him.' She tries to do him justice. 'My mother said it was first love – a silly, childish thing – but nothing I felt for Edward ever touched it. Nor any other boyfriend I had after the war.

'He was beautiful, you see.' And it was true: she had never seen a more beautiful young man, not in all her years of teaching nor among any of the farm workers who stripped off each harvest, their triangular torsos bronzed in the sun. But there was more to him than this. He radiated exuberance that summer: not cockiness, but a quiet awareness that when the war ended, the world could be his for the taking. He might only be a farm boy, but he was lucky: exempt from being called up, safe in Cornwall. A survivor. And he knew she was in love with him. That would give any seventeen-year-old a shot of confidence.

'I can't take it in. Does Richard know?' Judith looks shocked. 'Did you tell him and not me?'

'No, of course not.'

'And you said you went looking for him – for the baby?'

'Yes, I did.' Her tone softens – for Judith's hurt is understandable. 'When you and Richard left home.

'I went to the orphanage – but they had lost all of his records. Short of advertising for him to come forward – something that would have distressed your father and have severely strained our marriage – there was no way of looking at all.'

'It must have been horrific for you.' Judith's hands snake across the table towards hers, and her face is filled with compassion.

'Yes.'

'Always wondering.'

'Yes ... yes.' She is curt now, for she cannot bear this sympathy. No more needs to be said.

'I'm so sorry,' Lucy adds. Judith nods. But their words, well-meaning though they are, are inadequate – for how can they not be?

For a moment they just sit there. It is out there, thinks Maggie. My secret. She feels curiously deflated. Something so feared has occurred, and nothing dramatic has happened, after all. The kitchen clock still ticks with its usual regularity; a batch of scones cools by the Aga; and, in the fields, the cows will no doubt be grazing. The tourists, craving teas and relaxation, will be turning up any minute now.

'So ... what would you like us to do now?' Lucy is being practical.

'I suppose I'll have to tell Richard.' A knot forms in her stomach.

'Yes. He's not your only boy.' Judith gives a small smile, compassion tinged with something else, now: perhaps apprehension at how her brother will view this.

Her children's whole perception of her will change. Distorted by this single shift. She wants

315

to reassure Judith that she still loves her just as much as ever, but she does not know quite how to articulate it.

Her daughter clears her throat. 'I suppose that's why you're so determined not to leave the farm?'

'Well, a little,' she admits. 'It's just one of the reasons. But yes. I wanted to remain here in case he somehow made his way back.'

'I can see that.' Judith glances at Lucy. 'Well. That makes me even more determined that we should keep standing up to Richard – and absolutely certain that we should stay here.'

'What do you want to do about Mrs Coates?' Lucy voices a question Maggie wants to dismiss.

'I don't know.' She is weary, and suddenly confounded. 'I need to know why she's here. Why now? Does she want to rake over what happened? I'm frightened that, if I approach her, I'll only hear something worse.'

'She knows you're here. She knows you've seen her.' Lucy ticks points off on her fingers. 'What could be worse than what you've already gone through?'

'Discovering that she's been in touch with him – my baby – and that he's now dead? That it's too late, after all?'

The fear slips out before she even acknowledges it. And yet, hearing it articulated makes it sound so pitiful. She had a son she has never known – and, in all likelihood, will never know. But she is so wedded to the idea that she might somehow meet him that she would rather live in ignorance. She is a fool. An old self-pitying fool.

'He needn't be dead. He can't be dead.' Lucy

316

grips her hands as if willing her to be confident. 'What would he be – seventy?'

'Seventy on April the eighteenth this year.'

'And the men on your side of the family all live a long time.'

'Yes.' Maggie gulps a laugh of gratitude. Joe had been ninety-one; his father, Matthew, eighty-nine.

'I think you might need to talk to her ... but it doesn't have to be today, or even tomorrow. And we could go with you – or talk to her on your behalf?'

'That's a good idea,' Judith agrees.

'That's very kind of you, my dears.' She smiles at them both, for the thought is appealing. 'But this is something I need to do myself.'

She frees her hands from Lucy's grasp, aware that she is brushing off affection as she so often does when sentiment threatens. Spiky, that's what Edward said she sometimes was. She never explained that that was what happened if you learned never to trust anyone entirely. If the one person who should support you unconditionally – your mother – took your baby away.

Lucy is still looking at her.

'Thank you,' she adds. 'For offering.' And, she thinks, for understanding.

Her daughter puts an arm round her shoulders.

'It will all be all right,' Judith murmurs as she brushes a kiss, light yet perceptible, on the top of her head.

How times have changed, Maggie thinks. I used to do that to her: my usual goodnight kiss to Judith and Richard. Did I do it to the other baby? She must have, for she links that sweet, ineffable smell with him. She remembers other things, too: the whorl of his damp, black hair – a shock, for she had thought babies were bald – and the fragility of his fingernails; his tiny heart beating against hers – a light, surprisingly rapid beat. Is it enough? No, of course not. Yet they are the memories that have sustained her, over and over, for seventy years.

Thirty-seven

Maggie glances down as she steels herself to knock on the door of Yard Cottage. She has dressed for battle, a neatly ironed blouse, a slash of lipstick, freshly brushed hair. Her age-old anger burns. Emotions she had thought were long since tidied away jab, jagged and insistent. Who would have thought that hatred could be reignited like this? That it hadn't been extinguished, but has smouldered like a forgotten ember over seventy years.

Her steeliness falters when Alice opens the door: old age is not treating her kindly.

'Alice,' she says, and sees apprehension cloud her face.

'You'd better come in,' the younger woman says, and then the words seem to spill from her. 'I'm glad you've come. There's so much I have to tell you. About why I'm here and what I've been up to. So much that I think you'll want to hear.'

She looks nervous and strangely excited, but then starts fussing, pouring a cup of tea that Maggie refuses, for she is not here to exchange pleasantries or to reminisce. They sit opposite one another at the kitchen table, Maggie ramrod straight, the fingers of her right hand striking the table lightly as if playing the piano. Up and down they run over five imaginary keys.

She watches the other woman now and tries to see in her the frightened thirteen-year-old of her memory. The eyes are the same, though a dulled blue now, with none of that wide-eyed wonder at life on the farm. She has filled out: still slim, but with hips that take her by surprise. I never knew her as a young woman – or even properly as a teenager, she thinks. She has been frozen in time: forever a skinny girl, racing down sand dunes, clambering down from caves, and hiding in the barn. Her slippery shadow. Just the thought of her watching them makes the anger bubble up.

'So. It's been seventy years.' She needs to start somewhere. 'Seventy years in April.'

'I left just after Easter, lambing had finished.' Alice doesn't mention the baby at all.

'I still think about him you know. My baby.'

There. It is out there. She fixes Alice with her eyes and her voice comes out almost as a whisper: 'I think about him every single day.'

She pauses. The emotion she has kept bottled up for all these years risks rushing out, like the tide swamping a rock pool. 'I know I should be grateful to you for getting him to safety but I never wanted him to be taken away.'

Alice opens her mouth as if to protest, but Maggie is determined to have her say. 'I think it's been worse because, when I've tried to look, there was no means of finding him. The nuns had no trace, no record: no proof that he'd even been there. And so I've been in limbo. Much as I've tried to hope, I've no idea if he even knows my name or if he has anything with which to find me.'

Her voice escalates now, the pain and panic rearing up as she tries to convey the tragedy of her life: both she and her child may long for one another, and yet, with no paper trail, they can never be linked. There is nothing to tie them: the skeins have been snapped, if they ever existed. Her son may not even know that he was adopted – or that she exists.

She pauses and looks at Alice, whose expression is darkening. A flush of red spreads from the centre of her cheeks. She seems even more nervous, and when she speaks it is so softly that Maggie wonders if she mishears.

'Everything is going to be OK – but I didn't take him to the orphanage.'

'What did you say?'

This time, Alice enunciates more clearly: 'I didn't take him to the orphanage.'

The room constricts and whirls.

'Then what did you do with him?' Her voice comes out as a dangerous hiss.

'I wanted to take him to Will, but the vet wouldn't let me.'

'Patrick Trescothick?' She is bemused.

'Yes...' Alice falters. 'I begged him, but he said Will wouldn't want him. He knew of another farm though: a couple who couldn't have a baby. He said they might take him if I ... *helped* him.'

'If you helped him?' None of this makes sense.

Alice looks down at her lap. 'He ... he tried to

320

... interfere with me. I thought that, if I went along with it, the baby would be safe.'

The room shifts. Alice is red now. Patrick Trescothick? It doesn't surprise her. He had tried to corner her in the stable, the August after her baby. 'Don't pretend that you're a good girl,' he had said. For a moment she feels a shot of compassion, but her sympathy is buffeted aside by this blast of new information: that her baby never went to the orphanage but was taken elsewhere. She still can't quite comprehend it.

'So who brought him up? Were they kind? And how did Patrick Trescothick know them?'

'I don't know.'

'You don't *know?*'

'I don't know anything about the family – or I didn't at the time.'

'You left him there, but you knew nothing about them? Whether they were good people? The sort of childhood he would have?' Her voice escalates with incredulity. She left him at an unknown farmhouse with no idea about the family, and she never thought to tell her that she had done this – or to look for him years later? The thought is inconceivable. She defied her mother's instructions, and then lied to Maggie. The nuns would 'look after him really well,' she had said. Or was that quite what she had said? She can see her now, looking at her as she sat, tracing the pattern of her eiderdown and feeling faint, in her bedroom. 'They'll look after him really well. I know they will,' she had said. 'They', not 'the nuns'. And Maggie had believed her because she couldn't afford not to believe.

Her anger surges. Alice has no way of knowing if he was well looked after. 'Try to remember what you can of these people.'

'They were moorland farmers, much poorer than your parents.'

'And the farmhouse?'

'It was to the west of Rough Tor, near St Breward. He *said* they would look after him.'

'And you believed him? Patrick Trescothick?' She waits, remembering his handling of Clover, and the way he cocked his gun at Will. The implicit threat when he blocked her exit in the stables. His smell: whisky, old tweed, and a muskiness she would later identify as sexual, but at the time she thought was sweat.

'I didn't have much choice.' Alice's voice rises, and for the first time, Maggie senses some fight in her; some resilience. Her hands are clenched into fists and she is sitting straight. 'It was a terrible mistake, but I am trying to right that wrong. I've found the farmhouse and the family's name, Jose, and the name of your son – Will's son. He was – is – called Jeremiah.' Her voice cracks with emotion. 'And I am going to find him, if it is the very last thing I do.'

Jeremiah. The name means nothing to Maggie: she cannot square it with the child of her imagination. Her anger pushes up: a physical knot that swells and threatens to overwhelm her so that she feels as if she will choke. She cannot speak to Alice with kindness, though she knows she was just a child, and a child assaulted by the vet, at that. At some level, she senses that she wants thanks for tracking this unfamiliar Jeremiah down – and yet she has just a name: no address, no child, no way of knowing if he is dead or alive, let alone in Cornwall or even Britain. And, had she done as she was asked, there would have been no need for this searching. Maggie might have been reunited with him many years ago.

Her fury is overriding now: pressing upon her so that she wants to spew out words of hatred. She needs to get away before Alice drops another bombshell – or she says something she will regret.

She stands up, and in her haste knocks over her chair.

'Please don't.' Alice comes forward, and for a moment she thinks she is just trying to stop her from correcting the furniture, but she puts her hands on Maggie's to stay her.

'Please don't go. There's more that I need to tell you,' she says.

Maggie glances down at the thin, wizened hands imposing themselves on hers – and Alice removes them instantly.

'I know that Will died,' Maggie tells her, gripping the side of the table, concentrating on keeping her voice steady. 'My mother told me. Years ago, when my late husband started courting me. I had hoped that I could find him. But she had heard years before from Mrs Eddy. And she took great delight in informing me of the fact.'

'Do you know how?'

'No. No details.' She looks at Alice now, almost daring her to tell. The other woman's eyes are filmed with tears. For a moment she catches a glimpse of the small, lost girl who arrived here.

She rights the chair, and sits back down.

Thirty-eight

Then: 30 June 1944, London

London was drab. Sticky, humid and dusty, with a dirty heat that seemed to belong to cities. Not the crisp dry heat of a cornfield, the air sweet with the heady smell of crushed straw.

Everywhere was concrete, brick or stone. Towering masses of grey and white – or piles of rubble. Over the river and to the east it was worse. Aunt Olive, in Battersea, had had her terrace flattened by a doodlebug, and Will, sent by Annie to help her, had struggled to find it. Forced into a crater, all that remained was wood, tiles, bricks, broken-up furniture and, before they were dug out by the ARP warden, the remains of the family next door.

He'd never seen anything like it in Cornwall. The odd house blown to smithereens; the bombing in Bodmin; the gates at Tredinnick blown off their hinges. A chicken, blasted of its feathers, or a cow blown to bits. He gulped down a laugh. Black humour: that's what it was, wasn't it? One of the things the British were meant to be good at, that was supposed to be getting them through all of this.

War came to Cornwall as it came everywhere else: the skies filled with the drone of the B17 bombers and B24 Liberators, or the sound of a

Messerschmidt; the streets with soft-shoed GIs, with their tanks and their preparations for what they now knew was D-Day – the invasion of France. And there had been casualties. He still thought of the twenty-one killed at St Eval, when a bomb bounced into a bunker where they were taking shelter. But there had been no destruction – and no insistent, nagging anxiety – on anything like this scale.

He climbed the steps to Waterloo Bridge and glanced to either side: downstream to St Paul's, its dome majestic against the destruction of the East End; upstream to the Houses of Parliament, vast and golden, the face of Big Ben glinting in the sun.

He was glad to be leaving here. Relieved – until he received Alice's letter that morning – that his call-up papers had arrived. In a couple of days he would be on his way to a training battalion in Wakefield, and after that, who knew where? Italy, North Africa, France? The Hun was on the run, it seemed, and he was finally going to play a part. No longer a farm boy, but a soldier: battle-weary, scared, exhilarated, perhaps even victorious. Trained to kill, not to grow and rear.

It had been a mistake to come back here, apart from seeing his mum, though she wasn't the Annie he remembered. And this wasn't home any more. The war had fractured the Cookes: William, though nearly forty, in Italy; Robert – now six and a half – in Hampshire; the girls in Cornwall; and Annie, freed of her brood and unrecognisable without a clutch of children, now working as an ARP warden.

Even if his family hadn't been forced apart,

London still wouldn't be home. His heart wasn't here. The happiest time of his life had been last summer – when the fields were ablaze with corn, and he and Maggie Retallick were in love. Nothing could compare to what he'd felt then: that sickness in the pit of his stomach that softened as soon as she smiled, and that incredible sense of being alive that made everything – colours, taste, smells – brighter. The way he'd felt when he'd watched a film in Technicolor – but multiplied a hundred times.

Just the thought of her brought a smile to his face, while the memory of her curves – that dip of her waist – made him tingle with excitement. For a moment, he let himself remember lying in a sand dune, his arms round her, his head resting on hers, listening to the skylarks and breathing in the fresh smell of her hair.

'What are you thinking?' she had asked, smiling up at him.

And he had made something up because he would have felt stupid telling the truth. That he wasn't thinking anything at all, but was feeling it. Sheer happiness. He had been happier than he ever imagined he could be.

The drone of a doodlebug overhead. A steady *vroom vroom vroom* like an insistent motorcycle driving at a steady speed. They made him jittery, these new bombs, though he knew he only needed to run for shelter if the engine cut out. You could count to twelve before it struck, according to those more experienced than him, more jaded, or more willing to chance it. It hadn't helped those killed at Victoria Station the week before last, nor the scores left dead the day after, as they said their prayers at the barrack chapel on Birdcage Walk.

He glanced above. It was still going: flying towards Holborn to destroy somewhere in Bloomsbury or north London. He let out his breath and felt only a brief twinge of guilt that the fact he was unscathed meant that someone else might be harmed. His heart was thudding now, like a bird stunning itself against a window. These V1 raids had been going on for over a fortnight, and still he couldn't get used to them.

He wiped beads of sweat from his cheeks and started walking faster. Perhaps he should just go straight there now? Down to Cornwall – a mad dash before reporting to his training battalion in Yorkshire tomorrow. Could he manage getting there and back? It would be reckless or – what was it Maggie would call it? – *spontaneous*. The thought – which had buzzed at the back of his mind ever since he'd received the letter – nudged at him, increasingly insistent. As if he could ever be that foolhardy or brave. As brave as she.

The Will who had kissed Maggie in the sea, who had made love to her in a hay barn with her mother in the house less than fifty yards away, might have done this. But the one who had been shouted at by Evelyn Retallick, her eyes like bullets? That Will could only go back if he was sure that Maggie would welcome him there. Because this changed things, this letter in his pocket... In his heart, he wanted to jump on a train and race down there, and yet his head told him that doing so was not just logistically impossible, but stupid.

She hadn't written – might not even want him back.

For there was a baby, the letter said. The thought terrified him, to be honest, and yet he felt just the tiniest leap of excitement at the same time. Maggie and he had made a baby. And now it had been sent away. Alice hadn't said where. She had just said that Maggie had had a baby in April; that Evelyn was cross – which must be a polite way of putting it – and that they'd given it up for adoption. The letter was brief and written from a different address, as if she was worried that someone would open it. Cryptic except for that last plea – before the lots of love and the string of kisses. *Please, Will. Can you help?*

He wanted to go down, straight away. The thought consumed him as he crossed the Strand and turned east in the direction of the Royal Courts of Justice. He had to find this child – perhaps living with some different family – and persuade the Retallicks that he and Maggie would not just love it, but could give it a home.

Even as he worked it out it seemed ridiculous. What if Maggie didn't want it? She was going to be a teacher, and if she'd wanted the baby then surely she'd have written to ask for his help? She could have found Farmer Eddy's address and contacted him from her aunt's in Bodmin. He'd only left Cornwall at the start of May: plenty of time for her to tell him she was pregnant, or to tell him that, yes, she loved him still.

But there'd been no word since he'd left Skylark. At times, he'd wondered if Mrs Eddy had refused to pass on any post – he'd had so very little. But she was a good woman, and he couldn't imagine her doing this, even if Evelyn had asked.

He had written to Maggie, of course, but with little hope that the letters would get through. And as the bitter winter progressed, it seemed that he might have been mistaken. She no longer cared for him. Perhaps she loved someone else?

The thought plagued him so that he was abrupt with the cows, and their milk yield dropped. Once, he had kicked the stable door in a fury, and the intensity of his anger had shocked him. He knew that he had to get away from Cornwall, right away. When his papers came, he was back in London, scraping together work as a messenger boy and dreaming of that golden summer at Skylark Farm.

A double-decker bus rumbled past, and he crossed the street, walking along the curve of the Aldwych. It was a mistake to return, however briefly. He no longer belonged here. He wanted to be back in Cornwall, with Maggie. His heart swelled at the thought of what she must have gone through, alone. He hoped he had done enough, in this letter. He had tried to be poetic. *I remember our swim,* he had written, *and how we felt then. I remember the sand dunes and the storm against the casement. You have always been there, and I for you.* Doubt crept in. Perhaps he should add a bit more to let her know quite how strongly he felt? The letter wasn't sealed, but he had tried so hard to write neatly, had been so conscious that he wanted to impress her, he didn't want to spoil it. Surely she would understand?

The Aldwych was busy. Late lunchtime, and the girls from the Air Ministry were returning to their office: the street was bustling. There was a queue outside the post office at Bush House, a line snaking from the door. The woman in front of him smiled, the stain of her red lipstick somehow shocking against the grey of her skin, the cut of her cheekbones.

'Do you have a light?' Her voice was hard, her eyes frank. She seemed older than him, though perhaps she only seemed that way because of her extreme thinness, or the way she held herself, as if she hadn't relaxed properly for a long time.

He shook his head.

'Well, this is a bore,' she drawled, turning her back on him and shuffling forwards.

Another drone, another doodlebug approaching, the noise getting louder as it flew lower and lower. But this time it happened: the engine cut out.

A moment's silence – then 'Run!' He didn't know who screamed it, for several people seemed rooted in the queue.

He grabbed the woman and pushed her inside Bush House.

'There's no need to shove...' she began, but he wasn't listening – too distracted by the silvery swoosh of the falling bomb.

The force of the others powered them in. Crouched down, head shielded, he started counting: nine, ten. Images of Maggie cascaded: her hair, her smile, her laugh. Eleven, twelve. She will never know how much I love her, he thought, as he heard the *cruummmpppp:* the sickening thud as the bomb exploded, blowing the windows into slivers, peppering the walls with shrapnel, blasting bodies through the swing doors.

A woman landed in a heap by the table beside him: a sack of clothes, coated in glass, she started to cry loudly.

'Are you OK?' he called to her. Beside him, the lipsticked woman swore, her voice trembling, then managed to stumble up.

He moved through the billowing smoke to the first woman.

'Just bruised, I think,' she whimpered, stretching her legs as she tried to stem her tears. 'We were lucky.'

'Luckier than those.' He gestured towards the street, through the smoke billowing in from the blasted window.

In the smog outside, it seemed to be November: a mist had descended and a plume of smoke spiralled above the junction with Kingsway. The street was strewn with bodies: flung against the building, lying, crumpled, in piles.

No one seemed to be moving – though to the left of him, through the smoke, further away from the bomb and its crater, he could hear an eerie moaning. Loud moaning was a good thing, he had learned in his brief time back in London. It was when people moaned quietly that you feared the worst.

He made his way towards the sound, the dust thick in his throat, past banknotes floating down the street and a double-decker bus wrenched open like a sardine tin. Leaves had been stripped from the trees opposite – but something else was hanging there. He peered, and then retched, his stomach opening out onto the pavement. It was flesh, blown from limbs.

He was alive, though, wasn't he? He was *alive*. The thought burned as he groped his way through the smoke and down towards a voice that was crying. He had another chance. A curious hysteria took him over. He would go straight to Cornwall to see Maggie. Bugger the consequences. Would tell her immediately: that he loved her; and wanted her, and their child.

The moans seemed louder now, and for a moment he didn't hear the silvery whoosh of the glass window. Nor did he see it as it slipped from the fourth storey of the building, sharp and lethal, glinting in the sun.

It fell like a stone: straight and forensic, intent on dissection – and neatly sliced him in two.

Thirty-nine

Now: 23 August 2014

Maggie takes to her bed when she comes back from Yard Cottage. It is so unlike her that Lucy knows something is terribly wrong.

She knocks, then pushes open her bedroom door. Her grandmother is lying there, covers pulled up to her chin, face drained of colour and the skin pulled tight over her cheekbones. It is almost as if she is looking at a corpse.

'Granny?' Lucy perches on the edge of the bed and reaches for fingers that are as light and dry as bones.

'I found out how he died.' Maggie turns to her. 'Will – not the baby, though he may be dead as well, for all I know. He was hit by a sheet of falling glass... It happened in the Aldwych, of all places.' Her crisp, deliberate tone slips just a little. 'He had sheltered when the bomb was falling – and was only hit when he came out.'

'I'm so sorry...' Lucy starts, but her grandmother doesn't seem to be listening. The words are tumbling out.

'He had just turned eighteen. About to join up. Two days before setting off for training. It was only six weeks after he left Cornwall. Ten weeks after his son was born.'

For the smallest moment Maggie's mouth contorts and wobbles. It is over as quickly as it happens: this soundless howl. When Lucy next looks, her eyes have hardened into pips that gleam dark against her skin and the white of the pillow, and it is anger Lucy sees as much as loss.

She waits, wondering if she can ask about the baby. He may be dead as well, for all I know. She finds herself praying that this isn't so.

'Could she tell you anything about the baby?'

'Oh yes.' Maggie gives an odd, bitter laugh that is quite unlike her. 'She had quite a lot to tell me about the baby. About someone called Jeremiah.'

She is shaking, now, with what appears to be a potent mix of anger and grief, and her eyes have a fierceness to them.

'She never took him to the orphanage. She took him to another couple, somewhere on the other side of Rough Tor. She just left him – a tiny baby – with no idea of how he would be looked after, and no means of me tracing him.'

She pauses for a moment.

'I find it hard to forgive her for that,' she says. 'For just abandoning him there, and for not telling me earlier.' She looks at her granddaughter. 'If she'd told me then, or back in my twenties or thirties, I'd have scoured the moor for him. I'd have looked for a child his age, and I wouldn't have given up until I'd found him. I could have done so if she'd told me fifty years ago.'

'Did she say why she is here now? Apart from to tell you this?'

'Oh. She's here to find him!'

'But that's wonderful.'

'And what are the odds of that happening?' Maggie snorts. 'She has a name, but no correct address. No means of knowing if he's in Cornwall or anywhere else in the world for that matter. She doesn't even have any proof that he's alive. He's not dead, according to the records in Cornwall. But that doesn't mean he isn't elsewhere.'

'We could search together. I could help her.' Lucy glows with optimism. 'You told me not to live with regret, don't you remember? This is your chance not to do so: to make everything OK.'

'My dear Lucy.' Her grandmother looks at her, sadly. 'It's just too late, don't you see? I'm an old lady. And though I can't think of anything more wonderful than finding him, I couldn't cope with the disappointment of not doing so – or of discovering him and finding that he doesn't want to know me.'

She pauses and strokes the eiderdown, her eyes welling with tears before she wipes them away,

334

savagely. She is right, thinks Lucy. She is an elderly woman, and has almost run out of time.

If she thinks her grandmother will accept this quietly, though, she is mistaken.

'I cannot forgive her for telling me the truth so very late,' Maggie says, her voice starting to tremble. 'And I cannot forgive her for killing off my hope: the thing that has kept me going all these years.

'I've been imagining him walking around the headland, you see, or over the cliff path. But now I know he will never come walking up the track, to find me at my spot under the crab apple. He will never come searching for me.'

Lucy bends to kiss the top of Maggie's head, feeling her dry grey hair underneath her lips and the scalp below, as vulnerable as a baby's. And though she wants to reassure her that there are plenty of other reasons to keep living – not least her family and the farm, which has sustained her, despite all its difficulties – she knows that her grandmother speaks the truth. The possibility of meeting her son is the reason she has clung so tenaciously to life.

'Was there something you wanted from me, anyway, when you came in?' Maggie looks up as she clasps her hand, makes an effort to talk more brightly.

Lucy grimaces. 'I should think it's the last thing you'll want to hear at the moment ... Uncle Richard has just arrived.'

'I see.' Maggie lets out her breath.

'Mum phoned him last night. Don't worry. She didn't tell him about the baby: she was just furious about him putting in that planning application without telling us.' She thinks of the laminated notice Tom found, nailed to the gate, yesterday. 'Just discovering the lay of the land,' Richard had said when Judith rang, incensed.

'She's angry about the pressure he's putting on us too, particularly if this ice cream idea works out, and particularly because of your reasons for wanting to stay here. I think she wanted to have it out with him, face to face.'

'Well, that's sensible,' Maggie says.

'They're talking about it, downstairs.'

'Ah. Then perhaps I should join them.'

'Can you face it?'

'Not particularly. But this is my farm and I will not be sidelined. Besides, I need to tell him about the baby, don't I?'

She fixes a smile on her face. 'Give me a few minutes to think things through and put myself back together. And then I'll come downstairs.'

He doesn't take it well.

'A baby?' Richard's face twists in incredulity. 'Before you had Judith?' He glances at his sister. 'Did you know about this?'

'Not before yesterday,' Judith says. 'Don't look like that, Richard. Poor Mum's had to keep this to herself all these years. Believe me, no one's been keeping you in the dark about this.'

'Well *she* has,' he says, and for a moment he is a petulant schoolboy: a child who would protest that something wasn't fair, that she favoured his sister. His face folds in on itself, almost glowering in a bloom of rage. She doesn't feel threatened, but sad: for his look recalls past injustices, more imagined than real, and all those times she automatically blamed him – the boisterous, accident-prone boy who'd rush into things, not his more considered older sister. It pains her: his flushed cheeks and eyes flickering from her to Judith as if he thinks he will get some sense from her.

She offers her explanation: she was young, she was in love, it was a huge stigma, she never told them because there seemed no need to distress them. It was her only secret, kept tight all these years.

'No wonder you were always so harsh on me.' He is calming down now – the accusation stated as fact, though it still takes her by surprise.

'Was I?' She knows the answer.

'Always. I just thought you were hard on me because I was a boy.'

'You could be very difficult,' says Judith. 'Do you remember when you let the sheep out and chased them towards Padstow? Or when you camped out in the cave for the night and never told us, and Mum was convinced you'd drowned?'

But Maggie stops her. 'No. You're right. I was too strict with you. Too unforgiving.' She shrugs: an inadequate gesture of admission. 'Perhaps this was part of the reason. I'm very sorry if it is.'

She remembers a frequent feeling of irritation that he couldn't be more like Judith, and a niggling conviction that her other boy might have been very different from this one. How many times had she imagined how *he* might have behaved differently from this known, fallible boy? At Richard's most difficult – his late teenage years when he made it clear that he wanted nothing to do with the farm or with Cornwall – she would idealise her firstborn and, irrationally, wonder if this was her punishment. She had rejected one son and now the other was rejecting her.

She moves towards this big, bruised man, who is now leaning forwards, elbows on knees, head in hands as if trying to hide from her. She doesn't do hugs, but she wants to touch him, now. She lays a hand on his shoulder and gives it a tentative pat, feeling the warmth of his bulk. And then he surprises her, putting an arm round her legs and turning towards her: folding himself into her as he did as a child.

It is brief, this clutch, five seconds at most, but it is ferocious. She stands there, looking down at his head – a thick mass of hair like her father's, now sprinkled with grey. And she finds she is reaching out and running her hand over his head, as she did when he was a boy. Her heart swells. How long is it since he has shown affection like this? Not the dutiful hug he gives when he leaves, but this heartfelt gesture that he needs her. That, for all his bulldozing of her opinion and his bluffness, he does love her after all.

He draws away, rubs a hand over his face, clears his throat – for it seems this has been a sufficient display of emotion. He smiles, and his voice, a little hoarse, is more reasonable. 'And is this the reason you want to stay here?'

'Not entirely,' she says, as she sits next to him. 'It's my home and I'm tired. I want to stay here until I die. After that, I know I can't control what happens, though I'd love it to continue as a working farm.'

He looks deflated. His shoulders hunch around him, and he fiddles with his wedding ring, twisting it around his marriage finger – just as Evelyn did when she was nervous or at a loss for what to say.

'I've no desire to push you into anything. I was just trying to be practical: to look at other options that would allow you to stay here but lift the financial burden from you. Perhaps I got over-enthusiastic. Hard not to when you realise how much we could make from a development.'

'I don't want to live on a sanitised, non-working farm.' She feels her chest tighten: the words come out taut and cold.

'I can see that – and Judith's told me about the interest in the ice cream. The order from Kernow's is impressive. If we can get a commitment to that in writing, I'd like to invest: purchase the ice cream-making equipment; pay for the refurbishment of the old cowshed as a kitchen.' He smiles, and though she senses a touch of resignation there, a sadness that a lucrative development won't be in the offing in the immediate future, she can see that he is trying.

'Thank you,' she says. 'We'd appreciate it.'

Forty

Her grandmother's lost baby worms his way into Lucy's thoughts as she does the early milking and as she bakes and serves the customers: a solid stream of holidaymakers who climb the cliff and clamour for ice cream. He obsesses her, this Jeremiah: running and crawling from a grimy kitchen, then growing into a muddied schoolboy, all scabbed knees and crumpled socks beneath baggy grey shorts like a Cornish Just William.

This imaginary boy is there at Ava's bath time, as she pours streams of water down her niece's back, puts a wind-up frog in the bath and watches her scrutinise it. Was it a weekly tin bath that he had in his house, high on the moor?

'Ava swim?' says the little girl and, before she can stop her, plunges her head in.

'Ava – no.'

The front of her hair is soaked, but the toddler doesn't care.

'Oh. Well, I don't suppose it matters.'

Her niece repeats the process, blowing fat bubbles through the water and laughing in delight.

Did he do that, this Jeremiah? Or this? She floats two plastic yellow ducks, which her niece picks up automatically, then drops with a flat and satisfying splat. The toddler smacks the water, delighting in the sound that echoes around the bathroom and laughing with that gurgle peculiar to small children. Did Jeremiah laugh like that as a boy? She no longer sees Jacob Wright the whole time – though the guilt is still there: a dull ache, now not a gut-wrenching pain – but this boy of the fifties; this never-known, phantom child.

Lost love can be so painful. That and wondering what might have been. Never having the chance to discover. Her grandmother's warning whirls around her head as she mulls over her lost son and dwells on Maggie's regret. Her grandmother believes she has left it too late to risk not finding him, at eighty-eight. But Lucy has a future ahead of her in which to live life to the full, and to try and glean as much happiness as she can. Hasn't her father's suicide taught her that as well? That life is to be grasped, and any possibility of joy recognised and clung on to, not discarded, for there will always be darkness and the threat of too much darkness, here.

Ava starts to pour water from one cup to another, entranced by the ribbon of liquid, the slosh of the water.

'Oosey!' Her dark chocolate eyes – her grandfather's eyes – blaze with curiosity, and the wonder that comes of being not yet two and seeing the world afresh.

She wants to eat her up. Or at least to share this hope: this pure, uncomplicated excitement at life. Impossible for someone thirty years older, but oh! How she craves a taste of it.

She is supposed to return to work in three weeks, though the idea seems unreal, something that will happen to a different Lucy. Summer is ending; autumn inching closer, its presence felt in the crispness of the evening air. She needs to talk to Matt, and to speak to him, properly, face to face. To see if there is a hope of happiness, still, in their relationship, so that she never feels the nagging pull of regret that consumes her grandmother.

Time to make some decisions in her life.

Almost as soon as he arrives it is clear it is a mistake. He doesn't turn up until after midnight on the Friday and, despite her best intentions, she has slipped into sleep.

Her mobile doesn't work in her bedroom, and it takes a while for her to realise that someone is at the door.

'Bloody hell,' she hears Tom swear as she emerges from her bedroom and scurries along the corridor.

'It's all right; I've got it,' she says through his door. 'Sorry.' As she races along the flagstone hallway, the bell rings again.

Matt is standing there, managing to look both apologetic and a little indignant.

'Sorry to ring – but I've been waiting here fifteen minutes. Didn't you hear your phone?'

'It doesn't work in the house. I thought I'd told you?' She can only get a signal in the top field: something she thought she had mentioned, but he has obviously not taken in. She smiles, trying to be conciliatory, for this is the first time they have met since they parted, in late June, and she doesn't want his visit to start badly. Still, she is surprised his self-righteousness has emerged this early. Surely he should be the one trying to make amends?

He evidently realises he should be trying harder. From behind his back, he pulls a bouquet of burgundy peonies tied with grosgrain ribbon: the florist is a designer one in west London, the flowers a sumptuous, glossy red. Her heart aches a little at the gesture, and then at how he could have got her so wrong. This morning, she had filled a jug with cornflowers, knapweed and rosebay willowherb, broken up with fronds of feathery grasses. And she had thought there could be nothing more beautiful than them.

He reaches for her, and she expects a hug, perhaps a chaste peck on the cheek, but his mouth brushes the edge of hers. She springs away, unsettled.

'Sorry. Bit soon,' she mutters.

'No, fine. Of course.' He looks down, awkward, but not before she sees disappointment cloud his eyes.

'I could do with a hug, though.' She must make some effort, and she finds she wants to hold him, to see if she remembers. His body feels slim and wiry, and his smell is the same – mint, washing powder and warmed skin.

It is all so familiar, and yet she wants to wriggle free. Someone else has held him more recently: felt these arms round her, breathed in the scent of his neck. It's over with Suzi, she reminds herself. But had he really wanted that? He had crossed a line with someone other than her. Her limbs, recently soft with sleep, become stiff, almost rigid, and she finds herself pulling away.

In her bedroom, he tries to kiss her again, his mouth fluttering over hers like a moth beating against a lampshade. But it's all too much: Suzi – her legs, her mouth, her imagined cry – keeps crowding into her mind.

'I can't tonight.' She shifts away, gentle yet emphatically. She had intended that he sleep in the spare room, but somehow he is in bed with her, here.

'There's so much to talk about. We can't just rush back in to it,' she finds herself trying to explain.

'No?' He props himself up on one elbow, the lines between his eyes furrowing into a deep V.

'No. I'm still confused. I need to believe that it can work: that you won't do it again.'

He sighs. 'Why would I do that?'

'Because you did before.'

'But I've learned from that mistake. Besides,' he risks stroking her cheek, his hand trailing to her shoulder before skirting her breast. 'It would be different this time. We'd know where we went wrong, what we needed to do to avoid it. Make time for each other. Make sure we don't bring work home. Have sex–' He shoots her a different look then. 'I've missed you: far more than I thought I would, to be honest. And I'm not going to do anything to risk losing you again.'

She is silent, not knowing what to think. Had he missed her? Then why the five-week delay before phoning? She does not know what to say.

'I promise we'll talk properly, but can it be tomorrow?' She reaches for a practical reason. 'It's just I've got to be up in less than five hours' time to do the milking.'

'Can't they give you the weekend off?' He looks

344

disgruntled, the Matt who doesn't like the farm, or understand farming, all too clear.

'Cows don't take the weekend off. Tom'll do it on Sunday.' She pauses, taking in his evident disappointment. 'I'm sorry.'

'Well, you'll have tomorrow off?'

'We can do something in the morning, but I'll have to work in the afternoon. We get most of our customers on a Saturday. Last week I did over thirty cream teas.' She stifles a yawn, her exhaustion suddenly overwhelming. 'Perhaps you could help me – or just chill? The weather will be glorious, and there are some lovely walks.' He looks unconvinced, and she doesn't know what else she can offer. 'I know we need to talk and to try and make things better, but I'm sorry, I really do need to get some sleep.'

He lies on his back and stares at the ceiling, hurt pulsing off him.

'You won't be working tomorrow evening?'

'No, of course not.'

'So we can go out for dinner?'

'That would be lovely.'

Contrite, she rolls towards him and offers a smile – but no kiss. Then she turns her back, feeling as if she has been unreasonable, but craving the oblivion of sleep. An arm hangs over her waist, surprisingly heavy, and within stroking distance of her breast. He falls asleep quickly, but she lies, tense and wired, wanting to shrug his hand away, resenting his touch. It is only once his breathing deepens that she can slide away from him and slip into a fitful sleep.

She has been up for three and a half hours by the time he emerges the next morning. The cows have been milked, and she is giving Field Cottage a quick check over before the new guests arrive later that day.

She catches a glimpse of Alice, shaking bread-crumbs out for the birds in the garden, but the old woman scuttles into her kitchen when she sees Lucy glancing across. She looks nervous, and she is not surprised, for her grandmother can be for-midable when angry. She pauses on Yard Cottage's doorstep. She doesn't blame Maggie for refusing to listen to all she had to say, and yet it seems a wasted opportunity. Alice might have been able to tell her more about her search for Jeremiah, she is sure of it. If only she was willing to hear.

'I thought we could go for a walk on the beach?' Matt's voice cuts through her thoughts. He looks different. On his feet are pristine navy blue Hunter wellingtons with not one speck of mud on them.

'You bought some.' She gestures, suppressing the desire to smile, for he is making an effort. 'They suit you.'

'Do you think so? I'm not sure they're really me.'

'They're very you.' In his glossy wellies, skinny jeans, neat T-shirt and slim-fitting tweed jacket, he looks exactly what he is: an advertising creative playing at being a country gent. Topped with his heavy-rimmed glasses and two-day-old stubble, he looks as if he should be staying in a boutique B&B while attending a festival. He is, as Tom might say, a right townie.

'So – the beach?'

346

'Great!' She feels a sudden rush of warmth. Perhaps this will be OK. 'I need to be back for midday to bake some scones, but I'm all yours before then.'

'Two and a half hours?' He glances at his watch, peeved.

'Well, we'd better make the most of it, then.'

Try to make an effort, she reminds herself, as they march on down to the beach, and she hears herself chattering away to him in that relentlessly chirpy tone she never uses for anyone else. She reaches for his hand and swings it, but they have never been a hand-holding couple, and she quickly drops it again.

He pulls her to him for a quick hug, but that doesn't work either and, self-conscious, they break away. Soon, they find their rhythm: him walking in front, once the track narrows towards the sand dunes, her a couple of paces behind him. We have always been better like this, she thinks. Each in our own space.

Matt walks quickly, and as he strides on, legs out of kilter with hers, she compares theirs to her parents' marriage. Despite Fred's occasional dark moods, it was a good one: both trying to support one another and ease each other's workload as they brought up their young family and ran the farm.

They were easy in each other's company, too, and there was a definite spark. A memory of Fred taking out his silver trumpet and serenading Judith with some Miles Davis flits through her mind. 'Fred the Lips' he'd been called, when he'd played in the local silver band, and Judith had teased him: 'You've still got it, Fred the Lips.' 'I'll give you Fred the Lips,' he had roared, and chased her from the room, pouting grotesquely, before giving her a smacking kiss.

The teenage Lucy had rolled her eyes at Tom. It was clear theirs was a passionate marriage and, though the thought of them doing *that* made her cringe with embarrassment, as she grew older she sensed that this was something to replicate.

But perhaps they were too hard an act to follow. She cannot fabricate that unquestioning love and trust with Matt. Not any more. Not since Suzi, who blew the artifice of their marriage apart. *Perhaps it's for the best* he had said, as he'd left; and his comment keeps coming back at her, popping up whenever she finds herself almost believing it is possible. For it was the catalyst that has made her reappraise just what she wants in life.

They have reached the beach now. The tide is half out so that the sand dimples with silver and a windsurfer criss-crosses the fine strip of blue between the opposite bay and the sandbank with breathtaking ease. On the opposite cliff, a tractor prowls: a neighbouring farm baling his corn in an elaborate quadrille. In the field behind, cows amble through the grass, tails flicking away blue-bottles, heads dipping as they replenish them-selves before the four o'clock milking.

'It's gorgeous, isn't it?'

'It's all right,' he says. 'If only it would stay this way.'

'Oh, I don't know. I almost love it more on crisp days in the winter when the beach is empty and the sea rough, or whenever there's a gale

348

blowing. Anyway, are you coming for a paddle?'
She scrunches her toes into the soft sand, enjoying the warmth and, as she sinks deeper, the
silvery cool and then wet.

He looks down at his wellingtons.

'I'll paddle in these, I think. Can't bear the faff
of sand between the toes – and the palaver of
getting these back on again.'

She laughs, but of course he's not joking, and as
they stride out, she is corroded by sadness: sand
between the toes is what life should be about, isn't
it? Her throat catches, and she realises that if she
tries to talk, she will cry. It hits her, with utter certainty, that if she wants to be with Matt it will
mean relinquishing all of this: the rhythm of this
life. Its harshness, but also its sheer physical
beauty.

The tide laps around her toes and she breathes
in the sweet, salty air, fresh off the Atlantic, and
imagines it plunging deep inside her body, filling
her lungs, giving her strength. She could never
capture this smell in London: the fug of exhausts,
fried food, strong coffee and other bodies con-
suming her instead. She wants to bottle it, this
potent cocktail of discrete flavours – for there is
seagrass and gorse there too, and further up the
beach, just a tang of silage – that sum up this
place.

'Happy?' Matt calls to her – and, yes she is.
Standing here, drawing on this loveliness. But it
has absolutely nothing to do with him.

Later, much later, they finally make it out into
Padstow. Matt has booked a table at the upmarket

349

fish restaurant where Flo works, and where the prices make Lucy wince with anxiety; and she suggests a drink at The Wreckers on the way. A bit of Dutch courage, she thinks, for she knows that they will have to talk about their marriage properly – not just skirt around the issue as they did this morning, when she filled him in on her father's suicide, and her grandmother's secret. Besides, alcohol always helps her behave more amorously.

It is a glorious evening. The sun bathes the clouds in gold: the periwinkle sky has long since faded. The fishing boats bob in the harbour: all is safely gathered in. The debris of the day – the fish and chip wrappings, the melted ice creams, the broken crab lines – have been cleaned up so that what is on show is a sanitised Padstow, like the town her grandmother knew as a girl. Even the travellers who sell hair braids and loom bands around the harbour, to the consternation of the town council, have quietly ebbed away.

The tables outside the Wreckers are filled with holidaymakers enjoying a warm evening. Everywhere there are golden retrievers, and families who are smiling out of sheer relief at having fought their way down the M4, M5 and A30, and finally got to Cornwall for the bank holiday weekend. Matt watches them, as he sips his pint, and she knows that he is wondering how to bottle this goodwill and to express it in an advert. There is a look of detached amusement on his face.

He is not unattractive, this man who is her husband. In fact, she has always thought of him as good-looking in a neat, urban, almost feminine way. Of course, he is very different to the men she

350

was brought up with. And that was part of his attraction. A boyfriend who wore modish glasses and mustard cardigans, whose skin remained alabaster, because he preferred to spend his days in bars and galleries, shops and cinemas, fitted in with her vision of what an urban boyfriend should be.

If she'd wanted a farm boy or a surf dude, she might as well have stayed in Cornwall, she told herself. He was a type: the type that belonged to the world of PR, advertising and magazines. And being with him was an education: he might not want to explore the UK outside the M25, but he introduced her to the hip cities of Europe. She took more easyJet flights than First Great Western trains.

And all this was wonderful, of course it was, until Fred died, when it suddenly all felt rather irrelevant. But then Matt got her through those first weeks after his death. And when he proposed, six months later, she threw herself into planning the wedding with a certainty she hadn't experienced since that terrible phone call from her mother. Here was a future: something positive and hopeful, the perfect distraction from her distress.

It was an impulsive decision, she knows that now. A panicked one born out of a sorrow she had never before experienced; and a desire not to obsess about her dad's gashed and bloated body, offered up by the sea five days after his death. There had been a moment, a week before the wedding, when Tom had rung and asked if she was sure this was what she wanted. And she had been so scared of being derailed – of having to think about what she really wanted – that she had put the phone down on him.

She looks up and catches Matt's eye. He raises a quizzical eyebrow.

'So...' she begins but she doesn't get any further. Ben Jose is ambling out of The Wreckers, a beer bottle in one hand, talking to a man who she recognises as his younger brother. She spots him out of the corner of her eye and refuses to look at him, but her train of thought is gone. A hot flush creeps up her neck.

'Hey, Lucy!'

Bugger. She glances at Matt and winces in apology, then half-smiles at Ben.

'Are you all right?' He stands there, glancing from her to Matt. His long, tanned fingers, lightly holding the beer bottle, are inches from her lips.

'Ben, this is my husband, Matt. Matt, this is Ben – you know, who I told you about? Who's going to buy our ice cream?'

The two men nod to one another, checking each other out. She wonders what Ben makes of her husband and realises that, to her acute shame, she'd rather not know.

'So have you done any more swimming recently?' Ben breaks the heavy silence.

'No,' she says, painfully aware of Matt watching. 'I haven't had time. Besides, the tide's wrong, at the moment, for a cove swim.'

'I got into trouble swimming,' she finds herself explaining to her husband. 'And Ben kindly helped me out.'

'Ah. It was nothing. I'm sure you'd have been fine.'

'How serious was it?' Matt is bemused.

'Oh, not very... It wasn't worth worrying you,' she backtracks, feeling as if she has kept a secret from him.

'Right. Well – take care of yourself.' Ben stretches out his spare hand as if to touch her shoulder, then drops it without making contact. He smiles at Matt as if to compensate. 'Nice to meet you. Perhaps we'll be seeing more of you down here?'

There is another pause, painful in the extreme.

Matt gives a grunt that could be interpreted as a yes or a no and a non-committal nod.

'So. Who was he?' Matt comes straight to the point as they walk from The Wreckers towards The Fish Shed, the restaurant Matt has chosen. The sun has set now, and the temperature has dropped. There is a crisp nip in the air.

She reaches for his hand and he gives it a quick squeeze, then releases it and hooks his thumbs in his pockets. The distance between them feels impassable, though in reality it is no more than two feet.

'I told you. Tom's old school friend, who farms at Tredinnick. The one who's introduced us to Alex, who wants to sell our ice cream.' Her voice, high-pitched, strains to convince.

'Well, he certainly seems interested in you.'

'Don't be stupid.'

'And I think you know it.' His tone is amused, but it masks an edge.

'Matt...' They have reached the restaurant now, and she stops walking. 'He's an acquaintance: a

353

business contact. There's nothing going on with him. Besides which, you're hardly in a position to judge.' The pain spills out, despite her best attempts to control it. 'I'm not the one who shagged a colleague!'

'We're never going to get beyond that, are we?'

He looks at her – all pretence that they will remain entirely civilised blown away.

'I don't know,' she says, and her voice is thick with tears. 'I just don't know any more. I don't know about anything. But at the moment, I doubt it.'

The meal, of course, feels strained and dissonant: like a piece of music in which one instrument – a second violin, perhaps – persists in a different key.

'Well, this is nice,' she tries, as she searches for the least expensive item on a menu boasting pan-fried sea bass on a celeriac purée; roasted hake with potato fondant; pan-seared scallops with pancetta; langoustines with a Bloody Mary espuma and celery sorbet.

She finds a mushroom risotto drizzled with truffle oil.

'This is a fish restaurant. You're supposed to have seafood,' says Matt. His eyes skim the list and he chooses quickly, as he always does: no room for indecision. 'I'm having the turbot and, to start, the bouillabaisse.'

'Well, OK, then,' she says, scanning the price list. 'I'll have the salmon.'

'And for a starter?'

'Oh – shall we just skip them?' She wants to cut this meal short; be anywhere but here.

His face falls. 'I was looking forward to the bouillabaisse.'

'OK – a tomato salad, then, with a basil *jus*.' She shuts her menu and looks around for a waiter, eager to hurry the meal along or, at least, to change the subject.

Flo, apron tied tightly round her neat waist, her hair in a high ponytail, comes over to them. Lucy's embarrassment escalates further. The white damask tablecloths, the gleaming wine glasses, the polished cutlery, the bill that will top a hundred pounds easily: these are all at odds with the farm's financial difficulties; at odds with the world she inhabits – and where she feels at home.

Given the right company, she would be far happier perched on the top of a sand dune, the tide rolling towards her, with a bag of fish and chips and a takeaway cup of tea. In fact, she realises, and the shock makes her look down into her lap so that Matt won't see her expression, she would be far happier doing that on her own.

'Hello, Matt. Wondered how long you would stay away,' Flo says, her smile light and seemingly innocent. 'Lovely to have you down.'

'Thank you,' Matt says, and Lucy can see him wondering whether he is really welcome at all.

He spends the starter and main course detailing his excuses for his affair. He felt lonely when Lucy did night shifts, shut out when she was so evidently preoccupied with her patients. Of course it wasn't right, but he missed the old Lucy – the one who didn't bring her work home with her; who put him first for a change. Perhaps they

355

both need to make more of an effort with each other, he said. Realise that they have something worth keeping and try to find a way forwards from here.

She nods, smiles, bites backs the retorts that keep rising, unbidden– But of course I was pre-occupied when there were babies dying. Notices that he doesn't mention love or even acknow-ledge her pain. As she eats her salmon without tasting it, she plays along with the idea that in a fortnight she would be back at the hospital, caring for the babies she is terrified of hurting. That life could continue with her back in London. That she could pick up from where she left off: back in his life, back in his bed.

Just the once she mentions her fear of returning to nursing.

'Oh don't be ridiculous.' He is dismissive, barely seems to hear her. 'Nothing happened to the baby in the end, did it? You probably needn't even have mentioned it: just you being ultra-conscientious again.'

She swallows, pushing the memory of the wrong infusion from her mind. Agrees that, when she returns, perhaps they should reinstate date nights.

Yet even as she plays along with this, she knows she is spinning a yarn. She sees herself running to the Tube, incubating babies, administering in-fusions – and it is as if she is watching a character in a film. Fiddling with the cutlery, she looks at her hands, bronzed against the white damask, and sees that they are no longer the hands of someone who works in a sterile environment: who inserts cannulas into minute veins; who lifts limbs so slight she fears they will break at the touch. Her nails are clean, but a trace of earth is caught in the nick of a cuticle.

She sustains the fiction throughout the meal as they quaff a Chablis and share a raspberry semifreddo that is not a patch on Tom's. She orders a double espresso – the need to be responsive and not to plead tiredness suddenly important if she is make one last attempt to convince herself that they can stay married.

When they make love – at her initiation – it is as if she is watching that character in a film, once again. The real Lucy sees her body-double make the right moves, utter the right noises, lick and bite and suck and kiss. As her mouth snakes down his stomach, she wonders at him being so easily fooled, and then she looks up and catches his eyes, pools of tender darkness widening as she inches down. Sadness and guilt well, and she closes her eyes so as not to see him. In trying to make things better, she has only deceived him more.

'All good for you?' he asks afterwards as he spoons around her body. They have always fitted better together when lying down, though his neatness has always made her feel too ample: as if he needs a more androgynous wife.

'Lovely,' she says. And she turns her head into the pillow so that he won't see her silent tears.

Forty-one

She sleeps fitfully and, at a quarter to six, when she hears Tom's heavy tread along the landing, she slips quietly from her bed.

The milking parlour is cold at this time of the morning, the lights brutal after the gentle dawn of the farmyard. But she feels almost wired as she sidles up to her brother and accepts a mug of strong tea.

'Couldn't sleep?' He takes a final gulp from his mug and gestures that she should hurry up and drink hers. Outside, the heavy yielders – the cows that have had their calves most recently and will produce the greatest amount of milk – are waiting to be herded into their stalls for the milking to begin.

'Something like that,' she says and sips her drink, almost orange in colour and sweet with a spoonful of sugar. 'That's rank.'

'Thought you might need some energy.'

She wonders if he heard them, though the walls are thick, but his expression is unreadable. She nods, suddenly bad-tempered.

'Shall we just get on with it?'

The cows file into their stalls: two lines of nine flanking the sides of the herringbone parlour. Tom guides them in with a cry of 'home, home, home', while she sprays their udders with iodine and fits the quartet of cups to each teat. The feed

358

rattles down the hoppers and the cattle lower their heads. The milk drips down the tubes. The next two lines are ushered in.

There is something so reassuring about this, she realises: this endless cycle of creation and recreation that will carry on despite individual cows dying. Despite, even, the horror of their dad's death. It soothes her, this continuity: the rhythm grounding her like the steady beat of a heart. In London, the beat is light and quick: a flutter that peaks then falls, uttering her up, unable to sustain her. She breathes in the rich stench of manure and warm cow; of hay and ammonia. She *is* Skylark. She belongs here.

'You all right?'

Tom, back from leading the next line of cows, poses the question, looking uncomfortable. 'Just found a text from Flo last night at the restaurant... She wasn't spying ... but she said it didn't look as if you were having that good a time?'

She shakes her head, infuriated yet touched that they are concerned with her well-being. Her eyes smart with tears.

'Lucy.' Tom puts down the hose he had picked up to sluice the floor, and turns to face her. 'What are you doing with him?'

'Not sure I'm going to be with him much longer.' It is the first time she has articulated this.

'Really?' He raises an eyebrow.

'I just don't think I can do any of it any more – my marriage, London, my career.' He pulls her towards him and she finds herself crying, buried away in the safety of his chest. She smells straw and manure and the distinct scent of Petherick male that reminds her so much of her father. For one long moment, she lets herself believe that she is being held by him.

Eventually she pulls away, wipes her nose with the back of her sleeve and tries to get a grip.

'I keep thinking of Granny's advice. She warned me about regret: not grabbing a second chance if I was offered it. *Lost love can be so painful. That and wondering what might have been.* That's what she said. She was talking about her first love, and the baby that was taken away. But I can't make her feelings fit with mine for Matt. I can't love him in the way she loved Will. And he was unfaithful to me.' Her voice breaks. 'Whatever he says now, he crossed a line and wanted someone else. And I can see that that was actually because we weren't quite right, all along. If we split up, I just don't think I'll feel that intense regret.'

Tom strokes her hair, squeezes her tightly, his face flushed and troubled

'It's a lot to give up, a long-term relationship. Might mean you don't have your own Ava? I mean,' he tries to lighten the mood, though there's an edge to his comment, 'you are getting on a bit.'

'It might mean being alone, for ever.' She looks at him, baldly. 'Yes, I know. No husband. No children. But better that and be happy in myself, rather than being stuck in a relationship in which I don't want to be.

'When I think about regret,' she adds, easing away from his hold, calming her voice, 'I wonder what I'd regret most: giving up Matt or giving up on this new life here, helping to create a brighter future, being true to me.'

'And?' Tom asks, though he must know the answer.

'The farm wins,' she says. 'When I ask myself the question, Skylark wins. Every time.'

In the end, Matt makes it easy for her. When she returns from milking, he is waiting for her in the bedroom: the bed made, fully dressed.

'I've made a decision,' she says.

'Are you coming back in a fortnight?'

'I'll come and collect my stuff,' she says, and it is a relief to state this so frankly. 'But I'm not coming back permanently.'

He nods, taking in the finality of what she is saying.

'You've never really wanted me, have you?' he says, after a while. His voice is flat and without malice, though the hurt seeps out anyway.

'Of course I have!' She sits down next to him, hoping she sounds sincere, for she knows they were passionate once, albeit briefly. 'What makes you say that?'

He shrugs. 'I was the safe option. Your friend. The one you turned to after all those disastrous boyfriends; the one your dad liked. I'm not stupid.' He smiles, rueful. 'Think I always knew I was lucky to have you as long as I did.'

'Oh, Matt.' She puts an arm round him. Her cheek rests against his shoulder, soft skin resting against angular bone. He doesn't lift his arm and pull her to him as she expected, and she moves away, awkward. 'Well, I didn't think that, if it's any consolation,' she says.

The smile he returns is taut, his lips stretching

361

briefly. He leans forward and looks at the floor-boards, elbows resting on his knees. They seem to have accepted that it is over, and she feels an acute sadness but also, and more clearly, a strong sense of relief. Neither of them is fighting to make things better, and that seems to clarify things: to make it easier. Even at the very end, they do not feel sufficiently strongly to fight for their marriage to continue. They are resigned to it, all passion spent.

'It was always an issue, this place, wasn't it?' he adds, looking at her, and he seems to be on a roll now, determined to list the problems at the heart of their relationship. 'Your heart's here and you're happier, more contented, than you've ever seemed in London, whereas I know I just couldn't live here.'

He glances at the window, framing the rolling expanse of cornfield. 'I couldn't think of anything worse than all this...' he gestures, '...openness. Lovely now when the sun shines, but I just find it so bleak and lonely, so, well, *boring* for most of the year.

'We've hardly been love's young dream, either, have we, these past few months? Or the past couple of years. It's not great for your ego. Or your well-being. To know your wife doesn't want you.' He pauses. 'Well, you're a free agent, now. You can go after anyone you want. Even that Ben bloke,' he says.

The suggestion takes her by surprise. And she realises that, incredibly, he wants to be reassured.

'That's a bit like the pot calling the kettle black, Matt. And I've told you: nothing's happened.'

'But you'd like it to?'

'No!' Even as she says it, she wonders if she is lying.

'Do me the justice of being honest.'

'No,' she repeats. 'Actually, I've got so much on at the moment – so much to think about: Dad, Granny, us – that sex is the last thing I need.'

His breath comes out in one long sigh. Perhaps he is remembering last night, and her apparent enthusiasm. He gets up off the bed and looks down at her. It takes a while for her to realise that he is waiting, just in case there is a chance she might change her mind.

'When I go, that's it.' He looks at the floor, then back at her. 'So I'm going to check one last time: are you sure you don't want to make another go of it?'

There is a flicker of hope in his eyes.

'No. I don't,' she says. 'But that's got nothing to do with anyone else, and more to do with me realising who I am and what I need.'

It is important she is clear on this. That their ending is not just because of Suzi, or even Ben, but because their differences seem insurmountable.

'I'm so very sorry.'

'So am I,' he says.

Forty-two

Now: 29 August 2014, Cornwall

Lucy sits in the garden of Yard Cottage, waiting for Mrs Coates to stop fussing with the teapot. The elderly woman pours milk and then a stream of thick, dark tea.

'I'm afraid I don't have any sugar,' she says, apologetically.

'Really, Mrs Coates. It's fine.' Lucy is determined to befriend her and not reveal her frustration that she has waited seventy years to confess her secret.

'Oh.' The elderly woman flushes. 'Call me Alice, please.'

It is six hours since Matt left, and Lucy is sitting in this cottage garden because she has been dwelling on regret.

Her grandmother's refusal to risk finding out about Jeremiah, and her stubbornness in not talking to Alice, now seems more tragic than foolish. Their guest is leaving in two days – having already extended her stay by another three – and when she goes, the chance of any reunion, or reconciliation, will disappear with her. If there is any possibility of a happy ending – or even some closure – then this is the time to grasp it. She does not want Maggie to be left wondering what might have been.

'I expect you want to know why I came back now – after all this time.' Alice looks across at Lucy, seemingly calmer now that she is sitting.

'I think my grandmother feels unsettled by why you've decided to return now; and well, angry. But we – my mum, brother and I – are really grateful. We'd like to help find Jeremiah,' Lucy says.

Alice smiles, her thin lips dissolving into a brave wobble, but her hands fidget: her right thumb stroking her left one, over and over, in a nervous tic.

'I should have come years ago. But I had a reason for not being able to bear thinking about what happened. It was so traumatic that I think I managed to convince myself that what I did was, if not excusable, then understandable because of it.

'Then, just after Christmas, my sister died. She was eighty-five: younger than your grandmother. And Pam's death shook me more than all my other siblings – well, apart from Will's. Made me realise that perhaps I'd become complacent. I'd always assumed I had time to put things right, you see. But death – and illness – makes you realise that, perhaps, you haven't time.

'I had some bad news myself then – no, really; it's nothing – but it shocked me into realising that if I was going to track down your grandmother's baby, well, I had better get on with it.'

She looks down at her lap then, and her disappointment is almost tangible. Her chirpy tone fades. 'I have one more address left to visit, which I'll do tomorrow. If it isn't his, well, I don't know what more I can do. Perhaps, if you'd be so kind, you might help me – and carry on the search?'

She gets up and moves back into the house. For a moment, Lucy wonders if this is the end of the conversation. There was a finality to Alice's admission that she hasn't found Jeremiah. She waits, thinking of her frailty and the greyness that seems to mask her face. She has traipsed all over the moor, her grandmother said, and is now knocking on doors across Cornwall. No wonder, at eighty-three, she looks fatigued.

She comes back into the garden, however, clutching what looks like a letter: a cheap white envelope, with an address scrawled in a scratched and spidery hand.

'I was also prompted by this,' she says, putting it down on the table. The envelope, soiled with dust and with a crease down its middle, is addressed, in blue fountain pen, to Maggie Retallick: Skylark Farm, Trecothan, north Cornwall. There is no stamp and no postmark on it.

'It's from my brother, Will. Written, as you can see, to your grandmother. I found it in some papers in Pam's attic when I was sorting through her effects earlier this year.'

Lucy gives a shiver. 'What does it say?'

'Oh. I haven't opened it.' She looks shocked. 'That wouldn't be right. I wanted to give it to your grandmother if I couldn't find her son. I'd have given it to her before now – only she was so angry, so distressed, I didn't want to risk her not reading it properly.'

Lucy touches the envelope, stroking the lettering, puzzling over the crease. Perhaps it was folded and kept in his breast pocket: warm and safe, next to his heart? There must be a reason he never found a stamp or a postbox for what surely must have been a love letter? She tries to imagine its secret contents; itches to ease the envelope apart.

'I don't understand why it wasn't sent. Did he change his mind?'

'I've no idea.'

'Why did your sister have it?'

'It was in a bundle of letters belonging to my mother. She must have left them to Pam when she died.'

'Why would your mother have it?'

'I suppose it must have been in his things back at home – or perhaps he was carrying it when he died.'

Lucy looks at the envelope once again, trying to envisage its history.

'Do you know where your brother was killed?'

'In the Aldwych.' Alice's voice is quiet. 'Outside Bush House. He had just stepped out, safe, and a pane of glass sliced through him.' She pauses as if imagining the horror of the moment, then adds, more brightly: 'Do you know the place?'

She does. She had once gone out with a history student from King's, based on the Strand, and he had walked her along the curved street and pointed out the shrapnel lodged in the side of the building. A fact – recited in Henry's animated, adenoidal voice – swims up from the depths of her memory.

'Did you know that there was a post office, there, on the ground floor of Bush House? Do you think,' she tastes the words as her mind catches up with the idea, 'he might have been queuing up to post this when he died?'

Alice is very still. 'Well, yes. I suppose it's possible,' she says. The colour has gone from her cheeks, but she has become more animated.

'I did write to him, you see. In the May, once I'd moved to St Agnes, telling him about the baby.'

'You told him he was the father?'

'Not in so many words, but I told him Maggie had had a baby, and I asked him to come and help. I thought he might be able to help find the farm where I'd taken the baby; and help me get him back for Maggie. I wanted, and it sounds so childish, to try to make things right.'

'So perhaps this letter to Maggie is an apology – or a promise to come and help her?' Lucy is excited.

'I just don't know.' Her pale blue eyes start to water. 'I wrote to him at the Eddys' once I was with my new family, but I never heard from him. After he died, I learned that he had moved to London in the early May – and so I assumed he had never received it. I never thought it might have been forwarded. And when it occurred to me, much later, as an adult, my mother had dementia and there was no one to ask.'

Lucy sits, trying to piece together a jigsaw of possibilities, the parts almost fitting – but not quite.

'If he *had* received your letter, that might explain why your mother never sent this letter. She might not have wanted him to admit to being a father; might have wanted to protect him from my great-grandparents' rage.'

368

'I don't think she'd have sent it anyway. She knew he loved this farm, and she blamed your great-grandmother for sending him away. It sounds ludicrous, but as far as she saw it, they were indirectly responsible for his death. And I think she loved him more than any of us realised at the time. I don't think she could have passed any memento of his on – certainly not if it was on him when he died. But perhaps she couldn't bear to look at it either. And so it was stored, jumbled up with the other letters, for years.'

Alice strokes the envelope, tracing her brother's writing with her right hand, then hands it back to Lucy.

'I admit I'm intrigued to know what it says. It would be lovely if it brought your grandmother some small happiness. Please. Could you give it to her, from me?'

Maggie sits on her bench, underneath the crab apple tree, holding the letter. One finger traces the scrawl of the writing as she sees his slim fingers forming the words.

So he had written to her. He hadn't forgotten her, as she had always half-feared, or passed her over for somebody else. The buxom Land Girl had been a figment of her imagination. And he had loved her. She finds the crucial phrase. *I love you. There, I have said it.* For a moment she imagines him setting down the feeling: painfully self-conscious, wishing he could tell her in person.

She rereads that crucial phrase. Ridiculous that this should matter, after all these years. But, oh, how it does! She looks at the blue ink coursing over the once-white sheet of paper, and feels her heart strain with joy.

I love you. There, I have said it.

And what more needed to be said? I love you was all anyone needed to hear. And though Edward had told her, and her children and grandchildren over the years, still this elusive I love you is the one that has always mattered. The one she had never heard. For Will had never said it, despite her whispering it into his hair as they stood, clamped together, in the hay barn. *I love you, I love you.* Her voice had been savage, the knowledge shocking. *I love you, Will.*

A smile plays across her lips, floods her face. Will Cooke may have been too shy to say it, but he had loved her just as she had hoped, all along.

He had wanted to be with her, too. She scans the lines to double-check, but yes, he says it here. He wanted to come down to Cornwall and – oh! – he wanted to help find their child. Her throat constricts. What a waste. What a bloody waste! He would have come down if he had managed to send this letter, for she would have replied with a great, heartfelt yes. If he hadn't been caught in the aftermath of a bomb. If he hadn't been there, trying to send her this letter, they would have been together. A familiar refrain starts up: he wouldn't have died if he had stayed, safe in Cornwall, if he had never been sent from the farm.

She tries to imagine it. For one indulgent moment she forgets Edward; forgets Judith and Richard; Tom, Lucy and Ava – and tries to envisage that longed-for future with Will and her first, abandoned child.

370

The image – hazy around the edges, barely formed – shimmers, just out of her reach. A first love, cut tragically short – by the war and by her mother – will always be romanticised, after all. But, no. They loved each other with an intensity that would have carried them through the rockier parts of their marriage, she knows that. Theirs would have been a love affair that would have endured.

She thinks of what Lucy had said. Why hadn't he just come straight down to Cornwall to find her? Logistics? Or cautiousness? The stupidity of that decision and its consequences – hits her in the solar plexus, hard.

He had feared her mother: narrow-minded Evelyn, whose concern that her daughter's options would be narrowed by an illegitimate baby, and the associated social stigma, had ensured she forced him away. And perhaps she, too, was to blame. She had written, but when she received no reply – Evelyn intercepting her letters, she later learned – she had stopped: too panicked by the pregnancy, at first, but also too proud, too unsure of his feelings. That elusive *I love you* is wonderful, yes, but what if he had told her in person, seventy years before?

She turns back to the letter to reread a passage. Yes, here it is. What if she'd stumbled upon that sign he'd tried to give her? That he refers to here, in this letter, and that she must go to find now? *A small heart low down on a stile.* Hidden by overgrown tendrils of hedgerow, never seen, for the gate between the field and footpath has long gone and she has had no reason to clamber over stiles or inspect stile posts. And yet it has been waiting for her all these years.

She strokes the letter again. It warms her, this knowledge of his love. Her heart pounds, stronger than it has for months, flooding her with a relief that takes her quite by surprise. The warmth extends, just a little, to Alice. Her hatred – so clear in the last few days – barely smoulders; a damp squib that will never reignite. She is grateful for what she has tried to do – even if her lie and her failure to put this right for so long still confound her. And yet, a month after the birth, she had tried to do so. She had written to Will, begging him to help find their child.

In a few minutes, she will get up and thank her. Her visit has brought this letter. And Will's love gleams: hard and bright and pure. Nothing can make up for the fact she will never meet her baby, but at least now she knows, for definite, that it cannot happen. There is no paper trail, no means of contact. No reason to hope.

She has long known that her son was unlikely to find her, and the fear – intensely painful each time it struck her – was that he didn't care. But Alice's confession, somehow, eases that pain. He couldn't have found her, for he had no way of knowing where to look. He might not even have known that he was adopted: that he had some different mother all along. And while that would have once made her feel utterly bleak, at least now there is some certainty, some – what would Lucy call it? Ah, yes. Some closure.

She stands and, almost as a reflex, makes her way to the gate to look behind the farm, at the cliffs and the headland. No one walks towards the farm.

He will not come. And if there is no way he will find her, there is no reason to keep going. She is not sure how much longer she can carry on. She doubts she will see many more winters. She has had a good innings. Eighty-eight; eighty-nine in January. By ninety, it will be time to stop, for she knows she will start to slow down. She saw it with her father, Joe, who died at ninety-one. Fine until his ninetieth birthday, and then a catalogue of problems sapped his body and his spirit. Worn out. Just like her.

She will die not knowing if she has ever seen him, but knowing it is likely she hasn't. For she is still sure she would recognise him, and that has never occurred.

He might as well be dead. Perhaps he is. The thought – acknowledged many times – still chills her. And she will never know.

Forty-three

Now: 30 August 2014

The house is far from prepossessing. A 1960s ex-council house, by the looks of it: bleak grey-rendered concrete, plastic windows, a stark front garden with clumps of lavender, scrubby grass, a few moss-covered stones. It stands just behind the main road leading into the town: one of four

373

semis huddled together for comfort, braced against the wind gusting in from the Atlantic. The only houses on this thin slip of a side road. The only buildings this high for miles around.

You wouldn't choose to live here if you could avoid it, thinks Alice, taking in the rust bleeding from a water pipe and the satellite dishes fixed at jaunty angles. And then she turns and sees the view. The estuary gleams and, to the east, the moor glows russet-gold in the late summer sun. If you had a deep connection to this place, or were someone who had been brought up on the moor, or even if you were an outsider, someone who never felt they had belonged, who perhaps struggled with the fact they had been adopted – and her heart lifts at the thought of all these hypothetical possibilities – then perhaps you would welcome this isolation.

She parks the car, aware of a twitching curtain, and makes her way to number 4 Corporation Terrace. The gate clicks behind her and her stomach tightens as she walks up the path. This is the fifth address belonging to a J Jose that she has visited. Her last hope before accepting he has moved out of Cornwall – for she knows she will not have the strength to search for him else-where. The nausea has begun, and she is tired, so very tired, now. Ready to return home tomorrow. Lucy will carry on the search, but she will have to give up if this JS Jose is not the Jeremiah she has been searching for. Is not Will and Maggie's son.

She waits outside the uPVC front door, listening for any evidence that someone is inside. Just for a split-second, she considers leaving: for the thought that she will be met with a blank look – or worse, a youthful Jeremiah, a Jem or a Jez or Jezza – terrifies her. Better to retain some hope. To never know. But then she sees that a television set is on in the front room. And suddenly the blur of a figure is coming towards her through the frosted glass.

The door is wrenched open and she is disorientated for a moment. 'Oh, it's you!' she says, for this face is familiar. She stares at it, befuddled.

But something isn't right. 'I was looking for a Jeremiah Jose,' she begins. 'But I must have the wrong address.'

'No one's called me that for quite some time,' he says; and she sees now that they are not Will's eyes – his eyes if he had ever managed to reach seventy – but her own and those of her father, William. There is a hint of Will in his cheekbones, and of Annie in the breadth of his forehead.

'Bit of a mouthful, isn't it? Jeremiah? Only used by my late mother when I was in trouble – or now by the council when they're wanting money. I use my middle name. Have done ever since I was old enough to make a fuss.'

He keeps talking: a deep voice with a lovely Cornish lilt that reminds her of Uncle Joe's. There's a touch of Maggie's father in him, too, in the breadth of his shoulders and the weathered tan of his skin. And a little of Will, in the thickness of his hair. Nothing distinctly of Maggie and, thankfully, no hint of Evelyn.

She watches, piecing fragments of his relatives together, finding evidence of his parentage. Just lapping him up, drinking him in. 'I'm sorry,' she

375

says, for he seems to have stopped talking and is staring back at her, a look of concern on his face.

He smiles, and she realises that she might have been behaving in a way that was unsettling. He cannot know that the last time they met he was a newborn baby, held tightly in her arms.

'I just thought you looked a little shaken, my dear. Or perhaps it was my fault, gassing on as usual. Now. How can I help?'

Forty-four

Now: 31 August 2014, Cornwall

Alice looks around the neat, whitewashed bedroom to check that it is empty. It is as bare as when she arrived on 1 September, 1939, the day of their evacuation. Nearly three quarters of a century ago.

She is all packed now: roll-along suitcase and rucksack waiting by the door for the taxi; a flask of coffee for the journey; her copy of *Far from the Madding Crowd*, to be given to Lucy, left behind. It is time to go home. Coming here was such a wonderful thing to do, and though she could never describe it as easy, she knows that when she dies, it will be with a clearer conscience. No longer ravaged by painful memories. She could not have done more.

Of course, she will always feel a twinge of guilt for confirming Evelyn's suspicions. For a moment, she is back in the stifling scullery, with its cloying smell of wet apple, as Joanna peeled and quartered the fruit for a pie. It was the day Maggie returned to Bodmin; the evening after she had glimpsed her and Will, and she had pushed the maid to tell her the facts of life. 'Think of the cow and the bull; or the ram and ewe tupping,' Joanna had said, her eyes widening, her mouth a dark red cavern. 'Well, humans are the same.'

She had only watched them briefly in the barn, had run away almost as soon as she realised what she was seeing, feet whipping over the cobbles, heart thudding with fear. But she had seen enough. Her panic rose up in the scullery, and when Evelyn, catching her in the yard moments later, had asked what was wrong – was it something to do with Maggie? – she had nodded, in relief.

'And my brother,' she had blurted out.

Aunt Evelyn's forehead had creased. 'Will? What about him?'

Alice had shut up then, but it seemed she had said enough.

She must not obsess about that now. Better to try and relax before her journey. She settles herself on the bench and feels the morning sun on her face.

Here, if she looks around, she can see the parts of the farm she always loved: the beach, with its infinite rock pools; the fields, where she adopted her wild rabbit; the dunes, where, to the endless song of the skylarks, they had played hide-and-seek. She can hear them now; an antiphony, the melody picked up and flung back from one to another, as they mark their territory or – and she knows she is being fanciful – as they proclaim their joy at the extreme beauty of this place.

And then she does what she always avoids when sitting here: she turns to look back at the moor. The weather really does change everything. It glows, today, almost luminous: as different to the bleak landscape of her memory as the becalmed estuary is to the Atlantic churned by a storm. The brilliant sunshine makes the hills benign; softens their colours. And the whole is framed by the tendrils of a hedgerow, burgeoning in late summer with unripe blackberries, rosehips and the dulled black marbles of sloes.

She will be back in Fulham long before these berries are ripe. And that is as it should be. There is a nip to the evening air now: autumn inching nearer, the summer drawing to a close. She needs to be in London, for she was sick again this morning, and she is so very weary that even getting dressed – let alone hauling herself across the country – seems to be an effort. She needs to be near a hospital and her sons, Ian and Rob. Perhaps it is time to be honest. Time to admit that she is not so independent. That she needs them, after all.

Maggie sits underneath the crab apple. Alice is going this morning, and she had told her to sit here, as usual. Just stay there and relax, she had said. And please; don't get up.

She is irritable. She has better things to do with her day than just wait on a whim of Alice's. Does she want to be waved off? Good Lord. Perhaps she hankers after a more loving farewell than the last one she gave her. She does not want to do anything like hug. She is deeply grateful for her for bringing Will's letter, and for wanting to make amends, she told her as much earlier, but, really, there is no need to *wallow* in sentiment.

She will wait another five minutes and then she must get on. She has promised to do the baking today, so that Lucy can take delivery of the new ice cream maker and help Tom to install it. The farm is changing – diversifying – and all for the better, it seems. She looks up, watching the apples that hang heavy now, streaked with red. As a girl, she always loved autumn: season of mists and mellow fruitfulness and all that. But the end of August and beginning of September has long been tinged with the memory of Will going. She last saw him on 29 August, 1943: seventy-one years ago.

Restless, she leans forwards and pushes herself up. As she does so, she sees a familiar figure cycling down the track towards her. A flash of Royal Mail red, and, beneath that, in his incongruous shorts, those tanned, wiry legs.

His tyres skid to a halt, swerving on stones, kicking up dust. He looks slightly unsteady as he jumps off and rights the bike, so overladen it almost topples. Then, leaning it against the wall, he pushes open the gate.

'Hello, Sam,' she calls, surprised at the click of the latch, for the postman usually goes round to the kitchen at the back to hand over any letters. 'That's kind of you, but I was just getting up to start working. Really, there's no need.'

He is walking towards her quite deliberately,

and he is smiling. A tentative smile that broadens, as he gets nearer, until it can only be described as filled with joy.

'Hello,' he says, and his voice is more diffident than usual. 'I've been looking for you for a very long time.'

Forty-five

Then: 30 June 1944

Will started a second sheet of paper. He couldn't waste another piece, for this was filched from his mother, and yet the first attempt – written as soon as he had ripped open the letter from Alice – just hadn't been right.

He had had all night to think about it: his mind whirring with what Maggie had gone through in the last ten months – and with an endless ribbon of possibilities streaming into the future. His body ached with tiredness, though he felt clear-headed. Dawn broke, pale grey creeping under the edge of his blackout curtain, and he found he had barely slept at all.

It was six now, and he had half an hour to write this before he had to get up for his last day of work before heading off to the training battalion. Thirty minutes in which to convince Maggie that he loved her, and that he wanted to make things right. Trouble was, he had never found writing that easy: had always been more of a practical than a wordy type. He had tried to be poetic once before. 'Delicious danger?' she had said with a wrinkle of her nose. So, after that, he had stuck to actions. And there could have been no doubting his feelings, or so he'd thought.

He sucked the end of his fountain pen, barely used, but a present the first Christmas he arrived at the Retallicks'. Chosen by Evelyn, who had said everyone should have aspirations, even if they were going to leave school at fourteen.

Her aspirations didn't extend to him loving her daughter. He shuts out her face: those bullet eyes that bore into him when she had screamed at him. But he hadn't done it to spite them. Loving Maggie was inevitable: as likely as a January frost or a gale-force wind ripping leaves from the trees.

He should put all this down, shouldn't he? For this is what he was never able to tell her, and his tongue-tied inadequacy strikes him hard. He had felt it when he had chiselled that heart, low down on the stile leading to the beach, and scratched their initials to try to mark his feelings. He had done it the day after they first kissed, and wished he had made it bigger, bolder, less apologetic now.

He closes his eyes and suddenly he is back there, holding her in the sand dunes; listening to the sound of her breathing; smelling her sweet, soft hair crushed against his mouth. His arms are tight around her, and he can feel her breasts pushing against him, warm and firm. She looks up and smiles at him, then plants a kiss, her mouth open and inviting. A skylark chatters high up above them – a full-throated sound that eddies and whirls in one continuous, joyous loop – and he gulps down a bubble of laughter. And suddenly he knows what to write:

London   *June 30th 1944*

Dear Maggie,
Alice has written to tell me about the baby. I don't know what to say except that I want to try, to make things right, to be with you, if you will still have me and try to find our son.
I know we are young but I am eighteen now. Old enough to fight. And, I love you. There, I have said it, the thing I couldn't say all those times, when we kissed, or that last time in the hay barn. I think I have always done so: right from the start when you chased me over the sand, the day after we arrived. Or, at least, from the next summer when you taught me to swim and I was such a poor sport.
I'm embarrassed now. I've never written a letter like this before and I hope I'll never have to again. But I want you to know that I didn't forget you, or pass you over for someone else. I wrote, though I don't suppose any of my letters got through to you. And I drew a small heart with our initials, low down on the gatepost by the stile leading from the field to the beach. You should be able to find it. I didn't make it too big in case I embarrassed you, or if you didn't want it, but it should be there, all right.
I don't know if this will reach you and I only hope that if your mother opens it she can find it in her heart to give it to you. The bombing here has made me realise that life is fragile and if people find happiness, like I know we did, they should grab it with both hands.
I have never stopped thinking of you. Do you

382

remember that swim when we first kissed – and how we felt? Or when we leaned against the storm, hanging out of your window? Delicious danger we said and, yes, it felt like that at the time.

I'm starting training in Yorkshire the day after tomorrow and I'm sure real danger won't feel like that. It doesn't when there are doodlebugs overhead or I'm running down to the underground for shelter. Do you know what I think of then? Us – in the cornfields, in the barn, in the sand dunes – with those skylarks singing their little hearts out; celebrating us, or that's what it felt like. That's what I think of then.

I must rush to get this in the post. I do not know if you will want me, after everything you have gone through, but I do hope you believe what I say.

You can reply via the barracks at Wakefield – address below. You may never want to speak to me again, but please let me know that you've received this so that I can hope that you might believe me.

I love you,
Forever yours,
Will

Epilogue

Now: 30 June 2015

Lucy sits in a dip in the sand dunes, watching the tide roll towards her; lulled by the rhythm of the thud then slither of the waves on the shore.

An early evening in mid-summer: the sand is

still warm from the heat of the day; the beach is clear – for the schools haven't broken up yet, and the dog walkers have all gone home. She lies back, listening to the constant hum of the grasshoppers, the caw of the seagulls. High above, two brown specks hover, throwing a melody that spirals and shimmers: a seamless strand that sears through a mackerel sky and out across the deep blue of the bay.

It is a year since it happened. Since she made the mistake that would see her come hurtling down here. A year ago today, she found out about Matt and Suzi. Tomorrow it will be a year since she last worked as a nurse.

Jacob is doing well. She went back to the hospital in November to say goodbye to her old colleagues, and there was a card from his parents pinned to the noticeboard, thanking them for saving his life. A photograph of a baby boy was attached: still tiny, but unrecognisable from the jumble of bones and tubes she had left, dwarfed by a premature-baby nappy. He had beamed from the photograph, and she had given Emma a short, tight smile of thanks. For how could she not do? Without her checking, little Jacob would not be alive.

She was relieved to leave the cloying warmth of the neonatal ward, and the busy-ness of London. Happy to step off the train at Bodmin and breathe in the damp, lush smell of woodland; salt-lashed hedgerows; gorse-covered moor. Even when the weather was harsh – the puddles frozen to ice, the farm drenched by storms – she has never regretted coming back. There have been setbacks – Uncle Richard changing jobs and having to withdraw some of his investment; Tredinnick cutting their order in the winter – but Skylark ice cream is starting to grow in such a way that she can see their overdraft shrinking. They worked flat-out to fill Kernow's freezers from Easter, and she and Flo have been selling it at festivals and at the more popular beaches on bank holidays. Their fledgling business is burgeoning at last.

With the threat of financial ruin starting to lift, the farm has begun to feel more cared for. She and Judith ripped the peeling wallpaper from the hall in October and are waging a battle against rogue patches of mould. Her mother seems re-vitalised: buoyed by Lucy returning home, released from keeping the secret of her husband's suicide, from having to dissemble. But it is her grandmother who has changed the most.

Watching her getting to know Sam has been like seeing a couple falling in love. At first it was heady: Maggie infatuated, as if she couldn't get enough of her long-lost son. It might have been hard for Richard, had he been around, but Judith, with two children at home and her grand-daughter an increasingly talkative presence, has been mildly amused by such blatant favouritism, while aware that it couldn't last.

With time, Maggie has become less giddy. She still sees him three or four times a week – for they have years to catch up on – but she views him a little more objectively. 'I'm not quite sure about the beard,' she had confided, when he had flirted with a goatee. 'Do you think he's a bit alternative, after all?'

Lucy had looked at Sam, with the surf beads he

wears now he has retired from delivering the post, and the fortified roll-ups he smokes in his back garden, the sickly-sweet smell of weed over-powering the tamarisk. 'I'm not sure it matters if he is,' she had posited, for she is more willing to challenge her grandmother's prejudices now that Maggie is back to being her opinionated self. 'No.' Maggie had thought about it. 'I don't sup-pose for a minute that it does.'

She had got to know Sam better when they took a long train journey up to London, on a chill Tuesday in early December, to attend Alice's funeral. The church was fuller than she'd ex-pected: her sons, Rob and Ian, and her six grown-up grandchildren, visibly distressed rather than merely subdued. They hadn't introduced themselves beyond saying they had met her in Cornwall the previous summer, and if anyone noticed a faint resemblance between the dead woman and this nut-brown, wiry-legged man, it wasn't mentioned. But he later wrote, sparking a tentative email exchange with Rob, the elder son, and a card on his birthday with a black-and-white photograph of a young Will.

Being with Sam – listening to the story of his early years on the moor and of his marriage to Anne and adoption of their two children *(Funny: we couldn't have them; so I did what my parents did. Repaid the favour.)* – meant any half-considered plan to meet Matt for a drink was abandoned. And that was for the best. Suzi was replaced by a Cate, and though the news had initially rankled – he had waited how long before moving her in? – Lucy's sense of inadequacy disappeared far more quickly than she thought. *You don't want to think, later in life: Oh, if only,* her grandmother had said; and she doesn't, she really doesn't. Regret – wondering what might have been, never having the chance to discover – would have kicked in more clearly if she had returned to her old London life and left the farm.

And what of her? Does she dare risk falling in love again? She is wary, for she knows that love alone is not enough to secure her happiness. Her father's suicide has shown her that: he could not have been more loved, but he killed himself, still. And yet her grandmother has taught her that if she has a chance she should grasp it with both hands, trusting it will work in a way it couldn't for a young Maggie. *Wondering what might have been. Never having the chance to discover, well, I think that's the most painful thing.*

She has been thinking about this today, on the anniversary of Will's death. Running along the cliffs, she had stood on the headland: arms outstretched, with a stiff cross-onshore wind blowing, trusting entirely to its strength. Land's End was to her left, Devon to her right, the Atlantic stretched in front of her: aquamarine then teal, then a deep dark blue as it hit the horizon and the sky rose up and away. The edge of the cliff. The edge of her world. Dare she risk it? Believe in this exhilaration that could buoy her up and buffet away sadness? Below her, the spume swirled around the rocks, drenching a pair of mating seals; above, a pair of guillemots soared on the breeze.

Well, here he is now. A figure making his way through the sand dunes, holding packets of fish and chips, sharp with vinegar, soft and warm as a newborn baby.

'I thought tea would spill so I've brought beer.' He hands her a bottle. A tear of condensation runs down its neck.

He sits next to her, with the ease that comes from knowing someone for several years; and yet there is a tension in the inches between their thighs, in the small distance between them.

'To my great-grandfather.' Ben holds his bottle aloft.

'To Will,' Lucy says.

Author's Note

The idea for *The Farm at the Edge of the World* emerged from my love a specific area: the cliffs of north Cornwall to the west of Padstow, where I holidayed as a child. When I began to write about a Cornish farm that would be a physical refuge during the war, and an emotional one in the present day, it was inevitable I drew on my knowledge of this place, not least because the north Cornish coast was peppered with WWII airfields, allowing for the possibility of bombing, and I wanted it to be sufficiently close to Bodmin and Bodmin moor.

I have taken a few liberties with the geography, however, and introduced a couple of caves that don't exist as well as giving it a flavour of the land further to the west – more the Cornwall of West Penrith, the area from which my mother's farming ancestors originate. The Cornwall that feels as if it is at the edge of the world. I have also introduced dairy cows, though I know that the Camel Estuary is fringed with fields of barley and cauliflowers, and it is sheep that graze on the coast.

If I tweaked the geography and topography, I was deeply conscious of the need not to create historical inaccuracies. At one point, I detailed each of the bombs that fell on Cornwall during

World War II and tried to bend my narrative around one. And then I read Kate Atkinson's *Life After Life* and her author's note in which she states that she finds it hard 'to create an authentic atmosphere or narrative credibility if continually constrained. Fiction is fiction, after all,' she continues. 'That doesn't mean that I don't check things afterwards ... but sometimes to find the truth at the heart of a book a certain amount of reality falls by the wayside.'

She refers to being unaware of whether any bombs fell in the real Argyll Road in real life and I found that incredibly freeing: as long as I respected history, I could risk a little flexibility.

So a Heinkel did drop bombs in the deer park of Prideaux Place but I am unaware of whether the windows shattered in the main house; and a doodlebug struck the Aldwych on June 30, 1944, but among the many fatalities there was, of course, no Will Cooke.

I hope that this approach is acceptable. As a former news reporter, I have tried to get every detail right where it matters: obsessing about the types of plane that would have flown from David-stow airfield, and the date on which the Duke of Cornwall's light infantry would have left for north Africa, (March 23 1943); or the pesticide applied to drenched wheat reed; or the exact amount of milk produced by a cow. I am hugely indebted to the many farmers I have interviewed, some of whom have proofread my copy in a bid to prevent any mistakes creeping in. Should any errors have occurred, they are, of course, all mine.

Acknowledgments

I am hugely indebted to my publishers, Hodder & Stoughton, and in particular to my editors, Kate Parkin and Sara Kinsella, and their assistants Francine Toon and Sharan Matharu, who helped hone this novel into shape. Special thanks, as ever, are due to Lizzy Kremer, my unfailingly supportive agent, and to Harriet Moore, her clever assistant, who urged me to capture the Cornwall I love.

The Farm at the Edge of the World evolved from my love for an area of north Cornwall I have visited since childhood and from my mother's stories of summers spent running wild on Trewiddle, her grandfather's farm. I am hugely grateful to my mother, Bobby Hall, and to her cousin, Graham Howard, who whet my appetite with their tales of a world in which children built dens among the stacks at harvest, put chicks in the warming drawer of the Aga, and hid among the rhododendrons. My mother and my father, Chris Hall, fuelled this love affair by taking me on repeated childhood holidays to the area west of Padstow that is detailed in this novel.

Graham's intricate discussion of the risks of growing wheat reed helped inform my present day story, while my stepfather's brother, Mark

Evans, taught me about running an organic dairy farm. I am particularly grateful to Graham for his patience as I grappled to understand the mid-20th century process of threshing and binding, and to Mark and Will Pratt for allowing me to watch an afternoon milking. If I have come anywhere close to capturing the pressures of present day farming it is thanks to them.

A trio of octogenarian Cornish farmers, all teenage boys in 1943–4, provided invaluable descriptions of how to hand milk a cow or plough a field; and of the sound of a bomb whistling down a chimney or blowing off gateposts. I am hugely grateful to Clifford Butter, Robin Moore and Humphrey Eddy who welcomed me into their homes with grace and humour and allowed me to interview them for hours.

Major Hugo White of Cornwall's Regimental Museum was a courteous, knowledgeable and efficient guide to the movements of the Duke of Cornwall's 2nd Battalion, and vividly described being a Winchester schoolboy watching the Battle of Britain dogfights. Steve Perry and Rod Knight, at the Cornwall at War museum, situated at Davidstow airfield, gave me an invaluable sense of place and time.

Thanks are also due to three one-time evacuees I interviewed: Pauline Cocking, who was evacuated with her three siblings in 1939, and whose memories informed much of my early thinking; Norma Thomas, and John Beale. I am also grateful to Sarah McDonnell, Ian Johnson of the NFU in Exeter, and Alison Spence of the Cornwall Record Office, for providing links to contacts including these.

For my medical aspects of the present-day story, I am indebted to Gillian Bowker and Harriet Sperling, and to Jean Slocomb of Cancer Research UK.

Writing my second novel has been a steep learning curve and I am proud to be part of the Prime Writers, a group of authors who have all been traditionally published over the age of 40, and who have provided consistent support.

I am also grateful for the continued support of my extended family, not least in helping with childcare. Special thanks go to my mother, to my in-laws, Sue and Bryn Vaughan and to my lovely sister, Laura Tennant.

But my most heartfelt thanks, as ever, go to my husband, Phil, and to my children, Ella and Jack. Not only have they had to put up with my going to Cornwall without them but they have grown to love it almost as much as me.

The publishers hope that this book has given you enjoyable reading. Large Print Books are especially designed to be as easy to see and hold as possible. If you wish a complete list of our books please ask at your local library or write directly to:

Magna Large Print Books
Magna House, Long Preston,
Skipton, North Yorkshire.
BD23 4ND

This Large Print Book for the partially sighted, who cannot read normal print, is published under the auspices of

THE ULVERSCROFT FOUNDATION